Worries, Dan said, *are a lot like stones. There are heavy ones, like illness and death, divorce and bankruptcy. Then there are little ones. Carry around too many of them at one time and they create the same weight. Carry them for too long, and one becomes permanently stooped and joyless. You have to cast away those small troublesome stones and be grateful when you don't have big ones.*

Elsie sat outside in the early morning sun and reflected on her husband's words.

Ah. But the wisdom to determine what was little, and what was big.

The Weight of Stones

The Weight of Stones

Copyright © 2021 Roberta Sommerfeld

All rights reserved in all media. No part of this book may be used, reproduced, stored in a retrieval system or transmitted in any form or by any means without prior written permission of the publisher, except in the case of brief quotations used in critical articles and reviews.

This book is a work of fiction. Any resemblance to persons, living or dead, or places, or actual events or locales is purely coincidental. The characters and names are products of the author's imagination and are used fictitiously.

Cover and title page by Cara Dand (caradand.com)
Formatting by Rik (WildSeasFormatting.com)

ISBN (print): 978-1-7774541-2-8
ISBN (ebook): 978-1-7774541-1-1

Published by ThirteenBooks

Dedicated to those who encourage me to write.

Chapter 1

Elsie

September 1981

Elsie scrubbed the potato pot with short, vicious strokes. The saucepan, roaster, frying pan — all were thoroughly scoured, rinsed, wiped dry and returned to their cupboard shelves. Between each cleaning, she exhaled from the depths of her lungs.

Her family was supposed to be sitting around the large oval table in the dining room, sharing stories about their day — something she called "being cohesive" — but her husband was not yet back from the field, and the eldest of their four daughters was not home from a soccer practice that ended an hour ago.

Perhaps Leslie is trapped beneath a fiery vehicle with only seconds to live. Perhaps Dan is caught in the spinning reel of the swather.

Elsie sighed. Her mind's eye exploded with every disastrous possibility.

Her second daughter, sixteen-year-old Charlotte, looked up from her books spread out on the kitchen table. "I need to interpret a line graph of Ontario duck populations. It's a biology assignment and I'm trying to concentrate."

"You have a desk in your room." Elsie's voice came out more abrasive than she intended. She softened her next words. "Don't mind the sound of my worry." She usually enjoyed Charlotte's company in the kitchen.

Charlotte put down her pencil. "Worry is a total waste of mental energy."

"If only I could keep my imagination from spiralling out of control."

"Keep your mind and hands occupied." Charlotte often repeated Dan's advice whenever one of them became unreasonably anxious.

Elsie's temper flared. "You don't think my mind and hands are occupied?" She gestured to the six peach pies cooling on the kitchen counter.

Charlotte grinned. "Mom, my keen auditory perception can identify the source of your distress, and these sighs signal one of us could be in danger." Her tone was teasing. "Money troubles are the quietest — a quick intake of breath at an unexpected but necessary expense. Worry about illness or accident generates a murmur that increases in intensity — depending on the severity of the illness or the level of peril. Loudest is a combination of concern and impatience. It sounds like anger. That's you, right now."

Elsie laughed despite herself.

"Mom, you're an open book." Charlotte grabbed her pencil case. "But I'll go upstairs to my room and finish my homework there. I'm hungry, by the way. Can't we eat without them?"

"The Dewhurst family eats together." Elsie had rules. As long as she had breath in her body, there was never going to be the indiscriminate scavenging of food that was happening in households less disciplined than hers. She stopped still, relieved to hear the distinctive whine of Dan's old fuel truck approaching the house. "Paige. Wendy," she called up the stairwell to her younger daughters. "Dad's home. Wash up first, please."

Wendy, eleven years old and the most responsible of Elsie's daughters, was the first downstairs. She placed quilted sunflower-patterned placemats on the table in the dining room. Charlotte carried the yellow "every day" plates from the kitchen. Paige, the youngest daughter, grabbed the cutlery. Elsie removed the hot pots from the oven and transferred the food to colourful Pyrex casserole dishes, Wendy retrieved the bowl of cabbage salad and a jar of beet pickles from the refrigerator, and Paige brought glass tumblers and a pitcher of water.

The table-setting, a daily occurrence, was choreographed and synchronized to match the duration of Dan's washing up in the mud room at the back entrance of their house.

"Hi Dad," the girls chorused as he strode into the dining room. He was tall and thin and good-natured. *A good husband, an excellent father.* She didn't ask why he was late. Sometimes the reason was as mundane as being in a tractor on the far side of the field. She noticed he had a small streak of dirt over his eyebrow.

"Smells delicious, Else." Dan sat at the head of the table. "Anything new in Hatfield?" His smile faded at the sight of the empty chair. "And where might Leslie be?"

"Not back from soccer practice." Elsie couldn't help wringing her hands. "I wish she hadn't taken my car. The grid road was freshly gravelled yesterday. She won't think to slow down." *So easy to roll a car.*

"I bet she's hanging out with that Karen Anders and forgot the time," Charlotte said.

"Then let us pray for Leslie's safety as a prelude to our grace," Dan said.

Everyone bowed their heads but before the first word left his lips, Paige cried, "Listen!"

A different sound, deep and throbbing, crescendoed toward them. From outside, Good Old Dog barked a warning from his spot in the sun on the veranda. Everyone jumped to peer out the dining room window as a motorized tricycle moved slowly toward the house. Leslie was hanging onto the back of the driver.

"I'll take care of this." Dan was first out the door.

"Leslie looks like she could chew the ass out of a skunk," Charlotte snickered.

"Charlotte," Elsie warned.

She watched as the three-wheeler came to a stop. Leslie slid off and yelled something to Dan over the sound of the motor. She gestured toward the driver, whose face was black from mud and dust. Dan yelled something in return, his hands making a pulling motion. The driver shut off his machine.

Elsie stepped outside in time to see a young man follow Dan to the old fuel truck and climb into the passenger seat.

Dan rolled down the window. "We'll be back shortly." He drove out of the yard without any explanation.

Annoyed, Elsie turned her attention to Leslie. "What happened? Did you have an accident? What happened to my car?" She shot a triumphant glance at Charlotte, who had also stepped outside, to indicate her worry had not been needless.

"What happened?" Leslie screeched, as she made her way to the house. "Your car got stuck in some mud and Dad has gone to get it." Her long blonde hair was pulled tight into a ponytail and her forehead was smeared with sweat and dirt. Her legs were scratched red above her knee-high socks. At the back door, she tore off her shoes and socks and tossed them in a corner of the mudroom. "Grab me my housecoat from upstairs," she said to Wendy. "And a towel."

"Please," added Charlotte. "You forgot to add 'please.'"

Leslie slammed the bathroom door.

"Your father's supper is getting cold." Elsie forced a smile. "And we may as well sit. There's no point in letting a hot meal be spoiled for all of us." She quickly dished out portions for everyone and returned the casserole dishes to the oven.

"Who was that guy, Mom?" Paige asked.

"I didn't recognize him." Something about the boy was familiar. "I was going to ask your sister when she gets out of the shower."

"Reese Dunn," Charlotte said.

Elsie put down her fork. "That's one of the Dunn boys? Are you sure?"

"The middle one."

"The middle one?"

The Dunns. In her mind's eye, Elsie envisioned the family, dirty, secretive and angry. She blamed the wife and mother for not trying harder to fit into the rural neighbourhood.

"Selina Dunn. The woman has no control."

"Don't get started," Charlotte begged. "Don't do your 'I run a tight ship' routine."

"Some day, when you're a mother, you'll appreciate the discipline I enforce." Elsie ignored the eye-rolling between Paige and Charlotte.

Leslie entered the dining room, her hair wrapped in a towel. Her unblemished skin had a golden hue, her eyes were clear, her movements were graceful. Not for the first time Elsie marvelled at the beautiful daughter she and Dan had created.

"That was a mistake." Leslie lifted her housecoat to show her legs. "To walk in canola stubble without long pants."

"So tell us what happened. We're *dying* of curiosity," said

Paige.

"Absolutely *dying*," said Charlotte.

"Wait until I bring out your supper." Elsie carried the hot casserole dishes from the oven and watched as Leslie piled her plate high. Elsie envied the girl's metabolism.

"Stilling. Sorry. Coach Stilling kept us overtime. And Karen didn't have a ride home so I gave her one. And because I didn't want to be late for supper I took the short cut. You know, the road between the Fields' quarter and the Gladstones. And I got stuck in some mud. So I started walking across the field."

"Whose field?" Charlotte asked. "Fields' field?" No one smiled at her joke. "I see you caught yourself a hunk."

"A hunk? Reese Dunn? Not likely. You've got different eyes than I do."

"He brought you home, didn't he? Safe and sound. I think we should reward him."

"You reward him." Leslie's eyes flashed with annoyance.

Elsie was about to intervene when a sound outside prompted all of their attention to the window. "They're back," she reported.

"Don't make a fuss," Leslie begged. "Please."

A few seconds later, Dan called from the back door. "Any food left? I have a hungry young man here."

Leslie groaned and carried her plate of food upstairs.

Elsie eyed the peach pies cooling on the countertop. "Lots."

Dan was unable to coax Reese Dunn inside the house so she went outside. She noticed the boy's eyes, black-rimmed from dust, were an intense deep blue. She had never before seen a Dunn boy up close.

"Have a seat." Dan gestured to the porch step.

"I'll bring out some food," Elsie said. "It will be like a picnic."

She prepared thick slices of roast beef, gravy-smothered potatoes, corn on the cob and cabbage salad on two plates. She carried them out and handed one to Dan and one to Reese. She smiled at the boy, thinking it unlikely Selina Dunn was the kind of mother who initiated picnics on the porch.

"Perhaps some cutlery?" suggested Dan.

Paige ran inside for utensils.

Reese ate quickly and silently, balancing his plate on his knees. When he finished, Elsie brought him a large slice of peach pie, ice cream melting over the crust. She watched him savour every bite.

"Thank you." Reese wiped his mouth with the back of his hand. He handed her his empty plate.

"Thank *you*," said Dan. "For bringing our Leslie home."

Elsie watched as Reese mounted the three-wheeler. It roared to life and the sound vibrated off the windows of the house. Without a wave, or even a backward glance, the boy drove out of the yard, Good Old Dog half-heartedly chasing the machine. The sound diminished and eventually the yard receded into silence, leaving everyone standing around looking at each other.

"That Dunn boy turned out good-looking." The words were out of Elsie's mouth before she could stop them. "I wouldn't have recognized him," she added.

"It was hard to tell," Charlotte said, "what with that dirt and all."

"Well," said Dan. "That was a bit of excitement but I'd better get back to work. If I don't get moving now I won't get done tonight." He turned to Leslie, who had joined the group. "You can tell me your version tomorrow at breakfast. And you can wash your mother's car for her."

"I'm sorry I made you waste your time, Dad." Leslie's voice was suitably contrite.

"All's well that ends well." Dan handed her his empty plate. He came over to Elsie and put his arm around her waist.

"Elsie," he said. "I've found myself a hired man."

Chapter 2

Charlotte

September 1981

Once upon a time, Charlotte and Leslie had been the best of friends and the closest of allies. They had shared a bedroom, toys, books, and clothes. They had helped Mom in the house, Dad in the shop, and together they cared for their younger sisters whenever their parents had volunteer commitments.

That friendship ended four years ago when Karen Anders came riding into their lives on a school bus. Usually the only new faces on the bus belonged to kindergarten kids, but Karen was thirteen and in Leslie's grade eight class. She was a city brat, an only child. Her mother was newly remarried.

Nobody Charlotte knew around Hatfield had a second husband.

"Karen Anders is so exotic," Leslie had gushed after that first day of school when the family sat together for supper.

"Karen is an anomaly," Charlotte corrected, a word straight out of her grade seven vocabulary lesson. But that wasn't quite right either.

"She's a novelty," said Dad, his eyes crinkling with laughter. "Exciting to have a new girl for the two of you to pal around with, although I daresay the novelty will wear off at some point."

Mom had been sympathetic. "I am sure she is a little intimidated by the likes of you. Grade eight is a tough time to be transplanted. I remember when I was the newcomer to this community."

"You were twenty-two. Hardly a kid," Leslie had said, not

sarcastically enough to earn a reprimand.

Karen was a "shit-disturber." Charlotte hadn't known it then but she sure knew it now. Karen was the opposite of shy. She knew a lot about adult things and she wasn't afraid to share her knowledge. She liked to tell stories about her mother's marriage to Mr. Bristol, a man she referred to as "a gullible old bachelor."

Paige, who had been five at the time, overhead one of the conversations between Karen, Leslie and Charlotte, and repeated it almost word for word at the supper table. By the controlled tone of their voices, Charlotte could tell her parents were angry.

"I don't think Mr. Bristol would appreciate being talked about that way." Mom looked at Dad. "We need to put a stop to this."

"What are you going to do?" Charlotte asked. The novelty of Karen Anders was wearing thin, as Dad had predicted. It had taken less than a month.

"Please don't say anything to Karen," Leslie begged.

"Then I expect you to say something the next time she tries to tell you things," said Mom. "I can't say I'm not a little disappointed in you, Leslie. You can tell Karen that Mr. Bristol is a fine gentleman who deserves respect."

To Charlotte's knowledge, Leslie never had the chance to stand up for the Dewhurst family values of discretion and bravery. The next day on the school bus, Karen was livid. Apparently Mom had spoken to Karen's mother.

"Mr. Bristol is a man who deserves your respect," Charlotte said, in response to Karen's vitriol. "I don't think he would appreciate having his marriage discussed by the likes of you."

"Oh, you don't, do you?" Karen didn't say anything more and Charlotte was relieved the matter was settled, things could go back to the way they were. But that didn't happen. Karen had attached herself to the Dewhurst family and became a slow-acting poison intent on killing the loyalty between Charlotte and Leslie.

The sisters became guarded and a little less trusting. Charoltte's journals were sprinkled with complaints about Karen.

> Karen is especially relaxed with rules. I've often heard her ridicule Mom's attempts at family unity.
>
> That's what she does. She ridicules things other people value, thereby reducing everyone around her

to some level of anxiety, wondering how and when they will get hit. I have often been the butt of Karen's innuendoes.

Karen was athletic and forcefully encouraged Leslie to participate in every extra-curricular sport at their elementary school. In their freshman year at high school, the two girls joined soccer, volleyball and basketball teams, which required Mom and Mrs. Bristol to coordinate a driving schedule to pick them up after games and practices.

Mom tried her best, when it came to time and energy, to be fair to the rest of her daughters. The younger girls opted for dance and music lessons, but Charlotte, when asked what she wanted to do, declined any activity. She had not been a joiner. She particularly did not like sports teams.

She told herself she could have been a decent athlete had she cared enough to try. For her own lack of effort she blamed Karen Anders, which was foolish, as if "cutting off her nose to spite her face" was a good plan. Food was Charlotte's consolation during her years of puberty and she became larger than she would have liked. Instead of dealing with it, she became contemptuous of thinness and fashion — two things Karen represented.

> Despite Karen's disdain for our Dewhurst Family Rules, she likes to hang around our house. Whenever Mrs. Bristol is late picking her up, which happens often, or forgets where she is, which happened more than once, Mom invites Karen to stay for supper.

Charlotte noticed those invitations ceased when Reese Dunn was hired to work on the farm. *Was Mom keeping Karen Anders from interfering with the new family dynamic and making it farcical?* Perhaps Mom was more intuitive than Charlotte realized.

> My mother believes Reese's mother has no parenting tools. Selina Dunn's household is chaotic and her are children hungry. Whenever we drive past their rented acreage on the way to grandma's house, Mom comments on the Dunn's yard littered with dismantled cars and trucks. For some reason, that is Selina's fault.

> My mother believes a woman's job is to raise confident children, manage an efficient household, and to live within one's means. She thinks of herself as resourceful. She uses whatever tools she has to keep us in line. Food and guilt are two of them.
>
> My mother is very judgmental about "the tightness of one's ship."

Charlotte knew Dylan Dunn, the oldest boy, had dropped out of school when he was sixteen. He had a loud voice and a big truck. Rumour had it that he stole from farmers. The youngest boy, Kurtis, was scowling and rude. He was in Paige's grade at school and she had talked about him at home.

Reese, the middle child, had seldom been mentioned.

Charlotte wrote:

> Like me, he is a bit of a loner.
> Reese is somewhat like an onion. Not thick-skinned,
> just someone with several layers.
> I believe I am also like an onion.

She went out of her way at school to befriend him, and he was receptive enough, although their conversations were short and they did not hang out together.

Wendy and Paige had no reservations when it came to holding onto Reese's hands and asking to be swung around. They were affectionate, like puppies, and followed him. He tolerated their attention with good humour.

Charlotte envied the way Wendy and Paige welcomed him into the family.

Chapter 3

Leslie

September 1981

It was eleven o'clock in the morning when Leslie crept downstairs. She managed to elude her mother working in the kitchen and sneak outside without being scolded. At the periphery of the garden, she stopped. Dad was working with Paige, but Charlotte and Wendy were working with Reese Dunn — who was wielding a potato fork. He had become a leader of a potato digging team.

Leslie scowled. It had taken less than three weeks for Reese to infiltrate the family unit. Didn't she get enough of him at school, where he skulked the hallways and slouched, quiet and stupid, in the back of her grade twelve classroom?

"There you are." Dad called out and waved her over. "You can join my team. You know what to do."

Leslie had been harvesting potatoes for as long as she could remember. She pulled the resisting plants from the soil, shook off the potatoes clinging to the roots and threw the stalks in a pile by the side of the garden. Her father pried the remaining potatoes from the ground with the fork, and Paige rubbed the dirt off each one before classifying them into three piles — medium, large and those damaged by the fork. The smallest potatoes were left to decompose.

Leslie worked for several minutes in sulky silence, not unaware of laughter from the other team, annoyed that Paige had a hard time ignoring it and wouldn't work faster.

"How's the progress?" Mom asked, appearing outside.

"What do you think, Else?" Dad handed Mom a potato. "What do you think of our fine spuds?"

"They look good, Dan. Not so knobby as last year. And the skin is unbroken." She grabbed several from the damaged pile and put them in a pail. "I came to get Wendy. I need some help with lunch." To Leslie, she said, "Try to get more of the dirt off or they won't dry properly."

Leslie glowered. That had not been her job.

After Wendy left, Paige joined Reese's team leaving Leslie to work alone with her father. The row stretched out ahead. "Did we plant enough potatoes for the whole neighbourhood?" she groaned, straightening her back.

"All of us here have been working for an hour before you showed up," Dad said. The rebuke that she was lazy came out loud and clear.

Out of the corner of her eye, Leslie saw Paige toss a small potato at Reese. A second small one clipped him on the top of his head but Reese appeared oblivious. Leslie watched in spite of herself. After several minutes when Paige was classifying potatoes, he tossed one at her.

"Ow!" she yelped with great drama.

Reese dodged the one that came from Charlotte. He had an arsenal of walnut-sized potatoes in his coverall pocket. One after another, he pelted Charlotte with uncanny aim as she ran shrieking with laughter across the garden. Paige retaliated in Charlotte's defence but Reese was able to hold them both off.

Mom came running outside again, her eyes wild with concern. "What's going on? I thought someone was hurt, with all the screaming."

"Just a bit of fun," Dad answered, smiling. "It's over now."

Hill by hill, Leslie and her father worked their way toward the other team. The closer they got, the faster they worked. Leslie felt a trickle of sweat run down her back. Finally the last plant was pulled, the stalks thrown in the pile, the ground forked and the potatoes laid to dry in the sun.

"The perfect sized potato," Dad said to Reese, as they walked together to the house, "is one you can hold in your hand while you peel it. Those big potatoes are often watery with hollow centres. They don't last long in cold storage."

Potatoes 101, Leslie thought, following behind with Charlotte and Paige.

Reese sat at their table as if he belonged. He bowed his head in prayer as if thanking God didn't make him uncomfortable. Leslie was sure he had never been to church.

"The tradition," Mom said to him, as she passed around a bowl of corn niblets, "is after work we go out for supper in town and take in an early movie, if it's an appropriate one. Would you like to join us?"

"The invitation," Charlotte explained, "is based on the premise 'All work and no play makes Johnny a dull boy.' Or is it Jack?" she grinned.

"I'm going to pass on the movie tonight," Leslie said, before Reese could reply. "There's a party I want to attend. With Karen." She knew she was throwing a curve into her mother's carefully constructed plans, but really, all day with her family was too much.

"You can do both," Mom said.

Leslie was about to argue but Dad shot her a look.

The conversation during the meal twisted and turned on more and less interesting topics, but kept coming back to Leslie's attempted abdication of tradition, despite her not saying anything.

"You always said parties don't get going before eleven anyway," said Charlotte.

"And weren't you at a party last night?" asked Dad. "You can go out after the movie." He pushed away from the table. "Thanks for dinner, Elsie. I'm going to have a short nap. Everyone, take a break. In an hour, we'll bag those potatoes."

Leslie sighed. Her father's authority ended all skirmishes and rebellions.

Later that night, after Leslie returned home from the family outing, Karen came over.

"Did I ever tell you the joke about the woman stuck in mud?" she asked.

"I can't remember." Leslie applied eye shadow and gazed at herself critically. In the reflection of the mirror, Karen was reclining on her bed.

"A farmer came across a young woman stuck in mud ..."

Leslie rolled her eyes. *Here we go again.*

"'This is the third pregnant woman I've helped this month,' observed the farmer. 'I'm not pregnant,' said the woman, surprised."

Karen paused for the punchline. "'You're not out of the mud either,' said the farmer."

Leslie knew what Karen was insinuating but didn't want to give her the satisfaction by asking.

"I was wondering." Karen stood and looked out the window. "Reese Dunn is kind of cute in those overalls."

"Oh puleeze."

"Come here and look. You can see his blue eyes!"

"Get away from the window. He'll see us spying on him."

"Reese Dunn. Of all people."

"Dad said he's a godsend."

"I'll say. A boyfriend for Charlotte, a brother for you, a son for your father. And all he does is work, even on Saturday night. You know what would be fun?" Karen's voice rose in enthusiasm. "We could make him over. All he has to do is hang around us and Voilà! He's accepted. It could be our little experiment."

"I don't want to be part of your experiment."

Karen came away from the window and leaned close. "You can tell me," she whispered. "What does he talk about when he's sitting right in front of you?"

"He asks about you." A lie, of course. The truth was, Reese didn't talk much at all.

"So, tell me again how you managed to finagle a hired man for your father."

"Don't remind me." Leslie exaggerated a shudder. That day was still fresh in her mind.

She and Karen had stopped at the Dairy Queen after soccer practice. They had sat in front of the Anders farmhouse for several minutes while Karen finished telling a mean gossipy story about a girl in grade eleven, a girl they both disliked. Because she was late, Leslie chose to take the dirt road home rather than the longer route on the gravel grid.

The summer road had appeared dry at the outset but she soon discovered small puddles. She had forgotten all about the thunderstorm that had blown through three days earlier. Past a rise in the road, out of sight, there had been a low spot filled with water. Too late to brake and too inexperienced to get enough speed to maneuver through, Leslie panicked. The car fishtailed, lost momentum, and lodged securely in the mud.

Frustration welled up amid a burst of words she normally didn't use. Tentatively she opened the car door. She removed her running shoes and her socks and stuffed them in her backpack. Barefoot, she stepped out. Mud squished between her toes as she slammed the car door and walked to where it was dry on higher ground. She could see the rows of evergreens surrounding her family's yard two miles away.

Leslie put her socks on over her muddy feet. She put on her shoes and started trudging across the recently combined field. She tried to walk between the rows of canola stubble. Her school bag gained weight with every step and her feet, dirty inside her socks, were uncomfortable. In the distance she heard engines — a not uncommon sound during harvest.

As she approached the top of the highest elevation of land, she could see two three-wheelers tearing around, creating a dust storm in someone's summer fallow. The machines approached. The solo driver, a stranger, shut off his engine. Leslie recognized Reese and Dylan Dunn together on the other machine.

"So what do we have here?" the stranger said, with a grin.

"My car is stuck. I'm walking home. And I'm late for supper." Leslie added the last statement with the implication someone would soon come looking for her.

"Hop on. I'll give you a ride." The stranger laughed.

Dylan Dunn joined in.

"I can walk." Leslie thought they were all creeps.

"He's safe enough." Dylan gestured toward his brother. "She's all yours," he said, and climbed onto the back of the stranger's machine. Amid a roar of throttle and more crude laughter, the two took off.

"I can walk," Leslie repeated.

Reese stood beside his machine and remained silent.

Depending on her audience, Leslie had different renderings of her story. The version for her parents omitted the stranger's invitation to 'hop on.' The account for friends embellished the potential danger and maximized Leslie's cockiness. Her version for Karen had been downright lewd. But one mistake had been made in the telling. Leslie had shrugged off Reese's involvement in the situation and that omission had been picked up on Karen's radar.

Leslie had failed to mention how she almost tumbled off the

back of the machine when Reese shifted into first gear. How he stopped and had taken her school bag so she could hold on to him with both arms. How her cheek had bumped against his back as they bounced across the field.

What she had most excluded was how little she had been repelled by Reese's proximity.

Chapter 4

Elsie

October 1981

Elsie had splurged on the purchase of a tablecloth. It was linen, required ironing and hadn't been on sale, but it coordinated beautifully with the autumn-leaf place mats she had sewn a few years earlier. The tablecloth helped display her china, silverware and crystal to their full potential.

"Everything looks just lovely." Rose Dewhurst, Elsie's mother-in-law, was the first through the door.

Elsie gave her a hug, surprised at the sudden gratitude surging through her. Rose Dewhurst wasn't known to give compliments.

"Where are my girls?" asked Joe, who had followed his wife.

"They're quiet." Elsie went upstairs to investigate. Charlotte was reading, Leslie was lying fully clothed on top of her bed with her eyes closed, and the two younger ones were on the floor playing with Barbies, which made Elsie smile. It was nice to have children who still played with dolls.

"Your grandparents are here. They'd like to see you."

Judy Rasmussen, Dan's sister, arrived with her husband, Troy, and their three active sons, aged twelve, nine and six. The squealing became almost intolerable as the boys chased Paige and Wendy throughout the house.

"Let the men supervise." Judy, a tall woman with long hair and an infectious laugh, was Elsie's best friend and confidant. She followed Elsie into the kitchen and put on an apron. "What needs doing?"

Elsie pointed to a large pot of cooked potatoes ready for

mashing. "I'll transfer the rest of the food into serving bowls while you do that." She regarded her sister-in-law with fondness.

When the last guest washed up and found a chair around the table, Troy Rasmussen took photos of Dan standing with his carving knife and fork looking ready to attack the turkey. The boys make duck faces behind his back.

Dan put down the utensils and everyone bowed their heads. "Good and loving Father. We have much to be grateful for. Thank you for answering our prayers, Dad's heart surgery this past summer was successful."

Elsie's eyes moved to Joe Dewhurst. His absence on the farm had not been noticeable because Reese had helped fill it.

"Bless this food to our use. And us to thy service. Amen," Dan said.

"Amen," everyone chorused.

"Please dig in," Elsie invited.

Chad, her oldest nephew, hollowed the top of his mountain of mashed potatoes and filled it with gravy. In his haste to copy Chad, the youngest Rasmussen boy knocked over his glass of cranberry juice. Elsie didn't jump to her feet with a shriek — as was her first instinct — but forced herself to calmly blot up the mess with paper napkins.

As soon as it was reasonably polite she would soak her new tablecloth in cold water.

Or is the water supposed to be hot?

She pushed the question out of her mind as she attempted participation in the conversations around her, at the same time constantly scanning the table for bowls and platters that needed refilling.

Several times during the meal, Judy caught her eye and winked.

After the meal, Dan took his parents and Troy on a driving tour of his recently harvested land, a tradition from which he derived great pleasure. Elsie watched them leave. She hoped their eyes didn't glaze over like hers did when Dan talked about crop yields and future rotations.

She checked the washtub in the laundry room where the new tablecloth with the offending cranberry juice was soaking. The stain was dissolving satisfactorily.

Outside the younger children were playing and their voices rang with just the right timbre. Elsie debated asking Charlotte and Leslie to help wash up, but decided not to. Time alone to gossip with Judy was priceless. Elsie loaded the dishwasher while Judy filled the kitchen sink with water to hand wash the silverware and crystal and china.

"I wanted to invite Reese Dunn." Elsie picked up a dish towel. "But Charlotte said it would look odd, as if he didn't have his own family."

"I haven't had a chance to meet that young man of yours. What luck you found him, with Dad unable to help."

"Dan didn't want your father to fuss. Retired farmers can't resist the harvest." Elsie dried each piece of silverware. "When Reese first started, he was so shy he wouldn't look at us. It just about drove me crazy, seeing his eyes dart back and forth. I gave him lessons on how to make eye contact."

"You didn't!"

"I did, Judy. He was magnanimous about it — didn't act insulted or hurt. You know, if you can't look someone in the eyes, it looks deceitful."

"You're right about that."

"Dan says he never stands around waiting for direction but finds something to do, sweeping the shop or cleaning the windows of the combine. The first time Reese came to be paid, he claimed fewer hours than I gave him credit for. It happened a second time, and a third so I stopped keeping track and decided to trust he wouldn't cheat us. We gave him a bonus cheque when harvest was completed."

"Hmmm. And here's a farm going to be needing a young man in the future."

Elsie laughed. "According to your mother, the whole countryside is talking. Not to mention our neighbour up the road."

"Ah, the evil Lila Gladstone."

"Lila's not exactly evil. She's very friendly and does a lot of good in the community."

"The very worst kind. You're sabotaged with a southern accent and a smile."

"She does put on a bit of a drawl. The men lap it up. She puts her hand on Dan's arm when she talks to him. You should see him squirm! It would make you laugh. Did I ever tell you what she said to me after church one Sunday, shortly after Reese started working for us?"

"I don't think so."

"She confronted me in the church vestibule. 'I understand you have that Dunn boy working for you,' she said. Charlotte was beside me at the time, and I could see she was ready to leap to Reese's defence if I succumbed to what she calls 'Lila's sweet acrid tongue.' (I don't know where Charlotte comes up with these descriptions.) 'He's a good worker,' I replied. 'You're not worried he might steal from you?' asked Lila. 'Steal from us?' I said. That's when Charlotte jumped in and cried, 'Reese would never steal from anyone!' Lila got this funny look on her face and said, 'You don't think you might be inviting the fox into the hen house, Elsie?'"

Judy laughed. "Good old Lila Gladstone. Not known to mince words."

"Do *you* think I'm inviting the fox into the hen house?"

"He sounds more like a puppy than a fox. Nice he's fitting in, though. I do love an underdog story." Judy gave Elsie a look. "The rest of his family is still on the fringe, I suppose."

Elsie sighed. "I can't put my finger on it. They make no attempt to fit in. I mean, if they at least tried, I could give them points. But that yard! At the very least they could hide that mess of theirs behind a hedge."

The kitchen gained a semblance of order as they chatted. The china and crystal were returned to the buffet cabinet; each piece of silverware left on towels to ensure all moisture evaporated before being returned to the felt-lined storage chest. The counters were wiped clean.

"A walk?" Judy suggested, like she did every year.

The two women put on their jackets and issued instructions to Charlotte and Leslie to watch the younger ones — specifically the boys.

"It's Charlotte I most worry about," Elsie said, when she was sure they were out of earshot. They turned east at the crossroad.

"What's wrong with Charlotte?"

"She's in grade eleven and has no social life." Elsie sighed. "Not like Leslie."

"High school is made for girls like Leslie. University is made for girls like Charlotte. Give her time."

"I know. You're probably right."

"I hate it when kids mature too young. All they want to do is party. Remember how you had to put up with Leslie's sulks and tantrums because you wouldn't let her date in grade nine?"

"I remember. That was a tough year." Leslie had been noticed by the boys on the football team and invited to after-game parties. "Now she's a senior, with no one steady. And that's fine with us." Elsie stopped to adjust her scarf. "But Charlotte is such a loner. Dan and I suggested sports. Unfortunately, Leslie's best friend was at the house and overheard. She said 'Play soccer. We need big girls on defence.'"

"Ouch. Karen Anders is a piece of work,"

"That she is." It wasn't the first time Elsie had complained about Karen to Judy.

They approached the lane leading to the farmyard of Pete and Lila Gladstone. There were large stones heaped in a pile in the ditch.

"What's this?" Judy asked.

"I don't know. The stones weren't there the last time I came this way. Do you think the Gladstones could be building a monument or some signpost, or something? She's artistic, but some of her ideas are weird."

"We could drop in for a visit and ask."

"She'd welcome us with open arms. Lila is nothing if not hospitable. But let's turn around here and go back. I forgot to put on my walking shoes and these are starting to pinch."

They turned their gazes homeward.

"I've always liked the view of your farm from this angle," said Judy.

"Just another yard surrounded by evergreens. You can't see the house or the buildings. But you're right, it does look nice. Saskatchewan has a subtle beauty."

"Very subtle, some would say. Do you ever walk the other road? Past the Fields' farm?"

"Sometimes. But the wind always seems a little brisker from that direction."

"Do you visit often with your neighbours, Elsie?"

"The Gladstones go to the same church as us so we see them almost every Sunday. But the Fields, not so much. They like to party. They're nice, though," Elsie added quickly. Donald Fields sometimes made her uncomfortable. He was a little too friendly, a little too touchy. She was, perhaps, a little too prudish.

After walking several minutes in silence, Judy cleared her throat. "Do you ever think about having another baby?"

"No," said Elsie, surprised at the question. "Not ever. I'm forty, remember. And Paige is almost ten." She turned to Judy. "Don't tell me you're thinking about having a fourth."

"Past thinking. I'm pregnant again."

Pregnant! Elsie stood still and stared at her sister-in-law. Judy's grey eyes stared back.

Elsie came to her senses and gave Judy a hug. "Congratulations! That announcement caught me off guard."

"It caught us off guard too," Judy admitted, resuming their walk.

"Pregnant! I can't believe it."

"It took Troy a week to get over the shock. He's getting that vasectomy he promised."

"How far along are you?"

"Three months. We haven't made an announcement, so keep the news to yourself. You can tell Dan. Of course, my mother noticed I'm gaining weight." Judy laughed without mirth.

They turned south at the crossroad and could hear the outside voices of their children. As they walked up the driveway, Judy's boys raced to meet them. The youngest spontaneously grabbed Elsie's hand and swung her arm wildly.

Elsie smiled at her nephew and rescued her limb from dislocation.

Wouldn't it be lovely if Troy and Judy had a girl this time?

Chapter 5

Charlotte

February 1982

The blizzard began in the evening.

Throughout the night, tiny fingers of frigid draughts snaked their way into Charlotte's bedroom. She burrowed herself under the warm wool quilt Mom had made and tried to sleep, but the wind screamed and the house trembled. Charlotte's dreams were as wild as the storm and all but forgotten when she woke the next morning.

She checked the clock on the desk and saw it was after nine. Had she not set the alarm the evening before? In the kitchen below her room she could hear the rise and fall of relaxed conversation between her parents. She tossed her bed covers aside, stood, stretched and looked out the window. The sky was an intense robin's egg blue contrasting against the brilliant white of fresh snow. It was calm. No wind. She put on her housecoat and walked downstairs.

"Today is a gift from God," said Mom. "No busses are running."

The words sent a thrill through Charlotte. A day to do anything she wanted at home, even if it were only to watch daytime TV. All plans and appointments were cancelled or postponed. Meals were casual and random and simple, like scrambled eggs on toast for supper.

The words "I'd like to go to school," were out of her mouth before she could stop them.

Her parents looked at each other. Charlotte couldn't tell if they were puzzled, impressed or disappointed.

"I'll go start the tractor and clear out the yard." Dad put down his coffee cup. "There's a snow drift barricading us in. Unless we want to remain trapped, I'm going to have to clear the yard anyway." To Mom he said, "I have a few parts to pick up in town. I can spend the day fixing."

"You don't mind, do you?" Charlotte was sorry she had asked. Dad also might have appreciated "a gift from God." A day in which to do nothing.

"How can I refuse a girl who wants to go to school?" Dad grinned at her and grabbed his winter coat off the hook in the mudroom.

"I'll wake your sisters." Mom headed up the stairs.

A few minutes later, Leslie stomped down. "Just great," she hissed, inches away so Charlotte felt the spray of her spittle. "If *you* go to school and I don't, the teachers will think I'm a slacker."

"I doubt they'll notice you're not there." It wasn't the right thing to say, but lately, nothing was.

A few minutes later Wendy and Paige came down, protesting.

"I'm not going to fight with them," said Mom to Charlotte. "Let them be. They can stay and you can go. What's so important at school?"

Charlotte was secretly jealous of the town kids who got to spend creative, informal time with the teachers. She remembered returning to classrooms transformed with new bulletin boards and displays. But instead of telling her mother the truth, she said, "I don't want to be stuck at home with Leslie. What a bag she has been!"

"I beg your pardon?"

"Haven't you noticed how mean she's been?"

Charlotte knew why. Leslie had been refusing the hot chocolate and cookies Mom often had waiting for them after school. Charlotte could tell the sacrifice was making her sister a little crazy.

In a rare moment of vulnerability, Leslie had told her about the failed shopping trip to the city two weeks earlier with Mom, Karen Anders and Mrs. Bristol. It was supposed to be a fun mother-and-daughter day searching out all the formal wear stores for graduation dresses but Leslie had returned dispirited.

"I can't believe I'm two sizes bigger than Karen. She even looked great in the one with the big puffy sleeves." Leslie looked at herself in the mirror. "I think it's my shoulders."

"Not much you can do about the width of your shoulders."

"We'll see about that." A look of determination fixed on Leslie's face. "I'm going to lose weight."

Immediately defensive about her own extra pounds, Charlotte's moment of sisterly love slipped away.

"I don't understand your jealousy. You have everything. You're a walking cliché. Good looks, great figure, a fun personality, and athletic ability." After a comedic pause, she had added, "Reasonable mental acuity."

Along the route to town, Dad and Charlotte got stuck where a row of evergreens caught the snow and created a drift.

"Maybe this wasn't such a good idea," Charlotte said.

Dad grinned at her and hopped out of the truck. He grabbed the shovel from the truck box and started to dig. It wasn't long before Mr. Fields, the neighbour to the south, drove up.

"The municipal snowplows are out clearing the snow, but it may be a few hours yet," Mr. Fields said, tramping through the snow with his big high boots. He helped push them through and Dad and Charlotte returned the favour by pushing his truck. By the time Charlotte arrived at school, it was ten minutes into her third period history class. The room was dark but not empty, as she first thought when she entered.

"I'm showing a slideshow of my trip to the United Kingdom," said Mr. Potts, a middle-aged teacher, best known for putting students to sleep with his voice. This time with a small group of attentive students, Mr. Potts was so enthusiastic Charlotte decided her first trip abroad would be to England.

At noon she sat on a bench in the front hall, a spot usually occupied by the high school jocks who liked to command the view at the junction of two hallways. No one challenged her right to be there. *What would happen if I started to sit here on a regular basis?* She decided she wasn't brave enough.

Seemingly out of nowhere, Reese appeared.

"I'm oddly impressed you're here," Charlotte said as he sat beside her.

"Hello to you too." Reese unwrapped an unappetizing-looking sandwich, the kind sold at garage station convenience stores. "I failed a physics test." He took a bite. "The rewrite is today." He took another bite. "Of course the exam was scheduled before this storm came along."

"I bet you could have pushed the test off for another day by not showing up."

"And forget what I studied?" Reese rewrapped the second half of his sandwich and tossed it in the garbage. "Also, I didn't want to be stuck at home with my family."

"You too? I can't stand Leslie." Charlotte shifted her position on the bench to study Reese. "So, what's wrong at your house?"

"There's too much yelling going on."

"At you?"

Reese shook his head. "My older brother needs to move out and get his own place. He and my Dad get into it. I try to stay out of the way."

"Hang on four more months until you graduate. Find yourself a job and move out."

"I could move out tomorrow, if I wanted. I saved almost everything I earned working for your dad. I could get a part-time job and still finish school. If I wanted." The briefest of smiles flashed across his face. "But I want money for something important. I don't know yet what that is."

"You want to be prepared for any opportunity. I think that's smart."

Reese gathered his books. "Speaking of smart, congratulations on getting the Ottawa trip. I heard your name announced yesterday on the intercom."

Charlotte flushed with pride. "I had to write an essay on why I'm the best choice for the school. Looks like my argument was a compelling one."

"When do you go?"

"In April. I get to miss a whole week of school. But of course I have to talk about it at assembly. Get in front of the whole school and speak."

Reese shuddered. "That would be a nightmare for me. Well, I'm getting help in algebra, another of my weaker subjects. I'm meeting someone now. And then I'm going to ace my physics exam. See you later, Char."

Charlotte thrilled at the sound. Her very first nickname. Char.

"Good luck," she called after him. Her smile froze.

Karen Anders was walking up the hallway toward Reese, touching his arm and leading him into a classroom.
Not Karen Anders.
The school bully. A steamroller, a control freak. Karen Anders, who uttered words under her breath to Charlotte, words that left her uncertain and bewildered.
"Slut," Charlotte sometimes replied in return. Once she said it first.
She picked up her book bag and walked down the corridor, slowing to look inside the room. Reese and Karen were pulling their desks side by side.
Charlotte turned around and retraced her steps. She snuck another little glance. They were opening their textbooks.
She walked past a third time and this time Karen glanced up. Her face was long and horsey. She smiled at Charlotte.

"That's funny," Leslie said, when Charlotte returned home and told her all about Reese and Karen. "I phoned Karen this morning while Dad was plowing out the yard. She told me she was staying home."
"I'm concerned about Reese," said Charlotte. "The two of you made fun of him all last fall."
"Karen has since re-evaluated the situation. She thinks he might have potential."
Charlotte snorted. "What situation? Potential for what?"
"She thinks she can make him popular."
"How? By letting him hang around her?"
"Something like that."
"Make a silk purse out of a sow's ear?"
"Karen thinks it can be done," Leslie said, seemingly unperturbed with Charlotte's rising anger.
"She'd be playing with him."
"Of course she'd be playing with him." Leslie put her face close to Charlotte's. "If you had the chance to hang with the cool kids, wouldn't you take it?"
"I have no need to be validated by your 'so called' cool kids," Charlotte hissed. "I'm already a silk purse. And Reese is too."
"I'm sure he is." Leslie opened her bedroom door and gestured for Charlotte to leave.

The next day at school, Charlotte cornered Reese by his locker. "I need to talk to you. In private. About Karen Anders." She lowered her voice, although no one was within earshot. "She's using you."

"She's using me for what?"

Charlotte hesitated. Had she honestly thought he'd be grateful? Still, it would be wrong not to warn him. "She wants to make you over. Like a project."

Reese's face got red.

"Karen Anders is not nice." Desperation crept into Charlotte's voice. "I don't want to see you get hurt."

Reese slammed his locker shut. The echo of its sound reverberated down the hallway and it seemed like everyone in the school turned to stare at them.

"It's not your business, Charlotte, who I hang around with."

Chapter 6

Leslie

March 1982

It was another Saturday night sitting around Karen's house with a group of friends while her mother and Mr. Bristol were out. Leslie yawned. It was barely eleven-thirty. She could go home before curfew or she could hang around and hope something more interesting would happen.

She glanced over at the corner of the living room where Reese Dunn sat. It was the third time he had been invited to hang out with them. Karen's experiment wasn't working. He still looked like he didn't belong. But he was looking better than he had before. He wore his hair longer in a mussed-up tousled look and his new jacket emphasized the broadness of his shoulders.

As if reading Leslie's mind, Karen sat on Reese's lap and wrapped her arms around him possessively. She winked at Leslie. Reese looked more uncomfortable than ever.

In one clarifying moment, Leslie realized she hated her best friend. Always, always, Karen was one step ahead.

There had been the grad dress shopping fiasco in January. On the second go-round, Karen bought the dress Leslie 'sort of' liked.

When Leslie had complained, Mom said, "I'll make you a dress."

Leslie had hardly been able to swallow her fury. *A homemade dress? As if?*

Then there had been senior girls' basketball. The team was strong and had traveled to tournaments throughout the province. Leslie, as captain, had provided exceptional leadership, but Karen had been a total showoff on the court. Apparently scouts from several American universities and colleges were watching. Karen had strutted around off the court and bragged she had been approached and was about to negotiate a scholarship.

No one had approached Leslie.

Last, but not least, there was a hockey player Leslie had been trying to attract, ever since the beginning of the grade twelve year when he had been imported from Ontario. All the girls in Hatfield had crushes on him but Leslie thought she had the best chance of being the chosen one. Somewhere between his promises of "I'll call you" and his excuses of "I've got a serious girlfriend back home" her patience fizzled. Wondering if her chances had been diminished because she was a farmer's daughter, she rejected him before he could reject her.

"It's over," she told Karen, without going into any detail except she had done the dumping.

The hockey player immediately turned his attention to Karen who didn't even try to play coy. She slept with him, and told everyone. Leslie felt vindicated soon after, when the hockey player's attention turned away from Karen.

"I bet you feel cheap," she said.

"Your hockey player wasn't worth the effort," Karen had retorted. "Your hired man is better looking."

"He's not *my* hired man." And yet, to her consternation, Leslie felt a strange sense of responsibility toward Reese. There was something about him. Some sort of innocence Karen was going to take.

Leslie knew exactly how Karen operated. "The Big Pounce," she called it. She would get Reese alone and make him an offer he couldn't refuse.

As if on cue, Karen stood up and announced she and Reese were going to drive into Hatfield to pick up pizza. Leslie guessed the drive into town would take longer than expected and "The Big Pounce" would happen on the way.

"What does everyone want?" Karen asked, flipping through the phone book. "If I order now, it'll be ready when we get there. How hungry are we?"

While she was in the kitchen on the telephone, Leslie approached Reese. "I need to talk to you," she said to him. "Alone."

Unrehearsed, it was as good a line as any.

She pulled him into an empty bedroom and closed the door to execute her version of "The Big Pounce." He was unprotesting when she kissed him, making sure the length of her body was pressed tight against the length of his. In a fleeting moment of unreality, Leslie became aware an excitement had crept into the bottom of her stomach. "My legs feel weak," she whispered. She pulled Reese with her on the bed, their lips locked. It was an awkward position.

Reese broke their connection. "We'd better get back to the others," he said to her left nostril and rolled off her. It was the longest string of words he had ever said to her.

"No." Leslie rose off the bed and wedged a wooden chair beneath the doorknob. She pushed him on his back and unbuttoned his shirt. "Ssh," she whispered.

"Is this some kind of joke?" Reese made another half-hearted struggle to sit up, but Leslie pushed him back down. Her fingers were moving over his chest, lower to his stomach, sliding under the top of his jeans. She found the elastic band of his briefs. His breathing stopped.

"I love you," she whispered.

Reese jerked forward, throwing her off. He stood, buttoned his shirt, removed the chair and closed the door behind him.

Leslie shut her eyes. *Shit.* She heard the front door slam, heard his truck roar to life and heard the tires spray gravel.

It was going to be all over school on Monday morning that Reese Dunn had walked out on Leslie Dewhurst. Everyone would have a hearty laugh. Karen would laugh the loudest.

Shit.

Leslie sat in the dark room for several minutes.

"Came on a little strong did you?" Karen said, when Leslie finally emerged.

"Go to hell." Leslie picked up her coat and left.

Reese's truck, visible from the road but hidden from the Dewhurst farmhouse by a windbreak of tall evergreens, was waiting for her. Leslie was surprised — and yet she wasn't. She turned off her lights and parked behind him.

"You blew your chance to get laid," she said, climbing into his truck.

"Don't be so crude. It doesn't suit you."

Leslie suppressed a smile. "I said 'I love you.'"

"That's the stupidest thing I ever heard you say. And you say plenty."

"But not to you, though my family thinks I could be nicer."

"So why me and why now?"

"Why not you? And why not now?"

"Stop being flip." His voice held a glare.

"You want the truth? The truth is, I couldn't stand seeing you with Karen."

"And why should you care?"

They stared at each other for a long time before Leslie said, "I don't know."

She moved closer and held his face between her two hands. Softly, their lips met, barely touching. She could feel a tiny bit of whisker rough against her chin.

Reese pushed her away. "This is a joke. You and Karen are in it together."

"I'm not capable of such a joke."

"That's not what Charlotte says."

"Charlotte always expects the worst from me."

"Prove her wrong. Go out with me. In public."

Leslie hesitated. *How would going out with him affect her status at school? Reese Dunn was a far cry from the popular hockey player every girl wanted.*

"Your silence is deafening," he said.

"I'm thinking. I'm not sure I want a boyfriend right now."

"Okay then," he started his truck. "Thanks for your honesty. This kissing has been fun, but that's it. You can get out now."

"No. Wait."

If she went out with him, what happened at Karen's house wouldn't matter. It would be discounted as just a bit of drama, a build-up to a scene. She could go out with him once or twice, and break it off, as if she had come to her senses.

"Okay. You win. I'll go out with you."

"Tomorrow afternoon. Around two. I'll come to the farm and pick you up."

"Tomorrow?"

"Two o'clock. And don't go changing your mind."

"I think you're the one who's a chicken," Leslie said, sliding closer. "We don't need a first date." She kissed him again and melted. "I'd better go." She let herself out of his truck and into her mother's car.

At the farmhouse doorstep she looked back. Reese was standing at the end of the Dewhurst driveway, a long shadow in the moonlight, like something on the cover of Charlotte's romance novels.

She had a feeling in her gut it was going to get messy.

Throughout the Sunday morning church service, Leslie thought about cancelling. At home, she dug out the phone book to find his number. Charlotte looked at her curiously the second time and Leslie fought the urge to confide in her.

Reese arrived fifteen minutes early. She was up in her room getting ready when she saw his truck drive into the yard. Quickly, she pulled on jeans and a navy-blue bunnyhug. She tied her hair in a high ponytail. She wasn't going to dress up special for him.

"It's so nice to see you." Mom welcomed Reese into the house. "Dan and I were saying it's been months."

"Since my birthday last November," Paige said.

Leslie stood at the top of the stairs and listened. She heard her father get up from his recliner.

"Good timing," Dad said to Reese. "I was starting to think about spring. I could sure use your help again — that is, if you want the job."

Leslie heard Reese clear his throat.

"We could move into the dining room and have a proper visit," Mom said. "I made a chocolate cake."

"Don't you want to have a proper visit?" Charlotte brushed past Leslie on the way down.

Reese cleared his throat again. "I'm here to pick up Leslie. We made plans to hang out together this afternoon."

At the bottom of the stairs Charlotte turned in slow motion. Her eyebrows were raised in surprise. Her mouth was a round "O."

Leslie descended quickly and breezed into the kitchen.

"I thought I heard a truck." She suppressed the nervous giggle that threatened to rise out of her throat. "Reese and I are going out on a date." She stressed the word date. To Reese she said, "I see you didn't chicken out."

"I never chicken out twice in a row." His eyes locked on hers. Leslie returned the look.

"So." Mom's voice was unnaturally high. "What are your plans?"

"Just driving around. Maybe stop somewhere for a coke or something," Reese said.

"We're getting acquainted." Leslie used an old-fashioned phrase her parents would like. "We haven't been very good friends."

"You haven't been friends at all," Charlotte pointed out.

"No, we haven't," Reese said.

"Well," said Mom. "Well. Leslie, be home before six. And Reese. Would you like to stay for supper?"

"Uh. Thanks but I think I'll pass. Just in case this date thing goes badly."

"Just in case this date thing goes badly," repeated Dad, and everyone started laughing as if it was the most hilarious thing. "If the date goes badly, I hope you'll still work for me."

Leslie put on her pink ski jacket, the new one she had gotten for Christmas, the one with the fur around the hood. It was time to get Reese away from the adoration of her family.

She could sense five sets of eyes staring out the dining room window as they drove out of the yard. Only then did she move closer to him on the bench seat of the truck. She took his hand and examined his big blunt fingers and rough skin. She brought his hand to her lips and kissed the palm. She folded the fingers over, as if the kiss was something that could be dropped and lost.

Reese was staring at her. "You are so beautiful."

"You watch the road."

They drove down the main street in Hatfield, made a U-turn and returned in the opposite direction. They stopped at the Dairy Queen, bought soft drinks and sat in a booth. Two giggling grade nine girls ogled at them.

"The news of you and me will be all over school," said Leslie. "Niners have nothing better to do than fantasize about the love life of seniors."

"Do you mind?"

"We'll be talked about, but later nobody will care. That's how high school works. Some other couple will have broken up, or started up, or gotten pregnant." Leslie paused. "Nothing exciting happens in Hatfield."

"Then let's get out of here. Out of town. Drive to Milford."

"That's almost an hour away."

"So? I've got a tank full of gas."

They took the highway north. Every ten or fifteen miles they drove through villages with names like Stalwart, Victory and St. Cloud.

They decided they didn't need to drive all the way to Milford. Reese turned off at the road leading to Crystal Lake Regional Park. He left his truck in the public parking lot and they walked along the road around the perimeter of the lake. Despite the sun and the warmth on their faces, everything was still frozen. The snow was melting into lace patterns; icicles hung from the cabin eaves.

"Did you ever wish you had a cabin at the lake?" Leslie asked noticing some were nicer than her house on the farm.

"I've wished for many things but a cabin at the lake isn't in the top ten. But sure. Who wouldn't?"

"What would be in your top ten?"

"Number one is this. Being with you right now."

"Excellent answer." Leslie pulled him towards her, wanting his body pressed close to hers, his lips on hers.

There was a wolf whistle from someone they couldn't see and Reese broke the embrace. "I think I'd better get you back. I don't want your family to get the wrong impression of me."

Leslie laughed. "My family likes you more than me. Did you see all their faces when you told them we were going on a date?"

"Liking me as your boyfriend is a little different than liking me as the farmhand."

"I didn't realize we had decided you were my boyfriend."

"We can decide this right now, if you want." His smile was playful. "I'm an all-or-nothing kind of guy. Don't worry. I won't leave you here if you want to end this. I'll still take you home."

She was a little turned on. "Let's see how far this can go."

"Date went okay?" Mom asked, casually.

"I think so. We just talked." Leslie was surprised at how easily the conversation with Reese had flowed, once the dam had broken. *We'd better get back to the others,* his very first sentence to her, less than twenty-four hours ago.

She went upstairs to Charlotte's room and knocked. She wanted to say there was more to Reese Dunn than his white-trash family.

Her sister was lying on her bed with her eyes closed as if she were asleep. Leslie reached over.

Charlotte snatched her hand away. "You promised," she said, her voice half-strangled. "You promised you wouldn't play games with him."

"I'm not playing a game."

"I know you, Leslie. You think you're too good for him." Her eyes were swollen. "And apparently, I'm not good enough."

"I'm sorry. I don't know what to say. It just happened."

"Things don't 'just happen' Leslie. You make them happen and then act all innocent."

"That's not true. I don't have that kind of power."

"Girls who look like you *always* have that kind of power."

Chapter 7

Elsie

April 1982

Elsie's heart lifted at the sight of Charlotte walking confidently through the arrival gate at the Saskatoon airport. The week without her had been long.

Elsie hugged her girl. "It looks like you had a terrific time."

"I did. The best time." Charlotte squirmed out of Elsie's embrace and stepped inside the circle of family members.

"Everyone missed you," said Paige.

"Yes," Leslie said. "Even me."

"Can't say I missed any of you. Ottawa's a neat city. We did lots of sightseeing. And I made many new friends." As if to prove her last statement true, Charlotte called out warm farewells to the assortment of students who had flown with her. She hop-scotched between groups of people waiting at the luggage carousel, laughing and hugging.

"In an arena where athletic ability and good looks are secondary to a quick mind, I shone," Charlotte bragged, when the six of them squeezed into the family sedan. "*I shone.* One of the leaders told me I had a strong voice. People listened when I talked."

"You don't think you should hide your light under a bushel?" Leslie said.

"I might run for student president in May."

"Stupid old student government," Leslie sniffed. "Only losers are on that."

"Not true." Charlotte remained unperturbed.

"Why are you in such a bad mood?" Elsie asked, twisting her

neck to frown at Leslie. It was a warning, and didn't require an answer.

"Lots of things happened while you were gone," Paige said. "Wendy won a hundred-dollar scholarship from the music festival. I won a twenty-five-dollar scholarship and mom said I could keep it. But best of all ... try to guess ..."

"She got the lead role in the dance recital." Leslie's voice was monotone. "She's Alice in Alice in Wonderland."

"Why that's great!" said Charlotte. "What a bunch of high achievers we all are."

"Not all of us," said Leslie. "I myself, have achieved a standard of mediocrity."

"Ah, but you have Reese — and he is besotted."

Elsie thought "besotted" was the perfect word.

After the initial shock and surprise had worn off, she and Dan had gotten used to the idea of Reese in his new capacity as sweetheart. It had taken the younger girls longer. The trip to Ottawa had been a timely interruption in the feud between the two eldest girls. Perhaps the bad feelings were over. Elsie fervently hoped so.

As they drove past the road leading to the Rasmussen acreage, Charlotte asked, "Has Aunt Judy had her baby yet?"

"My sister is overdue and very grumpy," said Dan. "So let's not stop to visit."

"I can't believe how much easier the fourth one is."

Judy was newly home from the hospital. Troy had taken their boys to a matinee movie in the city so she could rest.

A considerate husband.

Elsie's visit with Judy could be a proper one. She brought gifts: a casserole, a few pink sleepers, and an assortment of cotton dresses barely used from when her girls were infants.

"I'm not talking about the delivery," Judy continued. "That still wasn't easy. But getting back into running the house." She gestured toward her relatively organized kitchen. "I can handle that. Remember how the first baby overwhelmed us?"

"I felt immobilized with responsibility." Elsie was glad she wasn't the one with a newborn. "However, this is still a first. A daughter! Rose Alice. Named after each of her grandmas."

"I really expected she would be another boy — to balance out your four girls."

"I have failed miserably by not producing a son to take over the farm." Elsie could laugh, now that Dan had put a stop to unwanted sympathy from well-meaning relatives. "Our first baby is turning eighteen on April 30th and she's asked to have a party. We said yes — but not without some reservation."

"I'm dreading those teenage years. Chad turns thirteen this summer."

"I'm dreading this party," Elsie admitted.

More than fifty of Leslie's best friends showed up.

Much, much more.

Dan and Elsie lost count as they hid in the dining room and watched the steady stream of headlights point right at them through the window. Good Old Dog barked incessantly until Dan went outside and locked him in the shop.

"I'm concerned about the sobriety of some of the drivers," Dan said when he returned. "There's a lot of beer being unloaded from trucks and trunks. I think I should go out there."

"I'll take the role of assessing drunkenness." Charlotte was still buoyant from the success of her leadership week in Ottawa. She left the house with a flourish but it was an annoyed Leslie who brought six car keys into the house and handed them to Dan.

"This should satisfy you. I told those drivers we'd find them rides home. Reese said he'd help. That he wouldn't drink."

Reese and Charlotte are keeping everything under control? Elsie wasn't hopeful.

She caught her two youngest daughters upstairs watching the party from their open bedroom window. The noise outside was loud and the language was intolerable. Elsie slammed the window shut and glared. Chastened, Paige and Wendy crept to their respective beds.

"Is it necessary for those kids to use such language?" Elsie asked when Charlotte came to report on the alcohol consumption.

"It is a sad commentary on our youth."

"I wonder if their parents know how they talk." Elsie ignored her daughter's sarcasm.

"They don't. As you don't know how we act when you're not around."

"I hate this," Elsie whispered to Dan. "Even Charlotte is insufferable."

Before midnight, she set out the buns, condiments, paper napkins, and a large rectangle birthday cake. The boys swarmed the table and devoured everything. She hastily made peanut butter and jam sandwiches.

"The more food we can give them, the less drunk they'll be," Dan said. "I don't feel at all comfortable with this."

By two in the morning, Elsie and Dan had had enough. They put on their jackets and roamed the farmyard. Dan engaged Leslie's guests in friendly conversation, trying to assess who was allowed their car keys. Elsie worried about Dan's judgement but she wanted the night to end. She watched as the partiers retreated into vehicles and drove away. An hour later, only three boys and two trucks remained. Dan drove the boys to their respective homes while Elsie waited anxiously for his return. The night sky showed the promise of dawn by the time she and Dan finally climbed into bed.

Late the next morning, Elsie cleaned the house and Dan supervised the yard cleanup. While the younger girls picked up garbage, Dan helped Leslie and Charlotte pick up empty beer bottles, which were — he reported to Elsie — in the oddest of places: under bushes, in the hedge, in the garden. Some bottles were broken.

Elsie stayed indoors. She pulled rubber gloves over her hands and dipped a rag into disinfectant-diluted hot water. The whole mudroom was stinking of sour beer. Someone, stupid and insensitive, had ventured into the shower stall with muddy shoes. Someone who thought Leslie's mother had nothing better to do on Saturday than scour the bathroom. Is this what she had been reduced to? Cleaning up strangers' vomit and urine?

There had been a time when Elsie had attended parties. She had never been part of the fast crowd, but she had laughed and flirted and danced. She had given no thought to those who cleaned before and after an event.

But surely, even the fastest of my generation hadn't been so — piggish.

She backed out of the bathroom on her hands and knees and gave the floor a final wipe.

"Spic and span," she said aloud, picking up her scrub bucket and venturing outside toward the front of the house, to the veranda. She could hear her daughters' voices in the garden. And Reese's voice.

Such a thoughtful boy to help clean up. Thoughtful like Dan.

Twenty years ago at the Ag Bag Drag, a dance put on by the University of Saskatchewan Agricultural students, Elsie Holden, born and raised in Saskatoon, met the young man who would become her husband. She was in her first year of Home Economics. He was in his second year of a two-year vocational diploma course. He noticed she wasn't having a good time and took her away from the crowd. Over coffee and conversation, they "hit it off" and soon became serious. Elsie's parents and sister told her she was crazy to marry a farmer, even if he were handsome and athletic. Elsie was glad she hadn't listened to them. She and Dan moved into a big old house in the country and she had thrived.

The veranda was one of the features of the house that had attracted her. It was where she had served the neighbourhood wives lemonade and pound cake. They had visited often, bringing lily bulbs in the spring and jars of home preserves and brightly hued gladiolas in the fall. Elsie had been charmed by the gentleness and wisdom of the older wives, entertained by the gossipy warmth of the younger ones.

How the time has flown. Now I'm one of the older wives. And people seldom drop in unannounced anymore.

"Mom." Wendy interrupted Elsie's reminiscence. "Dad wants to show you something."

"Well, this can't be good."

Elsie followed Wendy to the garden, empty except for the decomposing plants of the past year. Dan gestured toward the angel statue he had given her when Leslie was born. It had been beheaded.

Elsie wept.

"I could glue the head back on," said Dan, "if only we could find it."

"And so ends the first — and last — high school party at the Dewhurst farm," Charlotte said sadly.

Later in the afternoon, Dan drove to the liquor store with boxes of empty bottles. He made a show of giving the refund money to Elsie.

"We are going to use this money to help replace your mother's angel," he said to Leslie, whose hand had been outstretched.

Chapter 8

Paige

May 1982

"Many hands make light work," Dad said when he rousted Paige and her sisters up early out of bed one Saturday morning in late May. "We're going to plant the potatoes and peas for your mother."

"Slave labour, that's what we are," Leslie grumbled. "What are you going to do when we're all gone?" she said, louder.

"We'll worry about that when the time comes. We won't need such a big garden. You have fifteen minutes before we meet outside."

Paige got into her grubby clothes. She ate the scrambled eggs and toast Mom had prepared and was the first daughter standing outside.

Dad slipped her a five-dollar bill.

Paige was surprised: to be bribed or rewarded was unusual.

"It's like a big empty canvas." Dad gestured to the freshly tilled garden when everyone congregated outside. He carried two large pails full of red potatoes, cut into sections. "Each piece should have at least two or three eyes." He picked one up to show. He did that every year. Paige could tell he liked teaching them practical stuff.

"How come Mom isn't helping?" Leslie asked.

"Your mother is tired. She has a lot to do this month."

The reason Mom had too much to do was because Paige had the lead role in the upcoming dance recital and there were extra rehearsals with other dance age groups. Mom was driving Paige into Hatfield almost every day. Charlotte and Leslie both had their drivers' licenses but Mom didn't trust either one of them to be careful on the gravel roads. So instead of them being chauffeurs, they had more to do in the house.

They weren't happy about it.

"I think the soil might be warm enough for the corn and beans as well," Dad said. "Those seeds don't like a cold bed. But we'll get this big job out of the way today."

"There's always too much work to do on the farm," Leslie grumbled. "The town kids don't have to work on Saturdays like we have to."

"You are privileged and you don't realize it. There are a lot of people who have no clue where their food comes from."

"I like working in the garden," Paige said. It was true. She preferred being outside doing yard work than inside cleaning the house, which was what Mom was likely doing.

"Well I don't." Leslie kicked a small stone in the dirt. "One day I'm moving away and I'm never coming back."

Dad didn't hear that, or see the kick. Or maybe he did and intentionally allowed Leslie to blow off some steam. That was one of the differences between Mom and Dad. Mom always picked up the sword, seldom backed away from a fight.

Dad worked quickly, using a spade to open the ground for them to slip in the potato piece, eye side up. Row after row, they worked. The air around them warmed as the sun rose higher in the sky.

When the last potato was planted, out came the pea seeds.

Dad made long rows with the hoe. "Two rows each for you to pick and shell in July. I expect you four to cooperate."

"I have a summer job," said Leslie.

"Good for you. I'm sure you can handle both."

When the four sisters were done with the garden work and washing up in the mudroom, Leslie said, "When I leave the farm, I'm taking Reese with me."

Dad was not around to hear that statement.

"How do you know he would go?" asked Charlotte.

"Reese would do anything I asked him to do."

Paige was afraid that might be true. It was the one thing about him that was disappointing. She wished he didn't like Leslie so much.

She wished he didn't like Leslie at all.

Chapter 9

Leslie

May 1982

*W*hat a surprise. Karen.

Waiting by Leslie's locker.

"I've found a house in the city," Karen said, as if the rift between the two of them had never happened. "Cheap. Four bedrooms. A twenty-minute walk to the campus. A five-minute bus ride."

"I thought you were going to Oregon." Leslie had not missed Karen one tiny bit.

"I've decided not to go."

"But why? You were so excited about the scholarship. Basketball was your dream."

"The U of S has a strong team."

"Well, good for Saskatchewan." Leslie opened her locker and selected her chemistry textbook off the top shelf. She slammed the door shut. "Who else will be living with you?"

"My cousin Christina. You've never met her. And Carrie McCombs who graduated last year."

"I remember her. She's got short red hair and looks like an elf."

"We have to sign a lease. July first to June thirtieth. One year. And we need a damage deposit."

"So you only want me for my money? Well, I don't have any."

Karen smiled slowly, a smirk twitching on her lips. "Are you interested?"

"I'll think about it." Truth be told, Leslie hadn't thought much about school next fall at all. She had applied half-heartedly, and was accepted. She was only going because that's what her father wanted.

Karen walked beside her to class. "Can you think about it soon? Carrie and Christina are also looking for a fourth roommate. I'd rather it be you."

"Thank you. That's nice of you to say."

"I mean it, Leslie."

Their friendship was restored as if the hockey player, the grad dress, and the basketball rivalry had never come between them. Unfortunately, it also meant Karen was back to her old bossy ways.

"I never see you anymore, Leslie."

"You came to my birthday party. You saw me then."

But Karen had kept her distance and had not said a word to Leslie, not even "happy birthday" or "hello."

"It's like you dropped off the end of the world," Karen continued. "Our friends ask about you. I tell them you're in love."

"I'm not in love." *It's only chemistry.* But Leslie didn't want to protest too much and give Karen the advantage.

"I can't imagine being so mindless over a boy. And Reese is just a boy like any other." Karen leaned closer. "I bet you're doing it with him. You can tell me."

"I've got to go."

"We aren't done with this conversation."

"Oh, yes we are." Leslie walked away.

Karen was wrong about Reese. He wasn't a boy like any other. He had ideas and plans and the purest of motives about sex. The decency she so admired in him was the source of her frustration. She wanted to possess him in a way she had never wanted to possess another human being.

Leslie sat cross-legged on the freshly mowed lawn. The ride-on lawnmower was abandoned a short distance away, Reese's task interrupted when she had come outside to talk. Reese reclined on his back, shading his eyes from the evening sun. Anyone could see them from the house, but it was important no one could hear their conversation.

"Are you afraid of my father? Is that why we aren't ... doing it?" Leslie asked. She would have said something cruder, but Reese hated it when she talked dirty.

"It's called respect. Respect has more power than fear."

"So, if I wasn't Dan Dewhurst's daughter — if I were someone like Karen Anders — you'd be more ..."

"I would never sleep with someone I didn't love."

That love word again. "We don't need to get married. Making love is not such a big deal."

"It is a big deal. I want our first time together to be special."

"Our first time will be special. I'm not talking about doing it outside against a tree with mosquitoes biting our asses. Champagne and roses would be nice, Reese. We don't need the honeymoon suite."

"What's wrong with getting married?"

Marriage meant in-laws, permanence, a mortgage, babies. Hardly romantic.

"We're eighteen," Leslie said. "Let's go to school first, get jobs, travel. Let's wait until we're twenty before we talk about marriage."

Reese sat up. "Speaking of jobs and travel, I've been asked to join a custom combine crew after graduation."

"What?" This was the first she heard of it. "Who asked you?"

"Ralph Hiebert. He lives just ..."

"I know who Ralph Hiebert is. Why did he ask you?"

"Calm down. Your parents will hear us and think we're fighting."

Leslie forced her voice to a normal tone. "Did my father put you up to this?"

"Your father wanted to do this when he was young. He told me it would be a lot of fun and a great experience. Ralph's crew is in Texas right now and working their way north."

"What about me?"

"It would only be until this harvest starts. Eight weeks tops."

"You've given this some thought, haven't you?" Leslie's voice rose again. "Without bothering to discuss it with me." She stood up.

"Where are you going?"

"To talk to my father. He shouldn't be putting ideas in your head."

Reese grabbed her by the ankle before she walked away. "I won't go, Leslie. I was only thinking about it."

47

But the mood was spoiled and Leslie sulked the rest of the evening. She did not talk to her father the next day about Ralph Hiebert's offer. She knew what her father would say — and he would be right. She was being selfish for wanting Reese to stay.

On weekends they had a private place they drove to when they wanted to be alone, an abandoned farmyard surrounded by trees. Each time they parked they got a little closer to "going all the way." Each time it ended in a fight. It was always Reese who stopped.

"I am not a virgin," she told him, in case the reason for his reluctance was his perceived mutual inexperience.

"I'm just an old-fashioned guy," he said, after a pause. He didn't ask who or when.

"I don't know where you get this 'I'm just an old-fashioned guy thing' from," Leslie retorted. "I think you're scared."

"I am not scared."

She pulled him on top of her. "You could have me right here." Leslie ground her body into his. "You could do anything you wanted with me. You could touch me anywhere and I would let you."

Reese turned his face away.

"I am not the teaser!" she cried, pushing him off her and sitting up. "You are!"

"That custom combine crew. The one I mentioned. They're still asking. I think I'd better join."

"You'd run away from me?"

"Maybe it's best."

"Maybe you're just not into girls."

Reese turned on the truck ignition.

"I have needs, Reese. It's like an itch needing to be scratched."

He took her home without saying a word. She slammed his truck door and walked into the house without a backward glance.

If he wanted to see her, she would be unavailable. He would be very, very sorry for making her so angry.

"Where's Reese?" Leslie asked her father when he came home alone for supper on Monday. She had been hoping to see him, to smile at him ever so little, to cajole him into forgiving her.

"It was too windy for spraying. I gave him the night off. He

didn't say anything to you?"
"No, he didn't."
"Are you two having a disagreement?"
"No." Of course everybody in the house probably guessed something was wrong, but it would not do to confess why.
At school on Wednesday Karen said, "Rumour has it the big romance is over."
"Go to hell, Karen."
"It must be difficult having him in your house."
Reese hadn't been at the house. He also avoided her at school.
He'll get over it, Leslie told herself, replaying the fight over and over in her head. She did not believe this impasse could last one more day. But it did. Four days. Five days.
She got the point. Reese was not one to be bullied.

He was standing at her locker on the sixth day. She ignored him as she dialled the combination on her lock, deposited her books and slammed the door shut.
Reese said, "You name the place and the time and I will let you do anything you want with me." He moved closer. She could smell the scent of his body. "You can touch me anywhere and I would let you."
She put her arms around his neck and wept. She didn't care if anyone saw.
They drove out to their spot. In broad daylight, against a tree, with mosquitos biting their asses, they ended their fight.
It didn't get more romantic than that.

Chapter 10

Charlotte

June 1982

The lovers — for it was obvious to Charlotte that was what Leslie and Reese had become — were seated in the front row on the stage of Hatfield's largest hall. They were separated by the second letter of their last names: Dewhurst, Dirk, Dundrige and Dunn. Reese leaned forward often and glanced at Leslie.

How can Mom and Dad ignore what is right in front of their eyes?

"I can't believe there is no air conditioning," Grandma complained for the third time, fanning herself with the graduation program during the endless speeches and congratulations from Mayor Beck and all the other local and provincial dignitaries. Her voice managed to carry well.

"The new sports complex will be finished by next year," Dad told her. "Charlotte's graduation will be cooler. If God is merciful." The last words were only for Charlotte's ears, and she smothered a giggle.

After the graduates received their diplomas and certificates, the awards were dispersed. Leslie had admitted she hoped to win the Girl's Athletic trophy, but Karen's name was called instead. Charlotte didn't feel too sorry for her sister, the prettiest girl on the stage, but she would have preferred someone other than Karen to have won.

Charlotte caught a brief glimpse of Reese's parents two rows behind. The two looked older than the other students' parents. Mom nodded politely in their direction, and so did Dad, but when the ceremony was over, neither of Charlotte's parents made a move to greet them.

"They look like a pair of tired old hippies," Grandma said with a sniff. "And why don't they get their teeth fixed?"

Grandma never let an opportunity pass to express her displeasure Leslie was dating a Dunn.

During the summer months, Leslie and Charlotte worked as cashiers in a Hatfield grocery store. The two had to share Mom's little car to get to work and back and the assistant manager did his best to make their schedules compatible. The Dewhurst family sedan had become unreliable and needed an expensive repair.

Major expenses often had to wait until after harvest.

Reese had a job pumping gas at a service station in Hatfield. Sometimes he was enlisted to drive Leslie or Charlotte home after their shift whenever Mom needed her car. His friendship with Charlotte had been restored, although they never discussed Leslie.

"My boss is an asshole," he said. "He thinks he's being funny when he gossips about everyone, including his best customers. I can only imagine what he says about my family."

"That's the trouble with small towns. Everyone knows everyone's business. And their history. I can hardly wait to move away."

"I can hardly wait to quit this job and work full time for your father. I've asked Leslie not to come by the gas station. My boss will say something dirty. Obviously, she's better than I deserve."

"If it's any consolation, I hate my job too," Charlotte replied, a little rankled by his "better than I deserve" comment. "I've lost all my people skills. The rude, impatient customers always come to my till. I'm sure it's on purpose. And Leslie gets the nice ones. She is so damn flirtatious. The older women call her 'dear' and 'sweetheart' and they are all so friendly."

"I'm sure people like you too, Char."

"I'm sure they don't. Leslie says to be playful. When I try to be playful, it comes across as sarcastic and condescending."

Reese laughed, but Charlotte hadn't been trying to be funny.

It took Dad's truck, Mom's car, six Dewhursts and one rainy day in late August to move Leslie's stuff to Saskatoon. Her rental house, a small one-story tucked among tall Victorians, was in the university area. The kitchen was galley style, a narrow corridor filled with cupboards and appliances. The living room was small and dark. There were four bedrooms, two on the main level and two larger ones in the basement.

"We drew names. And this is my room." With a flourish, Leslie threw open a door on the main level and everyone crowded in.

"I have seen closets with more floor space," Charlotte said.

"Not unlike a dormitory room," Mom said kindly. "One nice feature — you have a south facing window. You'll get lots of sun."

The window was small and placed high. Charlotte stood on her tiptoes to look out.

"We could make hay bales out there in the backyard."

"Don't be negative," said Mom.

Charlotte wished she was the one leaving home to attend university. She wished she could live in the closet-sized bedroom and look out the window at the long grass in the yard. On the other hand, there were a few perks created by Leslie's departure. Everyone moved up one notch in the Dewhurst household hierarchy. Charlotte was to move into Leslie's old bedroom with its double bed, and window facing the farmyard. Wendy had the choice of her current room or Charlotte's old one, and she chose Charlotte's because she was promised new furniture and the freedom to redecorate. Paige got a room to herself, the second largest in the house, with two single beds. She'd have to share it whenever Leslie came home.

Everyone helped carry the furniture into the rental house. The old single bed, the chest of drawers and the desk had been Charlotte's. She was particularly sorry to lose the desk. It had been a faithful friend through nights of anguished journal writing.

She helped Dad put up a mirror above the chest of drawers. Mom called his attention to a leaking faucet in the bathroom so he headed off to the nearest hardware store to pick up a part. Bored because there was nothing more to do, Charlotte, Wendy and Paige decided to see how many minutes it took to walk to the university campus from the house. The rain had stopped.

"Don't get lost," Mom shouted from the kitchen, as they put on their shoes. She and Leslie started cleaning shelves in the kitchen before unpacking boxes of dishes and other odds and ends.

"We won't," Paige shouted back.

"Between the three of us we've got a functioning brain," Charlotte said, not loud enough for her mother to hear.

The air outside was fresh and Charlotte inhaled deeply. *It's a novelty to walk on sidewalks canopied by tall dripping trees instead of dusty gravelled roads.* It took ten minutes until they scampered across College Drive and worked their way between the old stone buildings, toward the centre of the campus to a green area Charlotte knew was called The Bowl.

"Fourteen minutes." She looked at her watch. "It's a fourteen-minute walk from Leslie's house."

Now that she was out of the shadow of her popular older sister, Charlotte was determined to make the most of her senior year. She had failed in her bid to run for school president; undeterred she participated in the school's governance as a member on council. On Friday of the second week of school, she stayed late and caught a ride home with another member on council who had to drive several miles out of her way.

The house was empty. A note on the kitchen table said: "*I have taken Wendy to dance. Paige is at a birthday party/sleepover. I am at a meeting (672-5546). Stew is in the slow cooker. Please serve with buns. Back after eight. Love, Mom.*"

A suitcase and filled black garbage bag sat by the foot of the stairs, which could only mean ...

"Leslie?" Charlotte called up the stairwell, but there was no reply. She helped herself to a bowl of stew and sat comfortably alone.

Twenty minutes later, Dad and Grandpa walked in. Dad wanted Grandpa to go home after eating, but Grandpa wasn't ready to "call it a day." Half an hour later they left together, still arguing.

Reese and Leslie walked in next, stuck close together, their bodies touching.

"It's been a long week." Leslie dished out a generous portion and passed it to Reese. "You have to keep up your strength," she whispered loud enough for Charlotte to hear, her hand moving to Reese's thigh.

"Please," Charlotte begged. "Get a room."

Reese's face turned red.

"How long are you home for?" Charlotte asked. "And what's with the garbage bag?"

"It's filled with laundry. For Mom. And I'm leaving Sunday afternoon."

"You brought your laundry for Mom? Pretty arrogant, even for you. She only washes clothes on Monday. I am *incredulous*."

"All my white socks and underwear are grey because I washed them with my new blue jeans. Mom said she'd try to bleach them white again and hang them on the line."

"She brought her laundry home for Mom!" Charlotte repeated, turning to Reese for backup.

"What *is* your problem?" Leslie demanded. "I'm home to help. I'm not expecting to be served like a guest."

"By the way, how did you get home?"

"Karen's cousin, Christina. But she hates driving on gravel roads so next time someone needs to pick me up in Hatfield when she passes through."

"I didn't know Karen had a cousin."

"Yeah. Karen is full of surprises." Leslie didn't elaborate. "Hey, after we're done combining for the night, we're going to a party at the Pit. Do you want to come along?"

The Pit. The meeting place for underage drinking teenagers. Charlotte had never been there, never been part of that particular crowd. "Yeah. Sure," she said. *A new experience,* she thought as she watched Leslie and Reese drive away.

Mom and Wendy showed up after eight like the note stated.

"No family cohesiveness today," Charlotte joked, in way of greeting.

"And likely not on any Friday," Mom replied, setting a bag of groceries on the counter. "Just the way this year's dance schedule works out."

"There's three new girls in my age group," Wendy said. "One comes from a little town a hundred kilometres away."

"That's dedication." Mom dished out the remainder of the stew. "An hour drive each way. I shouldn't complain about my little bit. Can you finish this, Charlotte? Wendy?"

Their reply was drowned out by Dad shouting "Yoo-hoo!" from the back door. He stepped inside the kitchen. "I sent my father home. Reese said he could stay late. He and Leslie are combining. I've quit swathing for the night and now I'm going to haul grain. There's a warm wind blowing, so likely we'll work late."

"I can make you coffee to take to the field," Mom said.

"That would be great, Else. I'll pick it up when I return with another load." He left again.

Charlotte told herself she hadn't really wanted to go to The Pit. *Just a bunch of drunks. There might be something amusing to watch on TV, instead of summer reruns.*

She told herself she wasn't the least bit disappointed.

Chapter 11

Leslie

September 1982

One September weekday afternoon, Leslie returned from classes and found Reese asleep on the couch. Her roommates were not home so one thing led to another. And another. Afterwards, she and Reese walked hand in hand to an Italian restaurant on the corner of Clarence and Eighth where they sat in a booth across from each other. Reese was playful and seductive, twisting spaghetti around a fork, making her laugh.

Leslie could hardly get back fast enough to her little house. She wedged her desk chair under the doorknob so her roommates couldn't accidentally intrude.

Reese left before sunrise the next morning.

She could hear her roommates loud and clear in the kitchen when she stepped out of the shower.

"I came home yesterday at noon and found him sitting on our front step," said Karen. "I asked him why he didn't come into the house. The door was unlocked."

"What did he say?"

"Said he wasn't going to walk uninvited into a girls' residence."

"Decent of him," commented Carrie, "considering Christina wouldn't know him from Adam."

"The two of them. Going at it like rabbits." Christina sniffed.

"She's going to get pregnant," Karen said.

Talking about me, as if I can't hear.

Leslie walked into the kitchen, a towel wrapped around her hair. "For your information — and not that it's any of your business — I am on the pill. Do you think I'm stupid?"

"Smart girls — and nice girls — get pregnant, too." Carrie, sitting at the little kitchen table, smiled up at Leslie. "The truth is, we'd all like to have what you have. We're just being bitchy about it."

"I prefer to have my freedom to see what's out there." Karen put her empty coffee cup in the sink.

"Yay for freedom," said Christina. She was fully made-up, hair styled, not like the rest of them who were more casual. "Well I'm off to class. Who needs a ride?" She left without waiting for a response.

"What's eating her?" Carrie asked quietly.

"She's always been abrupt." Karen shrugged. "Don't take it personally."

"Christina needs to get laid." Leslie was purposely crude. *You all do.*

"You need to get married," Karen said. "That would cure your sex drive. At least that's what my mother says."

"You talk about me at home?" Leslie was aghast.

"Oh grow up. Do you think anyone back home really cares about your love life? Speaking of home, I hear the weather forecast calls for more rain. Lover Boy will be back soon."

Lover Boy. How Reese would hate the label.

Leslie retreated to her small sanctuary of a bedroom and studied herself in the mirror.

Only recently had she gone to a doctor in Saskatoon for a prescription of the birth control pill. The doctor warned it would not be effective until her next menstrual cycle. What she and Reese had been using was less reliable. They were playing roulette, and so far they were lucky.

"If we were married," Reese had said when they discussed contraceptives, "you could go to university while I worked. If we were married we wouldn't worry if you got pregnant. Everyone would say congratulations."

"I'm eighteen years old."

"My mother was married at eighteen."

"No one gets hitched that young anymore."

The thought of his family was a deterrent. If only Reese came unencumbered.

She couldn't ever be Leslie Dunn. She just couldn't.

After the harvest was completed, the fields prepared for spring, the equipment serviced and parked in the Quonset, Reese found a full-time job in the parts department at a Hatfield machinery dealer. Every Friday after work he drove to the city and stayed until Monday morning. Leslie never asked her roommates if they minded, and she was especially careful not to comment when their male guests slept over.

She liked it best when she and Reese had the house to themselves. They made loud love in rooms other than her bedroom.

Her parents asked why she never came home anymore. Leslie suspected they knew what was going on, but avoided the subject. She told them she needed to study. She wasn't entirely lying. She did need to study. She was not a natural brain like Charlotte.

Her father had urged her to attend university and take Arts and Science classes.

"A general education never hurt anyone," he said when he helped her pick out classes: history, science, math, English, philosophy. "It will help hone your critical thinking."

Leslie's last exam was history and scheduled at nine on the last Saturday morning before Christmas. By the time she finished writing, her hand was cramped. She didn't phone for Reese who was waiting to pick her up, but walked home. It took twelve minutes at a brisk pace.

Carrie was there with Reese. "I have the bad luck of one last exam on Monday," she said. "At least I get an empty house to study in. No distractions."

"I'm not looking forward to three weeks at home." Leslie carried her suitcase to the vestibule. "My parents will treat me like a child and expect me to fit back into the family rhythm. But I'm not the same person I used to be."

Carrie laughed. "I feel the same way."

"Maybe we'll run into you in Hatfield," Reese said, pleasant and polite as usual.

"Maybe. But if not, have a good Christmas and I'll see you in January."

Leslie, half asleep and bleary-eyed, sat resentfully in the church pew. She never went to church in the city. She was old enough to make her own decisions about her faith — or lack of it. But there was no use arguing with her father.

On Monday, she watched her sisters catch the school bus in the early morning darkness. It felt odd to be home, like having a sick day. But she wasn't sick and her mother expected help with the housework, the shopping, and the Christmas baking.

"You could act a little more enthusiastic," Mom said. "You haven't been home to help for months."

"I came home in November for the church fall supper."

"Well, that's a Dewhurst tradition."

"This family has too many Dewhurst traditions," Leslie grumbled. "If you didn't make such a big deal about things, you wouldn't be so short-tempered."

"I beg your pardon?"

Leslie opened her mouth to repeat what she had said, but the look on her mother's face stopped her.

"Society thrives on routine and tradition, young lady." Mom's voice escalated. "If you should be so fortunate as to have a family of your own, you will find out. Unless of course you intend to remain as self-centred as you are now."

"I hate being here at home."

"It would be the easy thing — to drive you back to the city," Dad said, walking into the conversation and ending it. "But that wouldn't make it right."

On Tuesday, Karen picked her up before noon and they drove to Hatfield. They walked the hallways of their high school and ran into teachers who asked them, without much interest, how they were doing. Students swarmed around them — young girls who had moved up a grade said they missed Leslie and Karen on all the sports teams. The young boys flirted shamelessly.

After an early supper, Leslie accompanied her family to the school Christmas concert and endured hours of poor acting and off-key singing. Near the end, Wendy and Paige, costumed as angels in white chiffon dresses, white tights and pink ballet slippers, danced gracefully. Leslie was shocked to notice Wendy was no longer a flat-chested child.

She found Reese waiting for her at the back of the school auditorium.

"It went a lot longer than I thought," she said, daring him to complain or make a joke. But he did neither.

"Reese, Reese, did you see us dance?" Paige cried, still in costume, coming out of nowhere and throwing herself at him. Wendy was behind her, angel wings getting caught in the crowd.

"I saw. You were both great." He allowed them to hang onto him.

"Come on." Leslie pulled him away. "I need to have you all to myself, away from my family. I can't stand living at home." She led him out into the night as if they were fugitives escaping from banality of Christmas good-will.

They drove to their deserted farmyard, his truck providing the only venue for the unsatisfactory turn in their sex life.

"This is ridiculous! I miss sleeping with you."

"I've been thinking," Reese said, holding her in his arms. "It's time to get my own place."

Two days before Christmas they went apartment hunting. Leslie preferred the one with a balcony and two bedrooms, but Reese chose the more reasonably-priced basement suite.

"Unless, of course, you want to move in with me and share the rent. My offer of marriage still stands. I would make an honest woman out of you." He smiled at her hopefully.

"Not yet."

He signed a one-year lease, wrote a cheque for the damage deposit and a second for the first month's rent.

"That puts a hole in the old saving account," he said ruefully, handing her the spare key. "And now I need furniture."

"A bed. A table and a chair. That's all you need."

"I'm saving money for a ring. You deserve a nice big rock."

"It would be wonderful to live together." Leslie wrapped her arms around him and smiled. "But my parents would never allow that."

She sighed. Ten more days at home to endure. Returning to the bosom of her family was more difficult than she had expected. She could hardly wait for the second semester of university to begin.

Chapter 12

Elsie

December 1982

Because Dan's sister had offered to host Christmas dinner, the only special meal Elsie needed to prepare was for Christmas Eve and only for her own family, including Reese.

She had the evening planned. After a relaxed supper they would play board games like Monopoly or StockTicker and later they would attend the service at the Hatfield United Church. The following morning, after opening gifts and eating a leisurely breakfast, the six of them would drive to the Rasmussen acreage to enjoy Christmas dinner with Dan's family. Later they would visit the Holden side of the family in Saskatoon, eat a modest supper at Elsie's parents, and drive home.

Without warning, Rose Dewhurst insisted Dan and Judy bring their respective families for "one last Christmas Eve." She had been threatening for years to sell the family farm and move to Hatfield. Elsie suspected it was all a ploy to guilt everyone into subservience.

Judy complained to Elsie over the telephone. "I tried to explain to Mom how inconvenient this summons is, but you know her. She tends to dig in her heels if opposed and I end up feeling selfish and ungrateful. So now we have an hour's drive for supper and an hour's drive back, all with three very active boys and Rosie. Plus I needed the twenty-fourth to prepare."

"Stay overnight at your parents' house. Dan and I will do Christmas."

"No, Elsie. You've done more than your share of the holidays. I know you were looking forward to a non-hosting Christmas."

"Well, I don't have a baby to take care of, plus I have four capable girls to help me. You can do Easter. And next Christmas too, if you insist."

"Maybe my mother will change her mind again if she knows it means keeping us overnight and half the next day."

"Maybe." Elsie didn't hold out much hope.

"Some people, when you turn down their invitation, say 'too bad. I should have phoned earlier. We'll get together another time.' But not my mother."

"I told her we had already invited Reese for Christmas Eve."

"And what did she have to say about that?"

Elsie's anger rose at the remembrance of the conversation. "She said Reese should stay with his own family. You know, I'm going to be just as stubborn. If she wants us, she'll have to accept Reese."

"Way to go, Elsie. You rebel."

"You are going to give that Dunn boy the wrong idea," Rose Dewhurst said when Elsie phoned to confirm Reese's invitation.

"What idea is that?"

"That he's part of our family. He'll eat a lot. Teenage boys do. Judy is bringing her boys with their huge appetites, so I don't know if there will be enough."

"I can bring some extra food." Elsie thought of her own crazy last-minute preparations. "And a chair, in case you don't have enough of those."

Dan's mother did not catch the subtle sarcasm. "I suppose Leslie won't come if he's not invited."

"It would be rude to rescind on a previous invitation."

There was a dreadful sigh. "Very well." Rose Dewhurst hung up without saying goodbye. It took all Elsie's self-control not to slam the receiver down on the handset.

"Thanks for being a good sport." Dan put his arm around Elsie.

"I don't want to be a good sport," she said, shaking off his arm.

Christmas Eve was as cheerless as Elsie had expected it to be. There were no coloured lights on the house, no boughs of holly and no "fa la la la la." An artificial tree in the living room corner was decorated with dull, brittle ornaments. The table was set with paper plates and plastic cutlery.

Leslie arrived with Reese. He looked young and clean in a dress shirt, tie and vest — as if prepared for the test of measuring up to impossible expectations. He was barely through the door when Rose Dewhurst started barraging him with questions about his job, his future, his plans. His words became hesitating, his eyes started to dart around and his feet started to inch toward the door, until Judy — bless her heart — made room for him on the couch, handed him the baby, and steered the talk out of Rose's control.

The evening was awkward. Elsie thought a glass or two or three of wine could have made the visit tolerable, but Rose and Joe Dewhurst were abstainers and expected everyone to be. Conversations sputtered and died. The children were unusually quiet. After a decent dessert — plum pudding with orange sauce — the dining room table was cleared so Dan and his father could play Kaiser against Reese and Charlotte. Everyone else went downstairs to the rumpus room to watch *The Sound of Music* on the television. The movie showed the wedding scene and Elsie glanced at her watch.

"Look at the time!" she shrieked. Three capable women in the house and not one of them had nagged ahead to find the car keys, warm the vehicles, change the baby, end the game, turn off the TV, use the bathroom, find the coats, find the boots, lock the door, and run back in to check for fire hazards.

When they arrived, the church was overflowing and all the pews in the sanctuary were full. The eight Dewhursts, the six Rasmussens, and the one Dunn climbed the stairs to the choir loft and squeezed in at the back.

Dan grumbled because he couldn't see.

"Hush," Elsie whispered, grabbing his hand. "You don't have to see. Just listen."

As the minister's voice dramatized the familiar story, her body relaxed. In Elsie's nineteen years of marriage, she had missed only two Christmas Eve services: once when a sudden storm made road travel dangerous, and the second when a stomach flu kept Elsie home with Wendy, the two of them miserable together sharing a bed and a bucket.

Near the end of the service, everyone held out their candles that had been given earlier by the ushers. The flame was passed from one candle to another. The electric lights were turned off and the choir sang "Silent Night." Rosie was finally asleep in Troy's arms and the smallest Rasmussen boy stopped squirming. The minister gave the benediction, the lights returned, the congregation sang "Joy to the World" and the candles were blown out.

"Merry Christmas!" everyone said, shaking hands and hugging.

Young adults and children spilled out everywhere. People who did not regularly attend church made the effort on Christmas Eve. It was like a reunion.

Elsie became separated from her family. While waiting on the stairs, she saw Dan and Lila Gladstone talking in the vestibule. Not once, but twice Lila put her hand on Dan's arm. The second time, Dan took a step away and looked right up at Elsie, his eyebrows raised in apology.

Elsie's eyes moved onto Leslie, who stood tall in her high-heeled boots, hair piled on top of her head and looking grown-up. How had she and Dan managed to create such a beauty? Elsie was hard on the girl, knew every one of her faults, yet loved her unreservedly.

Reese, who was standing beside Leslie, said something to make her laugh.

"The significance of the Dunn boy's presence in church will not be lost on those members of the congregation who make a point of observing such things."

Elsie had not noticed her mother-in-law behind her, gripping the banister with a gloved hand. "Let them speculate all they want," she said flippantly.

"In peoples' minds, this is an announcement of engagement."

"They have time enough for that!"

"I hope so. I pray for you and your family. And Judy's family too. I hope Dan has his shotgun ready."

"His shotgun?"

"You know how people talk."

Elsie's eyes flickered over to Dan, waiting at the bottom steps holding out her coat.

"We don't have a shotgun," she said.

"Reese gave me this."

Leslie pulled back her sweater sleeve and showed Elsie and Dan the gold Seiko watch on her slender wrist. "I bought him a new coat." She grinned. "Well, technically, you bought him the new coat because I had to dip into the money you gave me for rent."

"That's a beautiful watch." Dan's eyes met Elsie's.

Chapter 13

Leslie

February 1983

"Girls!" Carrie burst through the front door of their little rental house, red hair bunched beneath her woollen hat. "How would you like to work in Banff this summer?" She tossed her boots into the closet and sat beside Leslie on the couch. "A girl in my history class worked there last year. She gave me the address. It's housekeeping. In a place called The Inn."

Christina snorted. "I can find a better job than that."

"But not in Banff," Carrie said.

"I wouldn't mind seeing the mountains," said Karen.

"I've already got a job, working at the grocery store again this summer," Leslie said.

"The grocery store again. Sounds exciting." Karen pretended to yawn. "Well, I'm in. And Christina, I know you're interested. You just won't admit it."

The three left Leslie alone to watch *Another World* on TV. She could hear them chattering in the kitchen, making rough drafts of the resumes they planned to send in the mail. At the last minute — and with no intention of going — Leslie included her hastily assembled resume along with the others.

"When were you going to tell me?"

Reese's body filled the doorway to her bedroom. By the controlled low tone of his voice, Leslie could tell he was very angry.

"Tell you what?" She looked up.

"About your job, a thousand miles away."

"It's not a thousand miles away. And I haven't decided if I'm going."

"I should be part of the decision process. This affects me too."

"I didn't want to tell you because of the way you'd react." She gave him a smile to temper her words. "You could, of course, come along. It would be fun."

"I have commitments," he replied. "I can't just drop them. I'm not like you."

"You're eighteen. What kind of commitments do you have?"

"I have that apartment leased in Hatfield. I have a job I like. And not least, I promised your father I'd help with seeding. I can't pick up and take off."

"Of course. I forgot. You're not flighty. Like me."

"How can you think about leaving me?"

"I won't stay the whole summer." Her voice softened at the look of reproach on his face. "Maybe being apart will be good for us. See how we're fighting?"

"We're fighting because you didn't tell me about the job. Don't you remember how you felt when I talked about custom combining?"

She had forgotten. Funny how, when the roles reversed, it was so much more difficult to be the one left behind.

"What about your old job at the grocery store?"

"That's the last thing I want to do!"

"Well, there are other jobs. You could work in Saskatoon. Doesn't someone have to stay in the house?"

"We're giving up the lease. Christina might not come back to school. I might live with Aunt Debra next fall."

"Oh." Reese paused. "Anything else you've neglected to keep me informed about?"

"I was going to tell you when the time was right. By the way, which of my roommates jumped the gun? Who told you about the job?"

"It doesn't matter. It came up in a conversation."

Leslie put her arms around him and held him tight. "That must have been embarrassing for you. I'm sorry I didn't tell you. Let's talk about it now."

She pulled him inside the room and closed the door. She knew exactly how to make everything right.

The packing up and leaving Saskatoon did not go smoothly. Christina said she would take care of finding someone to sublet the house for May and June, but she didn't. Things got a little heated as the month of April slipped by, until Carrie finally found someone from university who was looking for new "digs."

Then there was the packing up. How had they managed to accumulate so much stuff in eight months?

Leslie found a pair of Reese's boxer shorts under the bed.

"So that's where they went," he said, when she gave them to him. "I missed them on the chilly drive home. Just as I'm going to miss this old single bed." He loaded the bed and mattress in the back of his truck, along with the rest of Leslie's furniture. He tied everything down with rope.

"Remember," Karen instructed, before they drove away. "Everyone has to help with the big clean on Monday."

Monday came and went. Christina was supposed to pick Leslie up but bailed at the last minute. Leslie had no other ride to the city. The city phone had been disconnected and there was no way to get a message to Carrie and Karen. Leslie didn't blame them in the least for being pissed off. But it wasn't her fault.

Try as they might, it was impossible to fit all their luggage in the trunk of Christina's car. With four girls shouting instructions it took Reese several attempts — and that was after Carrie and Leslie sacrificed one suitcase each for the less dignified but malleable black garbage bags.

"I guess that's it," he said, slamming the trunk shut and turning to Leslie. His eyes were so blue she could get lost in them.

"I'm not going to Banff," she cried, throwing herself into his arms. "I've changed my mind. Open the trunk and get out my stuff."

Reese's face was buried in her hair. "We'll pass this test. We'll show your roommates our love is real." In a louder voice, he said, "I'll be up to visit on the long weekend in May." With no parting kiss and no backward glance he quickly walked away.

"Not a man for long goodbyes," remarked Karen, getting into the back seat of Christina's car.

"That little dramatic farewell scene was a nice touch on your part, Leslie." Christina mimicked, "'I've changed my mind Reese! I'm not going to leave you!'"

Leslie joined in with their laughter. If they couldn't get a rise out of her, they would leave her alone. As they drove westward, she pretended to sleep while they continued to tease.

Christina drove through the busy morning traffic in Saskatoon and did not stop for a pee break until they reached Kindersley almost two hours later. Every one of the three passengers was a little annoyed with her. After that, stops were regular: a snack in Oyen, fuel in Hanna and a sit-down lunch in Drumheller.

At Horseshoe Canyon they hiked into the ravine. The afternoon shadows deepened the contrasts of the layers of rock, but any pleasure in sightseeing and stretching their legs was diminished by Carrie nagging them to get back on the road.

"Can't we drive for more than an hour at a time? We're expected to arrive early this evening."

Calgary was full of stops and starts and traffic lights. Once they emerged on the west side, Christina stayed in the right lane and held her speed steady on the double lane highway, past the foothills and into the mountains, past Canmore and through the national park entrance. Banff appeared as one long main strip filled with neon-lit signs advertising motels, hotels and restaurants, none of which was The Inn. Christina drove through downtown and across a bridge.

"We've gone too far," said Carrie.

They retraced their route and looked again. Karen was the first to spot the sign. The Inn was a modern-looking building made of cedar and built-in tiers on the side of a hill. Christina drove the car to the front entrance and the four got out.

Carrie identified herself at the front desk.

"We've been expecting you." The clerk picked up the phone. "They're here," she said into the receiver.

Immediately a tall, lean man with dark-rimmed glasses emerged from an office.

"It's Buddy Holly," Karen whispered to Leslie, but the man overheard.

"No," he said with a laugh. "My name is Keith Hamilton. I'm the assistant manager." He shook hands with each one of them as they introduced themselves. "Is your vehicle out there?" he asked.

"My car," said Christina.

"Drive to the end of this building, turn right and go up the hill.

You'll find an older building, like a cottage. That's the staff house. It might be difficult to find in the dark but trust me, it's there. I'll meet you in about ten minutes and help get you settled."

It was hard to find the staff house among the trees. Once again, Karen had the keenest eyes.

The front door opened directly into the living room. There were empty beer bottles on the coffee table and an ashtray that needed to be emptied. Three unsmiling girls sat on a couch and scrutinized Leslie and her friends as they congregated with their luggage. One with short dark hair motioned toward the two garbage bags that had replaced two suitcases and snickered.

"Well, hello to you too," said Karen, speaking the words on the tip of Leslie's tongue.

There was a knock at the door behind them and Keith Hamilton entered the room.

"Lisa," he said to the girl with short dark hair. "Thanks for waiting. Could you help these girls get settled?" He appeared oblivious to the unwelcome in the room. He turned to Leslie and her friends. "Tomorrow, meet me in the lobby at ten for orientation. After tomorrow you start at eight. You'll often be finished by three." He paused. "Are there any questions? Everything is fine?"

"We're good," said Carrie.

"Then I'll turn you over to Lisa."

"He's hot," Karen said, after the assistant manager exited.

Trust Karen to say something inappropriate about the new boss. Leslie caught Lisa rolling her eyes.

"I don't know about you, Lisa," said Christina, "but let's get this 'getting settled thing' over with, so we can go find something to eat."

"No problem." Lisa got off the couch as slowly as possible. "There's a restaurant in the main building but it closes in ..." she checked her watch "... in ten minutes. I'd say you were shit out of luck."

The next day at ten, Keith led them to the housekeeping staff room located in the basement of The Inn. A big woman rose to her feet and hovered over the girls.

"This is Gaye," Keith said. He was only slightly taller. "She's in charge." He smiled broadly at everyone drinking coffee in the staff room.

"Find yourself a chair," Gaye said, after Keith left. "Break just started."

The other women in the room asked polite questions about where Leslie and her friends were from and how long they planned to work at The Inn. One woman offered Leslie a cigarette, but she declined. None of Leslie's roommates had been smokers and none of her family. Grandpa Dewhurst used to smoke, but he had quit after his heart operation.

"You." Gaye pointed to Leslie when the coffee break ended. "I want you to stay here. The others, I'll be pairing you up with an experienced worker."

"Here" was a laundry room in the basement. Shelves lined one wall and commercial-sized washers and dryers lined the adjacent wall. Two large tables stood in the middle.

"The towels are to be washed, dried, folded in a particular style and stacked in the shelves," Gaye said. "The bed sheets are sent away every evening and are returned, laundered and folded, every morning." She showed Leslie how to operate the machines and how to pack the dirty linens in large canvas duffle bags. "If you have any problems, get one of the girls to find me."

Laundry, dumped on the floor, seemingly appeared by magic when Leslie's back was turned. She kept the duffle bags stuffed with white bed sheets and the washing machines and the dryers fed. Folding warm towels kept her hands busy. It was hot, humid and noisy.

"And this is the slow season," Gaye said ominously when Leslie complained. "Just wait until July."

The lunch break was thirty minutes.

"What does Gaye have you doing?" Karen asked Leslie, as they prepared the two cans of soup someone in the staff house sold to them.

"Folding towels. My hands are starting to feel chapped. You?"

"Cleaning rooms. It's easy."

Mid-afternoon, Leslie's friends dropped by to see what she was doing. They were done for the day and making plans to pick up groceries.

"Please wait for me," she said.

Gaye came by shortly afterward and instructed Leslie to sweep and mop the floors of the laundry and storage rooms after the last load of towels was folded and stacked, after the duffle bags of sheets had been picked up.

"Why me?" she protested. "Why do I have to stay?"

Gaye, who stood six feet tall, looked down at her sourly.

"Because today, it is your turn," she said.

The next day was Christina's turn to be in the laundry room, and the day after was somebody else's, but the damage had been done to Leslie's reputation. According to Gaye, Leslie was lazy and a complainer. Gaye's eyes found fault in everything Leslie did or didn't do. The smallest of details — a wrinkle in the bedspread, a towel improperly stacked in the towel holder, a smudge on the chrome in the bathroom. Every day, something was neglected — matches, soap or water glasses.

"And we're not even busy yet," Gaye scolded. "Once the high season starts, you'll have to work a lot faster. And I won't have time to double check what you have done."

"It's not like this stupid job is a big stepping stone in the ladder to success," Leslie grumbled, when the others laughed at her.

She especially hated cleaning toilets. She wanted to gag when she found a drop of pee, a smear of shit, a pubic hair. She wore rubber gloves and when she was done wiping everything, she scrubbed her hands vigorously.

On the opposite end of the efficiency spectrum was Karen, who soon became Gaye's favourite worker. Karen's beds were perfectly made, her pillows fluffed, her towels aligned, her bathrooms pristine, and every ash tray, glass and soap properly displayed.

On her day off, Leslie sat at a table by a window overlooking Banff Avenue and sipped on a tall glass of iced tea. Being alone was a luxury she had never before appreciated. She watched as Keith Hamilton entered The Inn's restaurant. He disappeared into the kitchen and came out a few minutes later. She watched as he retreated to his office and closed the door.

It was not busy in the restaurant and for a brief time Leslie was the only customer. The waitress who had recommended the iced tea sat and chatted for a few minutes. They talked about life in the staff house.

The next time she had a day off, Leslie sat at the same table. She brought along a pen and writing paper and wrote two letters. The second was to Charlotte.

"We are no longer the new girls and all the beds in the staff house are taken. The workdays are not long — we are usually done before three, sometimes earlier. Gaye has us washing walls and inside cupboards and drawers. "Spring cleaning," she calls it. Yesterday, we were all outside sweeping the parking area! One of the girls from P.E.I got us all singing as we worked. That was kind of fun. I think the customers who heard us got a kick out of it.

"The girls in the staff house are mostly friendly. There is one who thinks she is the boss of the house because she's been there the longest. She's head waitress in the restaurant and barely tolerates us girls in housekeeping. Carrie says there's a hierarchical — did I spell that right? — order, like a class distinction. We chambermaids are at the bottom, the desk clerks are on the top. The waitresses are somewhere in the middle.

"There is one desk clerk who is really friendly. Her name is Gudrun. What an odd name!

"Not all the workers in The Inn live in the staff house. Some have their own place and some of the older women drive in from a little town east of Banff.

"Why don't you come here after you graduate? I could get you a job. Gudrun says there's always a shortage of workers during the busy season. I need to see a face from home. At least a face that doesn't belong to Karen, Christina, or Carrie."

Leslie put down her pen and turned her face to the window. She didn't want to acknowledge Lisa, who had entered the restaurant.

Karen laughed. "Really Leslie? Where is your head? This is not rocket science."

Leslie thought she had mastered the art of housekeeping, but apparently she had not. She forgot to leave a requested crib in one room and extra towels in another. Karen had walked in while she was being scolded by Gaye.

Leslie found a crib and wheeled it to the elevator. She delivered the towels. And because she didn't want to face ridicule from her friends in the staff house, she wandered to the lobby and sat in one of the chairs reserved for people who were not staff. *What would happen if Gaye caught me loitering?* From her vantage point she could see Keith Hamilton sitting in his office, staring at a stack of papers. His door was open, creating an illusion of welcome. She walked over and stood in the door frame until he noticed. His kind smile caused her face to crumple into tears. Keith got up, pulled her inside his office and closed the door. He handed her a tissue from the box on top of his filing cabinet and waited until she composed herself. He motioned for her to sit, which she did. When he took off his glasses and looked at her more intently, she fought off a second round of tears.

"I am so sorry," she apologized. "This is not who I am, not what I do." A few seconds passed. "Crying, that is." More seconds passed while she thought out her explanation. "Gaye hates me. She chewed me out in front of all the girls. I am the world's worst chambermaid."

Keith's expression of sympathy turned into one of amusement. "So you're the one who doesn't like to get her hands dirty. I'm sorry. I shouldn't laugh," he said hastily at Leslie's expression of outrage.

"I can get my hands dirty. I grew up on a farm."

Keith laughed. "I guess we're talking about a different kind of dirt."

"I'm not really a housekeeper type," Leslie said, an idea formulating in her brain. "I'm better at serving people, not making beds and cleaning toilets. Can I work in the restaurant instead? Or the gift shop? As soon as there's an opening, of course. I've never waitressed before, but at church back home I've served at teas. At home I cooked for our hired men." This was a slight exaggeration. "I was a cashier last summer in a grocery store. I'm sure the boss would give me a good reference."

Keith looked at her for a long time, as if assessing her worth.

"I'm sorry. I forgot your name."

"Leslie. Leslie Dewhurst from Saskatchewan."

"Ah, Saskatchewan. How about those Riders? Are you a big football fan?" He didn't wait for her reply but stood and paced the width of his office before speaking again. "As it happens, someone in the restaurant quit this morning and we're short-staffed. You can help and learn at the same time. Lisa can train you."

How easy to ask and have it granted! Even the mention of

Lisa's name didn't dampen Leslie's elation or hide her big grin.

"How are you for clothes? You must wear a black skirt, not too short, and a white blouse."

Leslie's face fell. "I've got a white blouse, but I don't have the skirt. Can I borrow one?"

"Not from me, I'm afraid." He wrote something on a card and handed it to her. "Here's the name of a clothing store downtown. They seem to carry everything we need. I think black slacks and skirts are standard gear for most servers in town. Charge the skirt to The Inn, I'll take the cost off your next cheque." He reached into his pocket and took out a keychain with a single key. "Here. Take my car, otherwise you won't get back in time. It's a standard shift, but as you tell me, you're a farm girl. It's a black Mustang parked in the back."

Leslie raced off to find his car. Out of nervousness she stalled it twice before she turned onto Banff Avenue. At the clothing store she bought the first skirt that fit. Back at The Inn, she parked the car and raced up the hill, clutching her package.

"Guess what!" she shouted to her friends sitting outside on the front step. "Tonight I am a waitress." She grabbed her towel hanging on a hook by her bed, and locked herself in the bathroom. She had less than forty-five minutes to shower, put on makeup, style her hair and iron her blouse and new skirt.

While she ironed her friends listened to how she got the job.

"Let me do your hair," Carrie insisted and pinned Leslie's wet hair into a bun.

Karen, who had been watching from the doorway, brought a pair of black shoes, not too high but a little dressy. "Here. We're practically the same size."

"I hadn't thought of shoes!" Leslie said. "Thank you, Karen."

Christina brought nothing and offered no help. "You're not the only one who hates being a chambermaid."

"Nothing is stopping any one of us from switching jobs," said Carrie. "We're all a little jealous Leslie thought of it first."

"You are not to do anything more than set up and clean up," Lisa said. "We call that bussing. And assist the waiters and waitresses when they get busy. Here," she grabbed a waiter by the arm. "Train her."

Taken by surprise, the waiter and Leslie exchanged embarrassed smiles. He had thick dark eyebrows. "Water is poured into glasses immediately after the guests are seated. I take their drink order. By the way, my name is Mike."

He showed Leslie how to assemble starter salads, told her when to remove unnecessary table clutter and when to replace ashtrays. The restaurant was never full and Leslie found it easy to keep up.

Later in the evening, couples or small groups came for coffee and the rich desserts for which the restaurant was known. At eleven, the doors were locked.

She had worked a double shift but she was not one bit tired.

Mike taught Leslie how to organize the restaurant for the morning's breakfast crowd. He vacuumed when the last customer left, and she wiped the tables and chairs. While she worked she pondered how she was going to end her career in housekeeping. By not bothering to show? Or by doing the right thing and giving Gaye two week's notice?

She decided to do the right thing.

The next morning, when she showed up to work, she found her rooms had been divided among the other workers. Briefly miffed, but mostly relieved, Leslie returned to the staff house and fell into her bed. She slept until the early hours of the afternoon.

Leslie had regularly phoned Reese collect from the pay phone outside the staff house, but now that she was waitressing six days a week, it was difficult to find a time neither she nor Reese was working. She wrote letters when she was alone in the staff house during the afternoon. She found putting her thoughts into words as satisfying as Charlotte had claimed it to be.

Leslie's routine consisted of a long leisurely walk down Banff Avenue, taking in the sights and smells of a tourist town waking up. Standing in the General Delivery line at the post office, she purchased stamps for her letters and savoured the anticipation of being handed a letter or two in return.

Reese wrote every few days, her mother once a week, and her sisters, often enough. Whenever Leslie received correspondence, she walked to the park across the street, sat cross-legged on the grass, and immersed herself in their lives. She saved Reese's letters for the last. Boyish in detail, he sometimes added a little gossip, although he was never mean-spirited. He always ended with "Please come home. I miss you."

At first Leslie thought it was her imagination. Waitresses, who had initially been friendly, became silent when she approached and burst into laughter when she passed. It reminded her of grade nine, this not so subtle method used to intimidate. She had never before been on the receiving end. Even at nineteen, and knowing how it worked, her self-confidence eroded.

How could this happen to a person who is popular?

Without explanation she was taken off the evening shift and put on the day shift. The restaurant opened at seven but she had to be at work at six-thirty. She wore a silly puffy-sleeved uniform with a white apron that tied at the back. The coffee-and-pancake crowd tipped less than the supper crowd.

A lot less.

She was not going to complain. Perhaps this was part of the rotation, like working in the laundry room.

One day, after spending the last hour filling salt and pepper shakers, Leslie was called to Keith Hamilton's office. Lisa was there, grim-faced.

"Have a seat." Keith closed the door. Leslie sat across from him while Lisa stood.

"It has been brought to my attention," Lisa said, reading off a clipboard, "that the other servers are unhappy with the way you hog the best tipping customers. It has been brought to my attention that you pour the last of the coffee without making a new pot. It has been brought to my attention that you are unfriendly to your co-workers — and you don't clean up after yourself."

"I wasn't aware I was doing that. Thank you for pointing it out to me," Leslie said. "If you see me doing something wrong, just signal, and I'll fix it right away." She pasted a smile on her face as the accusations continued. The one time she had slept in was discussed as if her tardiness was a daily occurrence. Her agitation increased.

"The evening waiters claimed you didn't 'tip out' the cooks and hostess their fair percent." Lisa used her two fingers on each hand to emphasize the phrase. "That's why we took you off that shift. There was a suggestion your tip cup seemed fuller than the rest."

"Stealing is a serious accusation," Keith said.

"Some of your petty complaints are valid," Leslie said quietly, her face burning with suppressed anger. "But I have never stolen in my life. And not 'tipping out' amounts to the same thing." She used her fingers in the same way, to mimic Lisa.

Lisa glared at Leslie for a very long time. Leslie returned the glare.

"Go back to work," Lisa ordered, the first to look away. "Keith and I have some things we need to decide."

Leslie returned to the restaurant wondering if the other workers knew. Who wanted her gone so badly they would lie? Well, she wasn't going to hide in the back room filling salt shakers. She held her head high and walked around with the coffee pot, smiling as if nothing were wrong.

A long time passed.

When Keith summoned her back to his office, Lisa was not present.

"Sit down." He closed the door.

So this is how it feels to be fired. Leslie hung her head in shame. She would have to return home in disgrace. If her honesty were questionable it was unlikely she would be assigned a job in the gift shop or even back in housekeeping.

Keith cleared his throat. "You've had a rough morning, so I'll keep this short. I think you're an outstanding waitress."

Leslie looked up.

"The customers like you. A lot. And that might be your biggest problem." Keith took off his glasses. His eyes were grey. "I've checked, and the complaints made against you are unsubstantiated. I've decided to let Lisa go."

Leslie thought she had misheard. "What? You're not going to fire me?"

"I'm not going to fire you."

On the basketball courts and on the soccer fields Leslie had been shoved around and called names. It was expected in contact sports, and part of the fun. But this form of roughhousing was different and she didn't like it. For the second time in less than a month, she cried in front of the boss.

"If you have any more problems, I want you to come to me," Keith said, handing her a tissue.

Leslie blew her nose in reply.

"If you need to take the rest of the day off, you have my permission. But to warn you. Lisa is cleaning out her room in the staff house right now. She is very angry. I wouldn't want you to run into her."

"I want to stay and finish my shift."

"Good girl."

"You are so nice." Leslie put her hand over her mouth, appalled she had said the words out loud.

Mike with the bushy eyebrows was put in charge and Leslie went back to evenings. The first time she was asked to work as hostess she wondered if this were a promotion or a demotion. Neither, it turned out. Just a turn, like working in the laundry had been.

Hostessing required a pretty dress. Somewhere among the hiking gear and sports shops, Leslie found an upscale boutique. She spent all her tip money on a black halter style dress. She thought she looked classy. She liked the way men ogled her. She particularly liked that she was finished at ten and did not have to vacuum when the restaurant closed.

Often there was a light on in Keith Hamilton's office when she finished her shift. It was as if he never stopped working. One night she lingered by his open door until he looked at her.

"Hello, Leslie. What can I do for you?"

"I never thanked you for not firing me."

"I'm sure you did. Come in and tell me how everything is going."

"I love my job," she said, sitting. "Mike is fair and the other servers ... well, they treat me better."

"They weren't nice to you before?"

A slip of the tongue. She had disliked kids at school who ratted. There was no need to get teachers or parents worked up about something that could usually be handled in the playground.

"Not while Lisa was in charge."

"Speaking of Lisa — was she gone from the staff house when you returned that afternoon? I wondered about that."

"I went for a long walk after my shift, just to be sure." Leslie smiled at the remembrance of wandering around in her milkmaid-style uniform. "But she was gone, every last bit of her."

Back at the staff house she had checked her own bed and food supplies for unpleasant surprises and retaliatory gestures.

"She had been a hard worker who kept everyone in line. She had worked here a long time."

Was there regret in his voice? Leslie couldn't be sure.

Keith leaned back in his chair. "So, Leslie Dewhurst from Saskatchewan, tell me about life on the farm. I've always been envious of country boys. They seemed to have more common sense than us city boys."

Having common sense wasn't exactly how Leslie would have described the boys back home, with their crude manners, big trucks, snowmobiles and hunting. "Redneck" was the word that came immediately to mind.

Reese was different, of course.

"Farm girls have common sense too. We can do a lot of things, like dig potatoes and drive cars with standard transmissions," Leslie said, remembering Keith's black Mustang. "I also spent last year living in Saskatoon, going to university. I think I have some city smarts too."

"So you'll be returning to student life this fall. What are you taking? What is your plan?"

Her plan? She didn't have a plan. Leslie grasped for something. Nursing like Karen? Pre-Law like Christina?

"Pre-Law." She hoped it made her sound smart.

"Ah. So you're a girl who likes to argue."

Leslie disliked girls who liked to argue. "No," she said.

And he laughed.

Reese had promised to visit during the long weekend in May but that hadn't worked out. He explained in writing that "as the bottom man on the totem pole I am on call at work in the parts department and have to be available to farmers during seeding." From her family's letters, Leslie knew he had been tracked down twice at their farm when the alternate "on call" person was "indisposed."

Reese's most recent letter stated he was coming to visit the third weekend in June. Leslie consulted with Mike, asking to book off Saturday and Sunday. With some difficulty, because the high season for tourism had begun, he granted her request.

On the night Reese was expected to arrive, Leslie scampered up the hill to the staff house and changed out of her restaurant work clothes. She half-dozed on the living room couch while she waited. She left the window open so she could hear his truck drive up the hill, or the pay phone in case he phoned. Each time the beam of a vehicle appeared, she stood by the window. But it was girls returning from a night on the town. The telephone outside the open window did not ring.

It was close to three o'clock Saturday morning when she heard Reese's truck. By the time he turned off the headlights, she was out the door, off the step and into his arms.

Reese pulled away. "I stink. A day of work and this long drive. I need a shower."

"No, you don't," she said, not letting him get away. "No, you don't. Let's go somewhere."

They parked off a quiet road and made love in the cab of his half-ton truck. They slept under a blanket that smelled vaguely of mildew.

"I need a shower. Can't you sneak me into your bathroom?"

"You never smell bad to me," said Leslie. "Let's find our own place and I'll shower with you."

She had no idea finding their own place would be so difficult. During high season, everything in Banff was booked on the weekend, even the most expensive suites.

"Why didn't you make a reservation when you knew I couldn't stay with you?" Reese's disappointment was evident in his voice. He sat across from her in a restaurant, eating breakfast. "You know this town better than I do. I could have borrowed a tent. We could have had a camping holiday."

"Why didn't you ask me?"

"Because I'm the visitor. I assumed you would take care of that."

"Let's not fight. Let's drive to Calgary. It's cheaper there."

"I didn't bring enough cash for a hotel room," he warned. "And the restaurants are expensive. And I need money for gas on the way home."

"I didn't take out enough either. And the banks are closed."

"This is ridiculous," said Reese. "Something we both looked

forward to, and didn't plan. I feel like a fool."

Back at The Inn, Leslie searched for Carrie and found her cleaning a room. After hearing the problem, Carrie immediately ran to the staff house and returned with sixty dollars.

"Tuesday morning I'll go to the bank and take out cash," Leslie promised. "I'll pay you back, with interest."

"No interest, just say hello to Reese for me. And have a fantastic time, you lovebirds."

Leslie imagined the knowing looks of the motel desk clerks as she and Reese tried to find a cheap, clean room with a kitchenette in Calgary.

"I hate this," she complained as they emerged from the second motel office. "You go in alone next time. You ask."

When he returned from the third, she could tell Reese was frustrated.

"So much for romance," she said.

"I'm really sorry."

At the fourth motel, Reese returned to the truck holding up key number sixteen on a chain. "It's not the cheapest, but I said we'd take it. I hope it's okay."

The room was dark and smelled of recent cigarette smoke.

"We'll call this our love nest." Leslie closed the curtains and put the chain on the lock. "This place will be our dirty little secret."

"Speaking of which ..." Reese stripped off his clothes. "I need a shower."

The bathtub with the rumpled shower curtain was not the sexiest place to make love. Still, they tried to joke as they lathered soap on each other while maintaining balance on the slippery tub floor, as they rinsed their hair and afterward, as they wrapped themselves in thin, cheap towels.

They fell asleep half-damp and woke with ridiculously kinked hair — which made them laugh on the verge of hysteria. A second shower was less awkward.

"If we got engaged this year, we could marry next summer," Reese said, as they were dressing. "We'd both be twenty. That's not so young. We wouldn't have to sneak around like this."

"I *am* tired of sneaking around," Leslie admitted, watching him in the mirror.

He turned to her. "I'd like to look at rings, to get an idea of what you like. I'm saving for something really nice. That's why I'm so cheap with everything else."

"Nobody our age has much money," said Leslie, moving to him and slowly removing the shirt he was trying to button.

"Don't you want to go out?" he protested. "Get some food?"

"Sssh," she whispered soothingly kissing him on the mouth, nibbling at his chin. Suddenly she stopped and buried her face in his neck. She felt a sudden chill.

"What are you doing?"

"I'm memorizing how I feel right now."

There was not a moment they weren't touching. Hand in hand, they walked along the downtown city sidewalks. When they lingered at the jewelry store display windows, Leslie pointed to the rings she preferred, the ones with clusters of tiny diamonds.

On Sunday, they walked in the park and sunned themselves on the banks of the Bow River. They bought a few simple groceries and ate in their motel room. They splurged and watched a forgettable movie in an air-conditioned theatre. All the time, touching, touching, touching.

"This old thing." Reese threw their bags in the back of his truck early Monday morning. "I guess this is the next thing that's going to cost me."

"I hope that's not how you refer to me," said Leslie with a laugh. "Something that's going to cost you."

"You are an investment." Reese took her hand and looked into her eyes. "It's not always going to be like this."

"I know."

"Someday I'll be able to afford all the things you deserve." Reese dropped her hand. "But for now we'd better hit the road. I've got a ten-hour drive ahead of me. And that's after I drop you off in Banff."

"You could have sent me back on the bus."

"As if I'd do that."

Their conversation on the drive westward became strained as if they were trying too hard to force optimism. In front of the staff

house Leslie suddenly panicked.
"Don't leave me!" she cried.
"Then come back with me. I'll wait while you pack."
"I can't."
"You can. Just walk away."
"I can't."
They clung together until Reese got back in his truck and drove away.

"*I have taken a second job,*" Reese wrote. "*I am working at the garage. Weekends. Please come home.*"
She wrote back, "*I'll be home in two months. If I stay until Labour Day, I get a bonus. I love you. I miss you.*"
He wrote, "*I don't care about your bonus. Come home sooner and we can salvage part of the summer. I would quit the second job. I want to be with you always. Please come home.*"
Please come home.

"I go jogging in the morning. Around nine," Keith said, on one of their late evening visits. "I stop at the restaurant first to be sure there are no emergencies, that the staff is present and happy, and then I check into the housekeeping department. If everything is a go, I have the morning to myself — more or less."
"When I was in high school I used to jog on the gravel roads before soccer season began, to get back into shape," Leslie said. "But when I started university, I stopped running. I don't know why."
She remembered how Reese liked the softness of her body.
"Would you be interested to take it up again?" Keith asked.
"Jogging?" Leslie laughed.
"You look like a girl who should run."
"What?"
"I apologize for my poor choice of words. You have the body of a runner. I think you would be good at it."
"I'll think about it," Leslie replied. She wasn't really interested in changing her relaxed morning routine.

Chapter 14

Charlotte

July 1983

*T*he *turnover is incredible.*

That sentence alone — written in Leslie's loopy handwriting — unleashed all Charlotte dreamed life could be. She imagined herself among rotating shifts of young people with no one knowing who she was, what she had done, or who she had loved. In Banff, she could reinvent herself.

The final months of high school had been tedious at best. Charlotte had never been part of the social scene, always in the background. Graduation, with its endless parties and ceremonies, only reinforced her belief she was an outsider. Letters from her sister were an unexpected lifeline. Leslie wrote about co-workers from England and Australia, Ireland and Brazil. Some worked only to earn enough money for the next leg of their travel. Charlotte wanted to be one of those people. Transients, Leslie called them.

Transience.

A quality foreign to farm kids, locked to the land, immersed in years of sameness. Same house, same neighbours, same classmates, same everything — year after endless year. Everyone knowing.

"I'm going to join Leslie in Banff after graduation," Charlotte announced at the supper table in late June.

"We thought you might," Dad said. "It's good to get away, if only to find where you belong."

Early evening of the last day of June, Charlotte waited at the Hatfield bus depot with her parents and little sisters. Her ticket to

Banff and two hundred dollars in travellers cheques were graduation gifts. When the bus arrived, everyone lined up to hug her. Dad slipped her another twenty dollars. At the end of the line was Reese. "For Leslie." He pressed a small bag into her hand.

In Saskatoon, Charlotte transferred to a bus that stopped in several small towns during the night. Sleep was sporadic at best. She arrived in Calgary in the early morning and had to wait three hours for the third and last bus to take her to Banff where her sister was waiting.

Leslie, smelling faintly of perfume, grabbed her in a tight embrace.

"You look different," said Charlotte, holding Leslie at arm's length.

"Do I? I can't see how. Nothing has changed. I'm just getting older. Come." Leslie picked up Charlotte's suitcase and led the way to a black Mustang.

"Wow." Charlotte ran her hand over the car's shiny black body. "They must be paying you well."

"Very funny. You know perfectly well I can't afford a car. This is Keith's. He lent it to me."

There had been no mention of "a Keith" in Leslie's letters. Charlotte raised one eyebrow.

"He's my boss," Leslie said, as she stashed the suitcases in the trunk. "And yours. So don't go reading anything into it. And don't go telling Reese and getting him all worked up."

"Speaking of Reese, I have something from him for you." Charlotte fished a tiny parcel out of her backpack and handed it to Leslie, who put it in her purse. "Aren't you going to open it?"

"I was waiting for a private moment."

"Aren't you curious? I am. Open it."

Leslie retrieved the parcel and unwrapped it.

"Earrings!" Charlotte said. "I hoped it would be an engagement ring."

"Reese isn't *that* unromantic to propose by proxy. The earrings are pretty though. I'll phone him tonight and thank him. How's he doing?"

"Only a shadow of the man he used to be — now that you're not around."

"Ah. You're teasing me." Leslie started the Mustang and put it into gear. "Tell me about grad."

Grade twelve graduation was, arguably, the most exciting event in a rural kid's formative years. But not every kid. Not Charlotte. What she had most dreaded was asking some random guy to be her escort. As a member of school council she had suggested abolishing the archaic tradition. The outcry had been huge. She knew she wasn't the only student to feel pressure, but the popular kids — who had no trouble attracting dates — ruled the roost.

Reese had escorted her.

"After all, he had a suit." Charlotte laughed. "One I had helped choose for his own graduation." The suit was a little tight in the shoulders but he had looked as handsome as ever, his hair curling over his ears. "I was proud to have Reese as my date even though everyone knew he was your boyfriend and not mine."

"Reese would jump through burning hoops if I asked."

"I'm sure he would," Charlotte admitted. "I hope he didn't think of me as such."

"Of course he didn't."

"I wasn't into the partying like some of the kids. But I did get to introduce the guest speaker at the commencement ceremony. A Mr. McAdams. Does that name ring a bell?"

"Not one chime."

"Well, he's an alumni of Hatfield. An activist. Big on peace."

"Did anybody ask about me?"

"Everybody asked about you." Charlotte decided not to mention the academic award she had won. "The light went out at Hatfield High after you graduated. Where are we going?"

"We're stopping for groceries." Leslie pulled into the parking lot of a modern Safeway store. It was jammed full of cars so she drove down a little side road and parked behind an apartment building. "Private parking," the sign said.

"Don't worry," she said. "This is Keith's."

"Him again. Do you get your boss's car often? Do others get to borrow it?" *Is Keith some creepy older guy trying to proposition my sister?*

"No one has a car. If Keith hadn't offered his we'd have to call a taxi, unless you wanted to carry your suitcases a mile down the road. He's very generous. To everyone."

"If no one has a car, how do people get around?" Charlotte

followed Leslie across a busy street.

"We mostly walk but some have bikes. You'll get lots of exercise, but your appetite is huge! All of us gained weight like crazy!"

"You didn't."

"I did at first, but then I lost it," Leslie said, as they entered the store and wandered the aisles. "Buy in small amounts. Some people will help themselves to your stuff. You'll be downtown almost every day for one thing or another, so pick up what you need when you need it."

A loaf of bread, a jar of peanut butter, some fruit, milk and cereal were all Charlotte wanted. The cost was high for such a small amount of food, compared to the prices she remembered from last summer's job.

"Here we are!" Leslie announced, as they drove up a hill and past the entrance to The Inn. She stopped in front of an old-fashioned cabin. "This used to be the registration office of the original motel but now most of the staff live here. I'm told it can house about twenty-eight people, four to a room, but it's never completely full — at least not while I've been here."

She unloaded Charlotte's suitcases. "You wait here while I return Keith's car."

Charlotte sat in the living room. The house was very quiet. "Where is everyone?" she asked when Leslie returned.

"Nobody hangs around. Whoever has the day off is already gone. The others are likely at work. Right now we're going to find you a bed."

"I don't want to room with Karen Anders."

"She's gone. So is Christina." Leslie glanced down the hallway. She opened a door. A sleeping girl grunted and farted. Leslie closed the door again.

"What do you mean gone?" Charlotte asked.

Leslie shrugged. "They left. Back to good old Saskatchewan." She opened a second door to a room filled with carelessly tossed clothing. "Looks like this one is full."

"Where's your room?" Charlotte asked. The news of Karen's departure erased the last reservation she had had about Banff.

"Here in this suite." Leslie opened a third door. There were two sets of bunk beds along corner walls and a bright kitchen in a little alcove. "This was occupied when we arrived in April. It's the nicest and the largest. I moved fast when there was a vacancy. That pissed a few people off." She laughed. "God helps those who help themselves."

"I wouldn't mind living here."

"We're full right now, but when I leave, I'll give it to you."

"Any rooms upstairs?"

"No," Leslie said. "The druggies and sluts live on the second floor. Not nice girls like us. They have a separate outside entrance. I hardly ever go there."

The druggies and sluts? Charlotte raised an eyebrow in question, but Leslie was out the door and down the hallway. "So where do I go?"

"In the first room. There's one bed empty. A top bunk. But let's not wake sleeping beauty yet. Here's your bathroom. And here's your kitchen."

The counters were filled. Food was dried on plates and counters. Pots were left on stove top burners.

"Here's a shelf you can have." Leslie opened a cupboard door and brushed out crumbs. She grinned at Charlotte. "Mom would be horrified if she saw this."

"I won't tell her. She's already worried about me. She keeps reminding me I'm only seventeen." She stopped. "My God, what is that stench?"

"It's here, in this garbage bag. What a bunch of slobs." Leslie twisted the bag shut and carried it outside.

Charlotte unpacked her expensive bag of groceries.

"The bin is outside, just so you know," Leslie said. "I'll make you lunch in my kitchen. I bet you're starving. Come."

"Your kitchen is immaculate in comparison."

"Only four of us share compared to eight in yours. Upstairs, there's one kitchen for twelve."

"I bet that one looks like shit." Charlotte followed her and sat at a small table by the window while Leslie prepared grilled cheese sandwiches. Leslie had never cooked for her before. "Where is my sister and what have you done to her?"

After lunch and clean up, Leslie suggested Charlotte thank Keith in person. Down the hill they went, through the back of the hotel and into the lobby. The desk clerk directed them to the basement where they found Keith discussing something with a very large woman Charlotte knew from Leslie's letters to be the formidable Gaye.

"This is my sister, Charlotte," Leslie said to Keith. To Gaye she said, "Charlotte's here to work at The Inn."

"I've heard much about you," Keith shook Charlotte's hand. His smile was warm and his grip was firm. He was not remotely creepy looking. "Leslie is very happy you're here."

"I am," Leslie agreed smiling, and once again Charlotte thought how much she had changed. *A nicer version.*

"We're short-handed and behind schedule," interrupted Gaye. "Could you start right away?"

Charlotte nodded. She couldn't very well refuse, knowing the poor impression Leslie had made.

"I was about to roll up my sleeves and help," Keith said with a laugh.

"I left all my stuff in the middle of the living room," Charlotte reminded Leslie.

"Yikes! That's right. I'll take care of it immediately. I'll get your bed ready for you. When you get off work I'll take you out for supper." Leslie dashed off without another word.

"Let's get at it," Gaye said to Charlotte. "Follow me, girl."

Charlotte stripped beds, first in one room and then another and another all the way down the hallway.

"We had a bus tour check out this morning." Gaye showed Charlotte how to make the beds with fresh crisp linens and replace the towels. "And another one coming this evening."

Gaye dusted, cleaned the bathrooms, wiped the mirrors and vacuumed. For a woman so large, she moved with efficiency. Charlotte had a hard time keeping up.

"You should be able to do a room in less than forty-five minutes," Gaye said, on their first trip to the laundry room to dispose of the towels and sheets. "Not if it's really dirty, of course."

Later she said, "Ideally, we should be finished before check-in time, but sometimes it can't be helped. None of us leave until all the rooms are completed. You're a good worker," she added.

"So, how is everyone back home?" Leslie asked, over spaghetti at a place called *The Place for Pasta.* "You can give me the latest update."

They had already talked about work, Keith, the staff house, and the girls upstairs.

"You remember what a drama queen Paige can be? Well, she had a fight with her best friend and they haven't talked for weeks."

"She's at that stage. And Wendy?"

"Can you believe she starts high school this fall? She's sewing all her own clothes."

"I hated sewing."

"Dad traded in the old combine for a newer model with a reverser. Remember how hard it was to get the old one unplugged?"

"I never helped much with the farm work."

"And the Gladstones have a new baby. A girl. Madison. We walked over for a visit. Mom carried a casserole and we brought gifts."

"Maddy Gladstone. Cute name."

"Mom is doing her usual. Fussing over everything. I can't think of anything more to report. Tell me what happened to your old roommates."

"They got bored. There's just Carrie left. She's coming along with us tonight when I take you bar-hopping."

"Did you forget I'm under-age?"

"That's not a problem. Nobody asks for ID."

"ID or not, truthfully, I want to find my bed and fall into it. I'm exhausted."

Leslie laughed. "You have the top bunk. You won't be doing any falling."

Charlotte wasn't one to monitor the degree or range of her emotions, but a week after her arrival she acknowledged contentment, *which is really just another word for happiness*. It had been an opportune plan to get away from Hatfield, to strike out on her own, and to rekindle her friendship with Leslie, a friendship made possible by Karen's absence.

The sisters coordinated their days off and explored the national park. They swam in the Basin, hiked Tunnel Mountain, rode the gondola, relaxed in the Hot Springs, and once, when Leslie borrowed Keith's car, they drove to Lake Louise.

Charlotte wrote letters home, assuring her family of her well-being.

She shared a bedroom with three other girls. One was from Quebec and so passionate about the separatist movement it was hard to argue with her, so Charlotte didn't. One was a health food junkie who rolled her own cigarettes and smoked marijuana out of sight behind the staff house. And one was Gudrun who despite a three-year age difference, became Charlotte's first best friend. They initially bonded over their mutual dislike of Karen Anders.

Charlotte and Gudrun joined the Presbyterian Church Group for Young Adults. It met Friday nights and provided wholesome fun, like canoeing and hiking and weekly coffee houses with folk singers.

Leslie worked on Friday nights and didn't participate.

One afternoon in early August, Leslie burst into the room Charlotte was cleaning.

"How would you like to go to Calgary on Monday? Keith is going to the city for meetings and he asked me to invite you. We could shop and look around. Keith said he'd take us to the tower for supper." Leslie's face was flushed with excitement.

"I don't have Monday off and neither do you."

"I can swap easily enough. And Keith can get Gaye to change your schedule. Please Charlotte, please. Keith won't take me along unless you go too." She made her eyes big and stuck out her bottom lip in a pout.

"I don't want Keith going to Gaye to ask for my day off," Charlotte said. "I can handle this myself." She thought for a moment. "Do you think this is a good idea? Won't the others accuse us of being the boss's favourites?"

"Does it matter if we are?"

"I don't want to be the subject of gossip and speculation."

At seven in the morning, the lobby of The Inn was busy with people checking out. No one paid much attention to Charlotte and Leslie who were waiting outside Keith's office.

"This is the first time I'll be out of the park since I got here," Charlotte said to Keith, as they followed him to where the Mustang was parked.

"Glad to provide the opportunity." Keith unlocked the driver's door and pushed the front seat over so Charlotte could squeeze into the back. Leslie rode shotgun, in the front passenger seat.

"What kind of meetings do you have?" Charlotte asked, as they drove down the hill. She could see Keith's eyes in the rearview mirror.

"The monthly meeting. Usually I go along with the manager but she's got something else going on. It's a boring day."

"We'll liven it up for you," Leslie said playfully. Her face was wide-eyed and innocent, a fake look Charlotte particularly hated.

They drove along the busy highway in the shadows of the mountains.

"What are your plans for the future, Charlotte?" Keith asked after several minutes.

"I'm going to work in Banff for a few more months. Maybe longer. I'm not eighteen yet and I don't know what I want to study. My parents didn't insist I enrol at university." *Like they did Leslie.*

"Taking a year off is not a bad idea," Keith said. "When I was your age, my parents wanted me to study business but I wanted to study the effects of alcohol on the immature brain. I was too young of course and I wasted my first year. I went to the University of Manitoba. I lived at home and worked at my father's furniture store on the weekends. Someone invited me to go skiing in Banff. In May, of all times! I never went home. I found a job. Eventually I became a bartender at one of Banff's exclusive hotels. The tips were generous."

"Were your parents upset?" Leslie asked.

"My father was furious. I didn't go home for two and a half years. Young men — and old men — can be stubborn."

"And then?" Charlotte prompted.

"I got hurt. A car accident. On icy mountain roads. I wasn't the driver and no one was killed but two of us were badly injured. The other guy was in a coma for a few days but he came out of it and fully recovered. I ended up in a Calgary hospital. For many, many weeks." He laughed ruefully. "I used to be heavier and muscular. I can't seem to put the weight back on."

"So you went home."

"I did. To convalesce. My mother said if I was going to sit around I might as well be studying. She drove me to the campus every day and picked me up when my classes were done. I was too stubborn to use a wheelchair, so I hobbled along with crutches. She also drove me to physiotherapy. I still have a limp when I get overtired."

"How old were you when the accident happened?" Leslie asked.

"Twenty-four. Actually, I am still a student. I have one more year to go."

"But aren't you the assistant manager?"

"A temporary assistant manager," Keith corrected. "Two years ago I was a senior desk clerk. Last summer I managed the restaurant. Johann — who's the real assistant manager, asked me to take over his job for this summer so he could return to Munich to visit his ailing father. When he comes back, I'm returning to Winnipeg in September to finish my degree."

Traffic slowed to a crawl.

"Something on the road ahead is causing backup. Construction, likely," Keith said. "Well, I've shared my story. What's yours?"

"We don't have a story." Leslie gave Charlotte a warning look.

"Yes we do," Charlotte said. "But our story is short. We're farm girls. Back home our fields are starting to turn from green to gold. Our father will be getting the machinery ready. Our mother will be canning or freezing garden produce." A wave of homesickness hit her unexpectedly. "The air is different in August. You can smell the harvest coming on. And our sunrises and sunsets are unbelievable. But you live in a prairie city, so you know that."

"Some prairie people feel oppressed when they live in mountain towns," said Keith, speeding up, the construction over. "I never have."

He drove with confidence in the morning traffic, his hand on the stick shift. Charlotte looked around with interest as they approached the downtown core. Calgary was the biggest city she had ever visited. Bigger than Ottawa.

"See that restaurant across the street?" Keith pulled over in a vacant spot with "No Parking" on a sign. He stepped out of the car so Charlotte could get out. "Meet me there at four o'clock this afternoon." He wrote the name of the restaurant on a piece of paper and gave it to her. "In case you get lost, you can ask for directions."

Charlotte watched Keith drive away.

"How did you get him to talk like that?" Leslie demanded. "I didn't know any of that stuff about him."

"It's a skill I have. It's called listening." Charlotte was pleased her sister noticed. "You might want to try it."

"How old do you guess him to be?"

"Twenty-seven, give or take a year. He looks older. Maybe the accident aged him. Do you want me to ask?"

"No. That's too personal a question and would look as if we're interested in him."

We are interested in him. "Let's stop here," Charlotte said as they approached a diner. "We haven't eaten breakfast."

They found a table by the window and ordered coffee and bran muffins.

"Have you ever said anything to Keith about Reese?" Charlotte asked. "I think Keith might like you more than as an employee."

"We never talk about our private lives. Until today." Leslie paused. "What makes you think he likes me?"

"Well, let's see." Charlotte held up her hand. "One, he lets you borrow his car. Two — he invites you and me for a day trip to Calgary. Does he ever invite anyone else? And thirdly, there is something in the way he looks at you. Something about you amuses him. I've suspected it for weeks."

"Honestly." Leslie's voice was curt. "We're just friends."

Charlotte let the topic drop. She and Leslie had been so close in July, she didn't want to wreck it.

She paid their bill and they ventured down the street and peered into windows full of mannequins dressed in fashionable fall clothes.

"Let's go in. Just to look," Leslie said, but every time they went inside "just to look," Leslie would find something to try on. She looked amazing in almost everything. Deep reds, blues and purples looked especially attractive on her. The salesgirls hovered; the older women gushed.

Charlotte was basically ignored. She sat on delicate chairs and rated her sister's choices. With some urging, she tried on a few dresses, but she was quickly discouraged.

"I don't have your sculptured shoulders, tiny waist, and long legs."

"You could be pretty if you tried."

"I'm more the functional type. You know — the Martha not the

Mary."

Leslie sighed.

Charlotte added, "The only reason I came was because you pleaded. And to carry your bags."

Keith took them to the Calgary Tower for supper. He insisted Leslie and Charlotte take the seats closest to the window in the revolving restaurant high above the city.

"Right now we're looking southeast," Keith said, sitting beside Charlotte. "Whenever my mother comes to Calgary, this is where I take her. She enjoys shopping, too."

"Our mother made our clothes," Charlotte said. "Or took all of us girls together for a sale day, like Bay Day, and we all got winter boots or something else practical."

"We haven't done that for years." Leslie gave Charlotte her warning look.

But Charlotte couldn't resist making her sister squirm.

"There hadn't been money for luxuries like professional haircuts when we were young. I remember the times our father summoned us into the kitchen with the battle cry, 'Rally the troops.' All of us girls attempted escape from the unflattering haircuts with the dreaded scissors."

"All of you girls? There's more?" Keith asked, laughing.

"Two more," said Charlotte. "We have no brothers."

"I have one sister. She's twenty-one and her name is Roxanne. She's a design student here at Mount Royal College."

"Why didn't you invite her along?" Leslie cried. "I'd love to meet her."

"I would have — if she were here. She's in Winnipeg for the summer."

"What does she hope to design?" Charlotte asked.

"I'm not sure," Keith replied. "It's a good question to ask the next time we talk."

The conversation went from design, to architecture, to environment. One topic bounced off another and to the next. Music, travel. Politics. Charlotte hadn't been so animated since the high school Ottawa trip, eighteen months ago. She loved anything cerebral.

"You have strong opinions for one so young," Keith said.

"Back home we tease her she's becoming our Grandma Dewhurst," said Leslie.

"It's not a compliment. Grandma usually criticizes."

"I meant it as one," Keith said. "It means you're a thinker."

As Charlotte had predicted, the trip to Calgary did not go unnoticed by the other employees of The Inn. She was bombarded by questions at the Tuesday morning coffee break. Worse yet, someone told her privately Leslie and Keith had been seen together a week earlier.

"I told you a long time ago I go jogging in the morning," Leslie said impatiently, when Charlotte confronted her during lunch.

"You said nothing about Keith!"

"We sometimes run into each other. We don't talk about intimate stuff. You saw evidence of that when we went to Calgary. Look. You don't have to make a big deal out of any of this. In less than a month I'll be back home and in Reese's arms."

Chapter 15

Leslie

August 1983

Had she really heard the words "Keith Hamilton" and "leaving soon" in the same sentence? Someone was obviously misinformed. Leslie had gone jogging with Keith earlier that morning and he hadn't said a word. They had met at their spot and had continued for three miles, over the bridge, toward the gondola lift. They had run — as they usually did — in silence. Keith was single-minded and intense.

Leslie excused herself from the restaurant and entered his office without knocking.

"I hear you are leaving us."

Keith put down the newspaper he was reading and removed his glasses.

"Is it true?" Leslie asked.

"My friend Johann is returning sooner than he planned, to resume this position and his apartment on the twenty-third. I will leave for Winnipeg shortly after."

"That's only two weeks away!" Even to her own ears, Leslie sounded like a petulant girlfriend who had a right to know his plans. "I will miss our run together. And our talks after work."

"I will too." Keith picked up the newspaper.

Dismissed, she resumed work. During the busy supper hours she pasted a smile on her face and faked cheerfulness. After the tables were wiped clean and the carpets vacuumed, she returned to Keith's office.

"I'm sorry I barged in earlier."

"I'm sorry you had to hear my news from someone else. I could have told you before your shift started."

But he hadn't.

"I can't imagine this place without you."

"Oh you will like Johann. He is one of my best friends."

"Why not stay and hang out with him?"

"Why not indeed?"

"I might leave early too. I was going to stay until Labour Day. But I need to find a place to live in Saskatoon. And I haven't yet chosen my university classes. I should probably take care of things."

"If the timing works out, I would be happy to give you a lift."

"To my home? Oh no! That's out of your way."

"It's good to see different parts of our country."

"There is nothing exciting to see back home unless you count a few sloughs and a hill or two." Leslie paused. "How soon do you need to know?"

Keith smiled. "Don't forget you have to give me two-week's notice."

"Won't that leave the restaurant a little short-handed if I leave?"

"There are always ambitious workers who take on extra shifts. And if the restaurant is a little short-handed at the end of August, well, that will be Johann's problem, not mine."

"And you say he's one of your best friends," Leslie teased.

The next day, Leslie came upon Charlotte reading in the living room. "Why didn't you tell me you had the day off?" she asked. "We could have done something together."

"It was unplanned and unexpected. Somebody needed to trade a day and this one worked best." Charlotte put down her book. "You have the look — like when you need to confess something."

"I have decided to go home early and get ready for school," Leslie said, sitting beside her sister on the couch. "I don't have a place to live."

"And you only became cognizant of this now?"

"I didn't give it much thought. But I do have a backup plan. That is, if Aunt Debra's offer still holds."

"Well, I'm going to stay here. I'm going to stay during the winter season and learn how to ski. Some of the best slopes in the

world are here and I should take advantage of it."
"Do Mom and Dad know?"
"Not the skiing part — you know how Mom worries. But staying has always been an option."
"Did you hear about Keith?"
"No! Did something happen to him?"
"He's going home. The permanent assistant manager is returning. You'll be having a new boss." Leslie hesitated, deliberating about giving Charlotte something to chew on. "And Keith has offered me a ride to the farm."
"Aha! The plot thickens!"
"There is no plot. Keith has become a friend and I might never see him again after this summer. Plus I'll be saving bus fare."
"It's a bad idea, Leslie."
"Give me your blessing, sis, and I'll give you my bed in the private suite."
Charlotte laughed. "A bribe for a blessing? I don't know, Leslie. But yes, I want your room."

After living four months in Banff, it was time to tie up loose ends and say goodbye to the friends she was leaving behind. Leslie could count them on one hand. Mike in the restaurant, Charlotte, who was obligated to be loyal, and Carrie McCombs, the last of Leslie's former roommates. Carrie worked full-time at the fudge shop in downtown Banff. Leslie did not remember her switching jobs and moving out of the staff house.

"I've been promoted to assistant manager," Carrie said, when Leslie stopped to visit. "And today I'm in charge. Which means, I haven't had a break all afternoon." She led Leslie into a back room and filled a kettle with water. She glanced back into the shop to see if she was needed.

"I'm heading back home soon. I was hoping you and I could share an apartment when we go back to university."

"I'm staying. I love it here."

"Charlotte is staying too. Have you heard anything from Christina and Karen? Are they going back to university?"

"I expected them to keep in touch, but I've heard nothing."

"Whatever happened with them?"

"It was a fight over some boy. Christina went off in a huff and less than a week later, Karen left."

"I can't believe nobody talked to me."

"You had your own problems in the restaurant," said Carrie. "Speaking of boys, I bet Reese is excited about you coming home."

Leslie had not told him. "I'm thinking about surprising him."

"Bad idea. No good comes from surprises. Better let him know."

"You're probably right."

She wrote Reese a letter as soon as she returned to the staff house.

I'll be coming home earlier than I said. I am not sure of the time, or even the exact day because I'm getting a ride with a friend. I'm tired of the mountains. I feel so closed in all the time.

I can't wait to see you. I love you.

On her last day in Banff, Leslie walked to the bank and transferred her savings to her Hatfield Credit Union. She cleaned out her kitchen cupboards and labelled what remained for Charlotte to use. In the afternoon she sorted through her clothes and gave away, or threw away, anything outdated or tacky. She managed to fit her newest clothes into her suitcase. An overnight bag, recently purchased, held enough for her last night in the staff house.

She spent her last evening bar-hopping. It was a half-hearted attempt to have fun; everyone was tired from Keith's farewell party the night before. No one threw Leslie a farewell party. She had not expected one.

Keith's Mustang pulled up to the staff house promptly at six in the morning.

"The air has a distinct chill," Keith said, as he helped stash her suitcase in the car's trunk. "Summer is over, time for school."

As they drove down the hill and onto the main road he said, "Say goodbye to The Inn." A little while later he said, "Say goodbye to the mountains."

"You sound sad."

"I am. I don't know when I'm coming back."

She tried to think of interesting things to distract him, but it was too early and she was not a morning person. Instead, they listened to the radio. By the time they stopped at a truck stop for breakfast, Keith was back to his usual cheerful self.

"I want this drive to be leisurely, not a marathon." Keith pulled out a map of the three western provinces. "I have the route planned. I've never been to Drumheller before. It was always a little out of the way. And Saskatoon, too. I hear it's a beautiful city. I especially look forward to seeing the farm you and Charlotte talked so much about."

"I'm excited to get back too," Leslie said, but the words sounded hollow. "Don't expect much. It's only a farm."

"Only a farm? You have no idea how lucky you are."

"I never looked at it as luck."

How easily they had talked in Keith's office, when five minutes was all the time needed to share a joke. How easily the conversation flowed when Charlotte had accompanied them to Calgary. But hours of just the two of them? Leslie was a little daunted.

Later, east of Calgary, she said, "I wonder what became of Lisa."

"I received a letter from her. She's alive and well and working in a resort in British Columbia. She filled me in on her life and forgave me for firing her." He turned and smiled at Leslie. "She will land on her feet. Her kind always do."

"What kind is that?"

"Lisa was an excellent supervisor, but she's a bully who wanted you gone for some reason. You seemed so oblivious to her tactics."

"I *was* oblivious."

"When she called you into my office, Leslie, you kept your cool. I was impressed. I asked others about what was really going on. Not everyone was afraid to speak against Lisa."

"Inside my head I was thinking all sorts of things," Leslie admitted. "But I didn't want to say them out loud in front of you." She leaned over and squeezed his hand. "I appreciated your support." She withdrew her hand and put it in her lap. "I'm sorry. I didn't mean to touch you."

"You only touched my hand, Leslie. You don't have to be sorry."

She couldn't drop the sense of formality that had always been between them. Even when they had gone running together, she had been aware he was her boss.

They reached Saskatoon late in the afternoon.

"This is a beautiful city," Keith remarked as they drove over the Twenty-fifth Street Bridge toward the university campus.

"If you turn here, I can take you past the house I used to live in while I went to school. It's only a bit out of our way."

They stopped at the Italian restaurant where Leslie used to eat with Reese. As soon as she sat, she felt the mistake. She was sure the waiter remembered her.

"Excuse me, Keith, but I want to call home to let them know where I am."

"Most certainly."

Outside the restaurant was a pay phone. She dialled quickly and put in several quarters. Paige answered, "Hello. Dewhurst residence."

"I need to talk to Mom."

"Mom's over at Grandma Dewhurst's house."

"What's she doing over there?"

"She drove Grandpa into the city for a doctor's appointment. Wendy and I made supper for Dad."

"Is Reese working tonight?"

"Not yet. Dad's swathing."

"I'll be home in about two hours."

"You're coming home today? Should I call Reese?"

"No! Don't call Reese!" It wouldn't do to have him waiting at the farm when Leslie pulled into the yard with Keith. "I want to surprise him. Paige? Could you get the spare room ready? We may have a house guest."

On the highway home, Keith and Leslie got stuck behind a slow-moving swather with flashing warning lights. By the time it turned off several miles later, there was a backup of vehicles.

"You have to be patient." Leslie told him about a trip home last fall when Christina recklessly passed a slow-moving vehicle and narrowly missed a head-on collision.

In Hatfield, she watched for Reese's truck. It would not do for Reese to see her riding in a black Mustang with a handsome man.

"Looks like a decent enough town," Keith said pleasantly, not noticing her agitation. "Clean and ..."

"Boring. Full of old people and young families."

"It looks safe."

Leslie laughed without humour. "It's safe alright. Everyone knows everyone's business. Turn north here. It's about ten minutes to the farm." Along the way, she pointed out fields of wheat, oats and canola, surprised at how knowledgeable she was.

When the car turned into the lane, Leslie could see her mother and sisters waiting on the front veranda. They stepped down and stopped in their tracks when Keith emerged from the car.

"Mom, this is Keith Hamilton. Keith, this is my mother, Elsie Dewhurst and my two younger sisters, Wendy and Paige." Seeing their faces were uncomprehending, she added, "Keith was the assistant manager at The Inn where Charlotte and I worked. He's on his way home to Winnipeg and he offered me a lift."

Her mother recovered first. "Well, this is quite a lift home. Thank you, Keith. And welcome. Can I offer you some refreshment?"

Leslie held her mother back as Keith followed Wendy and Paige into the house. "I'm not sure of his plans. It would be polite to invite him to stay. He can turn us down if he wants to keep on going."

"We can be hospitable," Mom agreed, following Leslie into the kitchen where Keith stood looking at the jars of freshly preserved peaches on the countertop.

"I haven't seen homemade canning for years," he said.

"The peaches are perfectly delicious this year. Sometimes they are woody and tasteless. It has to do with the right mix of sun and rain. And of course, the price has to be affordable. Otherwise, I wouldn't bother."

Leslie led Keith into the dining room with its big table and sideboard. The windows afforded a view of the west. Already the sky was a deep pink as the sun began to set.

"Dad will be home when it gets dark." Mom placed a pitcher of lemonade and a plate of cookies on the table. "Would you like to call it a day?" she said to Keith. "We have a spare room. You are welcome to stay here for the night."

"Why, thank you." Keith was quiet for a few seconds. "I will take you up on your offer and get an early start tomorrow morning."

"I'm up at six," said Mom. "I can at least put some coffee on and make some porridge for you."

"Porridge." Keith smiled. "I haven't had porridge since I was a boy."

"Glad we can take you back to an earlier time."

"It was my pleasure to get to know both of your daughters, Mrs. Dewhurst. Charlotte is one of our best workers. And Leslie was a wonderful waitress."

"Please call me Elsie. My daughters aren't quite as helpful at home but I've been told that will change. The teenage years are almost behind them."

Leslie managed to steer the conversation away from anything potentially embarrassing. Her mother talked about the neighbour who had an accident and how everyone chipped in to help with the livestock, about the wedding supper she helped prepare at the hall, about her garden and how lovely the dahlias were.

Keith listened with a friendly smile on his face, appropriately interested. His tall, thin body stretched out in the chair reserved for Leslie's father. They were still sitting at the dining room table when Dad returned from the field and Mom served generous portions of peach cobbler and ice cream. No one asked Keith to move to another chair.

It was after midnight when everyone headed up the stairs, Keith to the guest room that had most recently been Charlotte's.

"Have a safe journey." Dad shook Keith's hand. "With this early morning start you could be home by mid-afternoon."

Mom pressed a jar of canned peaches into his hand. "For you to share with your family."

"Thank you for your hospitality. I feel very welcome in your home."

Leslie walked him outside. "Thank you for the ride home. And for giving me a chance to prove myself at The Inn."

"Your talents were wasted in housekeeping. You are good with people, Leslie." Keith put his suitcase in the Mustang's trunk and wedged the jar of peaches in a corner.

"I'm going to keep jogging. Thanks for motivating me."

"Maybe we will meet again in a marathon."

"I hope so."

"I very much enjoyed your family, Leslie. Thank you for

inviting me to stay." Keith folded himself into the Mustang and was gone with only a quick wave goodbye before he turned onto the road.

And that, is the end of that.

Leslie suspected her parents were watching from the dining room window and she felt very uncomfortable. She strode into the house angrily. "Mom! I saw you spying on us."

It was her father who answered. "We didn't mean to spy, Leslie. Your mother and I liked Keith very much. Charlotte has spoken highly of him. He is a gentleman, for one so young. It was very kind of him to bring you home."

Somewhat mollified, Leslie said, "Well, Keith is a kind person." She started up the stairs to go back to bed.

"Don't you think you should call Reese?" Mom asked.

"I'll surprise him at work."

Paige was still asleep in the other single bed. Leslie crawled under the covers and stared at the ceiling. Even with her mother spying, Leslie had expected something more from Keith than that clumsy conversation by the car.

A tentative knock on the door woke her. Paige was gone. Mom peered anxiously into the curtain-drawn room. "You're up here so long." She stepped into the room. "Did something happen between you and your boss, Leslie?"

Leslie sat up and looked her mother straight in the eyes. "There was nothing going on. He was — and always has been — what were the words you used? A perfect gentleman."

Her mother closed the door, apparently satisfied.

Leslie turned over on her stomach and pressed her face on the bed. "It's over," she said to herself. "You will never see him again. There was nothing between you."

There had been something.

But if there had been something, why hadn't he said anything? Why hadn't she?

Reese's reproachful face appeared in her mind's eye, but Leslie wasn't ready for his passion and his talk of love.

"Leslie!" Her mother was back, her voice was urgent. "I need you to go to town. I'm out of vinegar. I need to get my dills done as soon as possible."

Leslie crawled out of bed and quickly dressed. At the bottom of the stairs, Mom handed her the keys to the same little car Leslie had gotten stuck on the summer road almost two years ago. She had been carefree back then. Reese and Keith had not existed for her.

At the grocery store, Leslie spotted Lila Gladstone and tried to dodge down an aisle. Too late. She had been seen.

"Well, hello there Leslie," said Lila, looking splendid in a linen sundress. "I can see you're back from your adventure. Banff, wasn't it?"

"Yes, Banff."

"And now school again. Your grandmother tells me you're going into nursing."

"Not nursing." Leslie wondered where her grandmother had come up with that. "I'm in Arts and Science, getting a general degree. I've never even considered nursing."

"Whatever will you do with an Arts and Science degree?"

Leslie was ready with her answer. "You need an Arts degree to get into law." *It isn't an actual lie. An undergraduate degree really is a prerequisite.*

"A barrister. Oh my."

This would somehow get back to the Dewhurst family. Lucky for her Charlotte was away. How she would laugh about Leslie's uninspired academic history!

Lila eyed the contents of Leslie's shopping cart. Three jugs of vinegar and one gallon of vanilla ice cream. Perhaps Lila would think Leslie was pregnant. *You never know exactly how rumours get started.*

"By the way, congratulations on your new baby," Leslie said. "I can't remember, boy or girl?"

Lila beamed. "A darling little girl. Madison Rose is her name. Pete says she's the spitting image of me. He's at home with her, giving me a break."

If grocery shopping was a husband's idea of a break, Leslie was never having children. She couldn't wait to get away from Lila. "I have to go. Mom is in the middle of making dills and she's out of vinegar."

"You'd better hurry home. I know our church luncheons wouldn't be the same without your mother's famous pickles."

Keith's black Mustang was parked in front of the farm house. Leslie wiped her eyes to make sure she wasn't hallucinating. She accidentally bumped the horn as she came to an abrupt stop.

Five solemn faces greeted her as she rushed in the house, tripping on the threshold and almost dropping the gallon of ice cream.

"What happened? Did you forget something important?" she asked Keith.

"Something very important."

Dad stood. "We had better leave these young people alone."

"Leslie and I can go outside." Keith took the ice cream from Leslie's hand and put it on the countertop, pushing aside several empty wide-mouthed canning jars to make room.

She was aware of the pressure of his hand as he gently guided her by the elbow to the door. She was aware she wore no makeup, her hair was in a loose ponytail and her clothes were less than unfashionable. They walked in silence down the lane leading out of the yard. Her heart beat loudly in anticipation.

They stopped beyond the grove of evergreens, out of sight of all the eyes.

Keith cleared his voice. Twice. "Sometimes I forget how young you are, Leslie," he said, facing her. "Nineteen? Right now you look fifteen and I'm a dirty old man."

"You're not the slightest bit a dirty old man!"

Keith smiled. His eyes searched hers. "I drove for hours, arguing with myself. I stopped, argued some more and turned around." He paused. "I need to be honest with you, Leslie."

A tiny seed of hope inside Leslie's heart pushed out a root, only to shrivel at Keith's next words.

"I have a girlfriend back home. I suspect she anticipates a proposal. I have given her reason to believe so." He paused for a very long time, before adding, "How can I be in love with her when I feel so badly about leaving you behind?" He took Leslie's hands in his. "While I was sitting with your parents, waiting for you to return, I asked for permission to court you."

"Court me?"

"They seemed a little reluctant. It appears neither you nor I shared our personal information. Reese, is it?"

For a second time, Reese appeared in Leslie's minds-eye.

Deliberately, she pushed him away.

"I don't want to talk about him with you."

Keith stepped closer, still holding her hands. "Your parents seem sure he's the one you want. What I want to know is, are *you* sure?"

How could she think straight with Keith right in front of her?

"If you know your own mind and you want me to leave you alone, I will. But if you have any doubts at all, give me a chance to plead my case." Keith took a step back. "I want to give your Reese some competition. If I don't pursue this, I will be haunted by my own cowardice."

"I want you!" Leslie cried. She pulled him close, his face to hers, closer and closer until their lips met.

Suddenly she was filled with indescribable sadness. She was kissing another man, and it meant more than something. She had cheated on Reese, something she had assured him and her friends and herself she would never, never do.

The embrace ended. "I can't kiss you again until I break it off with Reese." Her shoulders slumped.

"And I must break it off with Susan." He stepped back. "She's expecting to see me tonight. I'll phone you later. We can talk. It might be late."

"I'll wait."

They walked back to the house together. In front of her parents, she and Keith shook hands formally, before he got into the car.

"Keith? What exactly does it mean to court me?" Leslie asked when he rolled down his window for one more goodbye.

"Look it up in the dictionary," he said, with a smile.

Late in the afternoon Leslie let herself into Reese's basement apartment with the spare key he had given her. She put it beside the telephone and looked about.

His apartment was clean. His clothes were hung carefully in the doorless front closet. His casual shoes and his Sunday shoes were paired neatly, not thrown carelessly as hers usually were. Curious, she walked into his bedroom and looked in one of the dresser drawers. His socks were rolled together and his t-shirts neatly folded. She had never noticed before how meticulous he was.

There was a graduation picture of the two of them on the

dresser top. Reese's eyes squinted in the brightness of the sun. He looked happy and so did she.

"Reese." Leslie touched his face on the photograph.

She heard his footsteps coming down the stairs. She shot out of his bedroom and sat on a chair. She heard his key in the lock, saw the door swing open and Reese's look of surprise. He leaped toward her, pulling her out of the chair. He held her tightly and started kissing her. He kissed her lips, her forehead, her eyes, hungrily back to her lips.

Leslie's surge of desire did not return. She had worried it might.

Reese stopped kissing her and looked into her eyes.

She looked away, ashamed.

"What's wrong?" He released her. When she didn't answer, he asked again in a voice that was sharp. "What's wrong?"

She croaked like a frog's. "These last two years have been the best of my life."

"The best of your life," he repeated.

"But I have changed. I am a different person, with different wants and needs."

"But you have changed."

"Reese," she whispered. She stepped forward to touch him with her hand on his chest but he stepped away from her. Her tears started. "I am so, so sorry. So very sorry. I am not the one for you."

He licked his lips. "What do you mean you are not the one for me?"

"You made me promise. You told me not to keep you hanging on if I knew this wasn't going to last. Don't you remember? You made me promise."

"You promised it would last forever."

"I was wrong."

"Are you breaking up with me?"

Leslie nodded, the tears flowing unchecked.

"No. If we put our minds to it, we can make this work." Reese started to pace. His steps were short and quick. "I can fix this, but you have to tell me what the problem is. I need you to hang on. We can make this work."

"Reese, it's over."

"No, it's not. I need you to try. Give us a chance to get back to where we were." He stopped his pacing, came to her and held her, but she stiffened.

"Reese, I don't want to try."

"Don't make me beg," he pleaded, his eyes searching hers, his face, white. Unexpectedly, he shoved her away. "You don't want to try? What the fuck does that mean? You don't want to try?" His voice hardened. "You managed to keep me going four months with letters and promises. I wasted a summer waiting around for you."

"I thought I was coming back. But I changed."

"Yeah, you changed. In the last — week was it?" He strode over to the kitchen table and grabbed her most recent letter. "I can't wait to see you, Reese. I love you," he mimicked, thrusting it into her face. "So, who interfered? What is his name?"

"Reese," she said desperately. "We can still be ..."

"Friends? Friends? No, I don't think so."

The reality of what was happening twisted like a knife in her heart. To never see him again. To never hold him close again — the thought was unbearable. "Can't we still talk and see each other sometimes? Reese, please." She held out her hand to touch him, but he backed away another step.

"Get out of here. I never want to see you again."

"Reese!"

"GO!" He yelled so loudly the apartment walls shuddered.

Suddenly, she was afraid. She turned and fled up the steps and through the building door. She got in the car and drove away, half expecting to see his truck bearing down on her, forcing her off the road. Her breath came in great panicky gulps. Closer to home, her heart gradually stopped pounding and the gulps for air ceased. She was buoyant.

Like a helium balloon, she floated above herself.

Chapter 16

Elsie

August 1983

Elsie failed to cover the tomato plants in the garden and they succumbed to an early hard frost. There would be no jars of homemade chilli sauce to line her shelf of preserves, no cream of tomato soup made from scratch, no tomato paste.

"August twenty-sixth," she said. "The day all hopes were dashed."

"Don't you think you're being a little melodramatic?" Dan asked.

"I don't believe I am."

"Why don't you go visit Judy? Maybe she can help find your equilibrium. I can do without you for a day." He didn't wait for a response but retreated rapidly toward the shop.

"I'm going only to please you!" Elsie shouted at his back.

As she filled the gas tank of the car she spilled a little of the fuel on herself. Dan usually took care of fuelling the vehicles, but he had his own problems and she hadn't wanted to ask. Back in the house to change clothes, she caught a glimpse in the mirror of an angry-looking woman with wild hair. What did it matter anyway what she looked like? It wasn't as if she led a glamorous life. She was just a farm wife.

She clutched tight to all her angry thoughts as she drove the hundred or so kilometres to the Rasmussens' acreage. She knocked on Judy's door and walked in unannounced. The house was messy and smelled like shit.

"You're lucky you caught me home," Judy said, as she filled

the kettle and made room on the kitchen table for a teapot and two cups. "I was thinking about driving into the city to run errands." She sat on an old thread-bare sofa by the window and flipped her squirming daughter on her back in order to remove rubber pants. She unpinned the cloth diaper. "Ooh, this is a messy one!"

Elsie turned her face away. "Am I keeping you from something important?" she asked.

"Nothing is more important than you right now." Judy picked up Rosie, soiled clothes and all. "Excuse me for a moment while I soak this diaper in the toilet. And wash off this bum."

The kettle whistled. Elsie poured the boiling water into the teapot and added two bags. She wished she had asked for something stronger to drink than tea but it was barely mid-morning.

"Is everything alright at home?" Judy asked, when she returned with Rosie. "You and Dan didn't have a fight, did you?"

"It's not about Dan, although I *am* fighting with him. I just want to vent my rage. And I need a good cry."

"Vent and cry away. I'll be your shoulder."

Elsie sighed. "It's Leslie and Reese."

Judy looked at her with sympathy. "Yes, I know. Dan told me they broke up."

"Judy, we were blindsided! Leslie had given no warning she lost interest."

"Well, she is only nineteen. It happens. Better now than later — when she has children."

Elsie glared at her. A good vent invited no response, especially a well-intentioned one. "This Keith Hamilton had the audacity to ask Dan for permission to win Leslie's affections. Dan told him Leslie was serious about a boy." Elsie's laugh was bitter and coarse. "He should have sent this Keith packing."

"Give it time. This Keith might not last. Leslie may be back with Reese before you know it."

"She's not going back to university this fall. She won't tell us what she plans to do."

"Won't or can't?" Judy said, as she poured the tea.

"She's keeping her options open. Whatever that means."

Five days later, Elsie was back in her sister-in-law's kitchen. It was early afternoon — Rosie was napping and the boys were in school

— so Elsie asked for whiskey.

"You're only getting one," Judy warned, carefully mixing an ounce of alcohol with Pepsi and a few ice cubes. "I'm not sending you home half-looped." She handed Elsie the glass and sat across from her.

"Reese came to see Dan yesterday. I saw his truck drive in the yard. He parked behind the shed as if he were hiding. I ran to the shop. Oh Judy! I am so worried about him. He doesn't look well. He said he was sorry but he can't stay for the harvest. He's leaving for the Alberta oil fields. 'Take care of yourself,' was all I managed to say. Dan said, 'If you ever need a job reference, I'll give you an exceptional one,' and Reese said, 'thank you,' and drove away. Oh Judy! My heart is as heavy as a stone."

Judy's eyes brimmed with sympathy.

Elsie took a gulp of her drink. "I can't stop crying. When Wendy and Paige came home from school, I told them I developed an allergy to grain dust. I don't think they bought it. They know what's going on. They miss him too."

Judy stood and put her hand on Elsie's shoulder. "I know how you all feel about Reese. And now Dan's without help with harvest."

"We still have your father. And Leslie has promised to help. It's the least she can do." A wave of bitterness washed over Elsie. "Such a stranger she has become, waiting for Keith and his long distance phone calls. Did you know he paid someone to deliver flowers to the farm! Flowers! At this time of year! As if our house isn't surrounded by dahlias and glads I could cut and put in a vase. For free." Elsie stopped. Her glads and dahlias, like the tomato vines, were brown and dead.

"Leslie's young. Don't you remember being a self-centred teenager? I bet you broke plenty of hearts before you married my brother."

"Oh, I imagine I broke a heart or two," Elsie said, grudgingly. She took a second gulp of her drink and waited for the comforting whiskey warmth to flood through her.

The same afternoon, Elsie met Reese's mother coming out of the Hatfield Post Office. Selina Dunn turned her face away and walked past without stopping. She did the same thing to Elsie a few days later at the grocery store. There was no mistaking the snub.

Elsie told Dan about both encounters as she unpacked the

groceries. She had not intended Leslie to overhear.
"She looks like a rat." Leslie's face was twisted into ugliness. "Selina Dunn never gave me the time of day when I dated Reese. Imagine having her for a mother-in-law!"
"You certainly dodged a bullet." Dan put his arm around Leslie and led her away.
After that, Elsie was careful what she said when Leslie was in the house.

One morning, weeks later, when the harvest was winding down to the last hundred acres of flax, Leslie stated, "I'm moving to Winnipeg to share an apartment with Keith's sister, Roxanne. I have a plane ticket. I'm flying out on Thursday."
Elsie froze. Paige and Wendy looked up from their oatmeal porridge.
"I want to be near Keith." Leslie's voice was hard and expressionless. "And I don't need your permission nor approval."
"I heard you say Keith's sister was a student in Calgary." Dan's voice was controlled. "Has she already graduated?"
"She's taking one year off. She said she needs a break," Leslie replied, less defiantly. "One more thing." Her voice rose. "I have been invited to go to Hawaii with the Hamilton family during the Christmas vacation."
This caught Elsie off guard. She threw up her hands in exaggerated surrender.
"We can discuss this another time." Dan gave Elsie a warning look.
"The Hamiltons need to know right away. They need to buy the plane tickets ASAP."
"ASAP," Elsie said. "Don't you think this is presumptuous on their part? You barely know this boy."
"He's not a boy."
Leslie's voice was so cold that spoons scraping in the porridge bowls was the only sound in the Dewhurst kitchen for interminable seconds.
In a timid voice, Wendy said, "There's something Paige and I want to ask." Her eyes were big and her eyebrows were drawn in a worried frown. Elsie's third daughter. The one who seldom drew attention to herself. "There's auditions for the Nutcracker Ballet in

Saskatoon. Miss Louise told all the dance classes about it, and they need children for mice and soldiers and party girls and Clara and Fritz. It's this Sunday, the audition."

Elsie forced a smile and made the decision to rid the tension — Leslie —from her heart. The girl had at least been smart enough not to complain about the dirt and dust and the long hours alone in the combine.

"And you want to audition?" Elsie purposely made her voice sound enthusiastic. "I think that's a wonderful idea. And if your father's finished with harvest, he can come with us. We could make a day of it, have supper in the city, maybe visit Aunt Judy on the way home."

Dan took one look at the room filled with little girls dressed in body suits, tights and slippers and said he would wait in the restaurant across the street.

"I don't know how long this will take," Elsie warned. "How much coffee are you willing to drink?"

"Doesn't matter. I brought a book to read. And maybe there's another dad who looks as out of place as me."

Elsie felt a touch of remorse. "I'm new to this Dan. I don't know what to expect."

"Paige told me if she and Wendy get a part it involves a practice in the city once a week. Are you up to that kind of commitment?"

"Yes. Of course I am. What an opportunity!"

Elsie registered Paige and Wendy and watched while they were measured and put into audition groups according to height. A schedule was tacked on the walls. The smallest, youngest dancers were to audition first. Wendy and Paige had to wait.

"I have a husband here," Elsie confided to the woman beside her.

The woman laughed. "This must be your first time. We would never bring our husbands to this, dear. They just get in the way."

Elsie found Dan in the restaurant. "They are auditioning at different times. Paige is auditioning for party children and Wendy for soldiers. I talked to a mom who said this could be a long process. Why don't you drive out to Judy's and I'll phone you when we're done."

"Excellent idea." The relief was evident in his voice and on his face.

When Elsie returned, Wendy was already lined up to be ushered inside the studio. She looked back when the door opened. Paige gave her the thumbs up.

Elsie followed the waiting mothers to a room in the basement where she was told the dancers would exit.

"This used to be a church," one mother explained. "The dancers will be coming down those second set of stairs. And out there." She pointed to a door.

Elsie sat in a chair. Every once in a while she checked upstairs on Paige who had already made friends.

Half an hour passed before several girls came through the door. Wendy wasn't among them.

"That means your daughter survived the first cut," said the mother beside her, comforting her daughter. "Congratulations. They're doing a little choreography now."

The second time several girls came through the door, Wendy was among them.

"It's okay, Mom."

"Are you sure?" Elsie was unable to assess Wendy's level of disappointment.

"I'm sure."

Upstairs, Paige's group was lining up.

"Don't hold back," Wendy said. "Show off, Paige. Show off as much as you can."

Paige survived the first cut. And the second. Elsie's heart pounded. Wendy sat on the floor, twisting her hands.

The door opened a third time. Nine sad-faced little girls emerged, but not Paige.

"The rest are in," announced a woman to everyone still waiting. "The artistic director is determining who plays the girls and who plays the boys. And the understudies, of course."

"Understudies?" Elsie asked.

"The spares. In case a performer gets sick or something."

Another half hour passed before Paige appeared. She thrust a handful of papers at Elsie. "I'm Fritz!" she announced.

"Oh, that's wonderful," cried Wendy, jumping up and down.

Apparently, the part of Fritz was a huge deal, requiring more rehearsals than the other parts. Elsie studied the sheet which listed all the dates and times.

"Congratulations Fritz," said a mother to Paige. "I'm sure we are going to get to know one another well during the next six weeks. My daughter will be dancing Clara."

"Mom, Mom," Paige cried. "I want to tell everyone in the whole world."

"We'll start with your Dad. I'll phone him at Aunt Judy's right away."

Paige's news gave Elsie an excuse to contact Leslie in Winnipeg and Charlotte in Banff. Both were difficult to contact. Charlotte phoned back with her congratulations, but Paige ended up talking to Kim Hamilton, Keith's mother, who must have said all the appropriate things, judging from Paige's smile. She handed the phone to Elsie.

"Mrs. Hamilton asked to speak to you."

"I was told Paige is your youngest. You must be very proud of her." Kim's voice was warm.

"Yes, we are. Right now we are on a bit of a high with this dance thing."

"That is wondrously exciting."

"Yes. Wondrously exciting." From the cultured tone in Kim Hamilton's voice, Elsie had an image in her head of a tall, polished, sophisticated woman.

Elsie's high lasted. It was as if she herself had won the coveted role of Fritz.

She invited the whole family including Dan's parents, her parents, Judy and Troy Rasmussen, and her own sister Debra, with whom Elsie had a tepid relationship.

"But don't invite our kids," Judy warned. "They could never sit still for a ballet. It would be a waste of money. Troy's mother will watch them for us."

Charlotte booked time off as soon as she heard the performance dates in late November, but Leslie, when she finally returned Elsie's phone call, said she started a new job and could not take Friday off to fly home.

"And besides, the staff Christmas party is the same weekend," she added.

"A staff you barely know is more important than your sister?" Elsie hung up quickly. She burst into tears.

Paige cried too. "I'd be there if Leslie was on stage — even if I had to quit my job."

"Paige is the only dancer from Hatfield to get a part," said Wendy. "Tomorrow she and Miss Louise are going to be interviewed by the newspaper. Everyone at our studio is super excited."

"I bet." Elsie wiped away her tears. Not everyone was "super excited." Only the day before, while waiting for Paige at the dance studio, one mother said, "I sure wouldn't want to risk my life driving on that narrow highway through the winter storms."

"And I heard if you miss too many rehearsals, they take the role away and give it to the understudy," added another.

A third mother, whose daughter had consistently earned the highest marks in the ballet exams, exclaimed, "What a miracle Paige got a part."

A week later, after Paige's picture and biography appeared in the Hatfield newspaper, Lila Gladstone felt it was her "duty" to inform Elsie how Paige bragged on the school bus.

"Lila's last name should be Madstone or Sadstone." Dan laughed at his own joke. "Just let it go Elsie."

When Elsie vented to her sister-in-law, Judy said, "Welcome to the world of crazy ambitious parents. Be glad you don't have sons in hockey. You wouldn't believe what some parents shout out to their boys on the ice!"

"Of course it doesn't help that Paige is riding a high horse."

"She's eleven. Let her ride. This will pass soon enough."

Judy was right. Paige's success became old news and all that remained were the two weekly trips to Saskatoon for rehearsals.

Elsie reserved a hotel room close to the Centennial Auditorium. On opening night, dressed in their Christmas finery, the Dewhursts emerged from the hotel elevator to find all the relatives waiting in the lobby.

"Charlotte!" exclaimed Judy. "When did you get in?"

"I arrived by bus a few hours ago," Charlotte replied, submitting to hugs.

"Thank you all for coming." Elsie addressed the group. "It means a lot to Dan and I. And to Paige of course."

"Don't we look nice." Debra put her arm around Elsie. "Thanks sis, for the invite. I wouldn't have missed this for the world. And where is our little star?"

"I walked her over to the backstage an hour ago," said Charlotte.

"We don't want to be late." Dan steered the family out the hotel's main door.

"Relax, Dan." Judy laughed. "No one is going to steal our seats."

"I have all the tickets," said Elsie. "First balcony, seats in the centre, two rows of six." The cost was hundreds of dollars, but she would have paid for the moon.

"Leslie's going to be sorry she missed this," she said to Dan. From their excellent vantage point, they watched the theatre fill with people.

"I believe she will," he agreed. "But let's try not to make her absence into a big deal."

"Imagine all of us at a ballet," said Charlotte, as the lights dimmed.

The overture began. "I know this music." Dan sounded surprised.

"Shush." This was Elsie's first ballet too, and she wanted to take it all in, undistracted by small talk. She wanted to remember the music and the colourful sights of magical characters. However, the minute Paige was on the stage, Elsie watched no one else.

During the intermission, many familiar people from the rehearsals came over to congratulate the Dewhursts. "That girl of yours is going to steal the show," said one of the mothers. "The minute I take my eyes off my own daughter, I lose her in the group. They all look the same in their wigs and old-fashioned clothes. But yours is really acting like a bratty little brother."

"How is Wendy handling all this craziness over Paige's success?" Judy asked, when no one was in earshot. "Any signs of jealousy?"

"None Dan and I observed." Elsie watched Wendy laugh at something Charlotte said. "She's not one for the limelight. And she's always been close to Paige. Best friends *and* sisters." *Not like*

Charlotte and Leslie.
  Leslie. A shadow crossed over Elsie's heart. She thrust it aside.
  When the show ended and the characters took their bows, Elsie thought the clapping was a little louder for Paige than it was for any other character. *Or is my imagination playing tricks?* She was going to ask Dan, but he was talking to Troy Rasmussen as they exited their rows in the balcony.
  "This is from Leslie and the Hamiltons to make amends for not being here." Charlotte held a bouquet of red roses covered in clear cellophane.
  "How did you manage to sneak that in here without me seeing?" For the first time Elsie noticed other parents held bouquets as they waited for their dancers in the lobby. "I'm ashamed I hadn't thought of at least one rose for Paige," she whispered to Judy.
  "Oh Elsie," laughed Judy. "Let's not be hard on ourselves. It isn't as if we know the proper opening-night etiquette."
  "I bet Kim Hamilton knows the proper opening-night etiquette. I'm sure those flowers were her idea."

Early the next morning, Elsie retrieved the newspaper from outside their hotel door to read the review of the ballet. She scanned the article. "Paige, your name is mentioned."
  "You're the only one singled out," Charlotte said, looking over Elsie's shoulder. "Paige Dewhurst of Hatfield stole the show."
  "You're just making it up." Paige grabbed the paper. "See, it doesn't say that."
  "It implies it. I'm going to buy some extra copies of the newspaper." In a low voice, Elsie said to Dan, "and I'm going to give one to that bitchy mother whose daughter always gets the highest marks in dance exams."
  "No, you're not."
  "Oh, yes I am." But Elsie knew she didn't have the guts to stick it to anyone. She always felt remorse whenever she was vindictive.
  "Why don't you tack it onto the bulletin board at the dance studio?" suggested Charlotte. "Success is wonderful for the reputation of the whole studio."
  "Miss Louise is coming to watch tonight," said Paige. "And some of my friends are coming for the Sunday matinee."
  Elsie would have liked to watch all three performances like

some of the mothers, but that would have been too expensive — not to mention self-indulgent.

The telephone rang on Christmas Eve as the family was putting on their coats and boots to leave for church.

Dan was the closest and picked up. "Is everything all right?" he asked, his voice strangely odd.

Elsie put down her purse, ready to brace herself.

Dan's alarmed expression relaxed. He put his hand over the receiver. "It's Keith Hamilton, phoning from Hawaii. He's asking for our permission to ask Leslie to marry him."

"Oh my. Tell him no. It's too soon. We hardly know him. Leslie isn't even twenty."

"Yes," Dan said into the receiver. "You have our blessing."

"What are you thinking?" Elsie screeched, when he hung up the telephone.

Dan took her hand. "Leslie's very headstrong about all this. She will marry him without our consent, so we might as well act gracious. You know, it's commendable Keith phoned us."

"He's a smooth one all right."

"There's going to be a wedding," Paige sang as she danced Wendy around the room. "There's going to be a wedding."

"We can't tell anyone," cautioned Dan. "Keith hasn't asked her yet. She might turn him down."

"She won't refuse him," Elsie said sourly.

"Is he as nice as Reese?" asked Wendy.

"He's older and richer," said Paige. "But nobody's nicer than Reese."

Leslie's call came late the next evening after the last of the Christmas company had gone.

"Congratulations," Dan said and handed the phone to Elsie.

"Engagement is the time to get to know one another. Don't rush into anything."

"I would marry Keith Hamilton tomorrow if I could."

The words "marry in haste, repent at leisure" were on the tip of Elsie's tongue, but she restrained herself from saying them. Instead, she choked out "Merry Christmas darling. And congratulations," before passing the phone to Wendy.

But then there was a date. And a place.
September eighth. In Winnipeg.

"Could you have planned a worse time for us?" Elsie cried over the telephone, all pleasantries abandoned.

"I want to get married while the temperature outside is still decent. And I don't want to wait another year." The calmness in Leslie's voice sounded rehearsed. "We only got the church and the hotel banquet hall because of a sudden cancellation."

"If you married in your own church there wouldn't be a problem reserving a summer date. And you wouldn't interfere with your father's harvest." Elsie's voice was brusque with disappointment.

Leslie hung up and Elsie burst into tears of anger and frustration.

"She can't get married in her hometown! No! It has to be some big fancy hotel in Winnipeg!" she sobbed.

"My work can wait a few days," Dan said. "Let her have her day. She's young. We have to forgive her for being selfish."

There! Dan uttered the words Elsie had been holding back.

"I am so tired of hearing how young Leslie is." Elsie blew her nose. "If she's so young, why is she getting married? And if she's so selfish, why did Keith choose her?"

Later in the evening, after Elsie returned with Wendy from her piano lesson, Dan said, "You missed Keith on the phone, apologizing about the date."

"What exactly did our young Mr. Hamilton have to say?"

"He said we should have been consulted before any contracts were signed, before deposits were paid."

"I'm sure the concern in his voice was very soothing."

"We talked about budgets, expectations and guest lists," Dan continued, not responding to Elsie's sarcasm. "Keith made it clear we are not expected to pay for anything we consider too extravagant."

"Do we know the difference between extravagance and necessity? For the first time, I feel like a second cousin at a family reunion."

"It's a relief to see you haven't lost your sense of humour."

"I have, Dan. I really think I have. My heart is as cold as this frigid January air."

Chapter 17

Charlotte

January 1984

"Your sister phoned," said Gudrun from behind The Inn's front desk. She handed Charlotte a piece of paper with a number written on it. "It's not an emergency but she sounded eager to talk to you. Why don't you call her back now?" Gudrun pointed to the assistant manager's empty office.

Charlotte had not yet offered congratulations on the engagement. She had admitted as much to Gudrun, who pointed again to Johann's office.

"Don't put it off."

Leslie answered on the second ring. "Good morning! Rodgers, Dean and Associates. How can I help you?"

"Good morning!" Charlotte mimicked Leslie's gag-worthy cheerfulness. "It's me in Banff, returning the call. I'm supposed to be working, so you have to make it quick."

"I'm at work too. I can't tie up the line. Keith and I are coming to Banff in February for some skiing. I wanted to make sure you were going to be around."

"I'll be around."

"I've got something important to ask when I see you."

"Why wait? Ask me now."

"I'd rather do it in person."

"I'd rather you do it now. You have me curious. I suppose you want me in the wedding party?"

"Well. Yes. How do you feel about being my maid of honour?"

"Are you asking me to be your maid of honour or do you just

want to know how I feel?"

There was a long silence before Leslie replied. "I'm asking, of course."

"Well, thank you. I would be delighted."

"You are the person I trust the most. Have a good day."

Charlotte put down the receiver and blinked back tears. She was a horrible sister. She was sarcastic and couldn't control her anger. Five months ago she had called Leslie a bitch during a heated conversation over the telephone.

"And you turned off your feelings for Reese just like that?"

"I fell out of love."

"Suddenly."

"Breakups happen," Leslie had said, in a maddeningly patient voice. "Breakups happen all the time. Someone gets hurt, but everyone moves on more or less quickly. Reese will get over this."

"You two were talking marriage. He won't get over this. He's deep."

"And that would imply I am shallow."

"Ah. You're quick."

"You think you know him so well, Charlotte. But I know him better. He'll bounce back. He's practical. He won't throw himself off a cliff. Or blow his brains out."

"You are such a bitch."

And now, I have agreed to be maid of honour.

Charlotte hated hypocrisy.

Keith booked the nicest suite at The Inn. It was the nicest because it was the largest, with a kitchenette, some chairs, a decent pullout couch and a separate bedroom. Charlotte speculated about the sleeping arrangements for three, although it was none of her business. Perhaps Leslie and Roxanne would share the bedroom and Keith would sleep on the couch.

Charlotte had carried her outrage for so long, she wasn't sure she would be able to let it go. She wasn't sure how she would react the first time she saw Leslie and Keith together as a couple.

She confessed her fear to Gudrun, who said, "Time heals all wounds."

"I doubt it's true for everyone," Charlotte replied. "And for me, not enough time has passed."

Yet her anger vanished when Leslie walked through the glass doors of The Inn.

"So you've forgiven me?" Leslie asked, in response to Charlotte's warm hug.

"No," Charlotte said, because she hadn't. Not really. She was unforgiving on Reese's behalf.

"Charlotte." Keith swept her awkwardly into a hug. When he released her, he gestured toward a willowy brunette. "This is my sister Roxanne."

Roxanne had a droopy mouth and huge eyes peering out from under a mop of curly hair.

"Roxanne is also in the wedding party," Leslie said.

"Pleased to meet you." Keith's sister studied Charlotte without smiling.

"Likewise."

Charlotte helped carry their bags to the third floor and Keith unlocked the door.

"I have cleaned this suite a hundred times and not once have I sat on any of the chairs," she observed.

"Let's have a drink and everyone can sit," said Keith. One of his bags held ingredients for a makeshift bar which he set up on the kitchenette counter.

A knock at the door announced Johann holding a bucket of ice.

"Johann is my best man," Keith said to Charlotte. "The one to be partnered with you during the wedding."

"I am honoured." Johann gave a bow. "I have known Keith since we were both twenty years old and got into trouble together."

"What kind of trouble?" Leslie asked, looking up with interest.

"Let's not talk of days long past." Keith mixed drinks and passed them around. "The purpose of this holiday is to introduce Leslie to the fine slopes of Sunshine, Lake Louise and Norquay. I've got her enrolled in a beginners' class."

"Leslie is a natural athlete. She'll catch on quickly." Charlotte raised her glass. "To skiing!"

"Hear! Hear!" cried Johann.

The conversation that ensued was energetic and punctuated with laughter. Johann and Keith were like a comedy duo.

"I hear you ski often," Leslie said, taking Charlotte aside.

"I'm not bad. It doesn't require much exertion. It's because gravity does all the hard work." Charlotte laughed at her own joke. "I'll ski with you tomorrow after your class is done."

"You know, Charlotte, you could be quite pretty if you put your mind to it."

The insult, disguised as a compliment, came out of the blue and rendered Charlotte speechless.

"You'd look thinner if you stretched your neck and didn't slouch," Leslie continued. "I'll help make you over if you help me ski."

Charlotte excused herself soon after and returned to the staff house where she examined her face in the bathroom mirror.

She knew other girls spent hours trying to improve their looks, styling their hair to flatter their faces, choosing clothes to minimize body flaws — but she had accepted her fate in life as the least beautiful Dewhurst sister. She was not unattractive. That she knew. But would she have tried harder if Leslie hadn't been her sister? Always, always outshining the rest of them.

Leslie and Charlotte queued for the ski lift and maneuvered their way up the line and onto the track. The seat caught them and they swung out. Charlotte pulled down the restraining bar.

"Looks like Roxanne and Keith are deep in conversation." Charlotte gestured toward the Hamilton siblings four chairs ahead. She had not noticed them in the lineup.

"She dotes on him," Leslie said, with a sniff. "Keith is the Sun, the Moon and the Stars."

"Maybe that's how we'd be if we had a brother."

"I'd like to think not. Of course, Keith laughs when I complain."

"You? Complain?"

Leslie giggled. "Guilty."

"You get along with Roxanne okay?" Charlotte asked. "You're sharing an apartment." *Or is that what you tell Mom and Dad?*

"We get along fine. It's just different than being with people I've known all my life."

"How are the wedding plans coming along?"

"Keith's mother and sister are doing all the planning. I go with the flow. Of course, Mom is still upset about the date and the place."

Not to mention the choice of groom.

When the end of the ski lift came in sight. Leslie stiffened. "I'm having a hard time with my dismount. I fell twice during the lesson. Now I've jinxed myself."

"Watch what others do."

Keith and Roxanne skied off gracefully without a backward look. The next three sets of skiers also had smooth exits, but sure enough, when Leslie's turn came, she fell. The operator slowed the speed of the chair lift to give her time to scramble out of the way.

"I'll coach you," Charlotte said, helping Leslie to her feet. "I did the exact same thing when I was first learning." It was a little white lie to make Leslie feel better.

Leslie was more co-ordinated and confident the second day, and by the third day she insisted on keeping up with Keith at Lake Louise.

"Don't get ahead of yourself," Keith cautioned. "That's how accidents happen."

"But you've skied with everyone except me." Leslie pursed her lips in an exaggerated pout.

"I guess I have." Keith sounded surprised, as if he discovered a flaw within himself.

He went off with Leslie, leaving Roxanne to ski with Charlotte. The Lake Louise ski area was a huge complex of runs and lifts and it wasn't long before the two lost track of each other.

Accidentally on purpose. Charlotte found Roxanne to be humourless and reserved.

Charlotte had liked Keith well enough when he had been her boss, but as a brother-in-law, she wasn't so sure. He was too polished, too nice, too responsible.

He was not Reese.

"It's money."

"Exactly," Charlotte agreed, alone with Leslie in one of the ski lodges higher up the mountain.

Leslie took a sip of her hot chocolate. "Roxanne thinks she's better than us because her family has money. I always thought we were well off but seeing how some people live, our parents are stingy in comparison."

"Our parents aren't stingy. There's always food on the table and clothes for us to wear."

"Often handmade clothes," Leslie retorted. "And having money isn't just about food and clothes. Charlotte, this lifestyle ..." She waved her hand around. "Hawaii in December, skiing in February. I could get used to it."

"Keith is a far cry from the boy who drove an old truck, worked two jobs and lived in an apartment." Charlotte hadn't meant her voice to be sharp.

Leslie put down her mug and stared at her. "I wondered when you were going to get around to Reese."

"I'm still angry at the way you treated him."

"So you saved the confrontation for the last day? I guess I should thank you."

"Well, I'm also curious about your attraction to Keith. Is it his worldliness?"

Leslie's laughter pealed through the crowded cafeteria. People turned to look. "His worldliness, Charlotte? That is priceless."

"Do you love him?"

"Of course I love him. It's a different kind of love than what I felt for Reese. A more mature love. Keith takes charge. I like that. And you can't deny his charm."

"I admit he's very charming. But with Reese you couldn't keep your hands to yourself. I don't see you that way with Keith."

"With Reese, it was lust. You can't marry for lust."

She turned her head away and looked out the window in a gesture Charlotte took as a second of regret and remorse. But it wasn't. Leslie's gaze was resting on Keith and Roxanne talking to someone. Wherever they went — on the slopes, in the restaurants, or walking down the street — Keith was stopped by old friends and acquaintances. He introduced them: sister, future sister-in-law, fiancée. The last word typically generated a murmur of surprise, firm congratulations and a subtle appraisal of Leslie.

"Can't you understand just a little?" Leslie said, turning back to Charlotte. "Reese will always have a place in my heart. But Charlotte, I couldn't marry him. It was only lust."

She stood and waved as Keith and Roxanne entered the building.

In the evening, at a downtown pub, Keith was joined by many friends. Charlotte never knew anyone as popular as Keith. She could see Leslie was becoming bored with the conversation that didn't revolve around her.

"Your old roommate, Carrie McCombs, still works at the candy store. Why don't we pay her a visit before you return to Manitoba?" Charlotte suggested. "If she's not there, we can come back."

"Does she know I'm engaged?" Leslie stood and put on her long winter coat.

"I might have told her."

"Where are you two going?" Roxanne asked, her face curious as she intercepted their escape. "Can I come along?"

"Sure," Charlotte and Leslie said in unison but without enthusiasm. Roxanne didn't pick up on the hint.

The February winter air was crisp as they walked the half-block to the candy store. Through the window they could see Carrie standing behind the counter. Their entry was announced by a bell.

"Wow! Leslie! Look at you, I'd hardly recognize you anymore," Carrie squealed. "You look all grown up. And engaged! We were expecting an engagement, just not with Keith Hamilton. How did you manage to snag the boss?"

"Carrie," Charlotte interrupted, before anything more embarrassing could be revealed. "I want you to meet Roxanne Hamilton, Keith's sister."

"Hello Roxanne," said Carrie, without missing a beat. She extended her hand. "I used to work at The Inn with your brother. He was the best assistant manager I ever had. Now *I'm* an assistant manager." She laughed. "Who would have thought?"

She locked the door to the store and reversed the sign to CLOSED. "It's ten minutes until closing. I haven't had a customer in forty minutes. Of course, if anyone has an emergency, a burning need for chocolate, I'll let them in." As she talked, she took out two slabs of fudge and sliced a piece from each. "Tell me about the wedding plans."

"Charlotte is my maid of honour, Roxanne and Karen are bridesmaids."

"Karen Anders? What's she up to now?" Carrie asked, looking slyly at Charlotte. They had spent many an evening enjoyably dissecting Karen's personality, deciding she was passive-aggressive with sociopathic tendencies.

"She's in Saskatoon, working," Leslie said. "I think she wants to go back to school in the fall. She broke up with the guy she was following around."

"I wonder if he was worth the fight with her cousin," Carrie mused.

"So what kind of bridesmaid dresses do you have in mind?" Roxanne asked.

"Please, not too fluffy," Charlotte said. "I look ridiculous in fluffy."

"Absolutely not fluffy," Roxanne agreed. "We tall girls need something classic and stately." She looked hopefully at Leslie. "Let's have a look for dresses in Calgary before we fly home. If Keith thinks we have time."

"He *is* a stickler for staying on a schedule." Leslie tapped her watch. "And he likes to run the show."

"Excellent qualities in a manager," Carrie said.

They talked — about Carrie's job, Charlotte's job, future plans, travel, ambitions, and most of all, people back home — without once mentioning the Dunn family.

Roxanne yawned. "I don't want to be the party pooper, but I'm ready for bed. Is it the mountain air or the skiing? I can't seem to stay awake past ten o'clock."

Behind Roxanne's back Leslie shot Charlotte a look of annoyance. "Before we go, Carrie, I need your address. To send an invitation."

"I'm sure Keith has plenty of unmarried friends." Carrie wrote General Delivery on a card. "I should begin my diet right now. I've put on thirty pounds in six months. I have stretch marks."

Charlotte pushed the half-eaten fudge out of arm's range. Even if she lost thirty pounds in the next six months, she'd still be the heaviest attendant in the anorexic bridal party.

"Thanks for coming by. Nice meeting you," Carrie addressed Roxanne. "I'll talk to you soon," she added to Charlotte.

They returned to the pub but Keith wasn't ready to leave. He gave Leslie the key to the rental car. Roxanne, the girl who "couldn't stay awake past ten o'clock" decided to remain with her brother, so Leslie and Charlotte returned alone to The Inn and talked, not about Reese or Keith or lust or love, or how Charlotte could improve her looks, but about home and family.

It was the perfect way to end their time together.

A few days later Johann said, "When you have a few minutes, Charlotte, I would like to talk to you."

"I have a few minutes right now." She followed him into his office, wondering if she had done something wrong. She remained standing even after he indicated she could sit.

"One of our desk clerks has given his notice. Would you be interested in training for the job? And commit to staying for the busy summer months? There is a wage increase."

"That's funny. I've been thinking I'd like more responsibility and challenge."

"Perhaps someday you will be doing my job." Johann laughed. "Don't worry. I'm only teasing. I'm not going anywhere soon. Why don't you think about the job offer and get back to me in a day or so."

"I don't need time. When can I start?"

As it turned out, Charlotte wasn't the only one switching jobs. Gudrun, who had been a desk clerk for years, had always been interested in the culinary arts. In May she worked as a cook in The Inn's restaurant to see if it was something she wanted to pursue. Carrie quit her job at the candy store to replace Gaye who had given her two-week notice at The Inn.

Carrie, Gudrun and Charlotte shared the coveted staff house suite with the private kitchen. There was room for one more, but no one challenged their sense of entitlement as senior staff. They agreed, when the time came, they would vote on the lucky recipient.

During the spring and summer they talked about travelling to Australia, New Zealand, Thailand and Indonesia. Charlotte did not disclose her travel plans with her family. There was time enough, after Leslie's wedding, to give her mother something different to worry about. She and Carrie joined the local chapter of Weight Watchers and carefully weighed and measured their food. They cheered each other's successes, despaired together over relapses, and generally had an amusing time with a few of the young men who drifted their way.

Chapter 18

Elsie

September 1984

Charlotte walked into the sitting area of their suite at the Regency Hotel. Her hair was piled high on her head and her heavy dark eyebrows had been waxed and tweezed to half their size. Her silk gown showed off her slender body and her surprisingly long neck. She had lost thirty-eight pounds and had not said a word about it to anyone prior to her arrival home.
Has it only been a week?
Elsie had not recognized her own daughter when she picked her up at the bus station in Hatfield.
Charlotte's bridesmaid dress, which had been delivered to the farm earlier that month by Karen Anders, had hung like a sack. Elsie had to take the gown apart and reassemble it. She had spent hours basting and sewing but now the fit was perfect.
It had been difficult to know what to say about Charlotte's transformation, but now Dan, sitting on the sofa in their suite with Wendy and Paige, said, "Sweetheart, you are stunning."
"The bride agrees." Leslie took the attention away from Charlotte by walking into the room. "Goes to show, you really can make a silk purse out of a sow's ear."
"Charlotte has never been a sow's ear." Dan's voice had a tinge of offence in it.
"Relax Dad," Charlotte laughed. "It's a private joke."

Elsie, self-conscious in her expensive two-piece suit, was the last person escorted down the aisle of the Winnipeg cathedral. She sat beside Wendy and Paige in the front pew and watched Keith and his groomsmen walk out from a side door and stand facing the congregation. The pipe organist played the opening chords of the processional and Karen began her slow mincing walk. Keith's sister prepared for take-off and behind her was Charlotte. Elsie's eyes lingered on her daughter. With her head held high and a smile on her face, Charlotte made her way to the front, walking in the specific slow style that Paige had coached at home.

Karen, Roxanne and Charlotte, clutching cream-coloured bouquets, stood at the front of the church, each almost six feet tall with their high heels and big hair. Elsie thought the rose-hued gowns looked exceptionally striking on the brunettes.

The opening chords of *Here Comes The Bride* cued everyone to stand.

Leslie held on to Dan's arm. Veil-less, in a vintage hand-dyed court gown with extensive embroidery and lace, she could have graced any bridal magazine cover. She was as young as Lady Diana Spencer had been when she married Prince Charles in 1981.

As Dan and Leslie approached, Elsie pinched herself to prevent tears. She heard a stifled sob from behind her.

Judy, likely. Sweet, sentimental Judy.

"Dearly Beloved, we are gathered here today in the presence of these witnesses," said the minister. He continued speaking the traditional words but Elsie tensed when he came to the question, "If anyone knows of a reason this couple should not be united in Holy Matrimony, speak now or forever hold your peace."

In her mind's eye, Elsie heard a voice from the back yelling, "Leslie stop!" But it was only her imagination. The Reese she remembered was not into big gestures and impulsive actions. He would not disrupt Leslie's wedding day.

Dan nudged Elsie out of her thoughts to perform her one moment in the spotlight. She and Kim walked to the front and lit a candle together, symbolizing the unity of the Dewhurst and Hamilton families. Kim touched Elsie's hand gently and they both returned to their places.

The minister resumed. "Love is kind. It is not jealous nor boastful ..."

Love does not end.

During the vows Keith's strong voice caught in emotion as he stared into Leslie's shining eyes. "I, Keith Reginald Hamilton, take you, Leslie Anne Dewhurst, to be my lawfully wedded wife."

Leslie's voice was less audible, as if overcome with shyness.

The bride and groom exchanged rings and kissed to seal their verbal contract. While Charlotte and Johann and the newly wedded Hamiltons signed the registry, the much sought-after Winnipeg soloist sang joyously in a pure soprano voice.

One of Hatfield's finest singers could have sung as well for a lot less cost. But perhaps Elsie was unfair. Perhaps the soloist was a gift from one of Keith's many friends.

The wedding party posed for pictures in front of the altar for several minutes before the organist played the exit anthem. Keith and Leslie led the procession. The groomsmen and bridesmaids followed. Next were the Dewhurst and the Hamilton families. Everyone reassembled outside on the broad sidewalk and passing cars honked congratulations.

The day was cloudless and windless. *Harvest weather.*

"I'm going to tell myself it rained back home," Dan said, reading Elsie's mind. He guided her to their place in the receiving line. "I'm telling myself it's too wet to combine."

Before Elsie could reply, Judy passed through the line. "I say, well done you two," followed by Rose Dewhurst who said, "It's like a fairy-tale. How much is this costing?"

"Leslie was breathtaking. And Charlotte! I hardly recognized her," gushed Lila Gladstone. Patti Fields was right behind her. Elsie was surprised how the sight of these two neighbours warmed her. She gave Lila an extra tight hug and vowed not to make fun of her for at least a year.

"We drove up yesterday. Left the kiddies and their fathers behind," said Lila. "This is a girls' trip."

"I can't believe Charlotte! She used to be such a tomboy. That dress! It looks like it was custom made for her," said Patti.

For several more minutes, Elsie and Dan shook hands and hugged complete strangers. They watched as the bridal party stepped into a white limousine. A second limousine pulled up specifically for the Hamiltons and the Dewhursts. Elsie overheard Dan politely decline Rod Hamilton's suggestion about going somewhere for drinks, and asked instead to be returned to the hotel.

"I hope I didn't offend Keith's parents," Dan said, after they were deposited on the front steps of the Regency Hotel.

"I think Rod looked almost relieved his obligatory offer was turned down," Elsie replied. "And I am glad we have some private time. It's going to be a long day and I can't say I'm looking forward to it."

"We have less than two hours before we are to meet at the studio for family pictures," Dan warned, as they rode up the elevator together.

Amid the clothes carelessly tossed aside by the bride and her attendants, Wendy and Paige found a place to sit and watch TV. In the bedroom, Elsie kicked off her high-heeled shoes that pinched her toes, and removed her ill-fitting pantyhose and her too-tight suit. Some of the weight Charlotte lost had attached itself to her. As she pulled back the cover and stretched out on the bed, she thought longingly of her garden and her home.

She closed her eyes for a quick nap. Dan said she had forty minutes.

After an uncle of the groom blessed the food, the room was filled with waiters dressed in white and black. The head table was served first, an appetizer, something in a puff pastry. When everyone had been served, the emcee got to his feet and entertained the audience with stories of Leslie's childhood, which came across as quaint and old-fashioned. Dan and Elsie were portrayed as Ma and Pa Kettle. They laughed at themselves but Elsie was not amused.

The second course was soup and crusty bread. Again, after everyone was served, the emcee stood and entertained the crowd. This time it was the Hamiltons' turn to be roasted. Elsie suspected Kim's priggishness and Rod's "Good Old Boy" image were as exaggerated as hers and Dan's had been.

The third course was a presentation of art: two lettuce leaves and a thin slice of beet.

"You call this a salad?" Elsie said to Dan, who laughed.

The emcee called the Maid of Honour to deliver the toast to the bride. Elsie's heart fluttered nervously. *How Charlotte had anguished over writing this speech.*

"This has to be the perfect blend of honesty, and humour, and glorification." She had admitted she needed help. "I don't know if I'm up to the task. I'm still angry how easily Leslie dumped Reese."

"In a few years you'll forget Leslie's thoughtlessness and only remember your cruel words at her wedding. Write down all her favourable qualities. Here, I can help you. She's generous."

"That she is," said Charlotte, writing the word. "I remember how welcoming she was to me when I went to Banff."

"She's athletic."

"And she's very pretty. But has no sense of humour."

"She's not vain." Elsie ignored the last bit. "She doesn't spend a lot of time in front of the mirror. At least she hasn't in the past."

"Leslie is loyal. And she's hardworking."

"No. She's not." Charlotte put down her pencil and looked at Elsie.

"Remember how she helped out with the last harvest?"

"Only because Dad was without Reese."

"You can do this," Elsie had said. "You can find the right words without all the bad memories that go with them."

You can do this. Elsie stared at Charlotte standing at the podium, facing a ballroom full of strangers.

"Leslie is my older sister," Charlotte began, "but only by seventeen months. When I was younger, I wanted to be just like her. Sometimes I still do." She smiled at Leslie, who smiled back. "Not only has Leslie been a great sister," Charlotte continued, "she has been a great friend. She is loyal and generous and loving."

The speech went on. It was not brilliant and not totally honest, but it was a decent testimony of the bride's better traits. At the conclusion, Charlotte turned to her sister. "I love you Leslie, and wish you all the best." She held her goblet in the air. "To the bride."

The wedding guests stood. "To the bride," they chorused.

Elsie caught Charlotte's eye and discreetly gave her the thumbs-up.

When the formalities finished, Elsie went to the washroom where many women were waiting in line. A few recognized her as the bride's mother and offered congratulations. One woman offered her position in the lineup, but Elsie declined. By the time she returned to Dan, the tables had been cleared of the plates and cutlery.

"I'm glad our cost will only be for less than twenty people. Can you imagine the expense for a sit down meal in a city hotel?" Elsie rubbed her cheeks. "Now I can stop smiling. My face is so tight."

"We'll survive."

"I've reconciled myself to the fact Reese is out of the picture." Elsie smiled sadly. "Is it bad luck to talk about the ex-boyfriend on the bride's wedding day?"

"Not bad luck, just bad taste."

"I won't say anything more. I suspect I'll grow to love Keith. Apparently, he is quite the catch according to the women in the bathroom lineup." Elsie glanced over at Rod Hamilton. She could hear his voice carry over the noise. "I'm not too fussy about his father. I'm sure he is drunk."

Keith walked over. "The waiters want to move all the tables to the perimeter of the dance floor. I'll help move you to a table with a view of the action."

"Make room for more," Leslie said, with Patti Fields and Lila Gladstone trailing behind her. Keith claimed another table and pushed it close so Dan's parents, Elsie's parents and sister, the Rasmussens and the Dewhurst's friends could be together.

Like a small island in a sea of Hamiltons.

"Are you two enjoying yourselves?" Elsie asked Patti and Lila.

They nodded enthusiastically.

Charlotte wandered over as Keith and Leslie drifted off to circulate among their guests.

"My, oh my," said Lila. "I swear you have eclipsed the bride."

"It's the surprise." Charlotte laughed. "Every time I pass a mirror, a complete stranger peers back. It shocks me. I can't believe how makeup and hair style can change a face. Everyone expects Leslie to be beautiful and she is. But nobody expects it of me. Oh, gotta go. She's waving me over."

"How are you hanging in there?" asked Judy quietly to Elsie, who was watching Charlotte walk away.

"I can manage until midnight."

"Tomorrow morning, let's sneak out early and meet at the little corner coffee shop half a block from the hotel."

"Just the two of us? Count me in."

The lights dimmed and the crowd quieted. The emcee announced Mr. and Mrs. Keith Hamilton and everyone applauded as Leslie and Keith glided onto the dance floor.

"It's Ken and Malibu Barbie," Paige said, loud enough for

everyone to hear.

Elsie frowned at her, but the child had turned to talk to someone.

The second dance featured Dan with Leslie, and Keith with his mother. Rod Hamilton asked Elsie to join him on the floor and she took his arm. She used to be a graceful dancer. Rod was pleasant enough, held her casually, and returned her to Dan when the music ended.

Next the attendants were asked to join the six of them on the dance floor. Elsie relaxed back in Dan's arms, free to step on his toes.

The emcee thanked the guests and handed off his duties to the wedding singer. The entertainment kicked off with a rigorous rendition of *Footloose* and the dance floor filled with all the young people, including Paige and Wendy. The singer had a knack at getting them all off their chairs and onto the floor. There was music for all the ages: graceful waltzes, line dances, novelty dances and rock and roll jive. Elsie watched and danced. Whenever she watched, her sister was out on the dance floor. Debra, her arms and back slim, danced with Troy, Dan, Keith, and more than once with Rod Hamilton.

Debra can devote all her spare time to working out and looking attractive. She doesn't have children and a husband to care for.

"Would you like to join us?" Troy asked, holding out his hand. Judy was behind him. It was one of those novelty dances that required three people.

As Elsie danced, she watched her two youngest daughters. They were trying to throw their eldest Rasmussen cousin off balance. *Don't let him spin into the tables,* Elsie implored silently. As if reading her mind, Dan got out of his chair and said something to them. When the dance ended Elsie returned breathless but ready to scold.

"All the single women, please come forward," called the wedding singer and the dance floor filled with young women in short sexy dresses.

"It's the bouquet tossing!" cried Paige.

"We're too young," Wendy protested, as Paige pulled her out of her chair.

"All the single women," repeated the singer.

"Debra," said Elsie. "You go. Maybe this is your year." She knew she wasn't being kind as she pushed her sister out onto the floor.

A long drum roll fuelled the drama and Leslie exaggerated her time on stage. She flung her bouquet with athletic force. The flowers sailed through the air, avoiding the more aggressive girls, and hit a very surprised Wendy squarely in the chest. The Dewhurst table of friends and relatives erupted with cheers and whistles.

Rod Hamilton lurched over to Dan and Elsie. "You know what that means."

"Oh, I'm sure I'll have a few years yet," replied Dan.

"Four beautiful daughters. I'd have my shotgun handy."

"Oh, it is." Dan was pleasant enough but Elsie saw his fingers tighten on his wine glass.

"I've got an hour," said Judy, meeting Elsie the next morning. "Troy insists we should be on the road fairly early. I think my parents were awake, but I didn't knock on their door to find out."

"Thank you in advance for taking Dan home. I left him sleeping in the hotel, but his bag is packed and ready to go."

The waitress ushered them to a booth, poured them coffee and handed them menus.

"Tell me what you thought," Elsie said mischievously. "Did we stick out like two bumpkins?"

"You and Dan looked proud and handsome."

"I know a Hatfield wedding would have been modest in comparison, with the ceremony at our United Church and the reception at the Legion Hall. But I would have made it classy. There would have been laughter and love."

"It would have been beautiful."

"I hope Lila and Patti didn't think we were pretentious."

"I can't imagine a less pretentious couple than you and Dan."

They stopped their conversation to order whole wheat toast.

"I talked to Patti Fields," said Elsie, when the waitress left them. "She was excited to be present at what she called a 'big swanky wedding in a historical church and landmark hotel.' We country folk don't often have these opportunities."

"It has been fun. But tell me, Elsie, how did you manage to handle the financial end of it?"

Elsie sighed. "I'm not one hundred percent sure. Dan was upfront with Keith about money, right from the beginning. He suggested a dollar amount in an attempt to control the budget. I sure hope we don't get a rude awakening. A bill in the mail for ten thousand dollars or worse."

"I don't know how you could. Your share of the guests was small in comparison."

"I expected more of Leslie's friends from back home would attend. I thought Karen Anders mother would have come, but apparently she had another commitment. I know Charlotte was disappointed when Leslie's old roommate from Banff couldn't make it. And our friends and neighbours? Well, what can I say, it's harvest."

"Young people have such busy lives nowadays — and most of her friends are at university. So, how long were you in Winnipeg before the wedding?"

"I drove with Wendy, Paige and Charlotte on Wednesday. They missed some school, but they're decent students and it won't hurt them. We found a motel with a little kitchenette, but Leslie called it a hovel." Elsie paused. "Maybe it was. I'm afraid I've lost her. She's moved out of our sphere and into a new one."

"She's at that stage where everything her in-laws do is perfect. The cracks in their veneer will show. When those babies arrive, who do you think she'll want?"

"Not all daughters run to their mothers for help. You didn't."

"If my mother wasn't so judgmental, I would have. Troy's mother is the opposite. She volunteered to watch our two youngest in order to make room in the van for my parents."

"You certainly are at full capacity. Did I thank you for bringing Dan?"

"He's my brother. I don't get to spend enough time with him." Judy looked up as the waitress brought a platter of assorted jams and jellies and their order of toast. "Thank you."

"I don't think we've ever been away from home in September before. Dan managed to look relaxed for a man in 'harvest mode.' But I can't help worry. Every now and then we get a September of rain and an October of snow. It's these little reminders to 'make hay while the sun shines.'"

"Dan always rolls with the punches. I'm going to predict weeks of productive harvest weather ahead."

Judy always manages to say the right thing, Elsie thought as she spread jam on her toast.

"Wasn't it hilarious when Wendy caught the bouquet? Now you get to enjoy those beautiful flowers."

"Did you know Wendy made her own dress? I gave her a small swatch of material from Charlotte's bridesmaid dress and we went to four fabric shops in the city before she found a floral print with exactly the same shade of rose. At the Mikado. For two days she basted, altered, and sewed alongside me, until the dress fit perfectly."

"Wendy is such a talented girl. Hardly anyone sews anymore."

"She reminds me of myself when I was that age. Rather shy, very creative. What did you think of Charlotte?"

"Charlotte looked magnificent."

"Didn't she though? She's coming home with us and staying for several days to help on the farm before heading back to Banff."

Elsie waited for Judy to comment about Charlotte's lost weight, but instead Judy checked her watch. "I'm going to have to get going soon. I'm sorry I won't be there for the gift opening."

"I'm sorry too. I do better when there is a familiar face in view."

Judy reached across the table and patted her hand. "I promised my parents and Dan I'd have them back to the farm as soon as possible. I also talked to Troy's mother this morning — and she sounded tired. Just half a cup," she said to the waitress bringing coffee.

Elsie looked out the window at the quiet street. At this time back home they would be getting ready for church. She would be thinking about what to prepare for lunch.

"Montreal and Quebec City for a honeymoon," said Judy. "What an unusual destination! I suppose Keith speaks fluent French." She lowered her voice, even though there was no one they knew within earshot. "Did you ever find out what happened to Reese?"

"Charlotte managed to track him down but he didn't want to talk to her. He doesn't want anything to do with us." The thought depressed Elsie, so she changed the subject. "What did you think of Keith's parents?"

"Rod was a little intoxicated. Maybe that's why his wife looks so tense."

"I'm warming up to her. You know, Kim paid for all our hair and nail appointments. The spa receptionist brought us muffins and coffee while we chatted. Charlotte convinced me to leave a generous tip." It had been a girls' day of pampering that included Wendy and Paige.

"You and I don't spoil ourselves often enough. When did we become so practical?"

"Somewhere around the third or fourth baby."

"We choose to be the kind of mothers who put our husbands and children first."

The two women nodded to each other in mutual martyred satisfaction.

"There. That's the Hamilton house." Charlotte pointed to a large brick house in a mature and fashionable neighbourhood.

The street was lined with cars and they had to park almost a block away. Tall elm trees shaded their walk. Elsie noticed the grass around all the houses was a fertilized green and immaculately cut; flowers and shrubs had a look of professional design.

They entered the gate to the Hamilton's back yard. A kidney-shaped pool occupied one corner and Paige and Wendy disappeared to change into their bathing suits Charlotte had suggested they bring. Elsie went inside the house. An informal luncheon was set out in the dining room and an elderly woman who introduced herself as Keith's great aunt was in charge. She urged Elsie to help herself.

"Thank you. I'm looking for my daughter. I'm the bride's mother," Elsie added.

Leslie was sitting beside Keith on the sofa in the living room. They were unwrapping gifts. Roxanne was recording the information needed for thank you cards. Charlotte joined her.

Leslie stood. As she gave Elsie a hug, she whispered, "Keith's mother suggested we should wait for you — but there's been a change of plans and we're catching an earlier flight."

"There are no rules saying the mother of the bride must be present." Elsie knew of mothers who carefully noted who gave what or how much — but she wasn't one of them.

"You're not offended?" Leslie asked.

"As long as you're not offended when you discover Dad and I haven't given you a gift yet. We're waiting to see what you need."

Elsie wanted to give something special, like a homemade quilt.

After half an hour watching gifts being unwrapped, she wandered outside among the flower beds. She liked the cobblestone patios and paths, the ferns and vines, the dahlias and chrysanthemums. The backyard was huge for a city property, but nothing compared to a farm yard.

Did Kim pay someone to take care of all this or does she have a passion for flowers?

Elsie hoped it was the latter; something the two of them would have in common.

As she admired the plants, she discovered her parents and sister sitting together, tucked away in a corner patio.

"Debra has an admirer," said Elsie's mother, by way of a greeting.

"He's coming to Saskatoon on business and he has asked me out," Debra said.

Elsie wasn't sure how to respond. To be too enthusiastic implied something. Not enough could also be interpreted poorly.

"I was a little embarrassed when you pushed me out in the crowd last night to catch Leslie's bouquet," Debra said. "But I was also noticed."

"You're always noticed." Elsie chose to be magnanimous instead of jealous. "Tell me. Who's the guy?"

"An associate of Rod Hamilton's. I was walking back to our table and I was intercepted. Before I knew it, I was out on the dance floor."

Elsie wanted to hear more, but Leslie called out, "There you are! Grandma and Grandpa and Aunt Debra! I didn't want to leave without saying goodbye. Keith and I are off on our honeymoon." She had changed out of her dress and into a knit pantsuit.

"Very practical for travelling." Elsie threw her arms around her eldest daughter. The hug lasted a long time. She was surprised at how emotional she felt.

Elsie and her three younger girls arrived home late Monday afternoon.

On the kitchen table was a lengthy note, explaining Dan and

his father were harvesting wheat on the new quarter, Dan was hauling but not to the bins in the yard, his mother was going to deliver sandwiches to the field, they would keep the combines going as long as the wind kept up, and if they went late, could Charlotte take the night shift so Dan could send his father home?

Elsie smiled.

My husband knows me well. He has answered all the questions I would have asked.

She slipped out of her shoes and into her rubber boots. It was unseasonably warm outside and the soil in her garden was dusty dry. The hot glare of the late afternoon sun illuminated the reds and blushes of the tomatoes hanging from the vines, the greens of the peppers, the almost black zucchini and the pale yellow spaghetti squash. A long row of carrots with their feathery leaves waved in the breeze. Overripe apples had fallen off the trees.

Elsie returned to her kitchen with tomatoes, green peppers and kohlrabi, which she washed, sliced and arranged on a plate. She prepared scrambled eggs and toast, listening as Wendy played a difficult passage over and over on the piano.

After supper Elsie found Dan's dirty work clothes in the mudroom hamper and threw them in the washer. She liked to put his coveralls through twice. She unpacked the suitcases and sorted all the clothes in preparation for a full day of washing on Tuesday. She removed their wedding finery from the plastic bags and hung her cream-coloured suit and Wendy's homemade dress on the line to air out. Paige's dress was crumpled and stained. And washable. Elsie tossed it with the pile of delicates.

She touched the fabric of Charlotte's dress, feeling the familiar nubby silk.

It must have cost a fortune. Had Charlotte paid for it? Or was it a gift? Elsie had been tempted to ask, but resisted. *A dress to be worn once.* She sighed at the extravagance.

But she and Dan had become tightfisted. Maybe they needed to shake things up by wearing fashionable clothes, driving newer models of vehicles, purchasing art, remodelling their house. It was unlikely they would consider gambling in Las Vegas, golfing in Palm Springs, or flying to Hawaii — like Kim and Rod Hamilton.

I could make small changes.

Somewhere in the house was a picnic set for two, a Christmas gift from Debra in a poorly disguised hint to Elsie to add some romance to her marriage. It took five minutes to locate the basket. Inside were two plastic wine glasses and a corkscrew.

Paige, doing her homework at the kitchen table, looked up with interest.

"What are you doing, Mom?" she asked.

"I thought I'd surprise your father," Elsie replied, cutting cheese into cubes. "You and Wendy, make sure you're in bed before ten." She found a sleeve of saltines in the cupboard and added it to the basket. There was no wine in the house, but there was frozen grape juice. "Charlotte," she called. "Are you ready to go out to the field?"

There was a chill in the air, reminding Elsie soon all the garden produce should be harvested before the first killing frost. It had come early last year and she hadn't been prepared. She wasn't going to make the same mistake again.

The new quarter of land was less than three miles from the house. From the gravel road, Elsie could see the air was thick with dust and chaff as grain poured from the combine's outstretched auger into the box of the tandem truck. She found the approach leading into the field. Being careful to drive between the swaths, Elsie made sure both Dan and his father saw the car before she and Charlotte got out.

Dan jumped out of the truck, his face anxious in the headlights. "Is there anything wrong?" he asked.

Seldom did Elsie venture into a field at night, ever since the time she had driven into a shallow slough and gotten stuck. "Not at all," she replied. "I missed you. I want to sit in the truck with you and talk. Besides, I brought Charlotte. Like you asked."

"I'll give her a refresher lesson while you take Dad back to his vehicle. Then you and I can be alone."

An hour later, Elsie said, "I meant this to be romantic. But it is hardly that." She fed Dan cubes of cheese on top of crackers that crumbled on his overalls. She opened the Tupperware container of grape juice. "How's the harvest going?"

"This morning I took a sample to the elevator to be tested. Our wheat is number one and high protein."

They touched their plastic goblets in a toast to the financially significant news.

"So what brings you to the topic of romance?" Dan asked.

"I missed you."

Sitting with Dan in the truck in the dark, with the lights of the combine in the distance brought back a memory of when they were first married, sharing every detail of what happened during the day. Elsie told him about Kim's backyard, the pool, the garden paths with the cobblestone walkway. She told him about the gifts on display in the Hamilton living room.

"Keith and Leslie want to look for a house in Winnipeg as soon as they return from Montreal," said Dan. "I got the impression they plan to start a family as soon as possible."

"You have a better relationship with her than I do," Elsie said, and added hastily, "and that's okay."

"Have you thought about what we'll do once the girls are gone and we have time for ourselves?"

"We're too young to think of retiring."

"I wasn't talking about retiring. I'm talking about you and me. We'll have the winter months to have some fun. You won't be rushing around with the kids anymore."

"The cycle of life." Elsie didn't answer Dan's question. "Like seeding and harvest, it goes on and on."

"Would you like to travel? We're young. We're healthy."

"Paige will graduate in five years and we can talk about it then." Elsie was sure she would be happy to go away when the time was right. "In the meantime, let's enjoy our lives with the children we have left at home."

Chapter 19

Paige

November 1986

As she carried the Dutch oven filled with mashed potatoes down the stairs to the church kitchen, Paige's nose was pleasantly assaulted with the smells of everything delectable. Her mother was behind her with the roast turkey. Wendy, who had recently earned her driver's license, was entrusted to park the van.

Dad indicated where they should leave the prepared food. He had been at the church since early afternoon. He had taken on the job of chairing the committee that coordinated the annual fall supper. Mom complained of his endless meetings and phone calls to recruit workers, especially when it conflicted with harvest, but Paige was proud of her father's organizational skills.

She glanced into the hall which had been transformed into a beautiful dining room. Each round table had a centrepiece of dried prairie grasses artistically arranged in pottery vases.

"Lila Gladstone's talent put to use," Dad said. "I'll join you shortly. Your grandparents are waiting in the sanctuary. Grandpa has our supper tickets."

Paige went upstairs and located her grandparents. "What numbers do we have?" she asked, sliding in beside her grandfather in the pew. He put his arm around her.

"One thirty-eight to one forty-three," he said, checking.

A young man in front of them turned. "Number? What number?" His face was freckled and his hair was an unusual colour of palest orange. But Paige's attention focussed on his companion who also turned, and whose eyes lingered too long on her figure. He was very, very cute with a foxy kind of face, although his hair was nondescript. She gave him a smirk of a smile to show she thought he was too obvious with his eyes.

"My father devised a system to avoid congestion and long lineups," she said to the young man with the unusual ginger hair. "As the tables empty in the dining hall, numbers are called. If your ticket number falls in that range it's your turn to chow down." As if on cue to clarify her statement, the numbers ninety-nine to one hundred-and-twenty-five were announced. Several people stood and exited the sanctuary.

"Where do I get this number?" The young man with the unusual hair, checked his ticket. "Mine says the five-thirty seating."

"Here. I'll do it for you." Paige took their tickets and dashed out into the foyer of the church to have them numbered. Upon her return, she almost collided with her mother.

"I'm waiting for your sister. What's taking her so long?" Mom watched the front door.

"I'm sure she's fine."

Wendy appeared, like magic, to appease their mother's worry. Her cheeks were red, and her hair was dark against her skin of palest cream.

Just like Snow White. Paige was hardly ever jealous of her sister's beauty.

"I had to park two blocks away," Wendy explained, following Paige and their mother back into the sanctuary, removing her coat and scarf as she walked.

Paige noticed the exaggerated double-take of the foxy-faced young man when he saw Wendy. She nudged her sister, but Wendy appeared oblivious.

"How were the crops in this area?" the fox asked Grandpa, who responded enthusiastically to the question by going into detail.

Dad arrived and the conversation progressed from rainfall to harvested bushels per acre to the new variety of canola apparently everyone was talking about. Another farmer joined the discussion, which ended when the next set of numbers was called and the Dewhursts headed downstairs to eat their supper.

"That guy was totally checking you out," Paige said to Wendy. "The cute one, not the ginger-haired one."

"I don't like the looks of that one," Mom said. "His face is sly."

She pointed to a table being vacated.

Paige claimed it. She waved her family to go ahead and serve themselves first while she saved the seats. She hoped others noticed her unselfish gesture.

When her family returned, she scampered off, careful not to jostle anyone carrying a plate of food. "Here. Can I help you?" she asked one old lady, and pulled out a chair for her.

As Paige served herself generous helpings, she couldn't help thinking, W*hat a little pig I am.* She had a very healthy appetite, but she was active enough with sports and dance to wear off the calories.

She sat and bit into a pickle with a satisfying crunch, but it was not as good as her mother's.

"You didn't donate any of your dills this year?" she asked.

"A poor cucumber crop," Mom replied, in explanation.

Paige became aware of a pimply teenage boy carrying a tub of dirty dishes hovering by their table. Ross Kingsley. Grade twelve. Not Paige's type.

"Hi, Wendy," he said. "How are you doing with our physics assignment?"

"I'm done." Wendy cut into her piece of turkey. "But it took me a long time to figure out the math equations. I had to draw a diagram and figure it out from there."

"Maybe that's what I need to do. Draw a diagram."

Ross looked like he wanted to say something else and the silence became awkward. He moved to another table to gather more dishes.

"A nice boy," Grandma said. "His grandmother is a friend of mine."

A safe, unexciting boy. Paige looked up, aware of more hovering.

"Do you mind if we join you?" It was the two young men. The ginger was very tall, his foxy companion appeared small in comparison.

"Find a chair and sit," Dad invited. "There's room for you here if we all squeeze together."

"We're encouraged at this church to welcome strangers." Paige smirked.

"Strangers!" said the ginger, as he put down his plate. "That makes me feel like a cowboy riding my horse into Dodge. By the way, I'm Ian Kennedy and this is Alex Warren. We're both from St. Cloud."

"You're a long way from home." Grandma gave them the deliberate scrutiny only the elderly could get away with.

"That we are," grinned Ian. "About a forty-five-minute drive by truck. A much longer ride by horse."

"I bet you don't have a horse," said Paige.

"I do. Three horses, in fact."

"Three horses!"

"So, what brings you from St. Cloud to the fall supper?" Mom asked, interrupting Paige before she could wangle an invitation to go riding.

"A good question." Ian attacked the turkey with his knife and fork. "My parents had tickets and couldn't use them. When they heard Alex had a combine header he wanted to look at around here, they gave us the tickets. Business and pleasure."

"What better time than after harvest to remember what you need for next year," said Alex.

"What kind of header are you looking for?" asked Dad.

"No, Dan," said Mom. "I didn't object to farm talk while we were waiting in the sanctuary but not now." She turned to Ian. "Farm talk will dominate the conversation if I don't put a stop to it."

"I know what you mean." Alex looked earnest. "That's all we talk about at our house and it gets tiresome. So what could we talk about?" He glanced at Wendy.

"I want to know about the horses," said Paige. "Do you ride them?"

"Almost every day," replied Ian. "Sometimes a group of us wear our long black coats and our big hats and roam the range. It's kind of a hobby." He grinned. "But not Alex here. He got thrown once when we were kids and I can't get him back on a horse."

Alex was quiet but kept sneaking little peeks at Wendy while Ian proceeded to entertain them with cowboy stories Paige suspected were exaggerated for their benefit.

"We're going to get our dessert," Mom said, interrupting Ian in one of his stories. She helped Grandma out of her chair and proceeded to the pie table. Wendy and Paige followed.

"You're never going to get a boyfriend if you keep dressing like a nun," Paige whispered to Wendy.

Mom overheard. "And I would have preferred you not wear jeans and a tight sweater to a church supper. Sometimes I could just shake you, fourteen, going on eighteen."

Paige grinned. Truth was, she liked the way she was — bratty and brash and a whole lot of fun.

"Lemon meringue," said Grandma, ignoring the scolding. "Made the way Joe and I like it." She picked two pieces.

Paige perused the table. So many different varieties to choose from, all homemade.

"Can she bake a cherry pie? Billy Boy, Billy Boy," she sang softly, making Wendy smile.

Alex pulled out Mom's chair for her when they returned. "I haven't had homemade pie for years." He eyed their selections. "Are any baked by you or your daughters?"

"Not this year," said Mom, checking the pie crust with her fork, something Paige suspected she did every year to see if it were as flaky as hers.

"For the record, we make awesome pies," said Paige.

"I bet. So, what else do you do?"

"I like to read."

It was true. Paige read voraciously. She had recently discovered romantic novels with explicit sex scenes. If her mother ever knew the contents, she would be appalled. But since Mom didn't read anything other than cookbooks and the weekly Hatfield newspaper, Paige's appetite for lewdness went unsupervised.

"And you?" Alex looked at Wendy.

"She's a dancer," said Paige.

"You're the dancer," retorted Wendy.

Paige grinned. "She's a good dancer, but not as good as I am. She does make better pies."

"Wendy is the musician in the family," said Dad.

"The church congregation likes it when my granddaughter is the accompanist," said Grandpa. "Church gets out five minutes early."

Paige laughed. Grandpa was exaggerating, but only slightly. Wendy had a tendency to accelerate the tempo of the hymns.

"I teach piano lessons to four children," Wendy said. "I enjoy teaching, and I believe I'm good at it."

"You know," Mom's voice closed the conversation. "There are

people waiting to eat. We shouldn't be taking up space."

"We men are scheduled to help with the cleanup," Dad said to Alex and Ian. He turned to Wendy and Paige. "Make sure Grandma gets safely into her house. Walk her to the door, please."

Dan's parents had recently sold their house on the farm and had moved into Hatfield. As Mom had predicted, Grandma was no happier.

The four Dewhurst women retrieved their coats, adjusted their hats and scarves and ventured outside. A delicate snow was falling.

"Wendy and I can get the van and pick you up here at the door," Paige told Grandma.

"Nonsense! Do you think I'm an invalid?" the old lady retorted, but she smiled to show she wasn't angry. "It's a lovely evening for a walk."

Wendy led them to where the van was parked. Paige helped adjust the seatbelt around Grandma in the middle row and climbed in beside her.

"Such pretty girls you have," Grandma said to Mom. "It's too bad Charlotte put back the weight she lost for Leslie's wedding."

"Charlotte is smart and ambitious." There was a steely tone to Mom's voice. Paige suspected Charlotte's weight was a sore subject for her. "She started journalism school in Toronto. And she's working part-time."

"Brains won't help her catch a husband."

"I don't think she's looking for a husband," said Paige, forever loyal to her older sister.

Charlotte had traveled with two friends the spring following Leslie's wedding, first to Australia then New Zealand and finally Indonesia. She had returned safely but not the thin princess she had been when she left.

"Ian and Alex were fun," Paige said when she returned to the van after walking Grandma into her house.

"You do realize they are much too old for you."

"Oh, Mom. We're never going to see them again. It was just a moment in time. They probably thought we were boring."

"Why did you tell them I was a dancer?" Wendy asked from the front passenger seat of the van.

"Dancing is a little more exciting than playing the piano in church. I could have said you also play the organ."

"Enough!" Mom's voice harsh.

Paige hadn't expected her to catch the innuendo.

Sometimes she couldn't control the little devil inside her. She believed her job as a teenager was to make sure Mom's job wasn't easy. The Dewhursts were such a well-respected family in the community that the worst thing to happen was Charlotte's weight had returned, thereby making her less eligible to catch a husband.

No skeletons to rattle in our closets, Paige thought, with regret.

Chapter 20

Wendy

November 1986

On the Monday after the fall supper, the first thing Wendy noticed when she stepped off the school bus with two piano students was a strange half-ton truck parked in front of her house. Neighbours often stopped by for a visit or on business, but what she did not expect to see was Alex Warren sitting in the dining room drinking coffee with her father.

Alex gave her a friendly grin.

Wendy felt her face grow hot. Without a word of acknowledgement she stuck her nose in the air and walked past them, a piano student in tow, and pulled the parlour pocket doors closed. As she instructed her eight-year-old beginner how to play a C major scale, she half-listened to the male voices in the other room. Thirty minutes later, during a second student's stumbling version of *Oh Christmas Tree*, Wendy heard the back door shut and the sounds of an unfamiliar truck leaving.

The night before, Alex had slipped a crumpled paper napkin into her hand and had whispered, so discreetly not even Paige noticed, "Phone me."

If she had been brave and flirtatious like her younger sister, Wendy would have said she had never phoned a boy in her life and she wasn't going to start with Alex Warren. She would have combined insult and invitation all in the same breath. But she was neither brave nor flirtatious. She was a thick-tongued cow of a conversationalist and had said nothing.

She heard the sounds of the two Gladstone students arriving as she finished the second lesson. During her third lesson, she heard the sound of the first two students being retrieved by one of their parents. At six-fifteen, Pete Gladstone picked up his children and Wendy was done teaching for the week.

She sat at the supper table and waited for her father to bless the food before asking, "What was he doing here?"

She was unprepared for the barrage of comments that followed. Nobody had to ask who "he" was.

"He came to look at my combine header," Dad said.

"You old fool." Mom cut into the lasagna and passed out servings. "He came to look at your daughters."

Paige dug into her meal. "One of them anyway. He didn't get much of a look. Wendy just zipped right into the parlour." She stuffed a large portion of pasta into her mouth.

"He's one of those Warrens from St. Cloud who farm almost forty quarters of land," said Dad. "A father and two sons."

"I call that greed." Mom shook her head. "I can't understand why you admire people like that, Dan. And what did he say about your header?"

"It's too small for their combine."

Mom snorted. "And your daughter is too young. Does this man comprehend Wendy isn't even seventeen?"

Dad laughed. "If he didn't, he does now. You inserted it into the conversation at least twice."

"I don't think you take this seriously, Dan." Wendy could hear the exasperation building in her mother's voice. "Maybe it's time to review our policy on dating." Mom's gaze rested directly on Paige, who rolled her eyes.

"We know, we know," Paige said. "No dating until we're over fifteen. No dating someone who is more than two years older than us. And we have a curfew." She held a glass as if to make a toast. "Well, I'm going to be fifteen in less than three weeks and I've got a line-up of seventeen-year olds wanting to ask me out. And you know what they say about seventeen-year-old boys."

Wendy could never tell what intention was behind Paige's semi-sarcastic mouth.

"Tell me." Dad set down his fork and looked at Paige. He wasn't laughing anymore. "What do they say about seventeen-year-old boys?"

Wendy was relieved to see Paige had the sense to blush and turn away.

"His full name is Alexander Murray Warren. His birthday is July 28, 1963," Paige reported three days later in the privacy of Wendy's bedroom.

"How in the world did you find out all that? You could be a detective." Wendy was often amazed at her sister's resourcefulness.

Paige shrugged modestly. "Summer camp. Too bad you never went. You make lots of friends from all around. Anyway, I know a girl from St. Cloud. And I phoned her. Seems like she has lots to say about Alex Warren."

"I'm not interested in him, you know."

"Turns out her older sister dated the guy. Here, I wrote it all down." Paige held out a paper to Wendy.

"Even if I were interested, Mom and Dad would never in a million years let me go out with him."

Paige continued to hold out the paper until Wendy took it.

"He doesn't come recommended," Paige warned.

"Why encourage me?" Sometimes Wendy couldn't understand her younger sister's motivations.

A week passed and Alex was nothing more than a passing thought. And then, he called. She happened to be home alone.

"I don't know if you remember me, but I met you at the turkey supper. And again at your house. I was wondering if you would like to go to a movie in Hatfield tomorrow night?" Alex's voice over the telephone was pleasantly modulated.

"With you?" Wendy could hear her own heartbeat.

"Of course with me," he said with a laugh.

She hadn't meant to be funny. "I'm not allowed to date boys who are more than two years older than I am."

"That's no problem. I'm only eighteen."

"No you're not. You're over twenty."

He laughed again, as if she said the most hilarious thing.

"I'm sorry." Wendy tried to think of ways to say "no" without appearing rude. "This won't work."

"How can we say it won't work if we don't at least try?"

"I'm not allowed to try."

"Well then." He paused. "I'm sorry to have bothered you.

Goodbye."

The problem was, Alex Warren wasn't twenty, he was twenty-three. That made him very old. Older than Leslie.

A week later he called again, and this time Wendy was not alone. She was aware everyone in the house was listening to her side of the exchange.

"What did he want?" Mom demanded, her hands in hot soapy dish water, when the short conversation ended.

"He asked if I wanted to go to a hockey game tomorrow." Wendy picked up a tea towel. "But I have dancing."

"Right that you turned him down," Mom said. "He's too old for you."

Paige ran upstairs and returned with a dog-eared copy of *Mrs. Mike*. "In the olden days, young women married older men. Cathy is only sixteen when she marries. Mike is twenty-six." She thrust the book in Wendy's hand. "It's a first-rate story. You would like it."

Mom frowned at Paige before putting her hands, warm and red, around Wendy's face. "Alex Warren doesn't lack for looks and charm, I admit. But darling, you did the right thing when you turned him down."

Wendy gave her mother a forced smile. "I'm not remotely interested in that little stubble jump of a farmer."

Held in the United Church sanctuary, the Christmas recital was hosted by four local music teachers and consisted of violin, voice, organ and piano performances. Wendy was one of the teachers. When she stood to introduce seven-year old Connor Gladstone playing *Jolly Old St. Nicholas* and *Good King Wenceslas*, she saw Alex Warren sitting in the back pew. She had not noticed his arrival. He looked young, like some prep student from a private school, a tie tucked under his woollen vest. He smiled broadly at her and she flushed. She avoided looking in his direction each time she stood and introduced one of her students.

As a finale, the teachers performed *O Holy Night*. The voice teacher's soprano notes soared effortlessly above the violin, organ and piano accompaniment. When the applause ceased, the violin teacher thanked everyone for coming and issued the invitation to come downstairs to the hall for refreshments.

Wendy's first instinct was to recede from view inside the crowd but instead she confronted Alex Warren.

"Why are you here?" she demanded, determined to be assertive.

Alex grinned. "I was in the mood for a little holiday music. I certainly came to the right place."

"Who told you about this concert?" If Paige was the culprit, Wendy was going to kill her.

"You're so bristled, like a porcupine." Alex grinned.

Wendy's brain scrambled for a scathing reply, but her words were drowned out by the vociferous voice of Lila Gladstone.

"Wendy. Wendy. I've been looking all over for you." Lila strode purposely into the sanctuary, a styrofoam cup filled with coffee in one hand and a date square balanced on a serviette in another. She stopped abruptly when she saw Alex.

"You must be Wendy's young man."

Alex stood. "I'm Alex Warren from St. Cloud."

Lila looked him up and down. She turned to Wendy. "I was hoping your parents would be here, but I see they didn't come."

"They had something to do in Saskatoon with my grandparents."

"And I forgot what I came back upstairs to tell you." Lila laughed lyrically. "No matter. It can wait. Are you coming downstairs, dear?"

"Yes, right away."

"It was nice meeting you," Alex said.

"Charmed, I'm sure." Lila leaned into Wendy. "Keep your eye on that one, honey," she whispered. "He's a looker."

"Now you've done it!" Wendy whispered furiously, after Lila walked away. "She thinks you're my boyfriend. She's the biggest gossip around! She's going to say something to my parents."

"I could run after her and tell her the truth. That I wasn't invited. That I'm not your boyfriend."

"Not a bad suggestion."

"Or you could let me take you out," Alex continued. "I can't make my age shrink but I can promise to be the perfect gentleman."

"No." Wendy walked away but made the mistake of looking back. Alex hadn't moved. "You at least should have something to eat before driving all the way back home to St. Cloud."

"I think I might," said Alex, bounding after her. He followed her downstairs. "What time did you say your parents are returning? Perhaps I can take you out for supper."

"My sister is home alone. So no."

"She could come with us."

"No. And don't hang around me too much while I'm mingling. I don't know how to explain you."

"Say I'm thinking about taking lessons."

"No. I am not teaching you how to play the piano."

Two days later, Wendy dropped Paige off at the dance studio and went to the public library where she did frantic research and wrote pages and pages of notes for an essay that was due on Friday. She had accidentally mentioned the need to do research at the library on Tuesday to Alex.

"What a surprise!" he said, finding her hidden in a carrel. "Wendy Dewhurst." He bent down and whispered in her ear, "Let's talk in my truck."

"Only for a minute." She grabbed her coat and adjusted her red scarf around her head. She left her books on the desk and followed Alex. He started the engine.

"Where are we going?" she asked, alarmed.

"I'm warming up the interior. No point in us sitting here shivering." He pulled her over to him and kissed her. It caught her by surprise and she pushed him away.

"I've wanted to do that since I first laid eyes on you," Alex said.

"You can't just kiss me like that."

"Like what? Like this?" He kissed her again. A little longer. "When can I see you again?"

"I'm busy. I've got choir practice tomorrow night, dancing on Thursday."

"You sing, too?"

"I accompany the church choir."

"Say the practice went late."

"Not too late. My mother will worry and my father will phone the church. I hate to lie."

"Churches and libraries! How my friends would laugh at me if they knew."

It is easy to fool people who trust you.
"My mother asked why I sometimes smelled of cigarettes," she said. "I told her I had a friend who smokes. And she asked me who — and I told her Chelsea Siemans."

"Maybe you should develop a better friendship with this Chelsea. Use her as a decoy. Better yet, I can be Chelsea Siemans."

"I hate to lie."

"Tell your parents the truth — that you're seeing me."

"When I'm seventeen," she begged. But twenty-three minus seventeen still left six years age difference.

Wendy's birthday came and went on December 28th, and still she said nothing about Alex. The gold necklace he gave her was hidden in her diary box. Wendy trusted her mother not to snoop.

The real Chelsea Siemans invited her to a New Year's Eve dance in a small town north of Hatfield. It was one of the few events that admitted teenagers under the legal drinking age. Wendy asked to go and her parents appeared delighted she was developing a social life.

The small town hall was smoky and dark. Rows of tables lined one side and nets full of balloons hung from the ceiling. Wendy, Chelsea and a girl named Samantha Adams found a place to sit among a crowd of high school students. The music was lively and soon Wendy was asked to dance by someone from her grade twelve English class at school. She barely sat before she was asked to dance again. And again.

"We never knew you were so much fun," Samantha shouted as the group of girls danced in a circle trying to outdo one another with silly dance moves.

"I didn't know I was so much fun either," Wendy shouted above the music. She had consumed one drink and suspected she could be a little drunk, but she didn't care. She was having a wonderful time.

She forgot all about Alex until much later in the night when she discovered him standing at the perimeter of the dance floor. He raised his glass to her and smiled. She smiled back and swung her hips enticingly. She made her eyes narrow and her mouth pout, the way some of the other girls did. The boy with whom she was dancing pulled her closer, and Wendy realized he thought her performance was meant for him.

"Excuse me," Alex said, cutting in smoothly between the two. For the briefest of seconds it looked like a fight would break out. The other boy backed away.

Alex grinned. "Sorry I'm late. At least I got here before midnight."

The next dance was a slow waltz, the kind where two people swayed together. Wendy felt a flutter of excitement in her stomach. Tighter and tighter she held on. Closer and closer.

"Ten, nine, eight ..." the crowd shouted out. "Three, two, one... Happy New Year!"

The balloons, party hats and favours were released from their net.

"Happy New Year!" Wendy called out to all around her as Alex led her away from the crowd. "Happy New Year!"

"Come on," he said. "Get your coat."

"Where are we going?"

"We'll be back before anyone misses us."

Outside the front doors in the fresh, cold air, he kissed her until Wendy's knees threatened to buckle.

He released her. "I can't stay. I have to go. I love you."

Wendy rode on a surge of popularity when school resumed. It was as if she were noticed for the very first time. Boys stopped to flirt and girls wanted to hang around with her. None of it mattered because Alex's words echoed in her head. Ever since he said he loved her, she hadn't heard from him. Over a week had passed and she wondered if she had done something wrong.

Why hadn't he stayed at the dance with me?

When the boy from her English class asked her out, Wendy said, "I might have a boyfriend."

"You don't know?"

"I guess I don't," Wendy replied, annoyed at the boy for being angry, but more annoyed at Alex for saying "I love you," and leaving her.

Boys are so stupid. If she were gutsy like Paige, she would phone Alex and demand an explanation.

He showed up at her locker the next day at noon.
"Grab your coat. I'll have you back in time for your next class. Unless you want to skip."
"No, I won't skip," Wendy said, though the sight of him made her wild and careless.
They went to the Dairy Queen and ordered hamburgers.
"Why did you kiss me and then leave me at the dance?" she demanded.
Alex laughed. "If I stayed I would have ravished you. My friends call you jail-bait."
Jail-bait. "Why do you want to bother with me if I'm so young?" Wendy cried, stung.
"You are truly the most beautiful girl I have ever seen," he answered.

Ravish. Wendy found the word in the dictionary and blushed at its meaning.
At school she sought out her favourite teacher for some boyfriend advice.
"Miss Winters," she said shyly. "Can I ask you something?"
"Of course you can." The teacher smiled at Wendy.
"It's personal. About a boy."
"Is someone bothering you here at school?"
"No, nothing like that. There is someone who likes me. Who I like back. The trouble is, he's twenty-three."
"Oh." Miss Winters set down her pencil. "That's how old I am." She looked at Wendy. "Well, I'd wonder what was wrong with him. Can't he find a girl his own age?"
"I think he can. He says he wants me."
"Tell him he has to wait until you're out of high school. Tell him you're worth waiting for."
"I will. And I am."
"You might want to tell your parents."
"Yes," said Wendy. She was not going to talk to her parents about this. "Thanks."

As the frigid air typical of January locked in, Alex grumbled about the long drive to Hatfield and the small amount of time he was able to spend with her, most of it inside his truck where no one could see them. The first time his hand reached under her coat to unbutton her blouse, she pushed him away.

"No." Wendy mustered the courage to sound stern. "I am worth the wait."

The second time it happened her response was the same. He fell silent for a minute before saying, "I'm leaving in two days for Las Vegas. Would you like to come along?"

"What?" she asked, confused by this sudden turn.

"To Las Vegas." In exaggeration, he slapped himself in the forehead. "Damn! I forgot! You have to be twenty-one to gamble in Vegas!"

A freeze set in her heart, followed by an unexpected anger. "Well, have fun," she said coldly.

"Is that all you're going to say? Have fun?"

"Good luck?"

"Don't you want to ensure I'll come back to you?"

"What?"

"Make love to me."

Wendy glared at him and he stared back. She removed herself from his truck, got into the family van and drove home.

And that is the end of that.

Weeks passed. Weeks without subterfuge. It was almost a relief.

Wendy should be happier, but she wasn't. *Why oh why was doing the right thing so difficult?* She kept herself busy with hobbies and friends and piano and church.

"Wendy! Someone here to see you!" Paige's excited voice rang up the stairwell.

It was Saturday afternoon. Wendy was in the sewing room cutting material for a new dress. She removed the scissors mid-cut on the carefully pinned pattern. There was something in Paige's voice that alerted her.

"Wendy!" Mom's voice was sharp.

Alex was standing in the back entrance, holding a bouquet of red roses wrapped in clear cellophane. Paige, Mom and Dad were staring at him.

"Happy Valentine's Day." Alex thrust the flowers at Wendy.

She did not take them.

"How long has this been going on?" demanded Dad.

"Nothing has been going on," Wendy stammered. "I don't know why he's here."

"I came to say I'm sorry."

"Sorry for what?" asked Mom, stepping closer to Wendy.

"Sorry for what?"

"There's nothing going on," Wendy said to her mother. "There is nothing you have to be sorry for." Her eyes pleaded with Alex to leave it alone.

"You are too old for her," said Dad to Alex.

"I know," admitted Alex. His voice sounded miserable, and Wendy looked at him more closely. He looked wretched and desperate.

"I'm going to have to ask you to leave," Dad said.

"No!" cried Wendy, surprising herself.

"If he sincerely cared about you, he would leave you alone." Dad put his arm around Wendy, wedging her between him and Mom.

"Your father is right," Alex said.

"No," said Wendy, making her voice calmer. She drew herself up and stepped away from her parents. She faced them. "I am going to date Alex."

She had heard stories from girls at school who talked about drama at home — sisters who threw things, mothers who didn't speak for days, fathers who hollered, brothers who shoved. But Wendy did not come from a family like that. She had a father who said to Alex, "Why don't we sit down and have this conversation man to man," as if Alex were a problem that could be solved.

Everyone sat around the dining room table.

"You have to recognize our concerns here," Dad said. "When you have a daughter of your own, you might see this from a different perspective. Wendy is a very young girl."

"With no dating experience," Mom added.

"I'm going on eighteen," Wendy interjected.

"You turned seventeen less than six weeks ago."

"My mother married at seventeen. Not that I'm planning on marriage any time soon," he added hastily, visibly flinching from the look Mom gave him.

"Several girls in my grade have boyfriends who are older."

Wendy tried to shore up her argument.

"And two of them are pregnant," Mom said.

"Mom!" Even as she protested, Wendy knew it to be true.

"A man in his twenties has different expectations than a boy in his teens."

"Elsie," Dad warned.

"We don't have to give our permission."

"No, you don't," said Wendy. "But I will go out with Alex. I'd rather not do it behind your back."

Several seconds passed. Wendy did not try to guess what thoughts were behind the silence.

"Alex can come for supper tomorrow night," Mom said, reluctantly.

"And I can go out with Alex on weekends," said Wendy.

"One weekend night," asserted Dad.

"Friday night," said Alex. "I play hockey on Saturday night."

"No old girlfriends," said Paige.

Everyone looked surprised she was part of the bargaining process.

"I disagree. Wendy should be allowed to have other friendships," said Mom. "And so should Alex. This isn't going to be an exclusive sort of thing, is it?"

"I would never limit your daughter an opportunity for growth." Alex looked at Wendy.

For the first time she noticed the colour of his eyes. They were grey-green and beautiful.

Later, over the telephone, Alex said, "I wanted to take you out on a real date but I was afraid to push my luck with your parents. I would have given up my hockey game for you."

"That's okay." Wendy spoke quietly, aware her mother was listening in the next room. "It was the best Valentine's Day I've ever had."

"I hope you don't mind me saying this, but — your family is a little strange. I never expected to go through negotiations to see you."

"My parents are overprotective."

"Your mother doesn't like me much. I can tell by the way she looks at me."

"You'll have to change her mind."
"Is that even possible?"
Wendy didn't think so, but she kept her opinion to herself.

"Tell us about your family," Dad said on Sunday.
Wendy knew what her parents were doing. She had overheard Mom say they would kill Alex with kindness, a form of reverse psychology. Over pot roast and apple pie, they would touch on subjects allowing Alex to reveal his inadequacies until Wendy no longer wanted him.
"I'm the youngest of three. I live on a farm with my parents. We're the biggest farmers in our area."
Paige lifted an eyebrow at Wendy.
So Alex is a braggart. Wendy knew that already.
The next Sunday the discussion revolved around religion. Alex admitted he and his family were not church goers, that they had no affiliation with any denomination.
"What do you believe in?" Mom asked. "The god of making money?"
Alex laughed but Wendy knew her mother wasn't making a joke. The Dewhursts believed in tithing and service and stewardship. They were more than active in their church, and had raised their daughters with the same values, although Wendy knew she was the only one who took her faith seriously.
Alex did better the third Sunday even though his views on politics clashed with the Dewhursts'.
"Well, at least he has a view." Wendy was impressed with Alex's handling of her parents during a lively discussion.

Their Friday night dates were rather tame, as if Alex didn't want to take any chances with the opportunity he was given, but in early March his hockey team hosted a dance on a Saturday night, and he wanted Wendy to attend. St. Cloud was a long drive from home and Wendy was scheduled to play the organ in church the next morning. She fought hard with her parents to go and it was with reluctance they said yes.
It was Wendy's first public appearance as Alex's girlfriend. She sat beside him on a white bench at the St. Cloud Community

Centre and tried to follow the conversation. It was easy at first, but as the night progressed the music got louder and Alex kept shouting. He had a big stupid smile plastered on his face and his arm locked around the head of any teammate unfortunate enough to be sitting on the other side of him. Was this the way he usually acted around his friends, or was he drunk? Wendy was not impressed.

Alex hadn't warned her about the girls who came to talk to him. One sat on his lap for several minutes before dragging him out to the dance floor. Wendy sat alone. No one asked her to dance. After a very long time, she stood and walked to the back of the hall and found Alex with a different girl, one with frizzy hair, her petite body arched intimately into his.

Too intimately.

Alex's eyes met Wendy's. She walked past him and into the bathroom. There she stayed for a long time, thinking about what to do next.

He was waiting for her outside the door. The petite girl with the frizzy hair was gone.

"I want to go home now," Wendy said, walking toward the coat rack.

"You can't. It's early."

"I can, and I will." She spoke calmly but inwardly she was furious.

"Take my truck then." Alex fumbled for his keys in his jeans pocket and dropped them. Wendy picked them up and put them in the back pocket of her jeans.

"I can't drive a standard." She found her coat and slipped it on.

"Can't you do anything except play that damn piano?"

"Where's the telephone? If I call my dad, he'll come and pick me up."

"If you call your dad, your parents will never allow you to go out with me again."

"I can drive a standard." A woman's calm voice came out of nowhere.

Wendy turned.

"I couldn't help but overhear," said the woman. She tucked her arm into Wendy's. "I'm Eve McDougall. My husband plays hockey with Alex. These dances are not much fun when you're sober. I'm going home now too. Why don't you spend the night at my house?

We have a spare bed. Alex can drive you home in the morning."

"I have to go home." Wendy liked the feel of the woman's arm, reassuring her everything was going to be fine. "I have something important to do tomorrow morning."

"What's going on here?" A man joined their group.

"My husband," Eve said to Wendy. "Jeff, this is Alex's date. I'm going to drive her home."

"I'll come with you," said Jeff.

"No. Stay and have a good time with your friends. I'll be fine." To Wendy she said, "He's had too much to drink. Like Alex. They get like this every year."

"I'll come with you," Alex said ungraciously. "Wendy lives a long way away."

"The least you can do." Eve followed them outside to the truck parked along the road. Alex stumbled in the frozen ruts.

Wendy handed over the keys. She sat in the middle between Eve and Alex and fastened her seatbelt.

"You owe me for this," Eve told Alex, leaning over to look at him as she started the truck and put it into reverse.

"I'll pay you back in sexual favours."

"Stop talking nonsense. You should know better than to bring a girl like Wendy to this drunken brawl. How would you have gotten her home if I hadn't offered?"

"I hadn't thought that far ahead."

"No. You never do."

Eve is hard on Alex. Wendy was tempted to give his hand a squeeze but remembered the frizzy-haired girl arching her body into Alex's.

"Why didn't you push that girl away?" Wendy said.

Alex didn't pretend to misunderstand. "Glennie. She always does that. It doesn't mean a thing."

"To you, maybe," said Eve.

The statement and its implication hung in the air.

Several miles passed in silence until Eve said, "This isn't public knowledge yet, but I need to tell someone. I'm pregnant! I found out for sure yesterday."

"That's wonderful!" Wendy was grateful for this unexpected confession of intimate news.

"I'm due in early October."

"Good thing Jeff's a teacher," said Alex. "A farmer doesn't plan his babies during harvest."

"If my husband were a farmer, he'd know what was more important," Eve retorted.

A few more miles passed in silence before Alex grumbled, "I'm going to be sober when I get back to the dance."

"It's always about you, isn't it?" Eve turned her head to Wendy. "I've known Alex ever since kindergarten. We both peed our pants playing too long outside. The teacher had one spare pair." She laughed. "If there's anything you want to know about him, ask me."

"I'm finding out more than I want to know. And I'm not liking what I am discovering."

"Don't you want to know who got the pants?" Eve asked.

"She did," Alex said sourly.

When they arrived at the Dewhurst farmhouse, Alex got out of the truck to let Wendy pass.

"I appreciate this," Wendy said to Eve. "If I don't see you again, good luck with the pregnancy." She slid over and out the door. She turned away from Alex and left him standing.

Inside the house she poured herself a glass of milk and sat dispiritedly at the kitchen table. She heard the creak of footsteps on the stairs.

Paige. Wanting to hear about the dance. Wendy would tell her the truth.

But it wasn't Paige.

"You're home early," Dad said.

"It was crowded and noisy. I got a headache."

Her father poured himself a glass of milk and sat across from her. "Your mother used to get headaches at dances too. Did I ever tell you how we met?"

Wendy smiled. "Yeah. It was some dance in Saskatoon with a crazy name. The Ag Bag Drag."

Dad chuckled. "The agriculture students — of which I was one — hosted the dance every year. Your mother came with a group of girls. I could see she wasn't having any fun so I volunteered to take her home. Once we left, her headache disappeared and we ended up talking for hours."

"I must be like Mom. I'm better now too." Wendy smiled at her father, sure he suspected something was wrong. If he had asked, she might have told him the dance had been more effective in showcasing Alex's shortcomings than a month of Sunday suppers.

Alex arrived on time the next day as if nothing had changed. He carried a shoe box, which he gently put on the dining room table.
"I brought this for you," he said to Wendy's mother.
"For me?"
Curious, Wendy drew closer to see what was inside. When the lid was lifted, a little grey kitten meowed.
"We're not really cat people." Mom picked it up and held it against her chest.
"It's a girl kitten. If you don't like her, I'll bring a boy."
"She's so cute!" said Paige, claiming the kitten and carrying it away.
Alex followed Wendy's mother into the kitchen. "Let me help. I can set the table."
"We would much rather have a dog," said Mom, washing her hands in the sink. She handed cutlery to Alex, as if his offering to set the table were the most natural thing in the world. "Our dog died a year ago. I miss his barking when people drive into the yard."
"I could find you a good dog."
"We're keeping the cat," Paige called from the TV room.
Alex turned to Wendy and smiled, as if in triumph.
She didn't smile back. If only her family knew, they wouldn't be treating him so courteously.

The Friday date night went without apology or contrition. The following Sunday supper took place in a Chinese restaurant on the main street of Hatfield.
"Mom's in Winnipeg," said Paige, in explanation of the change of venue.
"What's in Winnipeg?"
Paige explained Kyle Daniel Hamilton, weighing seven pounds fourteen ounces, had arrived, eleven days before his due date. That Kyle was the second child for Keith and Leslie, and their daughter, Colette, was seventeen months old.
Alex appeared genuinely interested and asked all the right questions about the Hamilton family. Wendy wondered if he knew

Leslie — or of her. Leslie had been very popular in high school.

"Whenever Mom phones, she asks first about Princess, the cat," Paige said. "Is anybody playing with her? Is the litter box clean? She never asks if we're happy or if the toilet bowl is scrubbed. She won't admit it, but she's crazy about that kitten. Excellent idea how to butter her up, Alex."

"Oh, I didn't do it to butter her up." Alex looked embarrassed, as if he were caught in the act.

Later, after Alex left and the three Dewhursts returned home, Dad said, "At least he's not a mooch. Alex paid the tab when I wasn't looking."

"He's buttering you up too, Dad." Paige gave Wendy a wink.

Wendy had watched Alex play hockey once. She had stood alone in the cold arena, watching that the puck didn't come hurtling toward her. She had hated the way the players pushed and shoved and slashed at each other with their sticks.

None of the other players' girlfriends and wives had bothered to talk to her. Perhaps they hadn't known she was Alex's girlfriend. She couldn't remember if Eve or the skinny frizzy-haired girl named Glennie had been in the group of cheering spectators, but of course she wouldn't have known to look.

In spring it was different. Alex played baseball, and Wendy was his girlfriend. Watching him play was the only time she got to see him because he was so busy on the farm with seeding. The Sunday supper invitations were declined. Respectfully.

It was fun sitting with Eve on the bleachers cheering on the St. Cloud Devils. Eve told little stories about each of the players, most of whom were young husbands and fathers. She told Wendy Alex was not so much of a flirt anymore, that Wendy was bringing out all his admirable qualities.

One Saturday morning in late May, Wendy packed a picnic lunch and drove out to the Warren farm where Alex lived with his parents. For all the wealth he bragged about — and he bragged a lot — Wendy had not expected such a plain little house.

A tall man with thinning hair and a protruding stomach answered the door. "Come in, come in," he bellowed in a friendly

sort of way.
Alex's father.
Wendy offered her hand. "Pleased to meet you," she said, trying to make her handshake firm.

"Dad," said Alex, coming up the stairs. "This is Wendy Dewhurst from Hatfield."

"A pretty one," said Alex's father.

"They're all pretty ones." A tall angular woman appeared from another room. She motioned for Wendy to sit at a wooden dining table in front of a huge picture window. Outside was a large gravelled parking lot surrounded on two sides by silver-coned grain bins. From where she was sitting, Wendy could see a woman putting a small child into a car as an older child stood and watched.

"I wonder where she's going?" said Alex's mother.

No one bothered to reply. No one bothered to explain who the woman and children were. It was awkward. Alex was trying to make Wendy laugh from behind his mother's back. Wendy ignored him.

She was relieved when she and Alex left. It was the first time in weeks she was alone with him. They drove out to a field in a truck that was not his and waited in the half-ton for the Steiger pulling an air-seeder to stop.

"My brother Stuart," explained Alex, when the driver stepped out of the large green tractor. "The surly one."

Wendy laughed, thinking he was making a joke, but sure enough, Stuart got into the truck they had vacated and drove away, barely exchanging two words with Alex and not acknowledging her presence.

Alex helped Wendy into the tractor and she sat in the small buddy seat. He handed the picnic basket up to her. He sat beside her, adjusted some levers, and shifted the huge tractor into gear. They went lumbering down the field.

"Do you feel a little helpless, alone with me in the middle of nowhere?" Alex said, smiling at her.

"I was wondering how many other girls have sat with you in this tractor." Wendy remembered the girls at the dance. She especially remembered Glennie.

"There have been a few," Alex admitted. "But you are the only one this year. Other girls pale in comparison to you and your offerings. What's in the basket?"

"Egg salad sandwiches and chocolate cake. And lemonade."

"Should we stop somewhere, roll out a blanket and have our picnic?"

"I hope you're not planning on taking advantage of my helplessness," Wendy had purposely not brought a blanket.

"Not if you didn't want me to." He laughed. "I was going to ask if you're like the land, but it's a bad joke."

"Like the land?"

"Fertile and ready to be seeded."

Wendy looked away. Every time she was alone with Alex, they were one step closer to something that was inevitable. She often fantasized about making love to him. She had read some of the historical romance novels Paige had stashed. She imagined herself to be the helpless female, ready to be "ravished."

When she returned home later in the afternoon, her mother was outside transplanting bedding plants into the new flower bed.

"We sure have a nice yard." Wendy squatted beside her mother. "Some people don't do anything to beautify their surroundings." She thought of the ugliness of the Warrens' yard. In her mind's eye, she was planting trees and flowers to soften the harsh landscape.

"What's the point of having space if you don't intend to use it?" Her mother straightened and looked at her. "Alex hasn't been pushing you to be intimate, has he?"

Wendy got to her feet, her happy mood spoiled. When her mother said things like that, she felt dirty and ashamed.

"No mother," she lied. "He hasn't."

Wendy's high school graduation was at the end of June. Alex attended the processional, banquet and dance as her escort but Wendy told her parents she would go alone to the all-night grad party to celebrate with her friends. She was not telling the truth. Alex would not be going home and Wendy would not be celebrating with her friends. A room at Hatfield's brand new hotel had been reserved for a different kind of special night.

During the dance, Alex held her close and whispered, "From the moment I saw you sitting at the church with your parents, I wanted you. You are different from any girl I have ever dated."

"How am I different?" she whispered. But she knew. She was a "good girl" — and bad boys like Alex loved good girls, although they didn't deserve them.

Alex pulled her closer and whispered details of his planned seduction.

Wendy caught her mother's frown from the sidelines.

Go home now, she implored her parents. *I'm not your little girl anymore. Leave me alone and let me grow up.*

A bottle of champagne sat in a plastic bucket of cold water, the ice melted. With ceremony and a pop! Alex opened the bottle. On the night table between the double beds were two wine glasses. And two wrapped condoms.

Wendy couldn't help her eyes from straying to the night table.

"To the most beautiful graduate of 1987." Alex filled the wine glasses and handed one to Wendy.

Her hand shook as she took a sip.

Alex held her other hand and compared her small manicured one to his larger masculine one. "Pretend we're still at the dance," he said, taking the glass from her hand. He hummed her favourite song and they stood clutching each other in imitation of a slow waltz. He kissed her, unzipping her pastel-blue dress. It floated to the floor. She stood before him in her slip and panty hose and high heels. One by one, he removed the bobby pins from her hair.

Her hands trembled as she loosened his tie, unbuttoned his shirt and undid his belt. She could not do the rest. Alex quickly removed his shirt and pants and stood in his boxers.

"These are new. In honour of this special occasion."

She would have laughed if she hadn't been so nervous.

His eyes were steady on hers. "You aren't okay with this, are you?"

"I am okay with this." Wendy kept her eyes on his face, trying not to be embarrassed, the two of them standing together in their underwear.

He stared at her a long time, wrapped her in a hug, and whispered in her ear, "We don't have to go through with this. I've waited longer for you than any other girl. I can wait longer."

It was exactly the right thing to say.

"I don't want to wait," Wendy said.

Chapter 21

Paige

September 1987

The Hatfield High School principal delivered his predictable annual speech welcoming students back after the summer holidays. The grade nines — mostly skinny boys and tarted-up girls — were greeted with tepid applause. The grade twelves at the top end of the hierarchy were "invited" to make 1987-1988 the best year of their high school "careers." Little was said about the grade tens and elevens, the middle children, of which Paige was one.

"Get involved," the principal ordered and went on to recite some long and boring creed about respect and integrity.

Paige looked around her. She knew most students were not remotely interested in respect and integrity and academic success. All they wanted was to have a little excitement now and then.

"Blah, blah, blah," she said to her friend, Lacey Ray, sitting beside her on the gymnasium bleachers. There were boys to date and parties to attend. Her grade eleven year was going to be memorable.

The student government — the usual reps of good-doers from each grade — was next introduced. The leaders echoed the words of the principal. "Get involved, sign up, participate."

Blah, blah, blah.

The football players ran into the gymnasium and the student body erupted with cheers. The first game of the season was scheduled to be played that very afternoon and the pep squad generated anticipation of victory. Paige was only mildly interested in attending. She found the boys on the team juvenile and only interested in scoring — both on and off the field.

Just when she hoped the morning assembly was coming to an end, the principal introduced the seven teachers new to Hatfield High. At first glance all of them appeared old, conservative and severe-looking — until one broke out a killer smile. His name was Jorden Wilks and he was the grade eleven history teacher. He was not old. He had dark hair and dark eyebrows and dark eyes. Though he was wearing a suit and tie like the portly principal, the effect was the opposite. Jorden Wilks was sexy.

"He's cute," whispered Lacey.

"He sure is." Paige looked at her schedule. She would have Mr. Wilks last class before noon. And did she hear correctly? Was he also coaching the senior girls' basketball team?

"I'm trying out for sure," Lacey said, reading Paige's mind.

"Me, too."

"You know he's married." Grade twelve Cathleen 'Cat' Collard, in the row behind them, leaned over confidentially. "His wife is the mayor's daughter."

"It doesn't mean he will always be married," whispered Lacey to Paige, and they both laughed deliciously.

"What's his wife's name?" asked Paige, twisting around and looking up.

"Used to be Constance Beck. I imagine now it's Constance Wilks."

Paige phoned her oldest sister in Winnipeg. If Leslie thought it odd of her to call, she didn't say so. After listening politely to chit chat about Colette and Kyle and how exhausting small children can be, Paige asked, "Do you remember Constance Beck from your high school days?"

Leslie's memories were disappointingly vague. "She was one of those uptight girls who got high marks and won academic awards. Or maybe that was her sister. What about her?"

"She married a teacher. He's new at our school."

"That's nice. What else is new back home? Wendy and the farmer still an item?"

"Yes," Paige said. "I'll call Mom. She'll give you all the dirt."

Paige's blonde hair was swept off her face and into a high ponytail.

She wore new stone-washed jeans and a striped top that crept up her midriff, exposing her belly button whenever she lifted her arms — something she was careful not to do around her mother.

"Good morning, Jorden," she said, practicing her saucy smile into the mirror.

"Good morning, Jorden," she said three hours later, when he walked into the classroom full of waiting students.

"Class," he said, in a sweeping gaze. "My name is Jorden, but I would prefer you call me Mr. Wilks."

Alyssa Moore, sitting one seat in front, turned and frowned disapprovingly at Paige.

"Mr. Wilks it is," Paige made her face demure, her hands clasped in front of her.

Mr. Wilks began each class by asking questions to see how much they understood from the previous lessons. He asked questions to search out how much the students already knew about the day's topic. Then he lectured.

This was Paige's favourite part, watching him stride around the classroom reenacting scenes. He made history come alive and often made the students laugh. As he talked and gestured and postured, she noticed his lips were red and inviting.

He dictated notes, writing on the chalkboard all the hard-to-spell words, plus the lists of dates and treaties and partnerships. He was unlike last year's lazy grade ten teacher who made them read their textbook and make their own notes. Paige had skipped a few of those classes. She didn't plan on skipping any of Mr. Wilks'.

There was an assignment at the end of each class, often reading homework, but sometimes it was a research project where they had to form an opinion. Paige hated having to come up with an opinion on something that didn't interest her. She was much too busy with soccer and dancing, and helping with the harvest — although truth be known, she would be hard pressed to define exactly what she did to help her father.

"Dewhurst. Why do you think that first attempt failed?" Mr. Wilks asked, during one of his question periods.

"I didn't have my hand up." Paige, caught off guard, was flustered.

Mr. Wilks strode over to her desk. "Look," he said, holding up her battered paperback copy of *Gone with the Wind*. "If this history class were on the American Civil War, you might get away with reading this kind of trash. But we live in Canada, this is the Twentieth Century, and we're studying the World Wars. I'd stick to reading the text book, if I were you."

"Those wars are so boring."

"Boring!" His lifted a limp wrist to his forehead in the pose of a distraught female victim, his face an expression of tragedy. The class laughed with appreciation. Alyssa snickered.

Paige pulled herself straight in her desk.

Trent Bouchard, who sat behind her and who was one of the imported hockey players from Quebec, put a hand on her shoulder. That gesture alone should have erased Paige's embarrassment, but it didn't. When the class was finished she went to Mr. Wilks' desk.

"Why are you trying to make me look stupid?" she demanded, impressed with her own bravery.

The few students who were still in the room looked up at her loud voice.

"Do your assignments and read your text," Mr. Wilks said.

"Half the class doesn't read the text and you don't pick on them."

He lowered his voice. "Perhaps they aren't as capable as you." He turned away, dismissing her.

Trent Bouchard was waiting for her at the classroom door. He walked with her down the hallway.

"He didn't have to call my novel 'trash,'" Paige said sadly.

As the autumn days grew colder and soccer finished without the Hatfield senior girls' team making it to provincials, Paige began reading parts of *Remembering Our Past* so she would be prepared to answer questions with some intelligence. She went to the library to research a topic, to prove a point. Teacher's pet, Alyssa Moore, did it all the time and "fake-argued" with Mr. Wilks in class.

"Mr. Wilks. I think you misrepresented the role the Canadians played in that last battle," Paige said, when an opportunity arose. She tried hard not to appear confrontational and brash.

"I beg your pardon?"

Paige repeated the statement, feeling a little foolish. It sounded rehearsed and rote.

"And what battle was that?" A smile tugged at the corner of

Mr. Wilks' mouth. "I talked about a lot of battles."

Paige stammered a reply. Her brain had become a sieve. Every intelligent thought escaped. She was like a deer in the headlights.

"I think I would cry," Alyssa commented, after noticing a large red C minus written on the cover page of Paige's essay. "You're not *that* stupid."

"Well thank you." *And you're not that ugly.*

"I don't know why he has to be so hard on you." Trent Bouchard saw the mark before Paige could hide it. "I'm going to say something in class the next time."

"No. Please don't," Paige begged. "I'll talk to him about the essay."

That night she practiced what she wanted to say to Mr. Wilks, choosing the words carefully.

The next day she waited until there was no one in the classroom to overhear. "I don't understand why my mark is so low," she asked. Rather than get angry or defensive — as she had half expected — Mr. Wilks touched her briefly on the side of her cheek.

"You are too easy on yourself. Capable of so much more."

"But I'm working as hard as I can!"

"I don't think you are. Your essay showed a complete lack of understanding of the roles of the allies. Why don't you give it another go? I may be persuaded to upgrade your mark."

A rewrite? As if.

Paige scowled as she marched down the hallway.

She tried out for the senior girls' basketball team and made it. Of course she made it. She was a great player. And yet during practice when a less athletic girl fumbled or tripped during practice, Mr. Wilks said nothing — but when Paige made a mistake, he yelled, "Dewhurst! What was that?"

Brie Cody, a bean pole of a girl, looked down at Paige. "You must have done something to piss him off."

"I don't know what."

Christmas holidays came and went. When school resumed in January, Paige was determined to show Mr. Wilks she had an introspective brain. However, life was full of more interesting things to do than study.

In the middle of dance class she remembered her resolve. When her mother came to pick her up at the studio, Paige asked to stop off at the high school because she wanted to retrieve *Remembering Our Past* from her locker. She wanted to be prepared.

But it was not there. *I must have left it in the classroom.* She hurried down the hallway and stopped in the doorway. Mr. Wilks, wearing a sweatshirt and jeans, sat working at his desk.

"Dewhurst?"

"Misplaced my textbook. I see it right here." She plucked the book from the tray under her desk and waved it at him. "As God is my witness, I'll never be unprepared for history class again."

"Then you'll be ready for tomorrow's spot quiz." He smiled at her.

"You're kidding, aren't you? About the quiz?"

He snapped shut his briefcase. "Maybe. Maybe not."

Invitation was in his dark eyes. His voice was flirtatious. One step, two steps. She approached him, leaned down and kissed him.

"What are you doing?" he cried.

Crimson with humiliation, she hurried out to the van where her mother was waiting.

"What took you so long?" Mom asked. "I was worried."

Mr. Wilks did not call on her in history class. The next day and the next, even when her hand was raised, he would not meet her eyes. The days ran out and the semester ended.

On her report card, Paige found she earned a seventy-eight in history. Higher than she expected, but oh, so teasingly close to an A.

Chapter 22

Charlotte

February 1988

Charlotte knew something was seriously wrong at the very first hello. Her mother's voice over the telephone was strained and unnaturally high.

"Well Charlotte, she's made her bed and now she has to lie in it," Mom cried. "I knew he would take her away from us. He was bad news right from the start."

Not a death, not an accident, not a prognosis of irreversible bad health. Charlotte could hardly keep the hilarity of relief from her voice. Wendy, the Dewhurst darling, had eloped. There was little she could do to comfort her mother from so far away.

Still, the news kept her mentally off balance for the rest of the day. She had a difficult time concentrating in class.

"I feel a little nonplussed," she said to her reflection in her bathroom mirror as she brushed her teeth before bed.

The second call came from Paige.

"I can't understand the fuss. Wendy's on her honeymoon in New Orleans. Just like Scarlet O'Hara."

"Trust you to spin the story in the right direction." Charlotte laughed in spite of herself.

"Wendy drove to Saskatoon for her piano lesson. But instead of returning home, she phoned, said she's married and about to board the plane. Mom is furious with Dad. She thinks he could have stopped her. I was at school and had to hear about everything second-hand when I got home."

"Mom's not in earshot, I'm guessing."

"She and Dad had to drive to Saskatoon to retrieve the van, hopefully still sitting in front of the piano teacher's house. They're afraid it's either been stolen or it won't start." Paige paused. "It seems so unimportant, doesn't it? The van. We haven't had this much excitement in our family since ... since Alex came to the house on Valentine's Day a year ago. Did you ever meet our new brother-in-law?"

"Once. Last summer. Mom was teaching me how to preserve peaches. You and Wendy were gone, to Saskatoon for something. Clothes shopping, I think."

Mom had asked Charlotte to call Dad in for lunch. From behind the shop she heard an unfamiliar male voice and her father's melodic voice replying.

"Alex is giving me a hand," Dad had said, looking up as Charlotte approached. "We're tightening the belts on the swather. On his farm, someone else does this kind of work."

"Did I give you that impression?" A boy scrambled out from beneath the machine and wiped his hands on his jeans. He was sturdy-looking and not much taller than Charlotte's five-foot-eight. He was very cute.

"Hello." She held out her hand. "I'm Charlotte."

"Alex."

"Mom said to come in for dinner. You, too," she added to Alex, although her mother had not mentioned him.

"Thanks, but I'd better head back home. I was in the area on business and stopped in to see Wendy."

Charlotte watched him walk away. She hated to admit it, but she liked his swagger.

"That's a shame he couldn't stay," Dad remarked. "We were working well together."

"I'll help you, Dad. I'd rather be outside than inside on such a nice day."

"I'd like that," he said, picking up a rag and wiping his hands.

That memory flooded back. Charlotte remembered the sunflowers, planted randomly in small groups around the farmyard, were in full bloom. She also remembered her father had been uncharacteristically negative at lunchtime, saying things like "they" predicted the death of the family farm, "they" predicted large corporation farms would dominate rural Saskatchewan, "they" said farms like the Dewhursts' were too small to be viable.

"Who is this 'they' you keep talking about?" Mom had cried in exasperation. "I know you, Dan. You would hate all the stress. Too much land and too little time. What happens when the weather doesn't cooperate?"

"The Warrens paid almost two hundred thousand dollars for a John Deere combine," Dad, ignored her question. "It's not even brand new. Who can afford these things?" Under his breath he added, "I always thought oversized equipment compensated for a shortfall in another department."

Charlotte remembered the smile Mom had suppressed.

"So what did you think of Alex?" Paige brought Charlotte back from Mom's suppressed smile, Dad's pessimism, Alex's charisma, and the sunflowers in full bloom.

"I remember thinking, 'that boy is going to be trouble.' Looks like I was right. Who would have thought Wendy would have the balls to upset the Dewhurst applecart?"

"I want you to say that about me someday!"

"Oh, we expect it of you." Charlotte laughed. "But I'm slightly curious. How did Wendy ever manage to keep this a secret? It had to have been planned. Did she confide in you?"

"I had nothing to do with this. But Mom thinks I aided and abetted them. She's majorly pissed."

The third call came on Sunday evening and it was from Leslie.

"Wendy and Alex will be home in ten days. Dad says we should plan a reception. What do you think?"

"It's a great idea," Charlotte said.

"There's no way Wendy should be cheated out of a special day."

"I agree."

"We can throw together a decent wedding reception on short notice. Keith has agreed to take time off work and help organize. Can you meet us at the farm?"

"You *do* know I go to school plus I tend bar part-time? It's not easy to drop everything."

"Your school and work can be juggled. Tell everyone it's a family crisis. That's not far from the truth."

"When is this reception?"

"I'm hoping the first Saturday after they return."

Charlotte sighed. Maybe her family couldn't see it, but she had a life in Toronto. "I'll see what I can arrange."

Charlotte spotted her father searching for her among the crowd hurrying through the airport arrival gate. She waved and he waved back. Seconds later, he wrapped his arms around her in a bear hug and all the security of childhood came flooding back.

"Your mother would have come along to pick you up, but the house is full right now," Dad said on the drive to the farm. "It's amazing how a baby and a toddler can fill every space. Leslie and Keith have been home since Monday."

"I haven't even seen Kyle yet, and he's almost a year old."

"He's a quiet little fellow. Grandkids are great. A reward for surviving parenthood." Dad laughed. "We're so glad you could come."

"It was difficult to get away. I had to negotiate with my teachers about missed classes and assignment deadlines. And my job ..." Charlotte stopped. She never talked much about her job. Tending bar wasn't respectable in the Dewhurst family, but the tips were great and she wasn't dependent on her parents for spending money.

"Leslie has been helping your mother make arrangements and inviting relatives, friends and neighbours. There is to be a reception, a dance, and a late evening lunch. I am supposed to ask how you feel about being the emcee. You are Wendy's first choice."

"No." Charlotte did not want that assignment. Simultaneously, she was pleased and honoured. "Yes. Of course I mean yes."

"Where are the Hamiltons?" Charlotte asked, disappointed Leslie wasn't there to greet her. It had been years since the two had been together.

"Running errands for us in Hatfield." Mom expertly divided the dough into portions. "They'll be back any second. They wanted to be here when you arrived, but getting out of the house takes longer with children." She leaned over and kissed Charlotte's cheek.

"Dad said you were doing the catering for the midnight lunch." Charlotte took off her coat. She watched her mother form buns and put them onto trays to rise. *How quickly those hands can fold and pinch.* "Are you getting any help from Alex's family?"

"Helen Warren said she doesn't bake. But the Warrens will gladly pay for half the expenses."

"I don't know about gladly," Dad said. "They weren't enthusiastic about hosting a reception for the kids. 'Too much trouble' were the exact words, if my memory serves me correctly."

"We drove over last week," Mom said. "Just to get to know them. Alex and Wendy plan to find an apartment and live in Milford but they are living with Alex's parents for now. I feel sad about that."

"I'd better interview the newlyweds." Charlotte did not wish to explore the depth of Mom's sadness. "If I'm going to be emcee, I'd better get my facts straight."

"The Hamiltons are coming up the drive!" Dad announced.

"Welcome to the monkey house," Mom said. "Now you'll be hard-pressed to hear yourself think."

"Colette's a busy one, that's for sure," Dad said, as the back door opened and a small girl came charging toward him, arms outstretched, her boots leaving little piles of snow on the linoleum.

Early in the evening, Charlotte drove to where Wendy was living with Alex. Gently falling snow added to the difficulty of finding an unknown destination in the dark. Charlotte forced herself to be calm and double-checked the directions written on the back of an envelope: Thirty-six miles on Highway 68. Exit left after a curve. Three miles north, two miles west, half a mile south.

With luck, and a prayer, there would be a long row of bins.

And there is.

Charlotte sighed with relief.

A bungalow was illuminated in the yard lights. Facing it, a street's distance away, was an older house. Wendy hadn't said there were two houses. Charlotte chose the older one and knocked.

A tall, thin woman opened the door. "Wendy!" she brayed. "Your sister is here."

Wendy appeared and grabbed Charlotte in a hug that spoke a thousand words. "Come into the living room where we can talk."

Charlotte took off her boots and followed Wendy.

Helen turned off the blaring television and indicated Charlotte should sit in the large chair by the chesterfield. Helen parked herself in the kitchen in full view, as if she wanted to direct the conversation.

"Hello, sister-in-law," Alex said, joining Wendy on the couch. He looked pink and fresh, his hair a little damp, as if he just came out of the shower. He wore blue jeans and a white flannel shirt that had three buttons undone exposing his hairless chest.

Charlotte took out her notebook. *Cute couple*, she wrote. *Barely adults.* Wendy looked younger than her eighteen years.

"So, tell me how you met." Charlotte already knew the story from Paige, about the church fall supper, the roses at Valentine's Day, Princess the kitten. All was grist for a lively romance if she chose to go in that direction, but her audience included their mother, who would not care for the fairy-tale angle.

"Have you ever been struck by a lightning bolt?" Alex asked.

"Can't say I have."

"Love at first sight?"

Charlotte did not believe in love at first sight, but she did not say so. "Alex. What were you like as a little boy?"

"A spoiled brat. An 'oops' baby."

"A 'what' baby?"

"An 'oops' baby. You know. A surprise."

Spoiled brat, Charlotte wrote. She was aware Helen Warren was listening in the other room.

"For me, it was all about sports," Alex continued. "I played everything that was offered."

Athletic, Charlotte wrote.

She lifted her eyes to a huge family portrait hanging above the brown couch. Parents, two teenagers — and Alex, who looked to be about eight. "Your family?"

"We don't need all that," Helen interrupted, striding into the room. "One of the benefits of elopement is to escape all this crap."

All this crap, Charlotte wrote. "I plan to introduce us Dewhursts and make a bit of fuss. I don't want the reception to be unbalanced." She spoke pleasantly, hoping to disarm Alex's mother.

"How old are you?" Helen demanded.

"Twenty-two."

"Twenty-two. A child. And how much land do your parents farm?"

It was no secret. "I'm not sure," Charlotte said. "About fifteen hundred acres."

"Oh," Helen sniffed. "Fifteen hundred acres. Just hobby farmers."

Charlotte's smile froze. *You old bitch. How dare you?* If Alex heard his mother's jibe he pretended he didn't.

"I have an older brother. He and his wife Sylvia live right over there." He motioned toward the house visible from the living room window. "My sister Jessie lives in Milford. She and her husband run a hardware store. No children."

The interview continued without further incident or insult. Charlotte wrote names and dates and funny little anecdotes, but try as she might, she could not regain her objectivity or her sense of humour.

Around ten o'clock the telephone rang and Helen picked up. The conversation was brief and when it was over she walked into the living room and said to Charlotte, "Your father phoned to let you know there are blizzard warnings on the radio. You are not to stay late." She turned to Alex. "I guess you won't be hauling canola tomorrow after all."

"Lucky for me I came when I did." Charlotte's fake smile was still glued on her face. She had originally asked for a daytime interview on Thursday morning — and had been turned down.

She woke to the sound of someone in her room. In the darkness she could see her young niece, Colette, going through her suitcase and emptying a package of tampons. Charlotte picked Colette, amid a scream of protest, off the floor and carried her downstairs where Mom, Dad and Paige were eating breakfast.

"We thought she was with Leslie," Mom said. An apology.

Dad took Colette from Charlotte's arms. "Look at the pictures in the window, sweetheart." He pointed to snowflakes pasted to the glass.

"In *Mrs. Mike*," Paige said, "you had to put a rope around your waist so you didn't get lost going to the barn." She looked at Charlotte. "Blizzard. No buses."

Charlotte felt the thrill of those words. *A snow day.*

"I'm glad we don't have cattle to tend," Mom said, going to the back door and opening it. She gasped with a little shriek as a blast of the winter snow pelted her.

Colette giggled. She scrambled out of her grandpa's arms and asked for the door to be opened for her as well. Paige obliged. The storm hit full force in Colette's face and the surprise left her temporarily soundless.

"Paige!" Mom scolded.

Paige shrugged. "How will she learn except through natural consequences?"

Keith came down the stairs. "Wow," he said, trying to peer out the window. "I can't see a thing. I'd hate to have some kind of emergency in this weather."

"Daddy, open the door," Colette commanded. She squealed with laughter when the snow hit him in the face.

"Look what you've done," Mom said to Paige, who was remorseless with laughter. Mom reprimanded but Charlotte could see a grin tugging at her lips.

Leslie appeared next, disheveled and lovely. "What's all the noise about?"

"Mommy, open the door," said Colette, but Keith shook his head in warning.

"We should move into the dining room," Mom said. "We're getting packed in here around this little table."

"Did you get enough info?" Leslie asked, putting her arm around Charlotte's shoulders.

"They gave me something to work with," Charlotte replied, liking the feel of Leslie's arm. "But Alex's mother is a piece of work."

"I'm trying to think of some funny stories about Wendy," Paige said. "But it's hard. She was always the obedient daughter."

But not anymore, thought Charlotte.

"Do you think this storm will be over soon?" asked Keith.

"This is just a little one," said Dad. "My guess, it will blow over by early afternoon. Are you feeling claustrophobic?"

Everyone ignored Colette's request to open the door so she started to cry. Dad attempted to divert her by making clown faces with raisins in the bowls of oatmeal porridge, but she upscaled her tears to full tantrum mode.

"Now you've woken the baby," Leslie chided.

"I'll get him." Paige ran upstairs. She returned with Kyle. "Not smelling so good."

"He needs a change," Mom said.

No one offered to do the job so Leslie took her son from Paige and headed upstairs.

"So what do you do when you're stranded like this?" asked Keith.

"We bake," said Mom, trying to get everyone to move into the dining room. "Cookies, squares and loaves. You can help. It's quite cosy."

"It *is* cosy," Charlotte said, trying to assure Keith. "But I can understand why you'd be a little apprehensive." She pushed her chair away from the table. "I have some work to do. If anyone needs me for quality control of the baking, you know where to find me."

She retreated upstairs to the small bedroom that once upon a time was hers, that until one month ago used to be Wendy's. On the desk was her notebook from last night. She looked over her notes. She had to keep her personal bias regarding Alex's mother out of her program for Saturday's reception.

Charlotte observed the Legion Hall was too large for the motley crew of guests. Sixty or seventy people congregated in a room that could hold three hundred. *A smaller venue, like the conference room at the local hotel, would have created the reception's illusion of being well attended.*

On the Dewhurst side were relatives, an assortment of neighbours, and several friends from high school. Apparently, Wendy was the first in her class to marry. Alex had a large contingent of friends but few relatives and fewer neighbours. Paige supervised the guest book, and was a fount of information about who was who.

The bar was open and the guests mingled with the newlyweds during the social hour. Wendy did not wear white, but rather a dress in robin's egg blue. She was a splash of colour among the black, brown and grey so typical of rural fashion. The dress had been purchased that very morning because Leslie, appalled Wendy had nothing new to wear, had taken her shopping. The selection had been limited at the two clothing stores in Hatfield.

Alex wore a navy blue suit. He looked very dapper.

Wendy and Alex left the crowd to sit at the table on the stage.

It was a visual signal the speeches were to begin.

Charlotte surveyed her audience.

"Good evening," she said into the microphone. "My name is Charlotte Dewhurst and I will be your emcee." She paused for a few seconds and repeated the sentence. The chatter ceased. "Tonight we will celebrate the recent marriage of Alex and Wendy Warren."

When the applause ended, Charlotte introduced the Dewhurst side of the family and asked them to stand as their names were called.

"Good-looking family," someone catcalled.

Charlotte spoke next of Alex's family. She spoke in generalities, not saying what she really thought, that Murray was large and red-faced, Helen was pinched and grim, Stuart Warren was a younger and more angry version of Murray, and Stuart's wife, Sylvia, could not smile to save her life. Alex's sister and brother-in-law were absent and no one bothered to explain why. Charlotte mentioned their names and left it at that.

She called on Paige to make a toast to the bride. Paige managed to turn Wendy's virtues into obstacles for Alex. Wendy had a lot of virtues. Charlotte admired the way her youngest sister handled the crowd.

Speaking for Alex was his childhood friend, Ian Kennedy. He talked about the ways they got into trouble together. He talked about the church fall supper and the first time Alex set eyes on Wendy. His last words before relinquishing the microphone were, "I had never before seen Alex so dumbfounded."

Judy Rasmussen welcomed Alex into the family. Diplomatic as always, she brought the audience close to tears with her prayer for a successful marriage.

Charlotte invited friends and relatives of the couple to share stories. A mistake. It was soon evident several of Alex's friends had too much to drink and many rambling stories to share. Apparently, there were a lot of girlfriends in Alex's past. Ian Kennedy interrupted the most ribald one with a joke and managed to remove the offender from the limelight.

"Thank you," Charlotte whispered to Ian, who grinned back at her and said, "Glad to be of service, ma'am."

Lila Gladstone took over the microphone. "I would like to add my best wishes to a fine young lady and her new husband. I have watched Wendy grow up. She teaches piano to my older children and I could not be more impressed with her professionalism, her integrity and her compassion. Take care of her, dear Alex, and cherish her."

Lila was the last lingering voice; the speeches ended on a high note. Charlotte thanked the audience and announced the dance was to begin soon. More young people were coming through the door and the hall looked less empty.

"Great job as emcee," Keith said to Charlotte when she joined her family. "I don't think a professional could have done as well."

Pleased with his compliment, she said, "Thank you. I'm relieved now that my part in directing the reception is over."

She escaped to the less public washroom on the second floor of the hall. No one was in there and she appreciated the privacy to release her bowels, which was something that was becoming an issue she hoped wasn't chronic, like Irritable Bowel Syndrome. Just as she was finishing, she heard the door open.

"God! It reeks in here!" Someone entered the cubicle beside Charlotte.

"Ssh," cautioned a second person.

Charlotte decided to remain hidden.

"I can't stand her," said the first voice.

"It doesn't matter. It's over and done with. It's time you move on."

"She sits there and smiles and doesn't say a word." The girl in the cubicle attacked the toilet paper dispenser and flushed the toilet. "He'll tire of her fast enough."

Charlotte caught a glimpse of maroon in the crack between the door and the stall as the girl washed her hands.

"Get over him," the second girl said. "There's other guys out there, Glennie. Don't waste your time on him."

"But I still love him." The girl in maroon worked herself up to a wail that reminded Charlotte of two-year-old Colette contemplating a tantrum. "He came to see me before Christmas. I wonder what the new wife would say about that. He didn't say a word about getting married. I had to hear that from my mother, who was only too happy to stick it in my face. She never liked him."

"That must have been tough." Charlotte opened her cubicle door. "I'm Charlotte Dewhurst, the wife's sister." She washed her hands slowly. "Your visits with Alex have ended."

She was not without hope it was all a misunderstanding, half expecting the girl to say, "Alex? I don't know any Alex" — and the three of them laughing over the miscommunication.

But it didn't happen that way. Instead of being ashamed or embarrassed, a smile twitched on Glennie's lips. "I wouldn't be too sure of that," she said, her head bobbing like a chicken's.

Charlotte resisted the urge to slap her. In her mind's eye, she saw the situation escalate to the point where the two of them were throwing punches and rolling on the floor. Glennie, who must have weighed ninety-five pounds, looked like she could be a scrapper.

"Come on." The other girl pulled on Glennie's arm.

"Think of your sister," hissed Glennie as she was towed away, twisting her head to look back at Charlotte. "Think of her sitting at home alone with a bunch of kids — and she thinks poor Alex is working hard. But he's not. He always comes back to me, you know."

He always comes back to me.

The ominous words stuck in Charlotte's brain. By Sunday afternoon she felt she would burst if she didn't tell someone about the altercation in the bathroom.

Charlotte persuaded Leslie to join her in a walk. Before the two could make their escape, Colette spotted them putting on their coats and screamed to come along. They located her snowsuit and Dad retrieved a sled from a storage shed in the farmyard. Halfway down the lane they discovered the February sun was so bright reflecting off the snow it hurt their eyes, and they had to return briefly for sunglasses.

As they walked, Charlotte told Leslie about her bowels and the bathroom and the smell. Leslie laughed in all the right places and Charlotte felt a moment of close kinship. Before she continued with what was on her mind, she remembered the little listening ears and turned to look at Colette in the sled. The child was bundled so only her face was visible, her eyes closed against the sun. She was asleep.

Leslie's face softened as she looked at her daughter. "She looks like an angel when she's sleeping. And acts the opposite when she's awake."

"You are so patient," said Charlotte, although "resigned"

would be a more accurate word to describe Leslie.

"Keith wants me to be a stay-at-home-mom. It's such a hard job, Charlotte. As soon as Keith comes home after a full day at work, I hand the kids over to him. I talk about going to the gym, but I'm usually exhausted. Instead I take a bath." Leslie laughed, but it was without mirth. "Having a hot bath without being disturbed is a luxury nobody warns you about. At night I fall to sleep the minute my head hits the pillow."

She unwittingly provided the segue Charlotte wanted in order to discuss Wendy and Alex.

"Do you ever worry Keith would stray — because you're so exhausted?"

"Stray? Keith? Never."

"You sound pretty confident. Is it because you are still so desirable?"

"It's got nothing to do with me. It's to do with him and the high moral standard he holds himself to. I don't believe he is a cheating kind of man."

"Do you think Alex might be a cheating kind of man?" Not waiting for an answer, Charlotte told Leslie the rest of the story about what happened in the bathroom. "What should we do about it?"

"What can we do? Warning Wendy might be the very thing this Glennie wants — get the new wife all paranoid and insecure. Steal her happiness and let the marriage die a slow death before it has a chance."

"I hadn't thought about that. You're quite insightful. It would become a self-fulfilling prophecy."

"Something like that."

The two walked in silence for several minutes. Charlotte took over pulling the sled.

"Is there any special man in your life, Charlotte?"

"I got asked that question over and over again last night, as if my main goal in life is to catch a man. The answer is no. I've had a few dalliances, if I may call them that, but nothing to cause me heartache. I'm not a natural head-turner like you."

"Don't get defensive."

"I'm not defensive. It's an annoying question."

"Well, don't sell yourself short. Anytime you want a makeover,

I can help."

"You and your makeovers! That time I lost weight, it took every ounce of my will power and concentration. I can't imagine being a slave to one's appearance. Is it worth the effort? I really can't be bothered."

Several minutes passed with the only sound being the slide of the sled on the snowy gravel road.

"I've given myself permission to be the intelligent sister." Charlotte couldn't help slinging a dart.

"Ah," said Leslie. "Let's go back now." She took the sled handle.

Charlotte turned. She could see the Dewhurst farmyard surrounded by tall black spruce trees in the distance. *This place is so remote, so beautiful, so pristine. The white against the black.*

But her life was not here. She did not fit in. She never had.

"I'm ready to go home," she said. "Home to Toronto. To my studies and professors, to buses and dirty snow. Back to a place where a girl isn't an old maid at twenty-two."

Leslie laughed. "I remember wanting to escape the farm and the whole rural way of thinking. I guess I did get away. To Winnipeg. I thought I was so mature."

"I don't want my life to be an escape. I want it to mean something."

"You're young. Your options are endless. I envy your freedom."

"That's the first time you have ever envied me anything." It was a new and wondrous thought.

"Really?" said Leslie. "That's what you think?"

"I always think you feel a little sorry for me. Maybe I don't know you well at all."

"I believe you know me best of everyone."

"More than your own husband?"

"More than my husband." Leslie sighed. "Keith has impossible standards about everything. I'm always pretending to be a better person than I am. You don't know what kind of stress that places on me."

"So, what you're saying is Keith has set the bar high. If he were a jerk, you would be more relaxed about your shortcomings?"

Leslie laughed again, and it was lyrical and twinkling.

"And," Charlotte continued, "since I know you for the horrible person you can be, you are completely yourself with me?"

"Yes."

"I should feel honoured."

"You should."

"How did you manage to find the two most decent men in the world? If I remember correctly, you pretended the same moral high ground with Reese."

"Speaking about Reese, you're not back in touch with him, are you?"

"Of course not."

"What do you mean, 'of course not?'"

"I guess I meant he threw all of us out of his life. After your defection."

"My defection? That's good. If it makes you feel any better, sometimes I talk to him in my head. I tell him I'm sorry."

"Are you sorry? What about? Are you having regrets?"

Leslie stopped walking. When she spoke, her voice was cold. "No. I have no regrets."

Charlotte did not want to ruin the rare — albeit brief — solidarity with Leslie. It was time for a safer topic.

"So ... what do you think of Wendy's in-laws, now that you've met them?" she asked.

Chapter 23

Paige

March 1988

The Dewhurst farmhouse echoed with Wendy's absence.
How can a person, who moves so quietly and draws so little attention to herself, be missed so much?
More importantly, without Wendy to confide in, how was Paige going to navigate her high school "career" before she also could escape the farm? One year and four months to go. The countdown was on.
And then, a reprieve. Wendy resumed teaching piano lessons in the Dewhurst parlour and was persuaded to stay for supper and spend the night rather than drive back to the Warren farm in the dark. Once a week, for a short time before bedtime, Paige had her sister all to herself.
Once a week will have to do.
Dressed in their homemade flannel nightgowns, they exchanged private jokes and gossip. "Go to sleep, girls, or I will have to separate you," Mom called more than once, but Paige knew her mother was happy to have Wendy home.
"Remember that history teacher I told you about?" Paige asked, the second time Wendy stayed overnight. "The one who used to pick on me in class? Now he's the basketball coach and he acts like I don't exist though I'm one of the best players. I don't know what's worse — being picked on, or being ignored."
"Being ignored is better than being picked on."
Paige hated being ignored. "Well, I think it's a little passive-aggressive," she said with a sniff. If only she could tell Wendy about

the kiss. She was searching for an appropriate introduction to the subject when she heard a stifled sob. "What's wrong?" she asked. "Are you and Alex fighting?"

"No. Not fighting. I don't know how to tell mom and dad. They'll be so disappointed in me. I'm expecting a baby in September."

Paige sat upright in bed. "You *had* to get married?"

"Ssh. I don't want Mom to hear." Wendy's voice became defensive. "I wanted to marry Alex anyway. This just speeded up the process."

"Wow. A baby. How far along are you?"

"Eleven weeks. My clothes are getting tight. Mom and Dad are bound to notice soon."

"Let them think you're too accomplished a cook. The newlywed nineteen, it's called, the average weight a woman gains the first year she's married."

"That's not the point, Paige. It's the stress of not being honest. I don't think my anxiety is healthy for the baby. I have to tell them soon. What I'm dreading most is 'the look.'"

The look of disappointment, worse than any punishment. Paige knew it well.

She grabbed Wendy's hand underneath the cover. "For the record, I want to be the first to say congratulations."

"Thanks. I appreciate that." After a long silence and a few more sniffles, Wendy pulled her hand away, "I've made up my mind to tell them tomorrow morning before I drive back to Alex."

"Would you like me to be there?"

"This is something I should tell them privately. After you get on the bus."

"You don't want me to do something naughty to divert the negative attention?"

There was a smile in Wendy's voice. "Thanks. I appreciate the offer, but no."

All morning Paige thought about how the conversation had transpired. At noon, unable to contain her curiosity, she went to the school office and asked if she could make a long distance call to St. Cloud.

"Who are you phoning? And is it important?" the secretary

asked. "Unless it's a call home, it's against school policy."
"Look, as God is my witness, I'm not making a drug deal," Paige snapped. She had never been a favourite of the woman. "I need to phone my sister."
"Unless it's a call home, it's against school policy."
Paige swore under her breath.
"What did you say?" the secretary demanded.
"I said I'm sorry I wasted your time." *You old bag.*

Mom's face was grim when she picked up Paige from basketball practice. "Your sister is three months pregnant," were the first words out of her mouth.
"That's wonderful news!" Paige acted surprised. "A baby! Wendy always wanted to be a mother."
"This means Wendy was pregnant before ..."
"I can count, Mom."
"What will the neighbours think?"
A line borrowed from Grandma Dewhurst. Paige was shocked into silence.
"I'm going to phone Charlotte and Leslie tonight and prepare them," Mom said as they turned off the highway.
"Prepare them for what? Oh. The scandal!" Paige's voice was cold. Her mother's fear of being judged angered her. "Try not to act like the sky is falling in." She paused. "And on another note, when are you going to let me drive myself to dancing? I've been sixteen for months."
Wendy had been allowed the privilege. Even allowed to chauffeur on occasion.
"When I'm driving, you're less likely to get into trouble," her mother snapped.
Paige glared out the window. She kept her retorts to herself.

"None of you guessed?" Charlotte said, over the phone that same evening. "Why else would Wendy have eloped?"
"Why didn't you say something if you're so perceptive?" Paige looked around to see if her mother was listening.
"It's not my news to tell."
I've got a story to tell. Perhaps she could confide in Charlotte,

who was discreet.

But no. The "kiss" was better left untold. Charlotte might be morally compelled to tell their parents.

Life went on.

In March, under the competent coaching of Mr. Wilks, the high school senior girls' basketball team won the district championship and qualified for the provincial title. They travelled to Saskatoon for the tournament and stayed in a hotel, along with several parents acting as chaperones. The Hatfield team won their first two games but lost to a city team from Prince Albert in the semifinals. Mr. Wilks pointed out getting to the semi-finals was an achievement in itself, especially for a rural school with a small student base from which to draw talent. But the girls cried anyway.

In an effort to raise their spirits he organized a celebratory banquet at the nicer hotel in Hatfield. It was a dress-up affair and the girls were allowed to bring escorts if they wanted. Paige made a huge impression on her teammates by bringing Trent Bouchard. He was a big teddy bear of a boy, popular and kind.

Mr. Wilks brought his wife. Constance was plain, thin and a few inches taller than Jorden.

Paige watched them. They did not make an attractive couple. There were no glances of intimacy between them, no shared smiles about private jokes. *Not like how Wendy and Alex are with each other or even how Mom and Dad are.*

After dessert and coffee Jorden handed out awards. Paige's teammates were called to receive recognition, one after another, until it was obvious each girl was going to receive something. Paige waited and waited for her turn.

"I know all about being the smallest player on the court," Mr. Wilks said. "Don't let size fool you. Despite her diminutive size, this team member will be key next season. For Most Promising Grade Eleven, Paige Dewhurst!"

Dad nudged her forward. When she shook Mr. Wilks' hand, his touch crackled with electricity.

"Way to go, Shrimp," Trent Bouchard teased when she returned to her seat. He ruffled her hair.

"It's time," said Dad.

"Time for what?"

"Time to drive yourself to dance."

"Your independence is bittersweet to me," said Mom. "I will miss our private conversations."

Those private conversations usually consisted of a lecture or a rebuke; Paige would not miss them one little bit.

"I won't abuse the privilege." Paige used the words she knew her parents wanted to hear.

And for the longest time, she didn't.

But one evening after dancing she stopped at the school. She stopped because she wanted to see if Jorden Wilks was working late. And he was.

"Hello Mr. Wilks," she said, standing by the door frame. She remembered the way the electricity had sparked when their hands had accidentally touched at the banquet.

"Hello Dewhurst."

"I want to thank you for the basketball award." She took a few steps into the classroom. "For most promising grade eleven. Is that true?"

"I expect you will be a starter next season."

Paige licked her lips. The silence became awkward.

"Well," he said, standing and walking towards her. "I have to finish up here and get home."

"No. This is what I want to say." Quickly, she reached for him. He wasn't so tall she had to stand on her tiptoes. Not like Trent Bouchard, when he had kissed her goodnight after the basketball banquet.

"Look," Mr. Wilks said, breaking her embrace. "You can't come into my classroom and do this to me. Do you want to get me fired?"

"Whenever I see you, Jorden, I want to kiss your lips."

It was as easy as that.

If Jorden had wanted, he would have put an end to these shenanigans months ago.

Her parents had not been called into the principal's office to deal with their problem child.

She became the hunter and found many ways to put herself in Jorden's view. She dressed in clothes that emphasized her tight dancer's body, although at home she wore sweaters and bunnyhugs. She alienated some of her girlfriends by inadvertently attracting more than her share of the male population.

She didn't care.

Paige danced three nights a week. One night, during a break between a ballet class and jazz, she walked to the school and was unsurprised to find Jorden there, like he had been the other two times. As he brushed past her in his attempt to escape, he turned off the classroom light, as if to signal he was done, but Paige pulled him back inside the classroom and pressed her small body into his.

"I'm in love with you."

"You can't keep doing this." Despite his objections, he was pushing her into the darkest corner. His mouth was on hers, his hands were all over her body. It was exactly the scenario in one of her historical romances, *Sweet Savage Love*.

She did not expect the frenzy and quickness and pain.

"I'm yours forever," she said after it was over, and started to cry.

"Oh, my God. What have I done?" Jorden put his head in his hands and sobbed. This frightened Paige so much she stopped crying and took his hand. They sat on the floor in the dark for a long, long time.

After what seemed like an hour, Jorden said, "I saw you sitting in my class. So pretty and young. Exactly like the girls who wouldn't give me a second look when I was in high school. And you flirted with me. I tried to resist you. You are like candy. If anyone finds out, I would be fired. I would never be able to teach again, or coach any sport. I would never see you again."

"I won't tell anyone. I promise."

"Oh, but you might. A friend ..."

"I promise."

"We have to figure a way out of this mess."

"Is that what I am? A mess to get out of?"

Jorden kissed her face. "What I meant to say, is how can we leave this building? It's all locked up — I think — but the janitors might still be here. We can't let them see us. Where is your car parked?"

"I walked here. It's at the dance studio."

"Oh God. Or maybe that's better. I need to think ..."

Down the darkened corridors with only the security light to guide them, Jorden went first and Paige a few minutes later. Out the back door like two thieves they crept, around to the parking lot. Jorden got into his car.

"Get into the back and crouch down," he ordered. "Where can I let you off?"

"By the dance studio."

"No. Someone might see me. Damn this small town." He let her off two blocks away.

Miss Louise was still at the studio when Paige retrieved her bag but the other dancers were gone.

"We finished the ending without you. Where were you? I was worried." Miss Louise peered a little closer to Paige's face. "Are you alright?" she asked. "Boy trouble?"

Paige nodded.

"Can I help?"

"No. It's fine. Just a fight."

"Paige," Mr. Wilks called out, as she walked down the high school hallway past his classroom. "We need to talk about that essay you were researching," he said loudly.

Right. The essay. "You said you have a book I can borrow?" Paige asked, following him into the empty classroom.

He looked around and asked quietly, "When do you get your period?"

She blinked. This wasn't the question she was expecting. "Soon."

"How soon?"

"Maybe in two days or so."

"We should be good." He looked around. They were still alone.

"Are you afraid I might get pregnant?" Her eyes locked on his. "Jorden, I would love to have your baby." That wasn't true. She wasn't remotely ready to be pregnant and miserable like Wendy.

"That can never happen."

A student wandered in and Jorden handed Paige a book. "This might help you with your report," he said. "You should come up with a plan on how you want to proceed."

She hoped the book contained a message for her, but it didn't. It was only a decoy.

Jorden told Paige he walked to school every evening to correct papers and plan lessons. During Paige's forty-five-minute break between ballet and jazz she parked the family van somewhere along his route and he hopped in, undetected. It was Jorden's suggestion she park in a different spot each time so no busy-body with nothing to do would see nothing suspicious. Paige drove to a place out of town, where the trees enclosed an abandoned yard. The few minutes of privacy gave her a reason to live. Or so she told herself.

"I'd like you to run for school president," Jorden said, as they sprawled in the long grass, concealed by lilac bushes.

"Doesn't that require a lot of extracurricular work? I'm already too busy," she protested. "I have dancing, and soccer, and basketball."

"Do it," he ordered. "It's part of our plan."

Our plan. The words intoxicated her.

Paige's family expressed surprise when she told them of her decision to run for election. This annoyed her to no end.

"You never cared about politics before," Leslie pointed out over the phone.

"This isn't exactly politics."

Charlotte was less dubious and offered Paige advice — which was largely ignored. It was, after all, just another popularity contest. Her two opponents were girls who were not as pretty or as athletic as she.

Wendy, as was her wont, was supportive. She was the first person Paige told when she won.

In June, at the high school's general assembly, the 1988-89 school council was introduced along with its supervising teacher, Mr. Jorden Wilks. He hadn't said a word to Paige about this appointment.

The brief and sporadic minutes that comprised their illicit love affair continued, even after dancing ended. Paige applied for a summer job at a local fast food eatery and she worked three hours daily during the supper time. She was off at eight.

Her father expressed concern over her need to study for year-end exams but Paige pointed out she was an excellent and all-round balanced student.

With one tiny obsession.

All was bright in Paige's universe until Jorden casually mentioned he would be staying all summer at his in-laws' cabin at Crystal Lake. She turned her back on him so he wouldn't see her cry.

"See," Jorden said. "This is why I was reluctant to tell you."

"I don't want to go two months without seeing you!"

He took her in his arms. "I don't want to go two months without seeing you, either."

"Then do something!"

"I have more to lose than you if we are caught."

"Doesn't your wife have to work while you're at the lake?"

"She's going to commute. Crystal Lake is not far from Hatfield." Jorden sounded short whenever Paige mentioned Constance.

An idea sprung into Paige's head. "Crystal Lake is only a short distance from the town of Milford. My sister lives there. It wouldn't look odd for me to be in your vicinity. We could meet."

"No. It's impossible. No phone calls."

"We can at least try. Unless you're tired of me already."

"Never."

"Walk along the public beach around two o'clock in the afternoon. That will be your signal you're free. I will be suntanning on the beach." Paige knew how cute she looked in a bathing suit. "I'll come to your car and we can take off."

"I can't leave the cabin every afternoon to see you. The Becks would become suspicious."

"But sometimes you could."

Paige knew this arrangement was fraught with inconveniences but it was the best she could come up with.

On the last morning of school, Paige's grade eleven homeroom teacher talked about the restorative healing summer provided, that September was a month for new beginnings, that their senior year was their most important for achieving high marks.

Blah, blah, blah.

Paige kept twisting in her desk waiting for the spiel to be done and the class to be dismissed. When everything finally concluded, she grabbed her report card from her teacher's outstretched hand with barely a thank you and did not linger for goodbyes with her classmates. Instead, she sought out Jorden for confirmation of her plan.

His classroom was empty.

Reluctantly, she boarded the waiting school bus. As it turned the corner, she could see Jorden's car in the teachers' parking lot.

That evening at work she kept glancing at the door, willing Jorden to come in and order something. He didn't. When she completed her shift, she drove past his house. It was dark and his car was not in the driveway.

On July first, Paige's family congregated on the recently constructed stone patio in the back yard. The day was windless and not too hot. The new barbecue — a Christmas gift from Leslie and Keith — was displayed in its silver gleaming glory, ready to be fired up for its inaugural performance.

Wendy, her body bloated and her face puffy, reclined in the shade on a deck chair. She was warned by the specialist to rest if she wanted to avoid hospitalization. She was not a risk taker and she obeyed every decree. Alex brought Wendy lemonade, the ice cubes clinking musically in the tall perspiring glass.

A picture of domestic bliss.

In Paige's imagination, she was the one pregnant and Jorden the one who was solicitous.

As she buried her head among the peonies, inhaling their scent, she wondered what he was doing to celebrate the holiday. Probably driving a motorboat or performing on water skis — how any self-respecting Saskatchewan citizen with a cottage enjoyed the short, intense summer. She wished she had an excuse to drive to Crystal Lake. Just for a glimpse of him. But Wendy was here at the farm, not in the Milford apartment. And Paige had to leave for work in less than an hour.

"How are you feeling, sweetheart?" Dad put his arm around her. Of course he would notice her edginess.

"The first day of summer holidays and I can't relax. I should be doing something."

"Now that's an odd thing to say," Aunt Judy said, walking into the conversation. Paige had not heard the Rasmussen family drive into the yard. "I thought teenagers came relaxed and we parents had to motivate them."

Paige gave her a weak grin.

"It's Paige's job to take on the world," Dad said to his sister.

"She ran for school president and won. She dances competitively. And she'll probably be captain of the basketball team this coming winter." He moved to kick a soccer ball back at his oldest nephew.

"Not to mention this fall will be my senior year and I need an A average to get into nursing."

"Wow," said Aunt Judy. "No time to be a kid, eh?"

"Yeah," said Paige sadly. "No time to be a kid."

Her cousins wanted her to play with them but she was too old for all that. She excused herself to get ready for work.

"This is kind of you, Paige, to lend Wendy a hand," Mom said.

Paige felt a twinge of guilt, as if she had wished a high-risk pregnancy on her sister.

Every morning she drove to Wendy's apartment in Milford where she swept the floor, cleaned the kitchen and helped prepare Alex's supper. On Tuesdays she carried the laundry to the basement where the washer and dryer were located and did all the Warren laundry. On Friday she shopped for groceries.

She left after lunch while Wendy napped.

The anticipation — which had been building all morning — was almost unbearable.

She flashed her regional park pass at the entrance gate of Crystal Lake, drove past the picnic area and parked in the public beach parking lot. In the changing rooms she put on her bikini and strolled leisurely to the hot sandy beach. She found a space to spread her towel and positioned herself in the sun to bake, aware Jorden might be watching. She refreshed herself in the water when she became too hot. By two-fifteen, if he had not shown, her spirits wilted. By half-past, she was on her way home to get ready for her evening shift.

But on the rare days Jorden walked across the sand to signal his availability, fireworks exploded within her. After a time, when minutes felt like hours, Paige gathered her belongings and slipped into Jorden's car, parked discreetly by a bush, the back passenger door unlocked. She crouched under her towel until he came to her. Still hiding from sight, he drove her somewhere private for ten minutes, or twenty minutes. Once, thirty minutes.

Crystal Lake attracted the teenagers from the town of Milford, not Hatfield, so Paige felt relatively safe from scrutiny. Of course she was the target of unwanted attention from pubescent boys who she managed to wither with a glance, but one afternoon it was Alyssa Moore who attached herself to Paige like a bloodsucker. No amount of hints and rudeness dislodged her.

Suddenly, Alyssa leapt to her feet. "Hey, look who's there," she cried. "Hey, Mr. Wilks!" She turned to Paige. "Come on. It's Mr. Wilks."

Paige could tell Jorden was embarrassed and annoyed. As Alyssa babbled on and on, he caught Paige's eyes and shook his head. She didn't know if it was in frustration or to tell her they couldn't be together that afternoon.

"Goodbye, girls. Enjoy the rest of your holidays." He sauntered away.

"He is one of the best teachers at our school," Alyssa said. "Wouldn't you agree, Paige?"

Paige wanted to slap Alyssa for being such a dweeb.

On rainy days, Mom and Dad sometimes went to Milford. On days such as those, Paige stayed home because Jorden wouldn't be walking the beach. But one hot sunny day, her parents wanted to tag along.

"No," said Paige. "I want to stop at Crystal Lake on the way home and cool off. That would be a waste of your time."

"A swim in the lake. That's a great idea," said Dad. "It's too hot to do anything at home."

"The Fields had an air conditioner installed last week," said Mom. "I talked to Patti yesterday."

"It seems such an expense for the few days we get such weather," Dad replied. He turned and smiled at Paige. "The matter is settled. Off to Milford and then for a swim."

"No, really it's not going to work for me," Paige said.

Her father stared at her for a moment. "Well, your mother and I will go alone. We'll take the truck. You can stay home."

As summer drew to its midpoint, Paige suggested she might work for a year after high school rather than attending university. She had been thinking she could not leave Jorden. What she did not expect was the recurring fight with her parents.

"I don't want to be a financial drain on the family," she said.

"Honey, we have money enough for school," Dad replied.

"You need an education," Mom said. "A woman can't count on a man to support her." She shook her head. "It's too bad Wendy decided not to take her associate piano exam. After all her practicing. All gone to waste."

"Are you still thinking about going into nursing?" Dad asked.

"Yes," Paige replied. "After a year of living on my own."

"All that shift work." Mom shuddered.

"I'm not like you," Paige retorted. "I don't need my life scheduled to the last minute."

"You're selling your mother short," Dad said, ending what was bound to turn into a fight. "Your mother drops everything at a moment's notice to run around for all of us."

The month of August was mostly cold and windy but Paige went to the beach faithfully. Jorden did not show and she worried he had lost interest in her. Just before school started, summer had one last hurrah. The air temperature rose to over thirty celsius and Jorden walked on the beach. After a suitable interval of time, Paige hid in his car.

She heard his footsteps on the gravel; his hand on the latch of the car.

"Hello," said a strange male voice.

Paige held herself still.

"You're Jorden Wilks, aren't you?" asked a female voice coming closer. "I don't think you'll remember us, but we're the Bennetts. We were at your wedding."

"Friends of your in-laws," said the male voice. "We're heading there right now. We've never been to Crystal Lake before and we thought we'd check out the facilities."

Jorden's footsteps moved away — Paige suspected — to draw the Bennetts away from the car while she remained hidden. She could hear every word of the boring conversation. Jorden stood talking for what seemed like hours. Just when she couldn't bear the heat a moment longer, Jorden opened the door.

"I wouldn't leave a dog in a vehicle that long," Paige said in fury.

"Get out."

"What?"

"Those people are going to the cabin. They'll mention they saw me at the beach. So get out. I've got to come up with a reason I was here."

Paige cried all the way home.

Of course, Jorden had a right to be upset. He almost got caught. But he didn't have to talk to me like that.

Dressed in her orange and brown uniform, she forced herself to smile through the busy supper hours, taking orders amid ringing tills, trying to be patient with customers who kept changing their minds. No one would guess her heart was breaking.

Unexpectedly, Jorden stood in front of her. He ordered a single full meal, his eyes intent upon her face.

"How is your summer going?" A question any teacher might ask a student.

"Could be better," she replied. "And you?"

"Planning this term's classes."

"I bet that's keeping you busy."

"Busy at school."

She held out his bag of food and he handed her the money. Their hands touched. Her body started to throb in excitement.

"I like to work at night," he added.

Chapter 24

Wendy

September 1988

"It's a boy!" The doctor held the squalling newborn for Wendy to see.

"With healthy lungs," added the delivery room nurse as she wrapped the baby and handed him to Alex.

"My son," he said, as his free hand grasped Wendy's. He studied the little red face with the thick thatch of blood-matted hair. His eyes welled. "My family."

Jubilation, relief, empowerment. Wendy couldn't find the right word to describe exactly how she felt. No matter. Never in her life had she done anything as important as this. The unplanned pregnancy, the hasty marriage — both had happened for a reason. The universe was unfolding as it should.

"I love you so much." Alex stared at Wendy.

She stared back, falling in love with him over again.

"We need to stitch up your wife right now, Mr. Warren. Then the two of you can make some calls," said the doctor.

"The calls can wait." Alex's face was close to Wendy's, the baby in his arms. "Let's be just us. Once the first call goes out, the world will intrude."

Just us. She felt the strength of those words.

Alex protested briefly when another nurse took the baby out of his arms.

"I'll bring him right back," she promised. "I need to weigh and measure him."

"Make sure you bring back the same baby."

The nurse had laughing eyes. "There is only one other baby in the nursery right now and it's a girl."

Alex looked anxiously after her. He turned to Wendy. "Does our baby look like a Joshua to you?" he asked.

"He looks exactly like a Joshua Alexander Warren," Wendy said promptly, securing for posterity their first choice of names.

Alex stayed at the hospital and slept on a chair, his head propped on the side of Wendy's hospital bed. He woke each time the nurse came in the room to take her temperature and blood pressure, to ask about pain medication, to have Joshua suckle.

Early in the morning, amid the sound of an awakening hospital, Alex said, "I'd better find myself some breakfast and get cleaned up." An hour later he returned and said, "The farm claims me. I have to go." He kissed her.

"I love you," Wendy called to his back. The spell was broken.

Later in the day her mother and sister visited. The nurse brought Joshua to Wendy's room. His complexion was pink, his hair had been washed and twisted into one little curl.

"He doesn't have those bird-like features so common in newborns," said Mom, cradling the baby.

"'Monday's child is fair of face,'" Paige quoted.

A silly little nursery rhyme. But Joshua was beautiful, more so, now that he was eighteen hours old and not so red.

There was a knock on the hospital door and a young girl carrying a huge bouquet of flowers entered the room. She put the flowers on a table by the window.

"A cousin for Colette and Kyle. Congratulations," Paige read from the card. "It's from the Hamiltons in Winnipeg."

"The flowers must have cost a fortune," said Mom. "I'm sorry I came empty-handed." She stood and handed the baby to Paige. "Well, it's a short visit, but it's a busy time on the farm and I have supper to prepare. Dad said to give you this." She bumped noses with Wendy in a clumsy kiss. "I still can't believe you didn't let us know when you went into labour. I would have driven to Milford right away."

"We didn't tell anyone. We didn't want anyone to worry."

"Have Alex's parents been by yet?"

"I think they're waiting for a rainy day." Wendy's in-laws

didn't stop working for anything except inclement weather.

Paige handed Joshua to Wendy. "See you, sis."

Mom turned at the doorway. "If you have the chance, stay in the hospital as long as possible. I can't believe how quickly they expect you new mothers to recover. When I had each of you girls, I was in for a week."

Wendy didn't want to stay in the hospital any longer than necessary, although the visit had tired her. "Thanks for coming. Drive safely."

Her homecoming wasn't the event Wendy had envisioned. She wanted to revive that memory of the hours immediately after Joshua's birth, alone with her husband and her baby, but her mother greeted the three of them at the apartment door. Wendy's initial annoyance was short-lived. The aroma of homemade chicken soup aroused her appetite and she ate greedily while her mother hovered.

"I made you some sandwiches to take to the field, Alex," said Mom. "You'd better head back there. I'm sure they're looking for you."

"I'm sorry my mother is such a pain," Wendy whispered as Alex bent to kiss her. "Don't rush off."

He looked as if he wanted to say something to her, something profound. She waited, willing the words she thought were on the tip of his tongue.

"I'll take care of you," said Mom, interrupting the moment and taking the baby from Alex's arms. "You are not as strong as you think you are."

A clean nightie was draped on the bed. Wendy changed into it and pulled back the covers. The sheets smelled as if they had been dried on the clothesline. She wasn't sure if she should be embarrassed or grateful her mother had taken their personal laundry home. It didn't matter. Wendy was tired. The short trip home had depleted her energy.

Her mother took over, changing Joshua, singing to him, purposely trying to keep him awake so he would sleep longer during the night. Wendy saw her baby, wrapped tight in a swaddling blanket, his face sticking out like a candle flame, only when he needed to be fed. She knew her mother wanted to help, yet Wendy resented the intrusion. *It is important to set boundaries.*

"Mom, I want you to leave." The words burst out of Wendy with no preamble.

The negative reaction she expected did not happen.

Her mother laughed. "I need to go. I have a husband who needs me and a home. Not to mention one last child in the nest. But I will help you. For a bit longer. Just not overnight."

Together they decided she would arrive at the apartment around noon.

"I'll make supper and leave it for you," Mom said. "And once I am satisfied you are rested I'll leave late afternoon."

This worked well. On the fifth day, Wendy complained, "I'm tired of being cooped up. I want to go outside."

"Wonderful! I brought the baby carriage a few days ago. Your apartment caretaker helped take it off the truck and store it in the shed at the back. It's clumsy and inconvenient."

The carriage was an old-fashioned perambulator given to Wendy from Leslie who had received it from Kim Hamilton.

"I'm done having kids," Leslie had said during a July visit to the farm. "You can have everything." She had brought toys and books and boxes of clothes with Baby Gap and Mexx labels. "There's more, but this is all I had room for in the car." The perambulator had arrived dismantled; Dad had put it together.

"I wonder if this is a family heirloom," Wendy said to Mom as they walked together down the sidewalk, the leaves falling from the trees. "I wonder if Keith's mother would like it back for her own daughter to use."

"We'd better take good care of it. Just in case."

The two of them talked as they walked. Never before in her life had Wendy felt closer to her mother than she did on Joshua's first outing. They talked about marriage and home and most of all, babies. Wendy's mother was so smart, so practical and not at all full of scary old wives' tales.

"Well, kiddo, you're on your own," Mom said when they returned to the apartment. "This is my last trip to Milford to help. Next time I come as a guest. I brought along two frozen casseroles, but I can fit only one in your tiny apartment freezer. One is thawing in your refrigerator."

"I'm going to miss you."

"I'm sure you will." Mom smiled and gave her a hug.

Wendy incorporated the daily walk into her routine, even when the fall weather was less than desirable. She felt a little exotic pushing the foreign-looking perambulator. As she walked she looked at the houses for sale, returning often to her favourite, a big old house close to the town's centre. She walked past the Milford High School, and the ball park. At the grocery store, someone always held the door open for her. Same at the post office where she collected her mail. Gifts and cards of congratulations from relatives poured in.

Miss Molly's Dance Studio, located half a block off main street, was her turn-around point. Most often the blinds were shut, but the first time they weren't Wendy saw an old upright piano in the corner of the mirrored room. On a second occasion a young woman danced alone to slow and lyrical music. She looked to be Wendy's age. Their eyes met briefly before Wendy walked on, pushing Joshua in the perambulator.

That used to be my life not so long ago. Dancing and piano.
Where are all the young people my age?

They couldn't all have left town. Surely there was someone with whom she could talk? Someone else who had a baby, someone else who needed to take walks in the fresh air.

Three weeks after Joshua was born, Wendy attended the Thanksgiving service at the Hatfield United Church with Paige and her parents. People gathered around after to admire Joshua. No one made a snide comment about his early arrival.

Aunt Judy, Uncle Troy and the cousins were waiting at the farm. They handed Wendy a gift and she unwrapped little shoes, coveralls and a plaid shirt that fastened under the crotch.

"He's going to be a farmer," predicted Troy Rasmussen.

"We'll see," Wendy replied. "Alex has other dreams for his son. A professional hockey player, no less." She went into her old bedroom to breast-feed Joshua.

He slept in his bassinet during the meal, allowing her the luxury of a proper visit. Everyone was eating and laughing and gesturing with their forks while Wendy sat and listened and caught snippets of conversation. She was disappointed Alex had not been able to attend Thanksgiving dinner with her. She wondered how he was coming along with the harvest.

"How would you like to take a bus tour through the Maritimes?" Dad said to Mom. His voice was conversational, yet heard above the chatter. "Louie Brown from church is close friends with the owner of a tour company. The tour was sold out, but there has been a cancellation. We could take it for half price."

"What?" Mom said, blinking at this unexpected proposition.

Conversation stopped while everyone listened as Dad enthusiastically described the itinerary.

"But we're not finished with harvest yet."

"I'll be finished tomorrow."

"But all the fall work ..."

"Will be waiting when we get back."

"Mom. Go," Wendy encouraged. *How romantic to be whisked away by a husband after a long time of work and separation.*

"Go," Paige echoed.

"I don't like to leave you girls alone," Mom said, a warning frown developing around her eyes.

"I can stay here at the farm with Paige," Wendy said. "We can take care of each other. Alex will be finished with harvest any day now." *A lie.* "He could sleep here at night so we wouldn't be alone."

"We don't have much time to decide," Dad said. "Elsie. This is a bargain price. Someone else will snap it up."

"What an opportunity!" said Aunt Judy.

Wendy could see her mother's mouth was set in a straight line.

"I wish you had told me about this privately, Dan. I feel a little sabotaged." Mom stood and carried some dishes into the kitchen. After a few minutes, Aunt Judy followed.

"I should have told her about it when we were alone," Dad admitted, "but I couldn't wait. Louie's friend will hold it only for a few hours before he offers it to someone else. I'd better call him now and tell him we aren't interested."

"Better confirm with Elsie," Troy said. "Women sometimes need a little time to ponder things over. Judy might be persuading her as we speak."

Wendy didn't give that option much hope. Her mother wasn't given to whims and last-minute decisions.

Mom, smiling brightly, emerged from the kitchen with pumpkin pie. Dad looked at her hopefully but she shook her head no. At the same time, Joshua woke with a roar and Wendy went upstairs to change him and to breast-feed. By the time she returned downstairs, Dad had taken his parents and Uncle Troy on the annual crop tour, and Mom and Aunt Judy had retreated to the kitchen to gossip. Paige and the cousins were watching TV, so Wendy decided to go home.

She was surprised to find Alex waiting for her.

"I don't like coming home to an empty apartment," he said sulkily.

"I don't like being home alone all the time," Wendy replied, handing him the baby. "Mom sent leftovers for you, packed in the diaper bag. It's in the truck. I'll get it."

She dished out a healthy portion of leftovers, put it in the oven to warm and took the sleeping baby from Alex and placed him in his crib.

Alex cracked open a beer.

"Why are you home so early?" Wendy asked, sitting beside him on the couch. "Is everything all right?" She noticed how tired he looked.

"One of our drivers asked for the day off. Mom snapped — like she does — and the guy up and quits. He's the second one to quit this week."

Wendy's body tightened. *The Warren harvest will go on and on forever.*

"Everyone is yelling at each other," Alex said. "So I came home."

"That's typical for harvest." Wendy didn't want him to see how discouraged she felt by his news. "Everyone gets a little tense when things don't go right."

"Things are tense even when things do go right."

"You work so many hours, so many days without a break."

They sat together in silence for several minutes. Alex had his eyes closed and Wendy thought he might be sleeping. Suddenly he stretched his arms and said, "Wendy, the food smells delicious."

She removed his plate from the oven. There was turkey meat, mashed potatoes and gravy, her mother's famous stuffing, and peas and carrots from the garden. Her mother had included a small container of cranberry sauce.

"Dad isn't finished with harvest." Wendy sat across from Alex and watched him eat. "I think he has eighty acres left of oats. He took the time to spend Thanksgiving with us. Mom would have insisted he take a break."

So different from Helen, who would sooner be operating the equipment than stuck in the kitchen.

"Something happened though. Something out of the ordinary," Wendy continued. She told Alex about the proposed bus trip to the Maritimes and about her mother's reaction. "It put a damper on the rest of the afternoon. All of us wanted her to say yes."

"Why don't you and I go somewhere after harvest? Someplace warm and far away. You can pick."

Wendy clapped her hands in delight. "Disneyland!"

They flew to San Francisco in late November and rented a yellow car they nicknamed "The Banana." They explored Fisherman's wharf, Joshua's little dark head visible in the baby carrier, nestled under Alex's chin. They took the Alcatraz boat tour and ate in Chinatown. They drove down the coastal highway, Joshua strapped in a car seat, and stayed the night at Big Sur. The hotel was more expensive than expected and Alex grumbled a little. In Anaheim they explored Disneyland. Alex went alone on the rides. They drove further south, all the way to San Diego. They stopped when they wanted. Wendy breast-fed Joshua in the car while Alex stood outside and smoked.

"I am done with this habit." Alex threw his empty pack into the trash. "I have too much to live for."

"Good." Wendy hated the smell of cigarette smoke on his clothing.

"This is a second honeymoon," she said, nuzzling into Alex after a particularly satisfying lovemaking session. She could not remember ever feeling so content. Away from his family, away from hers. "Better than our first. Remember how afraid I was to return home?"

"I remember." Alex glanced at his son sleeping in the travel bassinet. "Seems to me Joshua came along the first time too. Someday, we'll take a trip just the two of us. Las Vegas maybe, when you're twenty-one. We could leave Joshua with your mother.

Your parents would take excellent care of him." Alex pressed his naked body against Wendy's.

Not Las Vegas. She had no desire to go there. Ever. Alex's last-minute invitation and ultimatum, when they had first started seeing each other, were forever etched in her brain.

Wendy resumed her lonely life in Milford. Alex was gone from the apartment Monday to Saturday, repairing machinery bought for "next to nothing" at auctions and later sold for a profit. Wendy packed his lunch in the morning and didn't see him until after seven in the evening.

On occasion, and without warning, Alex stopped in when he came to Milford for parts. If Joshua were sleeping, they made love. "A quickie," Alex called it. Sometimes they both fell asleep only to be awakened by an angry phone call from the Warren shop requesting Alex's immediate return.

"I understand the long hours in spring and fall, but during the winter there should be more time for us," Wendy said, spooning Alex in bed. "It seems like I get the short end of the stick."

"Trust me, you don't get the short end of the stick."

Wendy did not smile. "I'm talking about your time."

"You know." Alex turned to face her. "I've been doing a lot of thinking. Maybe it's time to build a house on the farm. Then I won't be gone all day."

Wendy sat up. "Do you mean that?" She threw open the bed covers. "I have a book of house plans in the closet!"

Alex grabbed her arm. "I can't look at them right now. I have to get to the shop. Stuart will have something nasty to say to me about being pussy-whipped."

"Oh big boo to Stuart. Stay, Alex. Stay the day. It's Saturday and it's storming outside."

"I can't." Alex rolled out of bed and slipped on his boxers.

Joshua was in the next room performing his new repertoire of sounds. Wendy opened the door. Joshua gurgled.

"Peek-a-boo!" cried Alex in a falsetto voice, and ducked behind Wendy. He jumped out and called out, "peek-a-boo!" Joshua giggled and Alex did it again. Joshua giggled louder.

"I think I will stay," Alex said, reaching for his son.

"I'll get the book of house plans," said Wendy, happiness

pouring out of her. "And when it's built, I'll fill it full of kids."

"And where would you like to build this big house of ours?"

"Not inside that oversized parking lot your family calls a yard."

"I agree. We can build outside the shelter belt, south, north or even west of the yard. If we build north or south, we can have our own driveway. That way no one will see when we leave the yard or when we return."

A week later, Murray and Helen Warren, Stuart, Sylvia and their kids, stopped by the apartment without warning. There was no time to clean the toilet, no time to sweep the floor. There was not enough beer in the fridge, and no pop for the kids, who stood awkwardly beside their parents. No one took off their coats though Wendy offered to take them. Within half an hour of small talk, Joshua was screaming. Wendy felt as if her anxiety had transferred itself to her son.

"He's a fussy baby, isn't he?" commented Sylvia for the second time.

"Actually he's an easy baby," said Wendy. "He might be going through a growth spurt. He's hungry all the time."

She took Joshua into his room, closed the door and changed his diaper. She ignored the rise and fall of the Warren voices as she nursed her baby, not particularly interested in returning to the crowded living room. She rocked him to sleep before putting him into his crib. Reluctantly she rejoined the group.

"You'd better tell her." Stuart had a mean smile on his face.

"Tell me what?" asked Wendy.

Alex avoided her eyes. "My parents would like a new house. They have kindly offered their old house to us for free."

Wendy looked at Helen Warren. "Your house is too close to the farm traffic. It's too dangerous. I need a yard for the children. And a garden."

"You need ...?" Stuart began.

"There is a garden," said Sylvia, interrupting. "Big enough to share."

"But Alex and I want ..."

"Alex doesn't have enough money to buy a pot to piss in, let alone money to build a brand new house," said Stuart.

"Now wait just a minute," said Alex, bristling.

"Helen and Murray deserve a new house after all these years on the farm, don't you think?" Sylvia gaped at Wendy.

"Of course they do," stammered Wendy, but Alex's parents didn't care about houses, or yards, or gardens.

"The farm can't sustain building two houses the same year," said Stuart.

"I guess not," said Wendy.

"You guess correctly," said Helen Warren. Her words signalled the end of their visit and the guests stood and grabbed their boots by the door. "Alex, we have that appointment with the lawyer tomorrow morning." Helen paused in the apartment hallway. "Don't be late."

Wendy stood in stony silence until the final stomp of footsteps could no longer be heard descending the apartment staircase. She burst into tears.

"I'm really sorry." Alex closed the apartment door. He tried to put his arms around her, but she rejected him. "Wendy. I had to tell them our plans. I couldn't very well take money out of our farm account without discussing it with them."

"I don't want to live in your parents' stinky old house." Wendy knew she was behaving like a child but she couldn't stop. "Why didn't you put up a fight?"

"I was blind-sided."

"Stuart and Sylvia got your parents all worked up to screw with our plans."

"Wendy, I promise you a house. A castle if you want. I have lots of money invested in our farm company. Never mind what Stuart says."

Wendy held up the velour sleeper that had been the gift for Joshua. "This was an excuse to stick us with bad news. I am never going to dress our son in this. I would be forever reminded of this night." She threw the garment on the table. "And what appointment with the lawyer do you have tomorrow morning?"

"Just to sign some papers. We bought three more quarters last fall. Didn't I tell you?"

Chapter 25

Elsie

July 1989

Worries, Dan said, are a lot like stones. There are heavy ones, like illness and death, divorce and bankruptcy. Then there are little ones. Carry around too many of them at one time and they create the same weight. Carry them around for too long, and one becomes permanently stooped and joyless. You have to cast away those small troublesome stones and be grateful when you don't have big ones.

Elsie sat outside in the early morning sun and reflected on her husband's words.

Ah. But the wisdom to determine what was little, and what was big.

She suspected she carried a lot of little stones, and that was a source of irritation for her family. Paige's "normal" teenage behaviour had started off as a little stone, and had quickly escalated. During her last year of high school, the girl had become increasingly secretive, her moods alternating between exhilaration and despair. Living with her had become intolerable.

"We need to see a counsellor," Elsie had said.

"Whatever for?"

"Your mood swings. I can't deal with them."

"What about your mood swings? You think Dad and I can't deal with your menopause?"

"Your Aunt Debra is manic-depressive. I believe it is genetic."

"I am not depressed!" Paige screamed at the top of her lungs.

Elsie had backed away. She took her prayers, written on tiny scraps of paper, to church with her every Sunday and left them behind on the offertory plate. She told no one what was going on. Not even Dan knew the full extent of their youngest daughter's rage.

Paige moved out of the house as soon as she finished high school. Elsie felt insulted and rebuffed, and had said so. Now she was afraid this was her permanent relationship with her daughter, although Dan worked hard to keep the line of communication open and pleasant.

"Give her some time and space," he had suggested.

The sound of a vehicle turning into the driveway interrupted Elsie's worry. With a crunch on the gravel, the vehicle came to an abrupt stop. The door slammed shut.

It's too early for visitors.

Elsie stood and walked around the house to find Patti Fields sitting on the veranda, hands covering her face. Elsie dashed up the three steps and touched her neighbour's heaving shoulders. Patti looked up. Her face was lined and drawn, making her look older than her fifty-three years.

"Did something happen to one of the kids?" Elsie cried.

"It's Donald. He didn't come home last night," Patti wailed. "Before he left he told me he wanted out of our marriage."

"No, that can't be true." Elsie pulled Patti up and into her arms. There had been no sign of tension the last time she had seen the Fields together at a social function not so long ago. Not that Elsie spent time contemplating the state of her neighbours' marriages. She barely contemplated the state of her own.

"I was hoping he was here," Patti said, struggling out of the embrace.

"I'm sure he's not." Elsie was surprised. *Why would Donald come to them?*

"I hoped maybe he and Dan were friends."

"You know Dan. He would have insisted Donald go home and patch things up. Can I get you some coffee? We can sit out back on the patio."

"Oh, I'd look like hell out in the sun." There was the briefest hint of a smile from Patti.

"What was the fight about?"

"There was no fight. We were eating supper. He said he had been thinking of leaving. I thought he was joking. I mean, who doesn't dream about escaping once in a while? So I laughed and said, 'Steak not up to your usual standard?' He left and I haven't seen him since."

"That's crazy. Why on earth would Donald want to leave?" Patti gaped at her.

Suddenly it dawned. "He's having an affair?"

"Men don't leave a warm bed without having another warm bed to go to. I think he's got another bed."

"But people out here don't have affairs."

"Oh, Elsie. You are so naive."

"I don't believe he is having any affair," Elsie repeated stubbornly. But a distant memory flickered. The first time she met the Fields, Donald had flirted. Elsie remembered the too long holding of her hand, his lingering touch had made her feel a little dirty. But that was decades ago and he had kept his hands to himself ever since.

"Do you know Carrie McCombs?"

"Yes, I do. She's a friend of Leslie's and Charlotte's. But you can't possibly suspect she and Donald ... Why he's old enough to be her father!"

"She's looking for a meal ticket, flashing her stuff all over town. All the men practically have their tongues fall out of their mouths wanting to take care of her and her two little girls. That's where I think Donald is."

There was a soft knock from inside the house. It was Dan peering out the dining room window. He opened it and said, "Why, hello Patti. I thought I heard voices."

"Donald left me, Dan."

"What the ...?" A few seconds later, Dan came to the door wearing a robe. He stepped outside, his thin legs bare. He looked at Elsie who shook her head ever so slightly.

This isn't a social call, she implored telepathically.

But Patti started wailing again. "I'm so pissed off with him," she sobbed. She stood and wept into his shoulder.

Dan looked helplessly at Elsie. She didn't like seeing another woman in his arms, no matter what the reason.

"Well, that's enough of that." Patti detached herself, as if sensing Elsie's discomfort. "I can't let myself succumb to self-pity."

"Donald will come to his senses," Dan said. "Maybe he's back at home as we speak."

"Do you really think so?" Patti's face brightened. "I told Elsie he's probably with that Carrie McCombs."

"Carrie McCombs?" The surprise in Dan's voice was evident.

"Is there anyone we should call?" asked Elsie, eager now to get rid of Patti. "Any of your children?"

"No. I won't phone the kids until I know what's going on. And it's too early in the morning to call the restoration spa to iron out this wrinkly old face. Right now I'm going to get a few hours of sleep." Patti stood, and without a backward look, got into her car and drove out of the yard.

Dan followed Elsie into the house. "Carrie McCombs would never keep a man overnight," he said. "She's a young woman with two very small children."

"So why would Patti suspect her?"

"You know Donald. He likes to be a hero. I think he was helping her."

"What do you mean, helping her?"

"You know, with the well water and stuff like that. Plowing the driveway when it snowed. I can't understand why a young single mother would live alone on an acreage." Dan looked at Elsie. "You never have to worry about the water and the snowplowing. I take good care of you. It's a conscious decision I make every day."

"Well, thank you, Dan. How romantic you are, for making me a conscious decision. Thank you for being my hero and not that of Carrie McCombs."

"Maybe Donald's depressed? Or bored with himself and he's blaming Patti. To tell the truth Elsie, I don't know him well at all, even after twenty-five years. But leaving a marriage now seems like a stupid thing to do. Their kids are gone and the Fields have time for themselves." Dan took her hand. "Let's be spontaneous. Let's pack the cooler the kids gave me for Father's Day. Let's go for a drive and stay somewhere overnight. You pack that racy little nightgown the kids gave you for Mother's Day."

"The kids didn't give it to me. You did. For my birthday." Elsie smiled, remembering her daughters' embarrassed faces when she unwrapped the gift. "And we can't go tonight. You have an RM meeting."

"Shoot. I forgot. Let's go somewhere for the day. We can be back here late this afternoon if we don't go far. How about Manitou

Beach?"

"A swim in the healing waters." Elsie went to find their bathing suits.

The south side of the long narrow lake was lined with hotels, restaurants and cabins. The north side was barren.

"During the twenties, thirties and forties, this lake attracted Saskatchewan's rich and famous," Dan said as they drove down the beach street.

"I did know that," Elsie returned. Dan was in one of his didactic moods. "How about going to the mineral pool instead of the beach?"

"I'm game. No sand in our swimsuits."

They paid their fees and separated at the locker rooms. Elsie found a changing room and struggled into her one-piece suit. She looked at herself critically in a mirror, and jiggled the fat on her upper arms.

She met Dan at the side of the pool. A tall, thin elderly man walked past with a short, plump elderly female companion.

Elsie giggled. "Look Dan. There we are in thirty years."

"It's a good thing to get old. Considering the alternative."

Elsie sat on the ledge and slowly lowered her body into the warm water. "It's relaxing to soak our bones."

"Our tired old bones," Dan teased.

No sooner had he spoken when a voice called out, "Dan and Elsie Dewhurst! Fancy meeting you here."

"The Irvings!" A smile fixed on Dan's face. Quietly, to Elsie, he said, "His name is Ted, but for the life of me I can't remember hers."

Elsie couldn't either. She felt a little exposed in her bathing suit, even though she was up to her neck in water. Dan and Ted talked about farming while she and Mrs. Irving talked about their adult children and grandchildren. Elsie resisted the urge to talk about Donald Fields, prime on her mind. She knew Dan hated gossip.

"We're going away again this winter," said Ted Irving, including the women in this new turn of topic. "We bought a fifth-wheel a few years back. Right after freeze-up we take off to Arizona."

"Oh." Elsie laughed. "My sister calls farmers like you Triple A farmers. April, August, and Arizona. Of course, she's just jealous."

The grass is always greener on the other side.
"I wish it were only April and August," said Mrs. Irving. "Those sixteen-hour days take their toll. And we're not getting any younger."

"How long do you stay away?" asked Dan.

"Five months," said Mrs. Irving. "We leave in early November and return before April. There's lots of Canadians where we stay. Lots from Hatfield. You'd be surprised how many."

"Don't you come home for Christmas?" Elsie asked.

"All that fuss and bother! When the kids come home, they play cards and drink our liquor while Ted and I do all the work and foot the bill. No, thank you!"

It wasn't totally different from when the Dewhurst daughters returned to the farm. Still, Elsie couldn't imagine being anywhere but home for Christmas.

Elsie phoned Patti as soon as Dan left for his evening meeting.

"I couldn't stop thinking about you all day," she said. "Did Donald come back?"

"No, he didn't. My sister is here right now. She's furious with Donald and we can't find the gun."

There was laughter in the background.

"I'm kidding Elsie. We don't have a gun in the house."

"Are you drinking?"

"We sure are. It's as good a thing to do as crying," Patti replied. "Why don't you come over and join us. We can talk about what rats we're married to."

"I don't feel right now Dan is very ratlike."

"We'll help you stir up some old memories of resentment and anger." There was more laughter in the background.

"I don't think I should." Then Elsie remembered what Dan said about being spontaneous. "Oh, what the hell. I'll be over in ten minutes."

She left a note for Dan.

Lila Gladstone was part of the group. Her voice soared above the others as the women shared opinions on almost every marriage they knew, including their own. Patti's sister and Lila interrupted each other so often no verbal thought was fully complete before the next voice was added.

Elsie accepted a glass of wine and tried to follow.

"Young divorcee, looking for someone to take care of her," Patti's sister grumbled. "And of course many men jump at the ..."

"I can't believe you don't know her," Lila said to Elsie.

"If you're talking about Carrie McCombs, I do know her."

"I wish all Donald did was ..."

"Those helpless types with their dimples and tight jeans, parading ..."

"We shouldn't jump to conclusions. We don't even know if there is another woman." Elsie's sentence hung heavy in the smoky air. All three women turned on her.

"What do you speculate happened here? Donald wouldn't have left if not for Carrie — or someone like her," said Patti's sister.

"Women think men are ruled by their penises." Elsie repeated something Dan had said. "And that's insulting to their intellect." The words were out of her mouth when she remembered, too late, she was there to console Patti. Not to be rational.

"You are delusional," said Patti's sister. "Have another drink. Have a cigarette too."

"Oh, I haven't smoked in years."

"You're married to a saint," Patti said to Elsie, "so of course you'd think men didn't look, didn't touch. But, you're right. As usual." The group was silent as Patti worked to pick out her words. "It's easier to blame someone like Carrie, who for all we know might be completely innocent. I have let my marriage fail by getting old and smart."

"We all get old," said Elsie. "Being smart is the only power we have left."

"Women lose their sexual power." Patti's sister turned to Lila. "We worried a lot when you and Pete moved into the neighbourhood. You were — and still are — too glamorous to be a farmer's wife."

Elsie laughed uneasily and accepted a third glass of wine. Dan had been taken with Lila and her big brown eyes and her energetic revitalization of the United Church.

By her fourth glass, Elsie was an active participant in a crude and soul-baring conversation, laughing hysterically one minute and

crying the next.
At eleven o'clock the phone rang. Everyone went silent. Patti's sister picked up the receiver. "Hello?" Her eyes flickered over to Elsie. "It's Saint Daniel," she whispered. "Are you here?"

They broke out into laughter. Elsie rolled her eyes and took the phone. "Hello?"

"What's going on over there?" Dan demanded.

"We're having a little celebration. No men."

"I'm coming to get you. Under no circumstance are you to drive home."

He hung up and was there almost immediately, frowning at the empty bottles and the overflowing ashtray. "I hope I'm not interrupting anything."

"Actually, you are," said Patti. "But that's okay. We have tried and condemned Donald. I realize now I'm better off without him." She gave a twisted smile. "See you, Elsie. And thanks for your support."

"I'm taking Lila home too," said Dan.

Lila obediently grabbed her sweater and followed him out to the truck.

"You can retrieve your vehicles tomorrow." Dan pointed to the Dewhurst van and the Gladstone sedan.

The three drove in silence. Dan helped Lila into the front door.

"Did you know this isn't the first time Donald has left Patti?" Elsie said when Dan returned to the car. "He's had other women before."

Dan said nothing so she tried again.

"Did you know Donald was so drunk on their wedding night, he passed out before he could ... you know."

Dan sighed. "It's not important we know the sordid and unpleasant little details about the lives of our neighbours. Be careful with whom you share things. And what you share." He parked in front of their house.

"Sometimes I get tired of your holier-than-thou attitude." Elsie slammed the truck door. She tripped on the back step but recovered her balance without falling. Upstairs, she stripped down to her underwear and fell into bed.

"Shouldn't Patti be a little worried," Dan said, looking down at her, his face expressionless. "Maybe it's time to alert the RCMP."

The police!
It was Elsie's first thought the next morning when she got up. *The police!* she thought again as she carried her cup of coffee to the patio.

How quickly she had jumped to conclusions, ready to assume Donald was off womanizing. But Dan had suggested something else. Had Donald, in his misery, decided to end it all somewhere in the bush or a farmer's field? Elsie had heard of such things, but they always happened to people she didn't know.

Patti had mentioned a gun.

The telephone rang inside the house and she hurried to answer it.

"Elsie. It's Lila. I've just come back from Patti's. Donald has been located!" The relief in Lila's voice was evident. Had the same fear occurred to her? "He's in Montana. Helena of all places. He's fine."

"What's he doing in Helena?"

"Took a motorcycle trip. God, he must have driven straight through the night."

When did Donald buy a motorcycle? A set of new questions entered Elsie's brain, but they weren't important and they weren't hers to ask. "Is he going to leave Patti?" she asked.

"I don't know." There was a long pause. "Elsie. Let's keep the craziness of last night amongst ourselves. I'm a little ashamed of the things I said about men. Pete is a good husband, just not a perfect one."

"I'm a little ashamed and embarrassed too. No one needs to know about last night. And please don't say anything to Dan about me smoking."

"It will be our little secret."

"Thanks, Lila. I'll tell Dan the news about Donald."

Elsie sat back in the chair and reflected about the previous evening. She had been included with a group of angry women — and she had acted out of character. It had felt good to be bad and vindictive. Last night in bed she had turned her back on Dan. Of course she had been drunk, but she needed to apologize.

Dan wasn't in the shop. Elsie walked around the yard twice but he was nowhere to be found. This was so unlike him, to leave the yard without telling her where he was going, that Elsie worried she had pushed him past his patience.

"Donald has been located," Elsie said when Dan came in for lunch. She didn't ask him where he had been. They talked carefully as they ate and did not mention the night before.

After lunch Dan sat in his chair and opened his favourite farm weekly.

"I'm thinking about getting a job off the farm," Elsie said, hoping to provoke Dan's attention.

He looked up from the newspaper. "What would you think about doing?" he asked.

"Just something to get off the farm. Something that will give me my own money." She hadn't thought far ahead and was purposely vague.

"If it's something you really want to do, well, that's fine. But I was hoping, now we have an empty nest, we could travel together during the winter."

"Isn't that just like a man, to put his own need for companionship over his wife's need for independence."

Elsie knew she wasn't being fair. Dan never kept her from doing anything and he wasn't stingy. She had been content to be a housewife and rarely felt a need to get away. He had appreciated the comforts she provided: nutritious meals, bedsheets hung to dry on the outside line, disciplined children with regular bedtimes, her companionship.

"Elsie. Let's not fight." Dan's voice was calm. "When what's happening to our neighbours affects our life, it's hard not to be afraid. But let's enjoy each other and love each other. We have everything we need to be happy."

He was looking at her with such tenderness and hopefulness, Elsie burst out crying. She had been thinking such horrible thoughts about him. He stood, put down the newspaper and invited her into his arms.

"I missed your closeness in bed last night," she sobbed. "And I know you want to travel. I will go with you the next time you ask."

With one arm still around her, he pointed to an advertisement of a bus tour in the paper.

"New Zealand," he said. "I'd like to go. I'm asking now."

Chapter 26

Wendy
May 1990

Helen and Murray acted quickly in 1989, purchasing their new Ready To Move house in February. A basement was dug in the spring and the house was attached in the summer, but the actual moving of their furniture and belongings took months.

Wendy, Alex and baby Joshua moved into the old Warren house after the harvest of 1989. By Christmas there were three families living together, their houses in a semicircle, the women watching each other and judging.

Charlotte nicknamed the yard, "The Warren Compound."

To Wendy it was a prison. She felt animosity from her mother-in-law and sister-in-law. She had never been disliked before, at least not openly, and it bothered her more than she cared to admit. In an attempt of reconciliation, she decided to host a special Mother's Day tea.

"The fact you keep trying to be their friend is one of the things I love about you," Alex said, when she told him of her plan.

"Love" was a word he rarely said. Those moments of tenderness had gotten lost in the last year.

"I'm going to make your mother like me, no matter what. I won't give up. What would make it special is if you dropped by. I know you're in the field, but fifteen minutes of your time is all I'm asking for. Please."

"She'd rather I make money." Alex gave Wendy a sudden hug that took her by surprise. "I know it's been tough."

On the Saturday before Mother's Day, Wendy delivered handwritten invitations to Helen and Sylvia. There was no need to give them too much time to think of an excuse to decline, or a chance to forget.

At the hint of a furrow in Helen's forehead, Wendy said hastily, "It's just a coffee break. Fifteen minutes."

When Sylvia received her invitation, she stared at Wendy as if waiting for the punch line of a joke. And yet, she was the first to arrive the next day. She brought her children who had not been included in the invitation.

"Where's Josh?" Sylvia asked, looking around the house.

"Napping. Giving me a break on Mother's Day, thank goodness. Otherwise I'd never get to sit." Wendy set a place for the children at the coffee table and prepared frozen orange juice.

"You're missing your nap too." Sylvia eyed Wendy's thickening girth.

"Yes, I guess I am," Wendy said. She was pregnant, but hadn't yet made an announcement to the in-laws. Her afternoon naps had become a Warren family joke, a secret exposed when on one occasion she hadn't answered the knock on the door and Stuart walked in, catching her asleep on the couch. Wendy had been mortified. Laziness was not to be tolerated.

Helen arrived, not bothering to change from her work clothes, and they all sat. Wendy poured tea for her guests and offered them homemade scones.

"Who was here visiting yesterday?" asked Helen. "Who was the tall blonde woman with the two children? Who was the man?"

"My sister and her family from Winnipeg."

"They looked like visiting royalty."

Sylvia snickered and held her dainty teacup with her little finger curled. "Would you like a spot of tea?" she said to Helen in a British accent and Helen replied, "I would be delighted."

Sylvia's children giggled. They smeared strawberry jam on everything and crumbled the scones.

The whole effect of the Mother's Day Tea — with the lace tablecloth, the china tea pot, the beautiful hues of cream and brown and red — was lost on Helen and Sylvia. Wendy should have listened to Alex and not bothered. She checked her watch. *Where is he?* She needed someone on her side to even the odds, to banish the feeling she was a silly girl with foolish ideas of grandeur.

"Well, I'm off." Helen left without saying goodbye or thank you.

Sylvia stood up and gathered her children by the back door. "What's this?" she demanded.

By the back door there was an open cardboard box, filled with packages of seeds sent by a Manitoba nursery. The diagram of Wendy's planned garden lay on top.

Damn! Why wasn't I more careful?

"I ..." Wendy stammered. "I'm going to have a little garden behind the house."

Sylvia snorted and shook the box so the seeds inside rattled. The plan fell to the floor. "We have a perfectly good garden for all of us. You had no problem harvesting it last year."

"You told me to help myself."

It took great effort not to slam the door on Sylvia's receding back. "You're welcome for the tea!" she shouted in the privacy of her house. She raced to the spare bedroom closet and found her overnight bag, the one Alex had bought for her twentieth birthday. She tossed in a change of underwear, toiletries, a sweater and the blue jeans with the expandable waist. She carried the bag to the truck and wrote Alex a note so he wouldn't worry. Gently she scooped the warm little body of her son and tried not to rouse him as she strapped him into the car seat, but he woke with a roar. He cried all the way to her parents' farm.

"I thought you had plans," Paige said, the first one out the door to help her.

"I had." Wendy deposited Joshua into her sister's arms and retrieved her overnight bag from the truck and went to face her family.

"I gave the bigger bedroom to Leslie's children," said Mom. "And Paige thought she might stay the night. If I had known ..."

"I can sleep in my old room. Josh and I can share a single bed." She turned to her mother and her eyes filled with tears. "Happy Mother's Day."

"You'd better tell us what's wrong," Mom said gently.

"It's not Alex. It's his family." She described the Victorian tea fiasco, including the ridicule.

"We look like visiting royalty?" Keith laughed.

Wendy laughed too. Suddenly it seemed funny.

"Next time you have a tea, invite me," said her mother. "I'd appreciate the effort."

"I know you would, Mom. Next time I will. It's funny how I make the bigger effort on the ones who refuse to be impressed."

"Most of us do that," said Mom.

Keith squeezed Wendy's shoulder. "Leslie and I made reservations at the nicest restaurant in Hatfield. Six-thirty. We would be honoured if you and Joshua were our guests."

"I would be honoured to accept."

Keith is always so thoughtful. Not like Alex who is selfish — like a child.

Alex phoned later in the evening. He did not complain that his supper hadn't been waiting for him, or that Wendy had taken his truck without asking. He did not complain about anything.

When she returned on Monday morning she saw he had cleaned off the table and had loaded the dishwasher with her fancy china. She took it as a clumsy attempt at an apology. Wendy carefully removed the teacups and plates. She hand-washed each piece. Alex would not have known the dishwasher was hard on the gold trim.

Why did they call it the terrible twos? It should be the terrible twenty months.

Wendy carried bags of groceries from the truck. It was late in May, and Alex was busy with seeding, spraying or doing other field work. She couldn't keep track of where he was or what he was doing. He was only home to sleep and eat. She had no relief from childcare.

She returned to the truck and unbuckled Joshua from his car seat. He made loud hiccuping sounds as she carried him into the farmhouse. He clung to her legs and wailed until she sat on the couch and comforted him.

"Let's have a nap," she said to him. "Mommy needs to have a nap." It was only eleven-thirty in the morning and she was already exhausted. She put the perishables in the refrigerator but left the rest of the groceries to be unpacked later.

Wendy carried Joshua to his bedroom. She looked out the window and her jaw tightened.

Alex often forgets things he doesn't want to do.
He couldn't remember the simplest of things — like her schedules and upcoming events. Twice she had reminded him her parents were coming today to help. Twice he promised he would have the soil worked up before they came, yet the ground where her garden was to be planted remained solid.
But it isn't too late. Maybe that's his plan, to work it up just before sowing. The seeds in the warm ground would swell immediately and send out their first tender root. Germination would be immediate.
Straddling Joshua over her hip, nap abandoned, she went outside to the shop hoping Alex would be there, knowing it was unlikely.
Her sister-in-law was on a ladder outside her house, cleaning windows.
"Sylvia," Wendy called from across the gravel driveway. "Do you know where Alex is?"
There was no reply. Wendy had to get closer and repeat her question two more times before she heard Sylvia say, "They had a breakdown."
A breakdown.
Her baby inside her womb twisted uncomfortably. A breakdown was an excuse for Alex to behave badly for the rest of the day.
Wendy returned to her house and phoned her mother. "Don't come. The garden didn't get worked."
"We're still coming. Dad can rototill it."
Wendy hesitated. The garden tractor had become another issue. "I might not be able to use the garden tractor."
"We can bring our own."
Wendy swallowed back tears. Her parents never asked too many questions and for that she was grateful.
Last summer she had been "invited" to share the communal garden with Helen and Sylvia though she wasn't yet part of the compound. Helen's interest was superficial. The real boss of the garden was Sylvia, who planned it, planted it on the one day Wendy was busy, and monitored what and when produce was taken. Wendy's job was to keep the garden weedless, which she did. Early in the morning twice a week she had driven to the farm to do her

share in the work. She had brought along a portable playpen for Joshua. He would pull himself up and watch as she worked.

The only time Sylvia talked to her, was to chide.

"Why did you pick the beans?"

"They were ready. You were gone to Crystal lake."

"They had room to grow," Sylvia retorted.

"If you like your beans woody and tasteless."

Wendy had picked Joshua out of the playpen and marched over to the shop where Alex was fixing. "When we move here, I want my own garden," she said, louder than she intended.

Alex's father and brother looked up.

"I want my own garden," she had repeated, in a show of stubbornness. "I will not be scolded for picking beans."

"What?" Alex had wiped his hands on a rag and guided Wendy out of the shop. She told him about the encounter with Sylvia, but his response was disappointing. "Just ignore her. She's a little nutty." He returned to the shop.

"Why are you causing trouble?" Sylvia had demanded the next time Wendy was working in the garden, getting right into her face. "Complaining about me to your husband. That I don't let you take things."

It had taken effort, but Wendy held her ground and willed herself to remain calm. She stammered an insincere apology, packed up Joshua and the playpen and drove home to the apartment. When she calmed down she phoned her mother.

"I can understand wanting your own garden. It's like having your own kitchen."

That had been ten months ago. The memory of her encounter with Sylvia still rankled.

She planned her private garden plot right behind the house, away from the watchful eyes of her in-laws. When she told Alex, he nodded in agreement. *Maybe he thinks I've become a little nutty, like Sylvia.*

Joshua played with blocks on the kitchen linoleum while Wendy prepared lunch. She added finely chopped celery and onion to the tuna and a dollop of mayonnaise. She was determined to be nice to Alex, to make his favourite sandwich. She wasn't going to be passive-aggressive.

She cut Joshua's food in small pieces and let him feed himself

while she ate half a sandwich. She changed his diaper and put him in his crib for a nap. He protested briefly but her weariness had returned and she didn't care if he cried. She needed a rest.
Just for a minute.
She lay back on the pillows of her bed and closed her eyes.

A persistent knock on the door woke her. She went and unlocked it.
"Paige!"
"I was going to stick my head inside and shout 'Yoo-hoo,'" Paige said, grinning. "But you lock your door? Why is that?"
"Alex's family likes to walk in unannounced, as if this were still the family home. I'll tell you about it another time. Where's Mom and Dad."
"Unloading the garden tractor. Where's Joshie?"
"Still sleeping. Exhausted from multiple tantrums." Wendy studied her sister. Paige had spent the last year living on her own in Hatfield, somewhat estranged from their parents, but almost always available for a visit with her sisters.
As if reading Wendy's mind, Paige said, "Mom and Dad dropped by and asked if I wanted to come along. And I did."
Wendy directed her parents and sister around to the back of the house. "I'll show you where I want my garden."
It was an ugly spot, full of quack grass and weeds. Perhaps, once upon a time, when Helen Warren was younger and had dreams of a different life, it had been an attempted flower garden. Or perhaps Helen had never been interested and had purposely left the area neglected and overgrown — a symbol of her non-ambition.
"Good thing this isn't too big," said Dad. "You're going to have your hands full, keeping it clean the next couple of years."
"I don't care. I want a space I can call my own."
"You never know where this rebellion might lead," Paige said, laughing. "Today a garden. Tomorrow, a job off the farm."
Dad started the garden tractor. The engine was loud, making conversation difficult so Wendy, Paige and Mom returned to the house. Alex was there. From the look on his face, Wendy could tell he was embarrassed.
"I'm really sorry," he said to Wendy's mother. "We had a problem with our seeder. I completely blanked out you were coming." He looked over at Wendy. "I should have taken care of

this yesterday."

Alex didn't often apologize. Wendy smiled at him.

"I'm going to get our tractor and help your father. The ground will be like cement and needs to be worked at least twice." Alex ran off and returned minutes later. "Sylvia left it in Milford for her parents to use."

"She did that on purpose," Wendy said furiously. "She knew I wanted it."

Alex retreated from the room.

"Don't get so riled up." Mom patted Wendy's arm. "It's not good for you or the baby."

"She does this kind of stuff to me all the time. Whenever I stand up to her, somehow I'm the difficult one who overreacts."

"Alex should deal with his family," said Mom. "Not you."

"Sylvia isn't his family. Stuart is. We're all a little afraid of Sylvia."

"Alex is on the garden tractor now," said Dad. "With four of us — and Alex, if he wants to join us — we can get this planted in a few hours. Or less." He glanced at the diagram Wendy handed him. "Sweetheart," he said, putting it down, "you don't need a garden this big this year. You'll be too busy. We'll plant short rows, enough for you to eat fresh for meals, and perhaps a little to freeze. Next year we'll help expand it."

What her father suggested made sense. Wendy nodded in agreement.

"Everybody, put on your rubber boots," said Dad.

"I'll get Joshie," said Paige. "I can hear him talking."

They let Joshua play naked in the fresh dirt. It wasn't long before Sylvia's two children came over to see what was happening. Wendy was annoyed by their intrusion, but her father included them in the work and fun. Alex was friendly and funny and cooperative. When the job was done he bathed Joshua while everyone else was getting supper ready. The day ended on a high note, but soon it was time for her family to leave.

"Thank you. All of you."

"Many hands make light work." Mom gave Wendy a kiss.

"We had fun," said Paige.

"Good luck with the rest of seeding," Dad said to Alex.

Wendy watched them drive away. She went to embrace Alex,

a reward for his congenial behaviour, but he turned away and reached for his hat on the hook by the back door.

"Aren't you staying?"

"No. I promised Stuart I'd keep the air seeder going all night. There's rain in the forecast."

Chapter 27

Paige

October 1992

"Paige Dewhurst! I always wondered what became of you."

The voice belonged to Lacey Ray. Paige hadn't seen her since high school graduation.

"Trent Bouchard," said Lacey, when Paige brought water to the table. "Remember him? He's living in Quebec and keeps in touch with me. Sometimes he asks about you. Now I can tell him. Waitressing."

"I'm a university student," Paige said. "I work part-time to cover my expenses." She looked at the others at the table. "Can I bring you something to drink besides water?"

"I moved to Calgary and I work in a clothing store," Lacey said. "I'm home for a cousin's wedding. I'd suggest we get together and catch up, but my weekend is so packed."

Paige didn't want to get involved in a conversation. The restaurant was full and there was a long line of people waiting at the door, but Lacey kept up a banal monologue about who got married and who had babies. Paige was not interested in the lives of her former classmates. It was when she was explaining the dessert menu that Lacey said, "Remember that juicy basketball coach? Remember how you had such a crush on him? Now's your chance, Paige. His wife is divorcing him. She caught him cheating with another teacher on staff."

Paige's lips paralyzed into a fixed smile. "Really?" She excused herself, walked out the back door of the restaurant and vomited in the back alley. Shaking, she returned to the kitchen and phoned Aunt Debra.

"Please come and pick me up," she begged. "I'm sick." She handed her tables off to another server and excused herself.

Aunt Debra was there within minutes, as if she had waited by the phone for this call. Paige would have died before she disclosed anything about her affair to her mother, but Aunt Debra had her own demons and ghosts. She understood married men and being alone, waiting. She was the only person — besides Charlotte — who knew about Jorden, and even if Charlotte and Aunt Debra put their stories together, they would only know half. But Aunt Debra knew enough to insist Paige stay with her at her apartment, knew enough to accompany Paige when she retrieved clothes, toiletries and schoolbooks, knew enough about men that some don't like to let go easily, knew enough to have the locks changed before allowing Paige to return home to her basement suite, knew enough to check up on her regularly.

Paige went through the motions of existing.

School.

Work.

Repeat.

Her mind was a desert where nothing flourished.

When emotion hit her, she alternated between rage, sorrow and embarrassment.

Paige returned from an early morning class to find Charlotte waiting outside her basement suite entrance. The sight was so unexpectedly welcome Paige burst into tears.

"Mom and Dad think I'm arriving tomorrow." Charlotte enveloped her in a tight hug. "I'm home for a week. But today I'm all yours. An early birthday present. I heard in your voice you needed a friend."

"But ... how did you?" Paige stopped. Charlotte had an uncanny ability to read between the lines, and an iron-trap mind for remembering schedules and dates. It was almost impossible to keep things from her. Paige removed herself from Charlotte's arms and unlocked the door. "His wife is divorcing him," she said. "She caught him cheating." Paige didn't elaborate who "he" was.

"Oh." Charlotte followed Paige down the steep narrow staircase. "No wonder you're stressed. The wife is gunning for you."

"She caught him cheating with someone who is not me."

Charlotte stopped midway down. She laughed.

"I don't see what's so funny. I am humiliated." Paige unlatched the door at the bottom.

"I'm sorry, but I can't help see the irony in the situation. Who would have thought the cheater cheats?" Charlotte stepped through the doorway and put a hand on Paige's shoulder. "Here. Leave your books and my suitcase and let's go for a walk. It's a sunny morning. And mild. You won't be getting any more of these days until spring."

"He said he wanted to marry me." Paige slammed her textbooks down on the small wooden kitchen table. "I believed him. Now I find I was this silly little toy he played with once in a while."

"I say good riddance! Come. Walk off your anger." Charlotte set her suitcase on the floor and gestured to the open door.

"The family fuck-up, that's what I am." Paige reluctantly followed Charlotte.

"Don't say that about yourself."

"I'm sure our mother thinks it."

They walked in the affluent university area. Charlotte talked cheerfully about Toronto and her new job at a radio station. She sounded content. There was no mention of anyone special.

Paige was silent, brewing in her own petulance. *What does Charlotte know about true love and suffering? Has she ever been in a serious relationship? Or any relationship for that matter?*

They ordered quiche at a homey little restaurant off Broadway and talked about how Wendy was handling her difficult in-laws. They talked about how the Hamiltons were doing, now that Keith's family was bankrupt and there was no more money for anything. That took Paige's mind off her own troubles for ten minutes. *Leslie's life isn't all wine and roses.* As long as they talked about their siblings, Paige could avoid her own disappointment.

"Aunt Debra wants me to move in with her," she said, when they resumed their walk across the Broadway Bridge and along Spadina Crescent. She pointed to a tall apartment building. "She says it's as close to the university as the place I have now. I'm seriously considering it."

"So when did you and Aunt Debra become such good friends?"

"Over a year ago. I started calling her. Now we have supper

together every Tuesday night, my day off from work."

"That's wonderful! I've always felt sorry for Aunt Debra, but maybe because Mom led us to believe only marriage and children would make us happy. What a crock of shit!"

Married to Jorden, and pregnant with his child was exactly what Paige wanted, but she couldn't say that out loud without being smacked on the side of her head by her feminist sister.

"You know what we should do?" said Charlotte, as they crossed the University Bridge on their way back. "Let's think of all the horrible ways we could torture this ex-lover of yours. In our imagination of course."

"I wish I could take a knife and cut off his overactive prick. I'd flush it down the toilet. In my imagination, of course."

What she could do was report him to the police. But she could not bear the shock and disappointment on her parents' faces when they heard how she had baited and stalked a young high school teacher. That was where her revenge lost momentum. It was all her fault. She had initiated everything.

Back at her basement suite, Paige said, "I can't spend the rest of the day with you. I have another class at two and I waitress at five."

"I know. I've brought along some work and if I get bored, there's a movie I want to watch. And maybe I'll give Aunt Debra a call and invite her out for supper." Charlotte paused. "Should we be concerned about this man? That he might stalk you? How many years has this been going on?"

How many years have I wasted? "Two years," Paige lied.

Charlotte gave her a piercing look, and Paige knew the steel-trap mind was calculating a different number.

Paige's last year living at home as a high school student had been intolerable. Everything her parents suggested to make things better filled Paige with uncontrollable anger. She knew her mother had enlisted her sisters' help and she pretended to listen to their advice.

"Make the most of your senior year at school," Leslie had said. In a lower voice she added, "Go to the Pit. Flirt with all the boys. Have sex with a few. This time in your life is short."

"Whatever you do, don't fall for the first guy who takes your breath away. If he's the right one, he'll wait. Get an education. Have some fun," said Wendy.

"Travel, that's what you should do," Charlotte had said. "Take a year or two, like I did and figure out who you are. You don't have to make up your mind right away about your future."

Paige had taken a year to make her decision about school but the furthest she travelled from the farm was to Hatfield. She declined Charlotte's invitation to work in Toronto and share a living space. Instead, she found herself a small furnished apartment and got a job as a receptionist in an accounting firm. Her wage was slightly above minimum and her rent ate most of her earnings. She avoided her parents as much as possible, but on the few occasions they were together, they pretended everything was peachy.

Paige was too proud to admit it, but that year in Hatfield had been bleak, worse than any year she had ever lived at home. Several days went by without seeing Jorden or speaking to him. Their trysts had been few and furtive. When she had been a high school student, she had been busy with sports, student government and dance. She had been able to see Jorden five days a week, albeit most often from a distance.

The trouble with Hatfield was its size. The town was too small. Everyone knew everyone else. It was easy to arouse suspicion.

Jorden accepted a position in one of the city high schools and Paige followed. He helped choose her lodgings and suggested a place with a private entrance so he wouldn't run into anyone. The rental they found had a back alley where he could park his car.

"Are you sure you wouldn't like a bigger place and a roommate?" Mom's distaste was obvious as she surveyed the tiny bedroom, the cramped kitchen and the old-fashioned bathroom with water pipes that moaned and groaned. "It's so dark here. And if a rapist jumped out at you in this yard full of overgrown shrubs, no one would see."

"Always the worrier," Paige had replied, forcing a smile.

"You wouldn't want to live in a house with a bunch of girls like Leslie did at your age?" Dad had asked. "We would be happy to pay for a better place."

"I'm happy here," Paige said, her voice rising. She did not want the obligation that came with accepting her parents' money.

A look of alarm passed from her mother to her father.

Paige softened her voice. "I go to school and I work during the supper hours at the restaurant. That's it."

She had a key made for Jorden. Often he was waiting when she got home. He brought bottles of whiskey and vodka. Sometimes he took pictures of her in provocative poses. Sometimes she was naked. During her second year of university, after a lovers' dirty fight, Paige emptied her tip jar and bought a one-way plane ticket to Toronto. It had been her first attempt to quit the addiction she called Jorden.

Charlotte had picked her up at the airport in a car she borrowed from a friend.

"I don't need to own a vehicle except in situations like this," she said. "I use public transportation. I live downtown. It's expensive, and it's not fancy but I like the location. Of course I'll buy a car once I get a job in my chosen career."

Charlotte lived on the fourth floor of an old building. Her living room overlooked a busy intersection. She insisted Paige sleep in the bedroom. "I'll sleep on the pull-out couch."

"Or we can share a bed. I don't mind."

Living in a big city hadn't changed Charlotte's personality one whit. She was the sister who cared, the one who pushed the boundaries ever so gently so Paige revealed more than she intended.

"Are you writing about the secret man in your life?" Charlotte asked, eyeing the Hilroy notebook Paige carried with her.

"Who said there was a secret man?" Paige replied. "Maybe I have a female lover. Wouldn't that knock the socks off the old ladies in the Hatfield United Church!" She realized too late she sounded defensive. Charlotte had been only teasing.

"I know something is bothering you. You'll feel better if you confess."

Paige knelt on Charlotte's threadbare carpet and gave a dramatic pause. "Forgive me father for I have sinned. I have committed adultery. I have slept with a married man."

Charlotte's eyes settled on Paige's face as if trying to determine the validity of that statement. "Rachel Paige Dewhurst. A married man? Where does a young woman your age find a married man?"

"Are you kidding me?" Paige was incredulous. "As if my world isn't brimming with bored, disgruntled husbands."

"So tell me about him." Charlotte pulled a wooden chair close to Paige and sat facing her.

Paige, who had had nothing better to do than fantasize during her constant wait for Jorden, recounted fictionalized stories she had written in cheap notebooks. That her lover was the older brother of a friend, it was love at first sight, his wife was shrewish and his kid was sickly. That he was honourable and would never leave his family.

"If he were so honourable, why did he start an affair with you in the first place?"

The logic of the question made Paige angry. Charlotte's voice was not unlike the voice inside her own head. She flew home shortly after.

Back in Saskatoon, her resolve to stay away from Jorden had lasted less than a month.

"You're seeing him again, aren't you?" Charlotte said, over the telephone.

"Why would you think that?"

"It's in what you don't say."

A second breakup six months later lasted two weeks. Jorden couldn't keep away from her and Paige couldn't keep away from him. *Isn't this how true love works?*

What had Charlotte said? The cheater cheats.

This time she wasn't ever going back.

What was she supposed to do now? Start her life over? Reinvent herself?

Chapter 28

Wendy

July 1993

"Hello kiddo," Charlotte said over the telephone. "I heard you got a piano."

"An old upright, with beautiful tone and touch." Wendy could see the piano from where she stood. It took up a whole wall in their living room. How Joshua and Beth had danced when she made the piano rock and roll!

"Well. Good for Alex. I knew you wanted one."

"A belated Mother's Day gift. Of course my dear sister-in-law insinuated Alex has a girlfriend and the piano is a gift to appease his guilt."

"A typical family gathering in the compound?"

"You're right about that. Nothing is so small it can't be blown out of proportion. Like Alex playing baseball. They say he should quit because he's thirty."

"Thirty? Oh dear girl, how do you keep your sanity?"

"I try to get away as much as possible. This week we have swimming lessons. I take the kids to the Hatfield pool where Mom meets us and watches Josh while Beth and I are in the 'Moms and Tots' class. We have a picnic lunch on the lawn. The kids love it."

"I remember swimming lessons at the Hatfield Pool." Charlotte's voice sounded wistful. "I miss all of you. If I hadn't used all my holidays to tour Europe this past spring, I would come home." She paused. "Is someone crying in the background?"

"That's Beth. She's been complaining of water in her ears. I'd better go before she wakes Josh."

"Enjoy the piano. And keep your head up, kid."

Wendy replaced the receiver on the handset and went to comfort Beth, but the little girl had fallen back to sleep. In the living room, the piano beckoned. Her fingers found their way onto the keys.

Moonlight Sonata. The minor melody suited her mood.

Of course she was curious about the tiny frizzy-haired woman who seemed to show up whenever Alex played ball, the same woman who had pressed her body so intimately into Alex's at the dance hall. The girl named Glennie.

Eve would have given advice had she not moved away with her husband to a small city in Alberta. She had always been honest with Wendy about Alex's history. And Wendy remembered her words.

"Glennie's from Milford, not St. Cloud. As a teenager, she managed to become part of our high school gang. Alex would break up with her but they'd get back together. It became a pattern that ended when Alex met you."

Unwittingly, Eve mentioned Glennie and Alex had been together on that Las Vegas trip.

"What was I to do?" Alex had said, when Wendy asked him about it. "Cancel out on my friends? The reservations were made before I knew you existed. And besides, you and I were not yet a couple."

"Yet I remember you asked me for sex days before you left."

"So there had been a little overlap. If you looked at it from Glennie's perspective, Wendy, you were the intruder."

"You really don't judge yourself too hard, do you?"

The resulting fight had lasted a night and a day before make-up sex finally resolved the argument. Beth had been born nine months later.

A happy child, conceived in anger.

Wendy knew she had to trust Alex if she wanted her marriage to succeed. He said he didn't have a girlfriend. He barely had time for his family the way it was — and he was always where he said he was. Wendy had no reason not to believe him.

The reflection of headlights appeared on the wall above the piano. Alex was home early. Wendy quietly closed the piano lid and met him at the door. His ball uniform was stained with the red rock of the ball diamond.

"I must be getting old. I had no desire to go to the bar after the game." He swept Wendy into a hug and whispered in her ear, "and Glennie showed up at the game."

That damn woman.

"I'll get you a beer." Wendy left Alex's arms and retrieved a Budweiser from the fridge. She handed him the bottle. "Why don't you come along to swimming lessons tomorrow?" She knew Alex loved spending time with her and the kids. "My mom could stay home. She doesn't complain but every day at the pool is wearing on her."

A look of temptation crossed Alex's face and gave Wendy hope.

"There's only three days of lessons left," she persisted. "Come along and see how the kids are doing. Better yet, be the parent in the water in the 'moms and tots' class."

Alex shook his head. "I can't. Stuart is on the warpath again. Sylvia complains to him you're using too much gas, running back and forth to Hatfield. They say you should stay home."

The blood rushed to Wendy's face. "Stuart and Sylvia. The bane of our life. If it isn't one thing, it's another. And this is not my home."

"Of course it is."

"Then remind your family to knock before they walk inside *my* home."

"Come on," Alex tried to put his arms around her. "It's not that big a deal. It's not like you're walking around naked or something."

"Do you ever take my side?"

Alex put down his beer. "I came home to you instead of going out with the team. I'm not in a mood to fight."

He looked tired and defeated and Wendy's anger left as quickly as it had erupted.

"I know," she said, putting her hands on his shoulders and massaging them. She was determined to be a good wife.

A week later, Wendy used the remains of the day to pick raspberries growing on the long row of canes that separated her house from Helen's. Joshua and Beth were asleep early and the evening was cool and refreshing. She wore a loose shirt, untucked over loose pants. She had an ice cream pail attached to her waist with Alex's best leather belt.

She had not asked Sylvia's permission for the berries, nor Alex's to use the belt.

As she picked the plump raspberries, so ripe they fell into her hand, a truck pulled up to the house and someone got out. She was about to see who it was when her mother-in-law called out, "Gord. We've moved the office. Come this way." Helen's footsteps crunched on the gravel. "My youngest son lives there now, with his family." Her voice lowered conspiratorially but still carried with perfect clarity. "His wife is spoiled and lazy."

Spoiled and lazy? Wendy straightened her back. Well, she wouldn't be called cowardly. She stepped out from behind the shadows of the tall raspberry stalks.

"Hi. I'm Wendy Warren," she said, and walked forward to shake the man's hand. "I couldn't help but overhear. I'm married to Helen's younger son."

"Gord," the man said pleasantly.

Wendy walked away, cradling the pail that was only one-third full.

A mother-in-law who wanted a relationship with her daughter-in-law would have rushed after her and apologized. Helen did not. The pretence was over.

When had this dislike for Wendy started? When had she earned the label "spoiled and lazy?" It could be any number of times, but most likely it was when she refused to deliver food out to the field.

When she first moved onto the farm she had been enlisted to feed the men during harvest. Determined to make Alex proud, she prepared roast chicken, beef or pork. She boiled potatoes, made gravy, cooked vegetables, prepared a salad and a dessert. Around four-thirty every afternoon, she organized two cardboard boxes, one for the hot food and one for the cold. She packed the food in quart sealers, wrapped the quart sealers in clean towels, strapped Joshua in his car seat, and drove Alex's truck out to the field where the men were working. The boxes of food were wedged against the door.

If the breeze were gentle, she spread an old blanket on the ground and passed out plates and portions to whoever arrived to eat. On windy days she used the half-ton end-gate as a table and the men stood around it. There was usually about five of them, but they never ate at the same time because the combines and the trucks never stopped.

What Wendy had started with great enthusiasm eventually came to wear her out. The whole process — cooking, packing the food, and taking it to the field — took at least four hours. It was dark by the time she returned home. There was Joshua to bath and put to bed. Wendy was so tired she followed soon after. The dirty kitchen and the unpacked cardboard boxes greeted her every morning. She put the dishes through the dishwasher, scrubbed the pots and pans, and started over again.

"You were the one who preferred the evening meal," reminded Alex, when she complained. "You said the noon shift interfered with Joshua's nap."

It was true. She had been given first choice. And if the harvest time had been of short duration, she could have endured the intensity. But the Warren harvest, with their endless acres of land, went on and on and on.

"My father comes home for meals," Wendy said, remembering the happy times around the table.

"Your father farms only sixteen hundred acres and all his fields are close to the house."

"For all the acres in your family's farm, no one is any better off," Wendy had pointed out. "And my father always made time for my mother and us girls." She remembered Leslie's September wedding in Winnipeg.

Wendy was pregnant with Beth her first spring on the farm. She suggested someone else deliver the suppers she carefully packed. Someone was always back and forth to the yard, picking up fertilizer and seed. It had seemed like a reasonable request but Stuart's voice had risen angrily as he looked at Alex, "Can't you control your wife?"

"That's what happens when you marry a baby with a pretty face," Sylvia had said, tossing a sneer at Wendy. "That's what happens."

The Warrens didn't believe in compromise, collaboration, negotiation. They believed in confrontation and intimidation. Living on the Warren compound was like living on a TV drama. For the thousandth time, Wendy wondered why Alex put up with it.

Why couldn't they move away and start afresh?

Ah. Because we have no money.

Alex had requested an increase in wages, not only for himself but for everyone. He had been denied. There had been no meeting and no discussion and he had accepted the result without pushing back.

Wendy smiled grimly as she washed the raspberries. She drained them and put them in a colourful bowl.

Unlike Alex, Stuart didn't play hockey or baseball. His children did not take swimming lessons in the summer, nor skating lessons in the winter. Stuart's family did not take vacations. Their idea of a big excursion was going to Crystal Lake for the day.

Sylvia had no social life. Her house was so clean she wouldn't have visitors for fear of messing it. She bragged about her three freezers full of food: one for produce from the garden, one full of baking, homemade bread, buns and desserts, and one for beef, pork, or chickens, all neatly butchered and wrapped.

Sylvia could never be called 'spoiled and lazy.'

Wendy was not a money manager like Sylvia, who could pinch a penny until it screamed. If Wendy wanted more money, she had to earn it herself. The piano in her living room gave her an option.

"Nix the piano lessons," said Alex, when she suggested teaching. "My parents don't want strangers coming in and out of their yard."

"Strangers drive in and out of the yard all the time. And I thought it was my yard too."

"Well, I don't want students coming in and out of our house. I'm sorry, but I don't. I want privacy."

"You're hardly ever here."

"And when I am, I don't want people in my house."

On a warm August afternoon, Wendy picked up Paige who happened to be visiting at their parents' farm and brought her to the Warren compound to stay a few days. It felt good to have someone on her side. Someone who "had her back."

"Don't let the Warrens beat you down," Paige said, after Wendy complained of money troubles. "Find another place to teach. What about the school in St. Cloud? Phone the principal and ask if you could teach there. Try the schools in Milford. What about the dance studio you told me about? Every dance studio has a piano. I bet the teacher takes at least one day off."

Wendy remembered pushing newborn Joshua in the old-fashioned perambulator, and looking in the window of Miss Molly's Dance Studio.

"Let's go now." She suddenly wanted to escape. "Let's go now to Milford. To the dance studio. You can play with the kids in one of the parks."

"No time like the present." Paige grinned. "I'll treat everyone to ice cream after."

Unsurprisingly, the studio was locked and the blinds were shut. Disappointed, Wendy turned away.

"If you want your daughter in dancing, watch the newspapers for the registration day," a voice rang out.

Wendy stopped. A middle-aged woman stood in the doorway of the hair salon located beside the dance studio.

"I want to talk to the dance teacher about a different matter."

"In that case, she lives there. Right above." The woman pointed to a door Wendy had not noticed before. "I think she's home. Entertaining. Her car is parked out back."

"Thank you," said Wendy and opened the door to a long flight of stairs. At the top was a hallway and two apartments. Wendy knocked boldly on one of the doors, which was opened promptly by a pretty young woman with wild auburn hair. A man appeared behind her.

"I'm looking for Miss Molly who runs the dance studio."

There was a flash of white teeth. "That's me. Molly Givens. What can I do for you?"

"My name is Wendy Warren. I used to teach piano lessons back home in Hatfield and I'd like to start again in Milford. I'm looking for a space to rent a few hours a week."

"Warren," Molly said after a pause, taking a step out into the corridor. "You're not married to Alex Warren by any chance?"

"Yes. I am."

"I used to party with Alex." Molly looked closer at Wendy. "I knew him well. A good husband, I hope?"

"The best," Wendy said, not shrinking under Molly's scrutiny, wondering how well Alex was known.

"What did you have in mind? For space, that is."

"If there's a time this studio is not being used, I'd like to rent it from you and teach piano lessons."

"How many students have you lined up?"

"None yet. I wanted to find a space first. Then I'll advertise." Molly threw back her head and laughed loudly. "Where are you from again?"

"Hatfield."

"I dated a guy from Hatfield. Didn't last." Wendy wasn't sure if that was good or bad. She didn't ask who is was.

"You know. Milford needs some new young blood. I don't teach on Monday. You can have the studio."

"Monday it will be. Thank you." Wendy headed toward the staircase and turned back. "I didn't ask about rent."

"See how many students you get first. We might be able to barter. You'd like to go home with a little money in your pocket at the end of the day, after it's all said and done."

Five students. That was all. Wendy had hoped for twice as many.

"Gotta start somewhere," Molly said, coming into the empty studio after the last one left. "Start small, but be first-rate at what you do. The private teachers here are territorial. A cutthroat occupation." She paused. "Would you like one more piano student?"

"You found me another?" Wendy packed up her treats and stickers.

"I'm talking about me." Molly sat at the piano bench beside Wendy. "Instead of paying rent, how about teaching me? I'd like to learn."

"I've never taught an adult before. It might be fun."

"I'll start next week. But tonight, how about a glass of wine?"

Wendy hesitated. "I can't stay too long. I need to take the babysitter home before the kids are in bed. And I can't start any earlier in the day because the babysitter comes right off the school bus at four."

It would have been so easy for Helen to watch Joshua and Beth for fifteen minutes while Wendy drove the babysitter home. But Helen had stated early on she was not a babysitting type of grandma and clarified her position by never being available even for short periods of time.

As September slipped into October, the glass of wine in Molly's upstairs apartment at the end of the day's piano lessons became routine.

"Who was the guy the first time I knocked on your door?" Wendy asked, the companionship making her bold.

"Jon? He comes and goes from the Alberta oil fields. It's nothing serious. I was married before, you know. Twice."

"Twice!"

"My first husband was a crazy musician and we travelled all over the place with his band, which of course was difficult because of my business. My rebound marriage was to a banker in Saskatoon. Absolutely no craziness there." Molly laughed. "Too boring."

"I've only ever had one boyfriend — and I married him."

"Alex. I'm curious. How does he feel about you working? As long as it doesn't interfere too much with his life, right?"

Wendy nodded.

"My current piano accompanist is getting married next summer and moving away. Would you like the job? I pay well."

The offer came out of the blue.

"I'll have to discuss it with Alex first." Wendy wanted the job and the extra income it provided.

"Tell me what will work for you and I can make it happen."

If only it were that simple. Wendy wished she was more like Paige, who had a "can do" attitude, who didn't think of obstacles and negative consequences and husbands who grumbled.

Molly smiled encouragingly until Wendy said, "Yes."

Chapter 29

Leslie

November 1993

Leslie sat cross-legged on Kim Hamilton's cream-coloured carpet. She alternated between drawing with six-year-old Kyle and cutting out paper dolls with Colette. Usually it was Keith's sister, Roxanne, who entertained the children in the living room while Leslie helped Kim in the kitchen.

"Susan got married last weekend." Roxanne's words might have gone unheard had there not been a lull in Colette's prattle. "Someone from her law firm."

Leslie remembered a picture in the family photo album, of Keith with his arm around a beautiful brunette, the one discarded in his life to make room for Leslie.

"Yes," said Keith. "I sent a card of congratulations."

Leslie leaned toward the lowered voices in the kitchen.

"She'd better start making babies soon. That old biological clock is a ticking away."

Leslie thought Roxanne, who was thirty-two and unmarried, shouldn't be talking about someone else's biological clock.

"I don't believe she wants children. She is very career minded."

"I guess you would know," said Roxanne.

"I can hear you," Leslie called from the living room. In her nine years of marriage she had learned to be forthright rather than question Keith later and offend him with her imaginings.

Roxanne came into the living room and gave Leslie a wink. "We didn't purposely exclude you from the conversation, Leslie." To the children she said, "You two go wash your hands. Brunch is prepared."

Everything in Kim's apartment looked photo-ready, especially her table settings. The brown centres of the cream-coloured Gerber daisies matched the linen tablecloth. The fine china was simple and classic.

"It's a shame to mess this up," Leslie said, the first to sit. "With children, there is always something spilled."

"Everything can be washed." Kim's voice was cheerful, as she carried the platters filled with food to the table. Scrambled eggs, bacon broiled to the perfect crispness, French toast dusted with icing sugar. The menu varied month to month, but the ritual didn't. First Sunday of every month, brunch at Kim's.

Leslie glanced at Keith. *Is he thinking of Susan? Is he still in touch with his former girlfriend?* He had said "is very career-minded" instead of using the past tense.

And what about his parents? Had Kim and Rod Hamilton resented Leslie's intrusion in their lives as much as the Dewhursts had resented Keith's? Ten years ago had he sat his family down and said something like, "I've met a girl who is important to me. I don't know how it's going to turn out, but I want you to accept her and help her. She's young and from a farm."

"But we love Susan!" they might have cried.

Leslie wasn't going to question Keith in front of his mother and sister about who said what and when. It didn't matter what had happened, did it? Leslie, not Susan, was the one sitting in Kim's sun-drenched apartment on a November Sunday. Leslie, not Susan, was a Hamilton woman — tall, slim and impeccably groomed.

"Would anyone like some more coffee?" she asked, as she refilled the cream-coloured coffee butler and carried it to the table.

"Were you jealous when you heard the news?" Leslie asked Keith, as they drove home in the early afternoon. She hoped her tone was playful.

"News about what?" Keith replied, without looking at her.

"Susan. Married."

"Who is Susan?" asked Colette.

Keith blinked his eyes in a manner Leslie took to mean he was annoyed. "She's a woman from my old neighbourhood," he replied in his happy voice, meant to distract Colette's sharp little mind from asking more questions.

"Colette has been invited to a birthday party." Leslie turned to her daughter sitting in the back seat. "Who's the girl, Colette? I forget her name. And what is the present you want to give her?"

Colette was not going to be derailed. "Was Susan a girl in your class, Daddy?"

"Yes, she was. She used to sit in front of me and I used to pull her pigtails."

Colette giggled. "Can we visit her?"

"Sure," said Leslie. "Let's visit her. Let's give her a wedding present."

She saw Keith's lips tighten. He would likely have something to say to her privately about her purposeful provocation. Maybe they would fight. It had been a very long time since the last one. Keith — cool, rational and analytical — usually managed to defuse situations before they escalated. There was little drama in their life. Leslie often felt like a child when she tried to engage him in an emotional debate. He rarely asked what she thought or what she dreamed, and the omission rankled.

"I think I'm bored," Leslie said.

"Why don't you take a university class?" Keith's response was immediate, as if he had been anticipating this moment and had worked out some suggestions. "Work toward that degree you started. Or have another baby. We can afford a third now."

"Have another baby!" screamed Colette with excitement.

"This is not a conversation I want to have in front of the kids." Leslie was only twenty-nine but she did not want to go through all the fuss and bother of pregnancy and childbirth, not to mention the endless sleepless nights with an inconsolable newborn, the terrible twos and the whining threes.

An unpleasant thought suddenly occurred to her.

Perhaps the real reason Keith had chosen to marry her had nothing to do with love and lust. Perhaps Keith needed someone who was young and fertile. Someone who lacked the ambition to be career-minded. Someone who didn't mind staying home and taking care of the house, the medical appointments, the bills, the yard, and the social engagements. Someone who took care of the domestic details so the man's attention could be on more important business.

As the mother of Colette and Kyle who were "blood," Leslie was treated with respect and affection, but she knew Keith, Kim and Roxanne did not confide in her regarding secrets and family history. Eighteen months ago, Keith said to her, "The worst has happened and we have lost it all."

"What are you talking about?" Leslie cried. Keith was not a person prone to exaggerate.

"The business, the houses, the cars, everything gone. My father forged signatures and invested in some risky ventures. He has been arrested for embezzling."

"Arrested! And we've lost everything? Why didn't you warn me? How long has this been going on?"

"Please." Keith's voice sounded oddly detached from his body. "I needed to come home to a house that was calm, not infected with fear and worry and accusations. I needed a normal family life away from the business."

Leslie's anger had instantly dissipated. "What are we going to do?"

"We are going to survive."

She took his hand. "It's only money. We can make more."

Leslie was proud of her response. She was not as superficial as people believed her to be.

Keith endured their losses with practicality and grim optimism — except once and that was when the *For Sale* sign had been hammered into the front lawn of his childhood home. His mother wept in his arms and his stoicism wilted.

An elderly woman had walked across the street. "Oh Kim. I can't imagine this house without you." The woman's husband joined them and before long there was a group of neighbours comforting Kim and Keith.

Leslie had slipped discreetly into the backyard, taking the children with her. This deep-rooted affection for their home was not her loss.

That same afternoon her parents showed up and whisked Colette and Kyle off for a little holiday while Leslie stayed to help sort out their new life. A few days later her father phoned and said, "Your daughter is a perceptive little thing. I have told her the truth."

"Keith and I know we can trust you to say the right thing. We have almost finished moving our personal belongings into a two-bedroom apartment."

"Your mother and I have talked things over and we would like you to come home until everything settles. I hope you don't mind if we extend this invitation to Kim as well."

Leslie suspected Keith had talked to her parents. When she mentioned the invitation he said, "It's a great idea. Besides, you know what a handful Colette can be. Your mother will need all the help she can get."

By the time Leslie, Kim and the children returned to Winnipeg, Keith had a job, Colette and Kyle were enrolled in a local public school, and Kim's new home — an apartment in downtown Winnipeg, had been furnished and decorated by Roxanne.

It had taken several months, but now all the bad "stuff" was behind them and the bankruptcy delegated to the status of "an inconvenience." It was time to forge ahead and make happy memories for the children.

For the first time, Leslie comprehended why she had chosen to marry Keith. She had never been able to put it into words, not to Charlotte or even herself.

Keith was resilient.

A memory, unbidden from the recesses of Leslie's mind, made her smile.

She and Charlotte had gone with their father on an errand that took them to an old hardware store in a distant town. At the back of the store was an odd-looking machine.

"A pinball machine," Dad explained. "It's a game. Metal balls are shot across a sloping board. Points are scored when the balls strike various targets." He inserted a quarter into the machine and demonstrated. He kept the metal ball in motion, racking up points, bells ringing with every interaction. "You get three tries," he said, as another metal ball sprang into action.

Leslie and Charlotte had been mesmerized. "Let us," they insisted.

Dad gave them a handful of quarters and they took turns playing while he made his purchases. The game was a lot harder than it looked and it didn't take long to lose the money. They persuaded their father to show them one more time how it was done. Several minutes passed while he kept the game in play. They could tell he was having fun.

They returned home late for lunch and when they explained their tardiness, Mom had been less than amused.

"You should have seen him!" Charlotte had cried.

"Yes, your father's a regular pinball wizard," Mom had replied.

Leslie always thought Keith was a lot like her father, dignified yet playful with his children. Keith was a good man, a caring man, a strong man. The Hamiltons were back on their feet, and all was well.

Bing, bing, bing.

Chapter 30

Wendy

August 1994

"Nothing like watching ball on a fine summer evening," Dad said, sitting beside Wendy on the ballpark bleachers. "Montgomery has always been a sports town. The ball diamond is well-maintained. No wonder it was chosen to host this tournament." He paused. "I used to play here when I was a young man."

"You used to play?"

"Yeah, I used to be a Montgomery Warrior."

Wendy stared at her father. This was something she had not known. "I'm glad you came with me, Dad. I hope it brings back happy memories."

She was contented and relaxed. Her mother had offered to keep Joshua and Beth at the farm so Wendy could watch without distractions. The children had been unable to sit still during the morning game. Despite their shyness, they had wanted to chase around the bleachers and onto the road with the other children. Wendy had not been able to concentrate.

Alex crouched behind home plate, the defined muscles in his thighs visible beneath his uniform. He was a superior player — and he knew it. He caught the pitched balls effortlessly and gracefully.

Wendy wished his parents would watch him play. Their absence had initially surprised her, but now, knowing the family dynamics and motivations, she understood sports did not make money, and that baseball and hockey took Alex's time away from the farm. Also, Stuart was jealous and petulant about almost everything Alex did. Wendy suspected it was easier for Helen and

Murray to ignore their talented younger son.

"Wendy. Hello," a tall red-haired man called out, climbing the wooden bleacher stairs.

"Ian," she said. "Come and sit with us."

Everyone in the row shifted to make room.

"I haven't seen you for ages." Wendy turned to her father. "Dad, this is Ian Kennedy. His parents farm next to the Warrens."

"We've met before. You were the fellow with the tickets for the church's Fall Supper," Dad said. "What brings you to Montgomery?"

"My sister and brother-in-law live here. I heard Alex's name announced over the loudspeaker and thought I'd check things out. How's it going?" he asked, with a nod toward the game.

"It's 3-2 for the Devils," said Dad. "Top of the fourth."

The Regina Red Socks batter tipped the ball, and Alex tore off his mask to scramble successfully for a catch. There was applause from the stand. Three outs. The Devils ran to the dugout.

The announcer's voice rang out. "No runs and no errors."

"So," said Ian. "Alex behaving himself?"

"You know Alex. He likes to show off for the crowd." Out of the corner of her eye, Wendy noticed Alex was out of the dugout and on deck. She used to be a little embarrassed at the arrogant way her husband strutted and posed, but now she liked it. There was something almost seductive in his stance.

"I guess the big news in my life is my parents are selling the farm. It's kind of a shock to me," Ian said.

"They are?" Wendy cried. Now this was news worth sharing with Alex. "Buy it and move home!"

"Sadly, not an option. I married a city girl who wants to remain a city girl. Besides, our farm is too small to make a decent living."

Alex was up to bat. He had a little routine, a little shuffle he did with his feet. He swung the bat a few times to stretch out his arms and posed at the plate. He hit the first pitch solidly out of reach of the second baseman and made it safely to first base.

"Sell it to Alex and me." An idea was formulating in Wendy's head.

The Kennedy yard was surrounded by trees. If Wendy lived there, she would be hidden from Alex's family. She had never seen the house but anything was better than where she lived now.

"Wendy!" Dad shook her. "Alex is hurt."

Alex was writhing with pain. The coach ran out.

"What happened?" Wendy cried, standing to see better.

"He collided with the second baseman."

Ian pulled Wendy back to sitting. "Look, he's okay. They're helping him off the field."

Another player from the team ran out to replace Alex on the second base. The game resumed. Wendy wanted to go to her husband, but both Ian and her father persuaded her to watch the game. It took forever, but ended 9-6 for the Devils.

"I think he dislocated his shoulder," the coach said, when Wendy was able to see Alex. "I've applied ice packs, but he needs to go to the hospital."

"It might be broken." Wendy had no experience assessing injuries.

"We'll go to emergency in Hatfield," Dad said. "I'll phone Mom and let her know we'll be late coming home."

Alex winced as he got to his feet.

As Ian and Dad helped Alex to the truck, a woman approached. It was Glennie. Wendy pulled the seat belt over Alex's bad shoulder and he whimpered.

"Oh, you poor baby," Glennie reached out, as if to touch him.

"Doesn't she ever quit?" Wendy cried.

"Just get me to the hospital," Alex moaned. His face was pale and there were beads of sweat on his upper lip.

"Looks like someone spent too much time in the beer garden." Ian gave Wendy a wink and led Glennie away.

At the hospital they waited for the doctor on call, then waited for an X-ray technician to confirm nothing was broken and that Alex had a serious shoulder injury. The doctor administered a shot of Demerol and soon Alex relaxed. His arm was wrapped in a brace slung around his neck.

"See your family doctor on Monday to discuss options for pain and possible future surgery. Here's some painkillers to tide you over," said the doctor.

"I guess you won't be playing ball tomorrow." Wendy was sympathetic. And disappointed for her husband.

Alex turned to the doctor. "Will I be better in three weeks? I'll be needed for swathing."

"Three weeks is unlikely."

Alex swore under his breath, but everyone heard.

It was after eleven when they returned to the Dewhurst farm. Wendy propped pillows around Alex in their bed, so he was in a sitting position. He wasn't able to get comfortable.

"Let's put him in your father's recliner in the TV room," Mom suggested to Wendy. "At least *you'll* get some sleep. You're going to have your hands full, with two little kids and an invalid husband."

Wendy helped Alex back downstairs. She wrapped a quilt around him and kissed him goodnight.

"He's worried what his brother is going to say," Wendy told her parents the next morning when she and the children sat down to breakfast. Alex was still sleeping.

"It's an accident," Dad said. "Surely his family understands accidents."

"What's anacident?" asked Beth, in her high voice.

"When Daddy was running to second base, he tried to slide, but he bumped into someone and hurt his shoulder," said Wendy.

"Some bones are like hinges." Dad demonstrated. "See, like your knee. It only moves back and forth like this. But your shoulder can move around like a circle. Like a ball inside a socket." He rotated his arm. "On your daddy, the ball came out of the socket, and the doctor put it back in. Your daddy won't be able to throw you in the air for a while."

"Can we stay here?" asked Joshua. "Nobody yells here."

Dad looked over the child's head at Wendy. "Do people yell at you?"

"They mostly yell at Daddy," Beth said.

"Perhaps we shouldn't discuss this in front of the children," Mom said, buttering toast for Joshua.

"They have a good idea about what's going on." Wendy's tears, perennially close to the surface whenever she thought about her life on the Warren farm, spilled from her eyes. Her children ran to her and put their short arms as far around her as they could stretch.

"I'm sad for Daddy," she told them. But she was mostly sad for them. "Run upstairs and bring the box of Kleenex from our bedroom. Please."

Joshua looked at her for a few seconds before he ran off with his sister.

It was on the tip of Wendy's tongue to confess the latest threat to her sanity, but she hesitated. She could never tell her parents what happened last week. They would pressure her to call the police.

Joshua and Beth had been playing outside while Wendy prepared supper. When she went out to get them, Beth was alone.

"Where's your brother?" Wendy had asked, but Beth only shook her head. Wendy was not alarmed at first. *Perhaps Joshua was on the toilet, or playing with his Legos in the basement.* But he was not in the house. Wendy went to Sylvia's house and to Helen's, although it was unlikely Joshua would have gone to either place.

Wendy's imagination created all sorts of scenarios. She ran to the shop half dragging Beth, through the yard to where the grain trucks were parked, to the dugout, down the driveway and out on the gravel road. Several minutes had passed and Wendy was frantic and incoherent with distress.

Then Stuart drove up in his big truck with Joshua beside him in the passenger seat. The child quickly scrambled out of the vehicle into Wendy's arms.

"How long did it take you to figure out he was missing?" Stuart drove away before Wendy could thank him for finding her son.

Joshua had cried when Wendy questioned him. No, he had not been harmed. Not been touched. Uncle Stuart had asked for his help on the farm. "He said just for a few minutes."

Wendy believed Stuart had taken Joshua deliberately to make her panic, but it would not do to tell her parents. Her mother would become sick with worry, her father would insist Wendy move home with the children. If her parents only knew how little encouragement it would take to return to the safe and nurturing environment of the Dewhurst family farm.

The children appeared with a roll of toilet paper and Wendy hugged them tightly. Over their heads, she said, "Did I tell you Molly Givens will have me accompanying the ballet class from four-thirty to six every day, and a couple of hours on Saturday? When the dancers start preparing for exams, I'll have more hours."

"Are you still teaching piano lessons as well?" Dad asked.

Wendy brightened. "I'm up to nine students. I'm going to be busy. Joshua starts hockey this fall too."

"Dad wants to take me." Joshua looked toward the TV room

where Alex was sleeping. "He wants to help coach."

"Who's going to be taking care of these monkeys while you teach?" Mom asked.

"I've got a neighbour girl hired. She gets off the bus at four and I start the first lesson at four-thirty. The bad part is, I don't get home until ten to drive her home. After the kids are in bed. But only one day a week is like that."

There were sounds of Alex stirring in the other room.

Wendy went to him. "I love you," she said softly, and touched his face.

His hand tightened around hers. "I need a pain killer. And I need to take a piss."

She found the pills the doctor had given and brought Alex a glass of water. She helped him to the bathroom. She closed the door and turned to her children.

"Poor Daddy. He's a bit sore right now. And he's grumpy because of it."

They nodded gravely.

"Maybe it's time I quit ball," Alex said, joining the family at the breakfast table. "The team is getting younger every year."

"If it's something you enjoy doing, it would be a shame to give it up," said Dad. "And you're as good a player as any of those young ones."

"And I would like to see you play at least once before you retire," said Mom.

"Are you sure you're well enough to watch the game this afternoon?" Wendy asked Alex. "Or should we head for home?"

"I told the team I'd be with them in the dugout."

They spent the rest of the day at the Montgomery Ball Park. The St. Cloud Devils lost 1-0 in the finals and Alex blamed himself. Between his discomfort and the loss of the provincial title, he had another sleepless night.

During his early days of recovery, Alex couldn't do much more than rest.

Stuart would walk into their house without knocking or ring the doorbell unceasingly if the door were locked, just to rant. "You stupid son of a bitch. You stupid son of a bitch. You had to have your sports. Now we have to carry you."

When this happened, Wendy took Joshua and Beth to the furthest bedroom and turned the music loud, so they wouldn't hear Stuart's angry voice. It was as if Alex's helplessness gave him the right to be abusive.

Who talks like this? This is not normal, having to hide in my own home.

She would do almost anything to get her children and her husband far away from Stuart; purchasing the Kennedy farm became foremost in her mind. A place where Wendy couldn't be scrutinized by Sylvia and Helen.

Wendy always waved at Ian's mother when she spotted her riding the lawn mower along the lane that led to the yard. Mrs. Kennedy, her hair tied in a bright scarf, always waved back. One afternoon, after Stuart's latest berating, Wendy drove Alex and the kids over to the yard. Two dogs and one cat came to inspect the visitors.

The house was a one-and-a-half-story structure. Wendy imagined what it could look like with a coat of paint and a good scrub.

"We're animal people," Mrs. Kennedy said cheerfully, as if she were able to read Wendy's mind. "Take a look around." She gestured to the yard.

There was a barn painted red and a fenced pasture for the horses.

"A little more than we need," Alex said to Wendy, as they watched the children exploring. "We don't have time for horses."

"Maybe Beth and Joshua would like a pony. They could take care of it." Wendy wasn't going to let a few extra buildings get in the way of her independence.

"The house is no hell."

"But no worse than the one we live in now."

"My mother always said the Kennedy land would fit in nicely with our operation."

"I want the bid put in our name, not the corporation's."

"Stuart informed me I can't buy fuck all. Those were his exact words. Fuck all."

"Well, you know where Stuart can stick it." Just the mention of Stuart's name enraged Wendy. "Maybe it's time we see a lawyer. And an accountant. To see what we can afford. I'm tired of your brother telling us what we can or cannot do."

"I don't want to rock the boat. My dislocated shoulder right now is enough of an issue with my family."

Wendy and Alex were unable to place an offer in their own name. No one bothered to explain the intricacies of the Warren Corporation, with its preferred shares and common shares. Instead, Helen Warren determined a price, wrote up a bid, and paid a visit to the lawyer representing the sale.

Wendy's hope dwindled. *Not many people liked the Warren family.*

No one said that, of course, but she sensed it.

Alex's shoulder mended over the months. At first he worked with his functioning arm, but by the time harvest was in full swing he had recuperated enough to operate a combine. He continued to allow Stuart to barge into their house, which made Wendy furious.

"Stand up to him," she begged. "Don't let him talk to you like this."

She could not understand why Alex put up with it, and when she pushed, he made excuses and became defensive.

The bids for the Kennedy property closed in October, and by early November Wendy's spirits wilted. She heard the farm had sold — to someone else.

"Maybe it's for the best." Alex tried to console her as she cried into her pillow. "Stuart said we'd bulldoze everything over anyway."

In mid-November, the Warren clan attended an event sponsored by the village of St. Cloud.

"We are not community-minded people but the supper is free and we know a bargain when we see one," Alex said to Wendy.

"Maybe it's time to volunteer for things. Instead of take, take, take. For the sake of Beth and Joshua," she added.

As they waited in the buffet line-up, Mr. and Mrs. Kennedy came toward them. Despite her disappointment, Wendy put a smile on her face, but Helen, Murray, Stuart and Sylvia Warren acted as one and turned their backs. Wendy had never seen a shunning before. It was not a discreet snub. She caught Alex's arm before he could do the same.

Mrs. Kennedy's friendly expression never wavered, but her face turned red as she walked past.

"Shame on you," Wendy said to Alex. "They can sell their farm to whoever they want." She didn't care his family overheard. She went over to Mrs. Kennedy and stammered out an apology.

"It takes a lot of guts to stand up to that crew," Mrs. Kennedy said. "I know how badly you wanted the place, dear, but we sold our farm to a young couple who want to keep horses."

"I am disappointed," Wendy admitted. "But you have to do what's right for you."

When she returned to her seat, no one — not even Alex — looked at her.

So I am to be shunned as well.

She returned from teaching piano lessons to find Stuart in her house, yelling at Alex. The kids were in the master bedroom, huddled together. Wendy closed the door behind her and comforted them, but they all could hear Stuart calling Alex "a stupid son of a bitch" over and over again.

"Tell him off," Wendy implored. "Punch him in the face. Stand up for yourself."

But Alex did not.

Wendy's rage built. *Are we not safe in our own house?* She disentangled herself from her children.

"Where are you going, Mom?" Joshua cried, panic in his voice.

"Stay here," she commanded, and marched into the kitchen.

"Get out of my house." Wendy's voice was deceptively calm.

"What did you say?"

"I said, get out of my house."

"You can't tell me what to do." Stuart took a step toward her.

Wendy did not move. "Get out of my house or I will phone the police."

"Who do you think you are? You are just a woman who came with nothing."

"And you're just a bully who's too stupid to ..."

She didn't have time to move. He grabbed her by the neck. Squeezing. In an instant, Alex pulled Stuart off and held her safe.

Wendy wriggled out of Alex's grasp. If Stuart thought he had subdued her, he was wrong.

"Get out of my house," she screamed. "I am going to charge you with trespassing and assault." She stepped closer to Stuart and this time he backed away. "I'm sick of the way you treat Alex and how you run the farm. You and your wife and your moronic parents. You stupid bully. Run to your stupid wife. Hide behind your mommy's back."

To her surprise, Stuart turned and fled. He slammed the door behind him. Wendy locked it. She could hear Joshua and Beth sobbing in the back bedroom, but she didn't go to them.

"Don't press charges," Alex pleaded. "Don't call the police."

"What a coward you are." She started to cry. Fast, furious tears spilled over her shirt and her pants, but less than a minute later she wiped them away and went to comfort Beth and Joshua.

She found her suitcase in the closet and pulled it out. She went into the children's bedrooms and tossed in clothes, toys and toiletries, careless of packing.

She phoned her parents. In a voice devoid of emotion, she told them what had happened.

"I'm coming to get you," her father said.

"No. I refuse to stay in this house one minute longer." All the time Wendy was on the phone, Alex stood beside her, his hand on her elbow.

"Do you want me to come with you?" he asked after she hung up.

When she did not answer he dropped his hand and helped the children put on their coats.

"Where we going?" Beth asked.

"You're going to have a little holiday," Alex told her.

"What about school?" Joshua asked.

"I'll phone your teacher in the morning and explain." Wendy willed her voice to be steady. "I'll help get you caught up."

Alex carried the bags and set them in the truck box. He buckled the children into their booster seats and kissed them. Wendy did not reach out to him when he came to the driver's side of the truck. She could see he was crying.

"You need to find us a place in St. Cloud," she said.

"What about me?"

"You need to decide whose family you belong to. I'm not coming back here."

Chapter 31

Paige

March 1995

Paige sat on a sofa inside the two-bedroom apartment on the fifth floor of a Prince Albert high-rise. She had three days off, no place to go and no one to be with, not even her roommate, Karen Anders. The two were employed at the same hospital, but their shifts were out of sync.

Or in sync, depending how you look at it.

It was almost like living alone.

Paige paid slightly less than half the rent, occupied the much smaller bedroom, and parked in the heated garage only when Karen took her car on a road trip.

How Leslie had laughed when she heard who Paige was living with. "Well, that's a blast from the past," she had said. "How's the old gal doing?"

"Why don't you phone her yourself and find out?" Paige had not wanted to gossip.

"Karen is one person I have no burning desire to talk to."

Karen had shown an equal disinterest in Leslie. Evidently, some friendships fizzled out.

Charlotte had been less amused than Leslie. "Don't tell Karen your secrets," she warned. "Think seriously about getting your own place."

Every once in a while Paige did think about getting her own place. She thought about moving to the United States or overseas, but she was too indecisive and apathetic to tackle the required paperwork. Besides, after years alone in a dingy basement suite and the opposite experience living in luxury with Aunt Debra, Paige preferred being high off the ground. She could never afford it alone. She needed a roommate who had money.

Three days off. And nothing to do.

She would have gone home to the farm but her parents were in Hawaii.

And her sisters?

Charlotte was too far away and Paige had never been close to Leslie. In fact, Paige was annoyed with her. The last time the four sisters had been together, Leslie bragged about her boring and routine sex life. *Bragged*! Bragged because she was getting some, and none of the other Dewhurst sisters were. Not even Wendy, who was separated from her randy little farmer.

Wendy.

Each time she witnessed her sister's overwhelming sadness, Paige's heart broke.

I could be of some comfort to Wendy.

She got up from Karen's red paisley sofa, stretched, and looked out the window. Below was a park filled with evergreen trees and dirty half-melted snow. The day threatened more snow.

At least it will freshen the landscape. Something optimistic Mom would say.

If she were planning to travel, she should get on the road soon. *Another thing Mom would say.* But instead of preparing for a trip to Milford, Paige sat, crossed her legs, and accidentally scuffed the edge of the coffee table. The carelessly tossed newspaper was open to the obituaries. Paige's eyes were automatically drawn to the faces of people recently deceased. A young and disturbingly familiar one caused her breath to catch.

Dunn.

She peered closer.

Kurt Dunn.

A sullen boy at school, who had often fallen asleep during class and woke to ridicule. No one had liked him.

Maybe a funeral that afternoon was exactly what Paige needed.

She washed her face, put on makeup and styled her blonde hair severely in a twist. In her closet was her silk blouse and dark skirt. In the grey light provided from the overcast skies, the blouse shimmered. It had been an expensive purchase. She added a little

more eye makeup and brightened her lipstick. She grinned at her reflection in the mirror. She wasn't going for Kurt Dunn. She was going for Reese.
Tarting up for a funeral.

Paige's bravado fled when she stood outside the funeral home. *Why exactly am I here?* The honest answer was curiosity, but that seemed inadequate if anyone rudely asked. She could say she was there to represent the Dewhurst family.

She pulled open the heavy wooden door and entered. She hung her coat in the vestibule and peered inside the chapel. It was not full. *An understatement.* Two dozen people. Maybe less. She hesitated, took a pew to herself and sat. She was overdressed in her skirt, blouse and polished high-heeled boots. *Well, it isn't too late to leave.* She could say to the gothic-looking funeral director standing alone at the back, "I think I made a mistake. Isn't this the Smith funeral?"

Paige half rose to escape but the family walked in from a side entrance and stood at the front. She sat down.

She would have recognized Reese's back anywhere. He and the man she assumed was his older brother stood tall in their suits beside their small and wizened parents. Behind was a woman with three children. Paige checked the obituary on the funeral card. The woman and children belonged to the oldest Dunn, not to Reese.

There was a welcome, a prayer, and a hymn sung with thin voices. Paige purposely kept her big voice subdued.

"Please be seated," said the leader in charge of the service. "I'd like to call Reese Dunn to deliver the eulogy."

Reese faced the crowd. His eyes swept over the room and stopped at Paige. A small frown flickered across his forehead.

Of course. People often say I resemble Leslie.

She shouldn't have come. It wasn't the place or the time.

Reese began to speak. His words hinted at his brother's many struggles and his too few successes. The speech was short.

There was a second hymn, followed by instructions for internment and an invitation to stay for refreshments. The service was done after a final prayer.

Paige remained at the funeral home. She sat at a table and was relieved when two young women joined her. One had dangly earrings and the other had turquoise glasses. Neither were pretty.

"Are you Kurt's new girlfriend?" asked the one with dangly earrings.

"No. A neighbour," Paige replied.

"We all thought he was going to make it this time. Then he goes and hangs himself."

Suicide! Paige had not given Kurt's cause of death any consideration. She felt ashamed. She wished she had been nicer to him when he had been in her class. She wondered if that small kindness could have made a difference.

"I lived in the same house with Kurt," said the other woman, taking off her glasses, wiping her eyes.

"I went to the same elementary school as Kurt," Paige said. "In Hatfield."

"What was he like back then?" the first woman asked. "Was he happy?"

Paige hesitated, scrambling for something positive to say, but neither woman appeared to expect a reply. They kept up a steady stream of chatter. Paige listened absently, thinking she had no right to be here. But she had started this, she would see it through.

Reese glanced her way when the family returned but he did not come to her. As she waited, she nibbled on egg salad sandwiches and matrimonial squares. It took until the room emptied and her table companions left before he walked over to her, "Do you mind if I sit?"

"Please. Do." Paige cleared her throat. "I'm here to represent the Dewhurst family. We are so sorry about your brother." *Well, that sounded awkward.* She felt her face grow warm.

"I'm guessing you're the youngest. Paige."

"Wow." Paige was delighted he recalled her name. "Do you remember how I used to follow you around?"

"I remember everything."

"Reese," said the woman with three children. "We're leaving now. The staff here will want to clean up. We'll be at the house." She stared at Paige but Reese did not make an introduction.

"Could we go somewhere to talk? I noticed there's a pub around the corner," Paige said when the woman walked away. "It shouldn't be too busy at this time."

In the vestibule Reese helped with her coat — Paige liked that

— and they stepped outside. Feathery flakes of snow were starting to fall. In silence they walked to the pub and sat across from each other in the corner.

Paige studied Reese's face as he removed his tie, balled it and stuck it in his suit pocket. His face was lean. His dirty-blonde hair was the same and only marginally shorter than it had been when he was young. There was a tiny line around his mouth.

He will be thirty-two in July.

"How did you hear about my brother?" he asked.

"Completely by accident," she replied. "As God is my witness, your last name popped out at me from the newspaper."

"Did it now?"

The phrase reminded Paige of her father and the way he spoke when he was amused. *Did it now?*

"You became one of the mysteries in our family," she said, after the waitress took their order. "That's the real reason I came to Kurt's funeral. We missed you. All of us hated Leslie for a long, long time."

Reese's face darkened with a scowl, the lines around his mouth deepened. "Leslie betrayed me."

"I know." Paige put her hand over his and squeezed. "I've been betrayed myself. I know how it feels."

"When I saw you in the chapel I thought you were her."

Paige laughed. "I'm too short and too fat." He didn't contradict her and she removed her hand. "Tell me about your brother."

Reese sighed. "Kurt has been angry for as long as I can remember. He was the most dysfunctional of my dysfunctional family — as diagnosed by my wife."

"Your wife?" Paige hadn't expected that. "Anyone I know?"

"Ex-wife. And I doubt it." Reese didn't elaborate.

"Any children?"

"I wanted a family and she wanted to make money. We could have done both, if only we had cooperated with each other. We had a body shop. It did well so we opened a second one in a different part of the city. She did the books and the hiring, I did the labour and the bossing. She bought me out when the marriage went south — and hired her boyfriend to do what I did."

"You do have bad luck with women."

Reese ignored the comment. "I invested my money and moved

into my older brother's basement. He's one Dunn who has successfully managed his life. Not all of us messed up. I suppose all of you Dewhursts are doing well."

Paige nodded. "Well enough." She felt relaxed and didn't want to spoil her mood by talking about her family. About Wendy.

They ordered a second drink. Paige glanced around as more people entered the pub, brushing snow off their coats. The empty tables filled around them and voices seemed amplified. Paige moved her chair so she was sitting beside Reese. She leaned in so she could hear him speak.

Sometime after the third drink he asked, "So who betrayed you?"

The words she had so tightly held inside, the words describing her relationship with Jorden Wilks, those words, and the anger that accompanied them, came out in a rush. The affair she once thought so romantic now appeared tarnished and sordid. All the time she spoke, Reese's blue eyes never left her face. "In high school, boys kept asking me out and I kept turning them down. I missed all the parties at the Pit. And I barely joined any university groups. None, in fact."

"Perhaps we should slow down." Reese said, when the waitress came around and Paige ordered a fourth drink.

"I want to get stinking drunk. I'll pay for your taxi home in compensation for your counselling fee." She laughed coarsely. "I lived my life for minutes with a married man. Even now I'm not sure if I'm over him. Isn't that a sad commentary on my life? Jorden betrayed me."

"He doubly betrayed his wife and children. The time he spent with you, he stole from them."

Paige turned away and the silence hung heavily between them for several minutes. Ashamed, she said, "I hadn't thought of it that way. I am a horrible person. And on the day of your brother's funeral I'm keeping you from your family."

"It's okay. I called them when you were in the bathroom. Are you hungry?"

"I could eat something."

The stores had closed and the streetlights cast a creamy glow in the dusk. The snow kept falling and the icy sidewalks made walking in high-heeled boots difficult. The drinks hadn't helped.

Paige held onto Reese's arm.

At an A & W restaurant, they ordered hamburgers with bacon and mozzarella cheese, loaded with mushrooms. Paige shared a plate of fries with Reese.

"Never once did I eat in a restaurant with Jorden. Too public."

"A teacher is supposed to protect his students, not rape them."

"Rape is too strong a word," Paige said, drawing in the deliciousness of someone being angry on her behalf.

"What would you call it?" Reese asked. "An adult taking advantage of a child."

"I was hardly a child. I pursued him. And right now I'm pursuing you." Outside the restaurant window the neon sign of a hotel beckoned.

Reese must have caught her glance because he laughed. "You Dewhurst girls certainly are forward."

"I want to stay with you tonight. I don't want to go home to my apartment." At the look on his face she added, "I'm not drunk. And I'm not a child anymore. I know what I'm doing."

His eyes held hers for a long time. "What are you doing?" he asked.

"Erasing memories," she replied. "Please."

Still he hesitated.

"Please," she repeated.

They registered as Mr. and Mrs. Reese Dunn. As soon as they entered the hotel room they embraced. *Just like in the movies.* His suit, her skirt, all tossed randomly in their haste. Her expensive silk blouse floated to the carpet. Paige pulled the pins from her hair and let it fall, loose and long.

She loved him. Had always loved him.

Paige woke shortly after midnight. She went to the bathroom and poured water from the tap into a paper cup and drank thirstily.

"What have you done now?" she said to her naked self in the mirror. She was not unhappy.

She slid back under the bedcovers and was instantly cradled in Reese's arms. He did not wake. She listened to his deep even breaths and felt comforted.

The morning light shone through the window. Paige slid out of bed to find her panties and bra. Reese was still sleeping. His face was serene in repose, the lines gone. *Poor baby. He must have been exhausted, what with his brother's suicide, the funeral, the eulogy. Me.*

"Leslie," he whispered.

The word she least wanted to hear.

He opened his eyes.

With all the dignity she could muster, Paige picked up her clothes and carried them to the bathroom. She dressed, ran her fingers through her hair and splashed water on her face, careless of her expensive blouse. When she emerged, Reese was still in bed, looking at her.

"My name is Paige."

"I know who you are. Don't go. Please. Stay."

"You called me Leslie!"

"I wasn't fully conscious. I'm sorry."

"I'm not playing second fiddle anymore. I'm worth more than that."

Quickly she pulled on her boots, her coat, her gloves. She shut the door behind her.

He had not tried to stop her. *He could have done that much. And where is my damn car? Of course. The funeral home. Several blocks away.*

A parking ticket was pinned under the wiper. She burst into tears. People walking by looked at her curiously, but what the hell. She was across from a funeral home. Tears were allowed.

Karen was eating breakfast when Paige let herself into the apartment. Dressed in her quilted, button-up housecoat, hair tousled and wearing no makeup, Karen managed to look sexy. Paige didn't know how she did it.

"Early to bed and ten hours of sleep. My skin is firm and my eyes are clear," Karen called out cheerfully, as if she could read Paige's mind. "But you, my dear, are another matter. Looks like you were on a real bender. One that lasted all night long." She peered a little closer. "Have you been crying?"

"My usual hungover look. I drank too much and I didn't want to drive."

"Very responsible of you. And the lover?"

"One of your discards."

"Which one?" Karen yelled as Paige headed down the hallway.

In the privacy of her bedroom, Paige removed her clothes. The blouse would have to be dry-cleaned. *Who knows what was on the floor of that hotel?* She placed it in a bag. She threw the rest of her clothes into the hamper. And then she allowed her brain to focus on the events of last night.

She had no idea on the number and quality of Reese's previous sex partners. She could be infected with an incurable disease. A Reese Dunn sperm might be penetrating a Paige Dewhurst egg right now. A zygote could already be present. She could be both pregnant and HIV positive.

Why hadn't Reese said anything about protection?

Why didn't I?

Because Jorden always took care of that. Almost as if he didn't trust me to be careful. Almost as if he never wanted anything to accidentally happen.

She put on her bathrobe and opened her door, glancing toward the living room. The telephone directory was sitting on the side table and Karen had moved right beside it, as if guarding it. She would be curious as to what Paige wanted.

"Do you need the bathroom?" Paige called.

"No. Go ahead," Karen called back. "Get rid of last night's evidence."

The hot shower soothed Paige. She lathered shampoo into her hair in time to the melody of an old musical. "I'm going to wash those men right out of my hair," she sang softly. She rinsed in gasp-worthy cold water.

Wrapped in her cotton terry bathrobe, a towel around her hair, she checked on her roommate. Karen was dialling the telephone.

"Hello Mom. Yes, just relaxing. How are you doing?" There was a long interval while Karen listened to the voice on the other end. She rolled her eyes at Paige.

Paige returned to her room and applied some moisturizer and foundation to her face. She put on some jeans and a pretty sweater and took out the blow dryer and styled her hair so it hung loose and casual.

"I'm going to run some errands," she said as she pulled on low-heeled boots and a hooded parka. There was a clinic at one of the strip malls down the main drag. It was a fair distance away, but the day was bright and warm and she wanted to walk off the remains of last night's liquor.

Karen waved her hand — a gesture of acknowledgment as rare as Paige's offer of itinerary.

How civilized we are to each other this morning!

As the elevator descended she thought of Reese. The memory of his hands and lips on her body was hard to dispel and for a long second she indulged in the recollection.

Yesterday she had blathered away about Jorden Wilks. All the bitterness had spilled out of her, and it was good. She had allowed herself to be honest and vulnerable. Being with Reese had felt so right.

Don't be stupid, Paige. Reese called you Leslie. Keep walking. Don't slow down.

But this was different. This was serendipitous. Finding the obituary in a newspaper she seldom read, to attend a funeral on her day off, to find Reese free from romantic entanglements and as eager as she to ...

... take a chance.

There were too many coincidences. If Reese were meant to be, it needed to unfold naturally.

There had been nothing coincidental or serendipitous about her relationship with Jorden. Every step of the way, she had planned the moments she could be with him. Paige had made Jorden happen.

Did she need to waste this beautiful Saturday sitting in a clinic?

She could drive to Milford and visit Wendy, which had been her original plan. Paige could babysit the kids so her sister could go out to the bar and show Alex she wasn't sitting at home pining.

If the clinic were full and the wait was long, she was going to let the chips fall where they may. Reese was honest and honourable. He would never do anything to hurt anyone.

He could have said no, Paige. He didn't have to take you to the hotel. If he were so honourable he would have said no.

Paige opened the clinic door and looked around. Inside were at least twenty people, waiting their turn. Some of them turned to look at her standing indecisively at the threshold.

Twenty people with coughs, snotty noses, and all sorts of contagious rashes and intestinal disorders.
Paige closed the door and walked away.
Milford it is.

Chapter 32

Wendy

March 1995

Wendy jumped at the confident knock on her apartment door. The rap didn't belong to Alex, who was tentative, or to Molly, who tapped a pattern. Wendy looked through the tiny peep hole and saw Paige. She threw open the door.

"What a surprise! You're my second unexpected visitor of the day," she cried, grabbing her sister in a hug.

"The second? Who's the first?" Paige extricated herself and looked around. "And — more importantly — where are the kids?"

"Alex dropped by and took them tobboganing on the hill by the church. He hates them cooped up all day." Wendy took Paige's coat and hung it in the closet.

"He could do something about that," Paige said, taking off her boots. "You can't live here the rest of your life, no matter how cheap the rent. I'm sure the Warrens have lots of money to invest in a house for you." She sat on the couch, tucking one leg under her.

"They only have money for the farm," Wendy said. From below, she could hear the sounds of music and tap dancing. Molly Givens was shouting instructions.

Paige stood and started tapping in her stocking feet.

Wendy smiled. "We've gotten used to the sound. In fact Beth is eager to start lessons next season. She has quite the rhythm. Joshua too. They must have inherited it from you, Paige. You were always an exceptional dancer."

"I was good, wasn't I?" Paige said, with a laugh. She stopped dancing. "Is Alex trying hard to be a decent father?"

"Alex has always been a good father. Joshua's hockey alone consists of two practices and one game each week. He hasn't missed one yet."

"How is that going over with Helen, Stuart and Sylvia?"

"I don't know and I don't care."

"I'm impressed how civilized you and Alex are, despite his family. Talking to each other like everything is normal."

Wendy turned away so Paige wouldn't see her tears. She fought them off. "A decent person would wait until a marriage settled one way or another. Not widen the gap and make a move. What kind of person would try to steal a man away from his children?"

"Who are you talking about?" Paige gasped.

"Glennie Sullivan. Sometimes I drive past her house to see if Alex's truck is there."

Paige put her arms around Wendy. "How long has this been going on?"

"Since New Year's Eve." Wendy disentangled herself from Paige's embrace and started pacing. "Alex wanted to be with us but I was so unforgiving I took his kids and went with Mom and Dad to Winnipeg. None of this would have occurred had we stayed."

She knew something was wrong as soon as she returned to Milford. A sixth sense. A dread. She had to pry it out of Molly, who averted her eyes and said, with great reluctance, "Glennie went after Alex on New Year's Eve. He left with her."

The scene played itself over and over in Wendy's mind. Alex — drunk, vulnerable and alone. Glennie, leaning into him, moulding her body to his. Teasing him. Whispering in his ear, soothing his bruised ego.

"Paige," Wendy cried. "Alex avoids things when he has done something wrong. For days after we returned, he didn't phone or visit. I'm afraid Joshua will hear about his father's indiscretion from a big-mouthed classmate. 'I know your step-mother,' a little girl might say. 'I don't have a step-mother,' Joshua might reply. In my head I hear cruel laughter. 'You will, soon,' would be the answer. When he's ten, and Alex and Glennie are married with children of their own, Joshua will ask me, 'Why does Dad like his other kids better than us?' By the time he's twelve, he'll blame me for leaving." Her voice escalated to hysteria. "Paige, no matter how the story is spun, I am the one who left the marriage. My imagination runs wild every time I think of Glennie and Alex together."

Paige held her tight until Wendy's hysteria subsided. It took several minutes.

"One step apart, leads to another step apart," she said sadly. "When I walked out on Alex, all I knew was I couldn't live in that house across from Stuart. I didn't plan on this. Is this how a marriage fails?"

"You're asking the wrong person. I've never been in a real relationship." Paige grabbed Wendy by the shoulders and shook her. "Do you want to fight for Alex or do you want this Glennie person to become your children's wicked stepmother?"

"I don't know how to fight. Molly thinks I should dress up in my sluttiest, go to the bar and flirt with other guys. 'Get Alex a little excited,' she said."

"That's the exact idea I had in mind."

"But I don't want my children hearing about me from other kids at school. Kids talk, you know. Even the little ones. Joshua asked me the other day, 'Mom, what are hooker boots? Benjie said his mom has a pair of hooker boots.' And last week he said, 'Kelly called the teacher a douche bag, and had to stand in a corner for the rest of the art class. Mom, what's a douche bag?'"

Paige laughed. "Thank God I don't have kids. I would be a terrible mother. I am such a selfish bitch and I talk like a prostitute." She paused. "Just out of curiosity, what did Alex say to you about Glennie?"

"He doesn't know I know. But Molly confronted him and what he said was, 'Glennie likes my company. My wife doesn't.'"

"Tell Alex you want him back."

"Except now I have two unresolved issues, the second worse than the first."

Over the sounds below of an advanced tap class in progress, Wendy could hear the distinctive thump of several feet coming up the stairs. Her family had returned.

"Kids are home!" she cried, throwing open the door.

Beth's face was red and her nose was dripping. Joshua was behind her, holding onto Alex's hand which he immediately dropped as he rushed past Wendy and into Paige's outstretched arms.

"Auntie Paige!" the children cried with enthusiasm, hugging

the aunt who kept herself present in their lives, and for that Wendy was grateful.

"Hello Paige." Alex stood awkwardly in the doorway. Wendy couldn't tell if he was happy or not to see his sister-in-law. He looked damp and cold in his work coveralls.

"Guess who was at the hill," shouted Joshua in excitement. "Ernie Westcott!"

"Ernie Westcott!" cried Wendy in mock excitement. "I bet you two had lots of fun."

"Who's Ernie Westcott?" asked Paige.

"He's my best friend at school," said Joshua.

Wendy glanced at Alex. When they separated, he had made no effort to find his family a place to live in St. Cloud, so she and the children had moved to Milford. Joshua had to switch schools mid-year and Ernie Westcott had been the first to welcome him. Alex's only contribution to his family's welfare had been his truck. The farm corporation immediately bought him a new one.

Wendy's heart hardened at the memory.

"Alex, why don't you stay here for supper?" said Paige. "I'll make everyone's favourite, mac and cheese. We can play board games after."

Typical of Paige to make things happen. Wendy didn't know if she should be annoyed or relieved.

"I don't know. I'm pretty wet. I couldn't find my Ski-Doo suit."

"I packed it away in a box last spring," said Wendy, stripping the kids down to their underwear. "You've been without it all winter?"

"Yeah, I have."

"Poor baby," Paige mouthed to Wendy behind Alex's back. Out loud she said, "I'm sure Wendy can find you something warm to put on." She pinched Beth on the bum and chased her and Joshua down the hallway. "Is it too early to give the kids a bath and dress them in their jammies?" she called back.

"Knock yourself out."

"Is it okay with you if I stay awhile?" Alex asked.

"Yes. We need to talk about the children." Wendy motioned for Alex to follow her to their living room. "Beth acted up in preschool last Wednesday. Slapped a little girl who took her chair."

"Well, good for Beth. Do you mind if I get out of these clothes?

I'll cover up in a blanket if you want."

"No, I'll get you my dressing gown." As Wendy passed the kids' room, she could hear Paige singing silly songs over the sound of the tub being filled. She admired how easily Paige orchestrated time for her to be alone with Alex.

All I have to do is ask Alex to move in with us. But what good is that? He hasn't changed.

Molly, in her reluctant role as spy, reported to Wendy last weekend that Alex had been out to the bar with Glennie. "I told her to leave Alex alone while he was trying to fix his marriage, and the polite version of her reply was 'it's none of your business. All's fair in love and war.'"

"Maybe when you're sixteen," Wendy had replied angrily. "But Alex has children."

"She's desperate to hold on to him."

Wendy had a sudden chill. "Glennie wouldn't get pregnant on purpose, would she?"

"I wouldn't put it past her. She *is* over thirty," Molly had said. "Don't hold on to your pride too long, kid."

If only it was my pride that keeps us apart.

Wendy returned with her housecoat and handed it to Alex. She watched him peel off his damp shirt and jeans. She was sure his boxers were uncomfortable too, but he left them on. He made a little pirouette in the feminine housecoat and she laughed in spite of herself.

Damn my pride. All I have to do is ask him to stay.

If only she could remove the stink of Glennie from her imagination.

"I was hoping you and Alex would be back together by now," Dad said two weeks later, after he and Mom returned from their vacation in Hawaii. "This has been going on too long. You and Alex have to come to some sort of decision. This limbo way of living is not healthy for Joshua and Beth."

"Dad and I want to pay for a marriage counsellor," Mom said. "We'll watch the kids."

"It's our gift to you," Dad said. "We've made a first appointment. If you don't like this fellow, we'll find you another."

"What if Alex doesn't want to go?"

"If Alex doesn't want to go, that will tell you something. Then you can ask to be guided through a divorce."

Divorce! Wendy's eyes filled with tears. *Shared custody of Beth and Joshua.* Her children, unprotected without her; Alex oblivious to the hatred his family felt for them.

Because divorce was how it would turn out. Alex didn't believe in counselling. He said it was a waste of time and money.

Chapter 33

Elsie

April 1995

One advantage to being fifty-three was being able to see the big picture. To know what was important in life and to mark time — not in seconds, minutes, or hours, but in decades, generations, and lifetimes. A little kindness here and there paid big dividends over the long haul. Elsie acknowledged she had not always been kind. She knew now how important it was to keep one's mouth shut. Not to predict. Not to criticize. Not to judge.

I have been wrong on occasion.

It was also important to not be quiet. To shout truth from the housetops. To be bold.

Sometimes speaking up is as important as keeping one's big fat mouth shut.

When her predicted-to-fail Warren marriage fell apart, the self-satisfied "I told you so" did not drip from her lips. Sorrow outweighed any other emotion. No one was more surprised at her reaction than Elsie herself.

Seven years ago she had spoken privately and passionately to Dan. "Alex is selfish, arrogant and opinionated. I hate him."

Alex was still selfish, arrogant and opinionated, but Elsie did not hate him. Not one little bit.

She told Dan she was driving to Hatfield. And that had been her plan — up until the moment when the grid road met the highway and she paused for several seconds at the stop sign. She turned northward, to the Warren Family Farm. To Alex.

The day was sunny and frigid. The fields around her were

frozen, and covered with a fresh blanket of unexpected spring snow. It was beautiful but Elsie's thoughts were not on the scenery as she sped along the highway. She was frightened by her bravado.

What am I going to say?

She had not phoned ahead. *Alex might not even be home.* She lifted her foot off the gas ever so slightly to rethink her course of action. Did she have a plan?

"God, give me the words," she said aloud.

The words for what? To encourage Alex to fight, or to let go without vindictiveness? Would his life be better without Wendy, without his children? Would his life be easier if he married someone else?

No. No. No.

"God, give me the strength to accept with grace and humility whatever happens," Elsie prayed out loud.

Inside the family compound, three houses spied on each other. No one came to their front doors to wave a greeting. No dog barked in warning. It was eerily quiet.

Elsie hesitated inside her car. *Are the Warrens a violent kind of people? Do they have guns ready and cocked by the back door?*

Dan did not know where she was. If something happened to her, if she vanished off the face of the earth, Dan would not know where to start looking.

Her imagination was running away with her common sense.

You've come this far. Don't chicken out now, Elsie.

She went straight to the large shop that dominated the yard and knocked on the door. Alex answered. He looked flabbergasted when she entered, and stood stone-faced and defensive, no doubt waiting for a round of criticism and attack. Stuart ran off muttering something about getting their mother. Elsie would have laughed had it not been so serious. *Such big boys, unable to stand up for themselves.*

"Can we talk somewhere privately?" Elsie said to Alex.

"The house."

Two minutes later she sat across from Alex in front of the picture window. He offered Elsie a can of beer and she accepted, even though it was still morning and she almost never drank beer.

She hadn't seen him for six months. He looked as sad and as unkempt as the house. His face was guarded. He was waiting for her to speak.

"You and Wendy belong together," Elsie said. "Dan and I want to pay for a counsellor. Please think about our offer before you turn it down. You owe it to yourself. Don't leave any stone unturned."

"I have made so many mistakes." Alex looked away.

"You have married the most forgiving of my daughters. She loves you." Elsie's eyes filled. "I have grown to love you too."

Alex stood suddenly. Helen was approaching. She looked formidable, her face made ugly by her anger. *Such a cold woman.* Every time Elsie had tried to be friends she had been firmly and unmistakably rebuffed.

"Please don't be too proud." There was more Elsie wanted to say but Alex's mother entered the house without invitation.

"Is this woman badgering you?" Helen asked Alex.

"No. We are having a private conversation."

Helen crossed her arms.

"I've said all I need to say," said Elsie. "I'm leaving." She grabbed Alex, hugged him tightly, and walked away.

There was nothing left to do but pray.

Alex, possibly inspired by some divine intervention, accepted the lifeline that was offered.

Chapter 34

Wendy

April 1995

*W*hose idea was it, to travel together to the city, saving gas, saving money? Alex was polite when he picked Wendy up at her parents' farm, but during the drive to Saskatoon they barely said ten words to each other. Not that they were angry. At least, Wendy wasn't angry. She was scared.

The marriage counsellor's office was in an old three-story mansion along the riverbank. A receptionist ushered them into a lamplit room where they sat apart on the same couch and waited.

A man entered the room.

"Hello." He closed the door gently. "I'm Richard Carey. You can call me Rick." He sat on the overstuffed chair facing them and took off his glasses. His eyes were dark and piercing but he had a friendly face. "How do you want me to help you?"

"I need help deciding what to do," said Wendy. "We have been living apart since November."

"I want to fix our marriage," Alex said.

"I want that too," Wendy added quickly. "But there are people in the way."

"Who is in the way?" Rick asked.

Wendy hesitated. This would be the first time she acknowledged she knew about Alex's affair. Once it was said aloud, there was no taking it back. She forged ahead. "A woman named Glennie. And at least three members in Alex's family."

"As long as these people are in Alex's life, you can't be married to him? Is that what you're saying?"

Is that what I'm saying?

"You really want to make an ultimatum?" Rick asked. "Be very careful now."

Wendy hesitated.

"Glennie was never a threat," Alex said.

"How can you say that!" Wendy turned to him.

"She means nothing to me."

"She sure means something to me!" Wendy looked at the counsellor. "She's his high school sweetheart. She's his 'booty call' since we separated."

"It's over," Alex said.

"Over until when?" Wendy cried. "Over until you need someone to tell you how great you are? Over until I'm too tired to make love, or your brother calls you pussy-whipped and you need to feel like a man?" Wendy turned to the counsellor. "I won't rest easy until that woman is married with three kids and lives on another continent."

Alex laughed.

"It wouldn't be so funny if I had a past lover who was obsessed with me." Wendy was furious with Alex. To the counsellor she said, "I don't have any lovers in my past."

"Why did you laugh just now?" Rick asked Alex.

"I thought she was trying to be funny."

"Sarcasm can hide a lot of hurt. Take Wendy's hand and listen to her when she tells you things."

Wendy glared. "Don't think I'm so easily charmed."

"Let's talk about trust," said the counsellor. "It's the most important foundation in a marriage. Alex, take her hand."

Rick's voice was soothing. As he talked, Alex took Wendy's hand and held it tight, even when she tried to pull it away.

Why didn't he come with me when I left that night? He should have insisted. We wouldn't be here now, if he had.

"Trust is hard to recover and it could take years," Rick said. "There's no room for backsliding. But without trust, your marriage is doomed."

Wendy realized he had been talking for several minutes and she had barely heard a word.

"I trust Wendy," Alex said. "Without her, I do bad things."

"Tell her," ordered the counsellor. "Look into her eyes."

Alex turned to Wendy. Reluctantly she allowed her eyes to meet his. That cockiness she used to love was there. That arrogance. But as they studied each other, something started to dissolve ever so subtly in his features. Beneath was a misery, a loneliness, a longing. Wendy's eyes filled with tears.

"I need you," Alex said. "Without you, I fall apart. I do bad things."

"That's quite a responsibility you've handed her, to be in charge of your moral compass. You may want to reflect on that."

Rick made a few notes and closed his book. "I'll see you back in two weeks. Monday morning at eleven."

They stopped for lunch at a fast food restaurant, oh so careful how they spoke to each other, as if they were strangers. Back at the Dewhurst farm, Alex helped Beth with her coat and rubber boots and hoisted her into the car seat.

"Are we fixed?" the little girl asked, her face optimistic.

Wendy's heart contracted.

"Not yet, darling." Alex looked at Wendy over Beth's head. "It takes time."

"Did you have fun with Grandma?" Wendy asked.

"We folded laundry and made cookies in her new kitchen. I'm bringing some home for Joshua."

"Laundry or cookies?" asked Alex, giving her a kiss.

"Daddy! Cookies, of course."

Two weeks later, Wendy again brought Beth to the Dewhurst farmhouse while Joshua was in school. Wendy waited for Alex so they could drive to the city together.

"That's an optimistic sign," said Mom. "At least you're not wanting to kill each other."

"Yet," said Wendy.

She wanted to discuss Glennie with the counsellor acting as mediator. Wendy had a lot of things to say on the subject.

Glennie was not giving up without a fight. It was almost as if she sensed Alex was slipping out of her hands. She had arrived uninvited at the Warren farm with a picnic basket full of food for the workers. Alex told Wendy all about it the day it happened and how he dealt with the situation by walking away.

"Walking away? That's not dealing with it!" *Be a man. Make yourself clear.*

Sitting on the couch in the dimly lit room, Wendy and Alex attempted to unravel Glennie's importance.

"She shows up wherever Alex happens to be. She's pathetic," Wendy said. "And you, Alex, take advantage of her. Shame on you."

"I told her I was working on my marriage."

Wendy suspected Sylvia and Stuart were aiding and abetting Glennie, in the hopes of forever getting rid of Wendy, the troublesome wife number one.

"I told Glennie to go home."

"And did she?" Wendy asked. "Or did she clean your house and do your laundry?" *And warm your bed?* But she didn't say her last thought out loud. She was sure Alex was sincere about fixing their marriage. To Rick, Wendy said, "The Warrens would be happy if I vanished and took the kids with me."

"I know they appear hard to Wendy," Alex told the counsellor.

"Appear?" Wendy turned to Alex. "They are hard people. And you never stood up to them for me."

"I *am* standing up to them. I'm taking time off to come here. Isn't that a first step?" Alex held her hand and started massaging her palm. He didn't let go even when she pulled.

"I always wondered why they didn't like me." Wendy surrendered her hand to his. "I always …"

"It's because you have a backbone."

"Let her talk," Rick said. "No interruptions."

Wendy started with the house she and Alex had been forced to live in, and the fight over the garden tractor, and how no problem was so small it couldn't be magnified. Everything seemed so trite. "If I hadn't had to share my life with Sylvia and Helen, perhaps my relationship with my in-laws might have been manageable."

She started talking about Stuart. How he would burst into their house, his behaviour becoming more and more outrageous — his yelling, his name calling, the time he grabbed Wendy by the throat and squeezed.

"There is no turning back on that." Wendy was angry at herself for not leaving before that had happened, right after the incident with Joshua and Stuart.

Alex hung his head. "I let you down."

In June they discussed Alex's relationship with his family. At first he tried to shrug off the events as nothing serious and he laughed at himself, but the counsellor prodded. "What happened next? How did you feel?" And it started to come out. Alex told stories about his mother's quick and humiliating temper, his brother's ridicule, his passive father, his resentful sister.

Wendy thought the counsellor pushed too much, even when Alex broke down in tears, but Rick didn't stop. Wendy had seen Alex cry before. Three times. He was emotional at the births of his two children, and the third time when she was leaving him. But these tears were different. These were angry.

"We have had a breakthrough," Rick said.

"Because I cried?" Wendy could tell Alex was embarrassed.

"You allowed yourself to be vulnerable. And you trusted you would still be loved by this woman."

"Does this mean we're fixed?" Alex asked, using Beth's term.

"It means we are getting closer," the counsellor said. "See you in two weeks."

"I have something I want to show you," Alex said.

"Is it a farm? A farm for us to live on?"

Alex's face fell a little. "No. Not a farm, but a house in Milford. The kids need a yard. And you need a garden."

"And what about you Alex? What do you need?"

Alex was slow to answer, but his words were the ones Wendy most wanted to hear. "I need you. And Joshua and Beth. I'm hoping soon you will ask me to move in with you. But if that doesn't happen, you still need a house to live in."

"Why don't we go on a date and look at what you want to show me? I'll get someone to stay with the kids."

"A date? Just you and me? With flirting and all that?"

"I don't know about 'all that.' But yes, a date."

"Rick said we should do fun things together. Sex is fun."

"He also said not to rush into anything. And isn't that how we got into trouble the first time?"

"If you mean the trouble that resulted in Joshua, I say ..."

Wendy put her hand over his mouth.

If only she could capture these carefree moments in a bottle, and take them out when she needed a reminder how to be happy.

There was no first date. They took the children along. The house had high ceilings, cream-coloured walls, three bedrooms, two-and-a-half baths, and an unfinished basement. Wendy especially liked the bright and airy kitchen with the pantry in the corner.

This house is too nice for me.

Through the back patio doors she could see Beth and Joshua had discovered a sandbox full of toys.

There was also a small garden with little wooden stakes marking rows. Seedlings were emerging.

"Who would plant a garden if they knew they were moving before they could harvest it?" Wendy asked, stepping outside on the deck.

"Somebody like you." Alex put his arm around her shoulders. They turned to look out the picture window in the living room. The realtor was talking on a large portable car phone.

"Do you like the house?" Alex asked.

"I do, but it looks expensive. How can you afford it?"

"I've worked full-time on the farm for twelve years. It's time I took some money out."

"Is it going to be a huge problem?"

"In my family, everything is a huge problem. Going to the counsellor opened my eyes. This is a first step. If they don't like me buying a house in Milford, maybe it's time I take my share out of the company and start fresh. Farming alone. Other people do it. Your dad does."

"Mom, mom," Joshua cried, in great excitement. He pointed out the living room window to a boy riding his bike on the sidewalk. "It's Ernie Westcott!" He opened the door and called out, "Hey Ernie!"

"That surely seals the deal if Ernie Westcott lives on this street," Wendy said to Alex. By the puzzled look on his face, she could tell he didn't remember who Ernie was. "Never mind." She kissed him affectionately.

"Are we going to live happily ever after?" Beth asked in her high voice.

"As your Auntie Paige would say, 'As God is my witness.'" Alex scooped the little girl in his arms.

"Happily ever after. Nobody can promise that," Wendy said. "It's just in fairy tales." She hadn't meant to be cruel. She felt ashamed at herself for the look of disappointment in Beth's eyes, but it was important to be realistic. Until the house transaction was finalized, every "i" dotted and "t" crossed, she wasn't going to hope too hard. Helen and Stuart could find a way to wrench it out of her grasp.

Truth was, Alex wasn't going to change overnight. For all his bravado, he had a long way to go in standing up to his family. Wendy had to prepare herself for an occasional backward slide. She had to be strong for both of them.

Not to mention Glennie, lurking in the shadows.

Chapter 35

Charlotte

August 1995

The landmarks were the same.

A slight dip in the road, the rockery to mark the Gladstone driveway, a double row of evergreens surrounding the Dewhurst farm and the long lane up the slight incline leading to the house. As Charlotte drove into the yard she could see her mother rising stiffly in the flower bed at the approach of a strange vehicle.

Charlotte parked the car and jumped out. "I see you have been giving the flowers a haircut." She enveloped her mother in a hug.

"And I didn't expect your arrival until late afternoon." Mom stepped out of Charlotte's arms. "You must have left Winnipeg in the wee hours of the morning." Her face was tanned and her blonde hair was laced with silver; she looked healthy and happy.

"I did. Wide-eyed at three and couldn't get back to sleep. I left a note for Leslie saying goodbye."

"You couldn't sleep?"

Charlotte cursed herself. She had forgotten her mother's worry. "Just those middle of the night irrational thoughts. Everyone gets them. Wow, look at your flowers."

The distraction was successful. She followed Mom along the paving-stone path, feigning interest at the newest plant additions as her mother listed Winnipeg Parks Rose, Globe Thistle, and Hosta. At the back of the house, sunflowers towered above the rows of vegetables.

"I planted some new varieties of cherries," Mom said as they ventured off the grass and into the dirt. "In a few years they should start to produce. And I had a great crop of raspberries. Enough for me and Wendy to freeze and make jam." She gestured to the canes. There were a few raspberries left hanging. Charlotte popped a couple in her mouth and thought of the wealth that went undeclared in a prairie garden. In Toronto, the cost of a tiny basket of tasteless raspberries was exorbitant. And potatoes! She remembered digging potatoes and throwing away the smallest; now they were considered gourmet by epicures.

"So what brings you home?" Mom asked, twisting off two heads of Buttercrunch lettuce. "You never said over the telephone. Just taking a break?"

"I'm taking time off from the station to consider my options. A sabbatical. Sort of."

"Really? A sabbatical already? I thought you loved what you're doing."

"I did. I do. But people change. And one does gets stale after a while anyway."

"Does one?" Mom gave Charlotte deliberate scrutiny. "Are you getting stale?"

"No." Charlotte's answer was short and did not invite discussion. "Where's Dad?"

"He went to Hatfield to pick up a part for the swather. He'll be back soon for lunch. Are you hungry?"

"I am." Charlotte followed Mom into the house and tossed off her sandals by the mud room entrance. Her feet were gritty from the garden. She wiped them off with a rag.

"Come see what's new," Mom said.

Charlotte stood, aghast, at the threshold. The comfy old-fashioned kitchen of her childhood was gone. The new cupboards were white, gleaming, plasticized laminate. The ceramic tile on the countertops added a hint of blue. The appliances matched the cupboards. It was pristine.

"Do you like it?" Mom asked, as she washed the lettuce in the deep white sink.

"Thirty thousand dollars," Dad said, before Charlotte could reply. "We did it this spring."

"The discussion of renovation. Now I remember." Charlotte hugged him.

"It was supposed to have been installed while we were in

Hawaii," Mom said. "But it was delayed until we got back. Inconvenient. But I managed."

Dad pointed out the storage areas, the bookcase where Mom displayed her cookbooks, the blue-and-white gingham cushions on the bench. A desk. The telephone.

"Ooh, cordless," Charlotte teased.

"Keith's sister Roxanne designed it," Mom said. "The kitchen, not the telephone." She removed a loaf of homemade bread from the cupboard and began to slice it.

"And I suppose you had the money saved ahead of time." Charlotte found some plates in the cupboard and started setting the table — which wasn't a table at all but part of something Mom called "the island."

"Pretty much," Dad said. "I don't like to borrow money if I can help it. How was Winnipeg? How are the Hamiltons?"

"How is Kim coping with the return of Rod?" Mom asked. "I think he was recently released from jail."

"Have two years passed already? Keith didn't say a word about his father."

"He wouldn't," said Dad. "He and Kim are reticent about personal affairs. I like that. It's none of our business."

Mom placed sliced ham, lettuce, cheese, cucumbers, mayonnaise and various mustards on the island counter.

Charlotte reached for the bread, but stopped when she noticed her father's bent head.

"Thank you, Lord, for this food, and bless the hands that prepared it. In Jesus' name. Amen."

"Amen." Charlotte couldn't remember the last time she had prayed.

"You haven't said anything about the impending arrival of our new grandchild," Mom said, assembling her sandwich.

"News to me," Charlotte replied. "Wendy and Alex sure didn't waste any time."

Mom and Dad looked at each other.

"Not Wendy and Alex." Mom stood and went to the sink.

"Wow. You would think Leslie would have mentioned that bit of news while I was there."

There was silence.

Charlotte's eyes widened. "Paige? Paige is pregnant? I didn't know she was seeing anyone."

"We didn't either," Dad said.

"What are the neighbours going to say?" Mom said, wringing her hands. "First Wendy and now Paige."

"None of the neighbours are as judgmental as you like to think," Dad interrupted.

"Your mother will have something to say," Mom retorted.

Dad sighed. "I'm sure she will."

"She still brings up the early arrival of Joshua Warren."

"And I am still apologizing for her bad manners," Dad said. He turned to Charlotte. "My mother is of another generation. Sharing her opinion is how she copes."

Charlotte managed to change the subject to the results of the recent provincial election, a safer topic under the circumstances. Inside she was reeling.

Paige is pregnant? Not that married creep from her past?

After lunch, she located Paige's phone number in Mom's address book stored logically in the top drawer of her new desk, and took the cordless telephone upstairs to her room. After five rings the recorded voice of Karen Anders transported Charlotte unpleasantly back to high school.

"It's me," she told the answering machine. "I'm at the farm for a few weeks. Paige, call me."

Charlotte woke to the zoom of a plane flying low over the house. She resisted getting out of bed until a familiar creak on the stairs indicated she was not the only one stirring. It was barely five in the morning, the sound of the plane ebbed and flowed. She threw a wrap over her chemise and headed down to the kitchen.

"Good morning," Dad said brightly, as he brewed some coffee. "The Gladstones are spraying for caterpillars on their canola. I checked our crop a few days ago to see if we have an infestation and we don't, but I'll have to check again. The trouble is, the helpful insects are killed with pesticides too."

"So what do you do if we have caterpillars?"

"Well, here's the crunch. The spray is expensive, sometimes more costly than the expected damage. The stressful part is to determine if and when to spray to minimize the losses."

"And if we don't?"

"The caterpillars eat the seed pod and the seeds don't develop."

"Did you sleep well?" Mom asked, entering the kitchen. She was dressed in her work clothes.

"Like a rock. Until the plane woke me."

"I'm glad to get an early start," Mom said. "Today I'm doing dills." She went to the basement and returned with a cardboard box filled with wide-mouthed quart sealer jars. She filled the sink with hot soapy water and started washing them.

"Remember the children's fable? The ants and the grasshopper?" Charlotte teased, watching her mother work.

"I do. And don't for a minute think you're not going to help." She handed Charlotte a pair of garden gloves and two plastic tubs. "After breakfast you can pick the cucumbers. Pick all of them, including the big ones. I can make relish later."

Fifteen minutes later, Charlotte found herself outside, crouched at the start of a long row of vines. The dew was still on the leaves. As she tossed the cucumbers into the first tub, she listened to the zoom of the plane and wondered how far the poison spray could drift. Dad said the plane was further away than it sounded. At least six miles.

Bees buzzed industriously. The vines were covered with little yellow flowers in various stages of maturity and Charlotte was careful not to get stung. Princess the cat lazed in the shade of a row of beets, her eyes narrow slits of contentment. In the August garden, amid sounds both man-made and natural, the tightness in Charlotte's chest dissipated.

During last night's conversation, she had been less than honest with her parents about why she was home. Her cheerfulness had been forced and if they noticed they had not pried. Perhaps they suspected a failed love affair and Charlotte's despondency about turning thirty. Two of her sisters were married with children, and apparently Paige was going to have a baby. That left Charlotte doubly bereft.

Manless and childless.

And now jobless.

Her typically steadfast sense of humour deserted her.

Bullied. Pushed out. Shamed. Disgraced. Humiliated. Call it what you will, Charlotte was on an imposed sabbatical.

She hosted — at least she used to — a little radio show called

Charley's Time, thirty minutes once a week, of talking to and about the next big name or group in the greater Toronto area. Mostly about musicians, but not limited to, Charley's Time had been on the air for seventeen months and had gained a loyal following. Charlotte did her own research, wrote her own interview questions, entertained effectively and — when necessary — ad-libbed brilliantly.

Six months ago, the station manager asked if she were ready to take on a summer intern. Charlotte said she was. It was a common practice and was, in fact, how she herself had come to be hired. She was part of the process that shortlisted five prospects, but the intern chosen, Charlene Faulkner, was not her first, second, or third choice. Something about Charlene rankled, and it wasn't because she was too pretty.

Charlene began her internship in April. She was supposed to assist everyone during her four months, but she was especially attentive to Charlotte.

It took a few weeks before Charlotte sensed something was wrong. At first she wondered if she were imagining lost memos and miscommunications, but in June her interview notes with names, dates and other pertinent information were misplaced within minutes of going on air.

"I left them on your desk," Charlene insisted. "I had you initial my corrections."

An inferior copy was handed to Charlotte ten minutes into the show. Although the show proceeded without a hitch, Charlotte had been rattled. The material she wanted showed up hours later underneath some books on her desk. She was sure the books had not been there during her frantic search.

Suspicions aroused, she became more careful, yet files, notes and contracts disappeared and reappeared. Meetings were scheduled, then rescheduled. Charlotte was stood up. She stood others up.

Paranoid, she imagined phone calls she didn't receive. Over and over again, in her mind, she conceived scenarios of deception.

"I'd like to speak to Charlotte. I'm sorry. Charlene is it? My secretary must have written your name incorrectly. I'm phoning to ...."

It wouldn't be hard to be victimized if one was trusting and naive. But try as she might, she couldn't prove anything. Charlene always managed to elude detection. In fact, she was able to exploit Charlotte's increasing incompetence.

Why hadn't Charlotte gone to the station manager, Bill McKnight, and said, "Our intern is trying to sabotage me." Was it pride? Was it shame, to be in the position she found herself? Embarrassment?

Bill had been her friend and mentor for years. She admired and respected him immensely.

All the "should haves" kept running through her mind: should have gathered evidence, should have taken notes with times and dates, should have recorded conversations, should have had witnesses.

Oh, the wisdom of twenty-twenty hindsight.

What she had done was confront her intern privately and angrily. How easily she was baited. How easily she played right into Charlene's hands.

Bill had called Charlotte into his office. Apparently, the confrontation was the last straw in a long list of Charlotte's unprofessional behaviour toward Charlene, who had documented that particular conversation, along with Charlotte's other acts of increased hostility.

Charlene claimed Charlotte had never liked her — which was true. She claimed Charlotte was a micro-manager, always double and triple-checking — which was also true. She claimed Charlotte called her a bitch — which wasn't true.

She had called Charlene an opportunist.

"Take some time off." Bill's craggy face was formidable. "It's been over a year since you took even two days." At the look on her face he said, "I'm not asking you, I'm telling you. You need a holiday. You work too hard."

"What about my show?"

"No one is indispensable, Charlotte. It's as good a lesson to learn now as later. The show can go on without you."

"Are you firing me?"

"Firing you? No. We'll keep in touch."

Charlotte spent the first three days waiting for the phone to ring, for Bill to say, "It's a mistake. Come back." On the fourth day she contemplated her options, one of which was to quit. Burn her bridges. Common sense stopped her. On the fifth day she packed her bags, loaded her car, and headed west. She had taken her time driving, trying to lose herself. She had not phoned ahead. Not until she reached Winnipeg.

Ten days had passed since the meeting with Bill.

By the time Charlotte finished picking the cucumbers, the plane had disappeared, presumably back to the airstrip where such crop-dusters refuelled. Mom had the house tidied, the lunch prepped, the dill washed, the garlic peeled, the canning jars, lids and rings sterilized and hot in the oven.

Standing side by side, elbows bumping companionably, Charlotte and her mother scrubbed the cucumbers to remove any dirt, and trimmed off the blossom ends. The brine simmered in a large heavy cooking pot on the stove burner. When the cucumbers were all cleaned and organized in Mom's system of large, medium and small, the brine was brought to boil.

Dad came in and poured himself a cup of coffee. He watched as Mom expertly stuffed cucumbers into a hot jar and Charlotte poured in the brine, placed the lid on the jar and screwed the ring tight.

"Not too tight," Mom said, demonstrating. "Otherwise I can't get it off later."

"People at church talk about your mother's pickles," Dad said to Charlotte.

"I hope my help doesn't change the quality," Charlotte joked.

"They're a little different each year. But always good," Mom bragged.

"Reese Dunn paid us a visit a while ago." Dad's voice was casual.

"Really? Reese Dunn after all these years? The last time I saw him was 1983, the summer I graduated from high school." *The summer I left home for good, although I didn't know it at the time.*

"Said he was in the area."

"Maybe he was hoping Leslie's marriage failed. Maybe he wanted to see if she was available for a second go-round," Charlotte said.

"He asked about each of you," Mom said.

"Well, Reese always was diplomatic. I'll give him that. So, how does he look?"

"Like a man," said Dad. "Capable."

"He lives in Prince Albert," Mom said. "We told him Paige lives there too."

A glimmer of curiosity ignited in Charlotte. *Maybe Reese would be up for a reconciliation. Maybe he no longer holds me partially responsible for Leslie's deception.* "I hope you got his number."

"We didn't ask," said Mom. "But I'm sure it's easy enough to find."

"Why don't we rent a cabin at Waskesiu while Charlotte's here?" Dad rinsed out his empty coffee cup and put it into the new dishwasher. "It's a convenient location for Paige and Wendy to meet us. Maybe Leslie and Keith would drive from Winnipeg. What do you think?"

"I don't know, Dan," Mom replied, stuffing cucumbers into a jar. "I heard those cabins are booked months in advance. I don't think you'll have much luck."

Dad gave Charlotte a wink over Mom's head. "It's worth a try anyway."

Mom and Charlotte picked peas later in the morning and shelled them after lunch in the shade on the east side of the house. In the early evening, while Mom was blanching the peas and packing them into pint-sized bags, Charlotte escaped from her mother's inexhaustible energy of canning and freezing, and went for a run, something she had started doing in Toronto to alleviate stress.

As she jogged along the gravel road toward the Gladstone driveway, Lila pulled out of her yard in a shiny SUV, stopped, and rolled down her window. "Charlotte, dear," she said. "So nice to see you again."

"Hello, Mrs. Gladstone," Charlotte replied.

"Oh my. Lila. Please." She laughed. "My eldest, Conor, is interested in journalism. That's your career, isn't it? We should have a talk about what it all entails. How long are you home?"

"Two weeks." *Hopefully not longer.*

Lila looked at her watch. "I'd better go. I have to chair a meeting at the church in twelve minutes. And there's a storm brewing in the west. I hope it's not a bad one. You don't want to be out too long."

Charlotte turned around. Sure enough, dark thunderheads were brooding behind her back.

"You get yourself home," Lila ordered. "You look wonderful," she added before she drove away.

No one can say 'dear' and 'you look wonderful' like Lila, Charlotte thought with amusement.

Thunder rumbled as the dark clouds approached. The wind increased as she raced up the driveway. Dad was outside with Mom, taking down the plants hanging in baskets around the veranda.

"We were starting to worry about you," he said. "The temperature is dropping. I hope it doesn't hail. I'm going to park the vehicles in the shed."

Within minutes, the trees and shrubs started twisting with the wind. Mom, muttering something about a power surge, ran into the house to unplug the appliances.

Charlotte headed upstairs to watch the storm approach from one of the westward facing windows. There was an opening in the evergreen shelter belt where she could see the horizon.

An electrical storm in the country is so much more beautiful than one in the city.

The yard light turned on as the sky darkened. Lightning flashed and thunder boomed.

"Get away from the window," Mom scolded.

Charlotte obliged for a few seconds but returned, unable to resist. The rain was an anxious patter that accelerated in pace until it came in sheets. The driveway became rivulets. The yard light shut off.

"Power's out," Mom called.

Suddenly, car lights gleamed, reflected in the slick surface of the lane.

"Someone's here," Charlotte announced, scurrying down the stairs in the darkness and flinging open the door.

It was Paige, drenched from running the short distance from her car. "Greetings and salutations," she said, stepping inside and dripping on the mat.

"Goodness!" Mom said. "Imagine driving in this storm!"

"It wasn't so bad until the last bit. I could see the black cloud right above our farm. I knew I was driving into something, but I didn't want to stop. I kept telling myself the car is the safest place to be in an electric storm."

As she struggled to remove her wet jacket, her zipper stuck, her t-shirt pulled up and Charlotte saw Paige's thickening waist.

"Well, you're safe now," Mom said. "How long can you stay?"

"Less than one day. I start the night shift tomorrow. I'll leave right after supper." Paige turned to Charlotte. "I got your message. Share a room with me?"

"Gladly."

In the candlelight, Mom served peanut butter cookies and milk as the storm blew eastward. It was cozy, like sitting around a campfire telling stories. Dad reminisced about a plow wind in 1976 that blew several empty grain bins off their foundations, and about the Edmonton tornado of 1987 when a cousin of Donald Fields was injured, his vehicle tossed like a toy on the highway.

"Isolated cases," Dad said. "We are fortunate here in Saskatchewan we don't get extreme weather often."

"We get blizzards," Paige said.

"And droughts," Mom added.

Dad grinned. "Tonight's storm came at the perfect time. We needed the moisture. All those canola pods will be filling. And better yet, I'm guessing those caterpillars were washed off." He stood. "I'm going to report the power outage, in case no one else has."

That night in bed, Charlotte told Paige all about Charlene Faulkner.

"My boss said, 'Take time off. Gain some perspective,' and so I am. Trying, at least."

"So you ran home to Tara to lick your wounds. 'We get our strength from the land, Scarlett.' Maybe there's some truth to that."

"Maybe." Charlotte couldn't tell if Paige was joking or serious. "I'm tired of thinking about Toronto and the radio station. And before you ask, the answer is no. There is no one special in my life right now."

"I wasn't going to ask."

"I'm glad Wendy and Alex managed to find their way back together." Charlotte wanted to move the conversation away from herself. "I know none of us were ever a big fan of Alex and yet none of us wanted him gone. However did Wendy manage to persuade him to go to counselling?"

"I'll tell you a little secret," Paige said, leaning on her elbow.

Her profile was visible in the yard light, the power recently restored. "It was Mom."

"Mom?"

"I don't know how or when, but Mom and Alex have developed a decent relationship."

"Now that I think of it, Mom hasn't complained once about him and I've been home now for almost two days."

"She's shell-shocked from the bomb I dropped."

It was the segue Charlotte had been waiting for. "To be honest Paige, I'm a little hurt you didn't tell me first."

"I avoid things. It was ... just that I'm ... embarrassed."

"It's not that creep, is it? The married guy who cheats. He didn't entice you back?"

"No. It's not him, I'll give you that much."

"What's the big secret?"

"It was a one-night stand. My baby's father is not in love with me," Paige said. "Of course I could never tell Mom and Dad that. I'll have to make something up."

"But someone has to pay child support. And who's going to take care of you financially while you're on maternity leave? Won't it be hard — being a single mother? You have to give this some practical thought."

Paige turned away, signalling the end of sharing confidences. "I'll think about it tomorrow."

"Two phone calls was all it took," Dad said, smiling broadly at Charlotte and Paige when they stumbled down for breakfast the next morning. "We have a cabin reserved. A cabin with three bedrooms, right in downtown Waskesiu." He paused. "How did I manage it, you ask? There was a cancellation and I happened to be the very next caller."

"Why can't everyone meet here instead?" Mom asked.

"Because when you're away from the house you stop working," Dad said.

"You tend to hover," Paige added.

"When did thoughtfulness become a crime," Mom complained.

"That's not thoughtfulness, that's subservience," Paige said.

"The garden ..."

"Will be waiting for you when you return," Dad said.

"Remember you promised you wouldn't be a slave to it?"

"But it's in its prime. I hate to see it go to waste."

"What needs to be picked?" Dad asked. "I can find someone who will want fresh vegetables."

"How long? For how long will we be gone?"

Charlotte wanted to enter the fray and offer her opinion against her mother, but three against one was mean.

"Four nights, starting Thursday. The farm and the garden will be fine," Dad said. "We check out Monday morning before eleven. Paige, how does that work for you?"

"If I can't find someone to trade shifts with me, I can commute. Waskesiu isn't far from Prince Albert."

"Which reminds me. One of your tires looks a little low. And when was the last time the oil was changed? I'll do a little car maintenance before you return to Prince Albert." Dad looked at Charlotte. "Your car, too."

"Oh, Dad." Tears welled in Charlotte's eyes. "Some things never change."

Chapter 36

Elsie

August 1995

Elsie stretched out on the lounge chair and closed her eyes. The sun was warm on her face and chest and legs. A paperback novel was splayed open on the table beside her.

She was alone. Charlotte and Paige were a few blocks away, exploring the boutiques and gift stores in the heart of the lakeside tourist town, and Dan was out walking. Elsie had nothing to do. Her family was right. Sometimes it was necessary to get away from the work on the farm, but it was also disconcerting — a word borrowed from Charlotte.

Being left too long with one's own thoughts gives opportunity to count worries.

She was trying to be a person who was carefree, but it was difficult. It required conscious effort, and it started by changing her vocabulary. Like saying "I am frustrated," instead of saying "I am angry."

She was "disappointed" Wendy and Alex preferred to tent in the campground rather than stay with them in the cabin. There was room for all of them. But greater than Elsie's disappointment was a gladness the Warrens were together and happier than they had ever been. The marriage counselling sessions were well worth the sixty dollars an hour Elsie and Dan had shelled out.

Every marriage can do with a little tune-up now and then.

The sound of a man clearing his voice jolted her from her reverie. Elsie's eyes shot open. Reese Dunn was standing at the bottom step of the cabin deck.

"Sorry to startle you. Charlotte's expecting me. Perhaps I'm early."

Charlotte had said nothing about inviting Reese. Elsie's brain became unscrambled; her instinctive hospitality surfaced. "Please. Come up and have a seat. Would you like something to drink?"

"Water would be fine."

Inside the dim cabin Elsie hastily pulled a t-shirt and shorts over her swimsuit, even though it was one-piece and covered her well.

"I still think of you with Leslie," she said, through the screen door. She put her hand to her mouth. *What a stupid thing to say.*

Reese handled it smoothly. "According to Charlotte and Paige, Leslie made the right decision. She didn't mention she saw me this spring, did she?"

Elsie emerged from the cabin with a glass of water. She handed it to him and indicated he sit on the bench across from her. She adjusted her chair to the upright position. "Leslie saw you this spring?"

"Not Leslie. Paige. She came to my brother's funeral in March." His blue eyes were keen on her face.

"I'm so sorry, Reese. Your brother died? Was there an accident?"

"He took his own life."

Annoyance at her youngest daughter surfaced. Elsie leaned over and touched his hand in sympathy. "Paige could have told me. I would have sent a card."

As if on cue, the sound of Paige's voice and Charlotte's laughter came from around the corner. Reese got to his feet.

Charlotte saw him first. "Reese!" She bounded up the stairs. "You're early. I bet you gave Mom a surprise!"

"That he did," Elsie said. "You could have warned me."

Charlotte hugged him and held him at arm's length. "How many years has it been? Twelve? The last time I saw you, I was heading off to Banff, after I finished school. Remember, you were my grad escort. I still have the graduation picture out on my bookcase. Everyone tactfully ignores my hideous gown."

"That dress didn't suit you," Elsie said, remembering. "You never wanted to go shopping. We would have found something ..."

She stopped, aware no one was listening.

"I went to your parents' farm to find you." Reese's face flushed red. He was staring at Paige.

"Ah." Charlotte pulled Elsie to a stand and steered her down the deck steps away from the cabin.

"Where are we going?" Elsie asked, puzzled. "I thought you wanted to see Reese."

"Those two need to talk."

"As do we all. It's been so long since we had a proper visit." Then the light bulb went on inside her brain. "Reese and Paige?"

"I think so. The look on their faces gave it away. I hadn't considered Reese at all. I had missed the clues."

"There were clues?" Elsie struggled to walk beside Charlotte. "Don't walk so fast. I don't have shoes on."

Charlotte stopped and glanced at her mother's feet. "Look at you and your red toenails!" She started to laugh.

"What's so funny? My toenails look beautiful."

"Oh, Mom," Charlotte gasped. "Life is too strange sometimes. You. Me. Standing behind a row of cabins. You and Dad — so patient. Surviving another family crisis. It doesn't seem fair, does it, we all have managed to disrupt your life."

"Speaking of your father, he's over there." Elsie pointed. Dan was talking to an elderly man sitting outside the door of the cabin registration office.

Dan waved and walked toward them.

Charlotte laughed harder but Elsie couldn't understand why.

"What's so funny?" Dan asked, with a smile. "What's the joke?"

"I'm not laughing," Elsie said. "Reese is at the cabin talking to Paige."

"Reese is here?" Dan asked. "I'd like to see him." He strode purposely toward the cabin.

Elsie could not keep up. "Dan. Wait!"

Before they reached the cabin they heard a car door slam and saw Reese drive off.

"Dan! Stop! Charlotte thinks Reese is the father of Paige's baby."

Dan stopped. He looked at Elsie for a long second but she could not read his mind. "Well, that would be good news," he finally said.

Paige was sitting on the deck, crying. "Reese wants to marry me."

"Of course he does," Dan said soothingly.

Elsie marvelled at the way he could handle their youngest and most tempestuous daughter.

"I said something about Leslie being his sister-in-law. I made him go away."

"He'll be back." Dan handed her a crumpled but unused tissue from his pocket.

Paige blew her nose. "I believe so." A small satisfied smile passed fleetingly across her face.

The Warren truck arrived and any questions Elsie wanted to ask were postponed. Joshua and Beth flung themselves into a frenzy of hugs, as if they hadn't seen their aunts and grandparents the night before, sitting around the campfire and roasting marshmallows in the campground.

"Look what I got." Joshua showed Charlotte a pocketknife.

Charlotte opened it. "Look. Beside a blade, it's got a nail file, and a cork screw for wine. Something for everyone." She smiled at the little boy.

Elsie excused herself from the crowded deck. Inside the cabin kitchen she rubbed her eyes.

Paige and Reese? She couldn't picture them together. *Reese and Paige.* Their names didn't fit.

Elsie spread butter on slices of freshly baked bread from the town bakery. She layered the cold cuts that had been purchased earlier from the butcher. The potatoes and lettuce, beans and beets had been brought from home.

"Mom, do you need some help in there?" Wendy called through the screen door.

"No, I'm fine. Have a good visit."

Elsie piled the platter high with sandwiches. She added water to the frozen lemonade concentrate inside the pitcher and stirred. She assembled a salad and added a buttermilk dressing. The voices outside rose and fell in excited rhythm, but there was no sudden exclamation, no indication Paige's news was being told. Maybe Wendy already knew Reese was the father. Maybe everyone had known and kept it a secret.

And Leslie? How is that going to go over?

"Lunch is ready. I just need some help bringing it out," Elsie said, purposely thrusting Leslie from her mind.

As soon as she returned home, she planned to call her sister-in-law. Judy would understand Elsie's roller coaster ride of emotions. It had been too long a time since they last talked.

Chapter 37

Leslie

September 1995

When Colette and Kyle returned to school, Leslie got her life back. She was freed from the demands of children wanting attention. Mundane domestic duties were pleasurably done in the silence of the house. Leslie had time to go to the gym three mornings a week, time for personal shopping and time for her monthly luncheon dates with Kim and Roxanne.

All was well.

Until she received a letter from her mother.

A letter, handwritten, meant bad news. Not urgent, middle-of-the-night-phone-call bad news but nevertheless something unpleasant for the person receiving the correspondence. Often it was a criticism, written in the gentlest of motherly language. Leslie thought it was cowardly — a way to postpone confrontation, a way to avoid honest reaction.

She ripped open the envelope with growing agitation and read:

> Dear Leslie,
>
> By writing this letter I am giving you a chance to think in private and react positively in public. I know I can count on you.
>
> Paige is expecting a baby at the end of this year. Reese Dunn is the father. We are hoping they can work something out and perhaps make a go of it as a couple. Preferably, a married couple. For that reason he will be included in our family

events.
I know this is going to be awkward for you but Paige and this baby need our support. More importantly, they need to be part of a complete family unit.
I am writing to ask that you don't diminish Paige's chances with Reese. A word of encouragement from you might go a long way.
Love,
Mom

Well, well, well. The chickens have come home to roost.
Her mother's words were cold and artificial, phrases chosen carefully not to inflame. "Think in private, react positively in public. A word of encouragement might go a long way." This was a probably a third or fourth draft.
Wouldn't it be refreshing to read what my mother really thinks?
Leslie tossed the letter away in disgust. It fell on the carpet and she stepped on it.
Reese Dunn is back to haunt me? And her mother, second guessing Leslie's reaction that — what? She would be jealous?
Not likely.

Leslie prepared fried chicken and mashed potatoes for supper. Keith came behind her as she was making gravy and wrapped his arms around her.
"Is something wrong?" he asked softly.
"I got a letter from my mother this morning."
"Really? What's the problem this time?"
So Keith too had her mother figured out. Leslie looked to see if the kids were in earshot. They weren't. "The identity of Paige's baby's father has been revealed," she said dramatically.
"Oh?" Keith dropped his arms. "I didn't know she was expecting."
"Neither did I. But that's not the problem. It's the baby's father."
"Someone we know?"
"Our former hired hand. Reese Dunn."
"Oh." There was a long pause. "That will be awkward. Wasn't

he your boyfriend as well?"

"What's awkward?" Colette came bounding into the kitchen.

"Carrying all this stuff to the dining room," said Keith. "Your mom made a special supper and your favourite vegetable. I'll help you set the table."

Later, after the children were asleep, Keith said, "Why don't we go visit your parents for Thanksgiving? We could leave early Saturday and drive back Monday. We haven't been to the farm for over a year. And I'd rather not go at Christmas in case the roads get bad."

How like Keith to take the bull by the horns and face the inevitable.

He put his arm around her. "Your parents would be thrilled. They haven't seen Colette and Kyle since last New Year's Eve."

Last Christmas, her parents had phoned to ask if they could come to Winnipeg for a New Year's Eve visit and bring Wendy, Joshua and Beth. Leslie had not been overjoyed. She and Keith had plans to attend a big gala at a fancy hotel in downtown Winnipeg.

When she had objected, Keith said, "We can go to the gala next year. It's not often we get to spend New Year's with your family. Phone your mother back and tell her we are delighted."

Leslie had sulked. She was cold in her welcome. She had not known Wendy and Alex had separated. *You would have thought that particular bad news was worthy of a handwritten letter.*

Keith had bought balloons, whistles, party hats and blowers that unfurled. As the hours in 1994 ran out they had played old fashioned games like twenty questions and charades. Joshua surprised everyone with his accurate pantomimes. Everyone put on a happy face. Everyone except Leslie. She regretted she hadn't been nicer, more enthusiastic.

In response to Keith's question about Thanksgiving she said, "It's the long drive I hate. And only for one day? It hardly seems worth it."

"Are you worried about running into your old beau?" Keith asked. "This kind of thing happens all the time. Movies, TV sitcoms. Siblings marry past lovers all the time. Elvis has a song. 'Little Sister' I think it was called." He hummed a bit and sang the chorus.

"Thanksgiving at the farm," Leslie said, surrendering. "Why not?"

"We can get this whole uncomfortable situation with Paige and your old boyfriend out of the way." There was a pause. "And Leslie. You might try harder to be as close to your sisters as you are to Roxanne."

Leslie opened her mouth to protest.

It wasn't that she didn't like her sisters. But ... Paige was too loud, too crude, too cute, too little. Wendy was too timid, too nice. If Leslie had married Alex, she would have set him straight from the outset. But of course, she wouldn't have been stupid enough to get herself pregnant in the first place.

Leslie was closest to Charlotte. So what if they didn't hang on the telephone for hours at a time, talking about the good old days. So what if months and months went by before they saw each other. Charlotte was the sister who knew Leslie best. When they got together, they always could give tit for tat.

Whatever that means.

Between Winnipeg and Hatfield, the Hamiltons traditionally stopped at a small-town restaurant that served, according to Keith, the best hamburgers in the world where the patties were juicy and the buns homemade. A second stop, two hours further west, was at an antique store along the highway. It was a dusty little place full of treasures. Leslie purchased a piece of depression glass to add to Roxanne's collection.

They arrived at the farm mid-afternoon. Leslie could tell Keith was eager to help with the harvest but was too polite to rush through the small talk with Mom, who served them hot chocolate made from scratch and brownies smothered with icing. While Colette and Kyle devoured the brownies, Leslie inspected the new kitchen Roxanne had designed. It was a vast improvement over the old one.

"Where did you put my work clothes?" Keith asked, interrupting the tour.

What is it with men and farms? Leslie thought as she retrieved the bag from the car containing his grubby jeans and old shirt. *Must be some primal instinct.*

"Is Paige here?" Leslie asked, after she saw Keith on his way.

"Napping," Mom said.

On cue, Paige came thumping down the stairs. The side of her face was creased from being pressed into a textured surface.

"Congratulations on your recent engagement," Leslie said.

"Thank you."

"When's the wedding so Keith and I can save the date?"

"We haven't set a date."

"Did you get a ring?"

Paige held out her hands, her fingers swollen. "Do these look like hands meant for an engagement ring?"

So it's going to be like this. Leslie turned to her mother. "How's Dad doing?" she asked. "Is he almost finished?"

"We're getting close. We had a cool August, rain in September. Reese has been a huge help. He took time off work to help us."

Some things never changed. Reese Dunn was still the hired man. It was as if the last fourteen years hadn't happened.

The mention of his name took Leslie back to when she was seventeen. She remembered how she wouldn't talk to him, thinking she was too good for him. What a superior little snot she had been. Reese had acted "hard to get" and she had accepted the challenge. *Well played, Reese.*

She had changed a lot since then. She had learned compassion and humility. According to Keith, going through a bankruptcy had been good for them. To start over again, and to accept the changes in their lifestyle. Would Reese see the change in her when they met again? What would he think? It was not improbable he still had feelings for her.

If he kissed her, would her knees go weak?

Leslie pushed that last thought out of her mind. A kiss could never happen. Keith would ask for a divorce and would want custody of the kids. There were some lines that could never be crossed, some things for which compassion and humility were null and void.

"Is Reese excited about being a father?" she asked Paige.

"More excited about being a father than being a husband. Oops, did I say that out loud?"

"Why do you always put yourself down?" Mom's voice was sharp. "He wouldn't marry you just because," her hands fluttered at Paige's belly.

"Oh, yes he would. He'd marry me because it's the right thing to do. Because he cares about you and Dad and the farm. And maybe, just maybe, to get back at Leslie." Paige's eyes flashed. "I haven't any illusions, you know. I'm not afraid to call a spade a spade."

"I'll go outside and see what my kids are up to." Leslie could see her presence was adding fuel to a fire she never recognized had existed. She slipped her feet into some old loafers by the back door and escaped. From outside the house she heard Mom scolding Paige.

Leslie followed her children's voices out to the back where the silver grain bins were lined up in a row. The auger was in place for the next load.

"You stay away from that when its running," she said to Colette and Kyle.

"We're not stupid," Colette retorted.

"We're waiting for grandpa," Kyle said.

The tandem truck drove into the yard with Keith in the driver's seat and Leslie's father as passenger. Dad leapt out, agile as a young man, while Keith inexpertly backed the truck and hoisted the truck box. Her father started the auger and pulled open the sliding door on the box. The grain poured out and he caught a handful.

"Oats," he shouted. "A hundred bushels an acre!"

"Grandpa, grandpa," shouted the kids. "Can we go with you?"

Keith looked first at Leslie and shook his head. "Tomorrow, when I'm familiar with the combine I'll give you a ride," he yelled above the sound of the auger.

When the grain was unloaded and the auger stopped, the men were off. Colette and Kyle chased the slow-moving grain truck out of the yard. Leslie followed them halfway to the road. She paused idly by her mother's flower garden, the plants no longer green except for one with tiny purple flowers. She had never developed the passion Mom shared with Wendy for growing things.

I wouldn't know lupins from lobelia.

Inside the house, the washing machine in the mudroom was spinning a load and her mother was folding towels.

"Here. Let me help," Leslie said.

"You can make up the beds in the west room for you and Keith." Mom removed sheets from the dryer. "We put out an air mattress for the kids. I moved Reese into Charlotte's old room."

"Can't he share a room with Paige?"

"We all agreed, with the kids here, not until they are married."

Leslie snorted. "Why close the barn door after the cows have escaped?"

"I can hear every word you say." Paige stepped out from the kitchen.

"He's a good man, Paige." Leslie hoped Mom noticed her words of encouragement.

"But not good enough for you."

Leslie rolled her eyes. "Is there any button I can't press?" She climbed up the stairs, the bed sheets in her arms warm from the dryer. As she tugged the fitted bottom sheet on the double sized mattress, she thought longingly of her new king-sized bed back in Winnipeg with its six hundred count Egyptian cotton sheets.

She looked out the bedroom window as the tandem truck turned into the yard, bringing another load of oats. This time neither Keith nor her father were driving.

Leslie became conscious of her heart beating. She had to see Reese without an audience of gawkers. She had to get this dreaded moment out of the way.

The stairs squeaked as she descended, potentially alerting the others of her intention. Her children were inside the TV room at the bottom of the stairs. They looked up.

"This TV sucks," Colette complained. "It only gets two channels and the picture is fuzzy."

"Read a book," Leslie ordered. "Play a game. Watch a movie. Here, grandpa has some tapes." She peeked around the corner. Paige was in the kitchen with Mom.

Leslie ducked into the parlour and out through the seldom-used front door, closing it softly behind her. By the grove of trees that separated the house, garden and yard from the shop, quonset and bins, she stopped.

Reese was wearing jeans and a blue chambray shirt, the sleeves rolled up to expose his forearms. His body was lean and strong looking. His blondish hair was curly on the back of his neck.

As if he sensed her presence Reese stopped the auger and turned slowly. Five seconds, ten seconds, they stared at each other.

Leslie reduced the distance between them in purposeful strides. Ten feet away, she stopped and wet her lips with her tongue. "I want to apologize for being a little bitch. I want us to accept each other as in-laws." It was not the speech she had rehearsed in her mind.

Reese nodded and restarted the auger.

Leslie walked away. She wanted to feel his hand on her shoulder to stop her, but it didn't happen. She turned once to see if he were watching her, but he wasn't.

So this is to be my punishment? To be held at arms' length, to be tolerated?

At the very least, she had expected anger.

Paige was standing on the steps of the house. She walked straight at Leslie and wordlessly brushed past her as if they were in a crowded hallway and not outside in the open with all the space in the world. Despite her stoutness and awkward gait, she walked quickly.

Leslie was unable to stop herself from following. She ducked behind a building and watched Paige go to Reese, his arms enfolding her fat little body as if he were protecting her. He looked directly at Leslie and she shrank back into the shadow thinking she couldn't possibly have been seen. She scurried back into the house.

The kids were watching a movie and her mother was peeling potatoes.

"What can I do?" Leslie asked, her heart still pounding.

Her mother handed her the peeler.

"Aren't these an awful lot?" Leslie gazed into the pail.

"Leftover potatoes can be fried for Monday's hash browns," said her mother. "I try to plan ahead when cooking for a large number. Like the ham we're having tonight. It can be served cold tomorrow alongside the turkey and the ham bone made into a soup on Tuesday."

Leslie found the potatoes large and awkward to hold while she peeled. "How is it really going with Paige and Reese?" she asked.

"What do you mean?"

"Do you think they have enough in common to make a marriage work?"

"Just as much as you and Wendy have with your husbands. Reese is patient with her. He is exactly the kind of man she needs."

"Does he have a decent job to support her?" Leslie remembered how stingy Reese was. "Have they talked about the wedding date at all?"

"Paige suggested Valentine's Day. She wants to have a wedding in one of those warm countries, like the Dominican Republic."

"She would hardly have time to lose all that weight before a Valentine's Day wedding." As soon as the words were out of her mouth, Leslie recognized how mean-spirited they were. "I'm sorry." In silence she put the peeled potatoes on to boil and helped her mother assemble the rest of the supper.

"I never liked the idea of Paige living with Karen," Leslie said, trying to restore the intimate conversation with her mother. If one started with a confession of vulnerability, it usually worked.

"Karen has been very supportive of Paige and we are grateful. I don't know what happened between you two, but you used to be close. She was your maid of honour at your wedding."

"Charlotte was my maid of honour," Leslie corrected. She didn't know either what happened between her and Karen. They had drifted apart and discovered they didn't like each other after all.

Supper was in shifts; there was no cohesiveness. Leslie sat twice, first with her father and her children, and with Keith an hour later. He devoured his food as if he hadn't eaten for days.

"This harvest thing is all one big game to you," she teased. He looked happy.

When it was Reese's turn to eat, Leslie made herself scarce. She unpacked the suitcases and put out the kids' pyjamas. Colette and Kyle stayed downstairs to eat more of Grandma's apple pie.

After Reese left, Leslie and Paige cleaned the kitchen while their mother prepared for Sunday's Thanksgiving dinner. They worked together in silence.

How does Mom do it? This gong show, this family reunion.

The house was full: aunts, uncles, cousins, sisters, husbands, grandparents and kids. All needed attention and recognition, their glasses filled and their palates satisfied. Even Wendy and Alex were there, although they could not stay the afternoon.

The only person missing was Charlotte.

The last time Leslie had talked to her, Charlotte was back to work, on her show. Charley's Hour it was called — or something like that, although Leslie remembered it was only for half an hour. She had never bothered to listen to the tapes her sister had sent, but she was sure the show was decent.

Apparently, Charlotte had not been dispensable after all. Leslie remembered how her sister had worried. When everyone was seated at one of the three tables crammed into the dining room, Dad said grace, thanking the Lord for the bounty of food they were about to eat. He asked each guest to think about something for which they were thankful.

"Reese and I have an announcement to make." Paige stood.

"Two actually." Reese stood beside her, smiling.

"It's been hard to keep the first bit to ourselves, but we wanted to wait until the whole family was together."

"Well, tell us girl," said Aunt Judy, laughing. "Don't keep us in suspense."

Paige looked around the room. When her eyes flittered on Leslie for a brief millisecond, there was a self-satisfied smile on her pudgy little face. "Reese and I are having twins!"

Everyone sitting around the table cheered. Some of them stood to shake Reese's hand. Leslie managed to choke out a response that indicated enthusiasm. *No wonder Paige is so huge.*

"The second bit of news," Aunt Judy prompted.

"Oh, that was it." Paige laughed a twinkling laugh. "Twins."

Everyone had a twin story to tell. No one remembered only Paige had spoken about thankfulness. Leslie had planned to say she and Keith were nicely back on their feet, *thank you very much.*

"Almost finished harvest, Dan?" asked Grandpa Dewhurst.

"About seventy-six acres. Should be done tonight, with the help of my sons-in-law here."

"One son-in-law," Leslie corrected. "The other, soon to be."

Everyone ignored her.

With a house full of people and no one watching, it was easy to catch Reese alone before he drove out to the field. Leslie stood in the middle of the driveway and he stopped the grain truck.

"Reese," she said, when he rolled down the window. "Congratulations on twins."

"Thank you. But I can't take credit. Paige is doing all the work." He started rolling up the window but Leslie motioned him to stop.

"Please don't keep giving me the cold shoulder. I understand. You're happy. You're going to be a father and a husband."

"Keith is a decent fellow. You did well, Leslie. Thank you."

"Thank me for what?"

"For being right. You were not the one for me."

The image of his face, wild with anger — and something else — registered in her mind's eye. Leslie shook her head to disrupt the scene. "Well, I'm not sure if my little sister is the right one either. She's impulsive and unpredictable."

"*She's* impulsive and unpredictable?" Reese laughed without warmth. "I hardly think that my happiness — or Paige's — is foremost in your mind. Paige needs me. You never did."

Satisfied she had hit a nerve, Leslie said, "You always were so damn honourable."

"You say that like it's a character flaw." Reese put the truck into gear and Leslie stepped back. He drove out of the yard and left her feeling deflated.

She was happy with her life. Wasn't she?

Chapter 38

Paige

October 1995

Reese couldn't have done better in Leslie's presence if Paige had written his script. Nevertheless, she gave a sigh of relief when the Hamilton sedan drove out of the yard. She looked up at Reese standing beside her and wondered what he was thinking. He would tell the truth if she asked. His inability to deceive was one of the many things she found reassuring about him. But her parents stood with them outside on the cool October morning and any personal conversation would have to be postponed.

"They're coming back," Mom said loudly. "They must have left something behind."

But it was not the Hamiltons who drove into the yard.

"Why, it's Donald," Mom exclaimed, as a middle-aged man stepped out of a dark green car. "Donald Fields."

"Our neighbour to the south," Paige said to Reese.

"I remember."

"Well, look here." The man smiled at Paige standing on the veranda. "All grown up."

"Good morning, Mr. Fields," Paige replied. He didn't mention her huge belly and she was a little disappointed. She wanted to shout to the world she was having twins.

"And this is Reese Dunn, my soon-to-be son-in-law," Dad said. "Reese, this is Donald Fields."

Reese stepped down and shook Donald's hand.

"Come in for coffee," Mom invited.

Donald shook his head. "I'm off to pick up Patti's parents from her sister's. They flew in a couple of days ago from Edmonton to celebrate the last Thanksgiving at our house."

"The last Thanksgiving?"

"Patti and I have decided to sell the farm."

"You're selling the farm?"

"Patti and I dithered with the decision all summer. I'm tired of farming my little patch of land. Patti's tired of all the yard work and the big garden. We want to buy a house in Hatfield, or maybe a townhouse with no yard work at all."

"Your children don't want the farm?" Dad asked.

"No. They say there's no money in it. They like their city lives."

"You and Patti seem too young to retire," Mom said. "We'll miss you."

Paige saw tears form in Mr. Fields' eyes. He blinked. "We don't want to sell to any of these big corporate farms. Before we list it with a realtor, we thought we'd ask our neighbours if they're interested in buying our place."

"We are."

The words had come out of nowhere. Paige looked around to see who had spoken. Everyone was looking at her. "I'm sorry. Did I say that? Of course we're not thinking about buying a farm."

Reese took her hand. "We are interested." He swallowed. "To look at it, anyway."

"Well." Donald stepped back into his car. "I see you have lots to talk about." He winked at Paige. "Have a good day."

They watched him drive away and then her parents and Reese turned to Paige in choreographed slow motion.

"I had no idea you wanted to live in the country."

"I didn't either," Paige admitted. She couldn't tell if Reese were angry or not. "I'm sorry."

"It's not a bad idea," said Dad. "I believe they have three quarters. Enough to get you started. We'll go look at the house tonight."

"No, Dan," said Mom. "Not tonight. They have company. Patti's parents. Tomorrow is soon enough."

"What's the house like?" Paige asked. She couldn't remember if she had ever been in it. The Fields' children had been older than the Dewhurst girls. And her parents, friendly enough with their neighbours, hadn't been ones to visit back and forth.

"A bungalow. Built in the fifties. Sturdy enough with big windows," said Dad. "And the farmland has a nice slope to it. It's a decent property."

"Fields' field." Paige remembered Charlotte's joke from a time long ago, when Reese came to the farm for the first time. "Dunn's field," she said, testing the sound of it.

Reese looked at her, puzzled.

"Are we deciding your future for you?" she said, hugging his arm.

"Just a little."

"You ran your own business in Prince Albert. Farming is a little like that," said Dad, leading the way back into the house.

"Well, technically, my ex-wife ran the business." Reese followed. "I did the labour."

"Books and labour. When you're a farmer, you have to be able to do both. And more. Manage your time, plan your money, buy equipment, negotiate prices. Fix equipment, work long hours."

"Don't scare him off, Dad." Paige grabbed Reese's hand and led him up the stairs and into her bedroom. She wrapped her arms around his neck. "I am so sorry to put you on the spot. I can't understand why I jumped in. I never had any intention of living on a farm. Especially not next door to my parents."

They sat on the bed, side by side.

"Isn't this what engagement is about? Working out details?"

"There are so many things we need to talk about. Like where we want to live and how many children we want to have and who's going to take care of our parents when they get old."

"We don't need to know all the answers before we marry," Reese replied. "Some things fall into our lap. We have to be open for opportunities."

"Buying a farm — even a small farm — is a moment of reckoning."

"You and your moments of reckoning," Reese said, with a smile that melted Paige's heart.

She was never going to doubt he loved her.

The first life-changing moment of reckoning had been five months ago when Paige emerged from the upscale Prince Albert apartment bathroom wretched from retching into the toilet bowl.

Karen had been sitting on the paisley sofa. "You do know you're pregnant. I've suspected it for weeks."

"I think I am." Paige wiped her tearing eyes. She sat beside Karen and waited for criticism.

"I was pregnant once. I had an abortion. I've always regretted that. Now here I am. Thirty-two, no husband, no children." She looked at Paige. "You're young. Don't make the same mistake."

"I won't."

"I am not going to ask who, or why, or exactly what caused an intelligent woman like you to be careless. As long as you don't ask the same of me."

"I won't."

"Would it be a good idea to let the father know?"

"No," said Paige.

"Well, I disagree." But Karen did not push further, and Paige was grateful.

A sudden fear stabbed through her. Had Karen and Reese hooked up once upon a time?

As her figure thickened, her resolve not to tell Reese weakened. She suspected he would want to do the right thing if he knew. But what kind of burden would that be for him — to be forever tied to the younger sister of his first love? And this wasn't his fault. Paige had initiated everything. She had taken advantage of his grief and his need for comfort. She was an immoral person.

Fate had taken over. Reese was brought to her at the Waskesiu resort town. The expression on his face had been delight when he first saw her, fading to something else as his eyes moved to her torso. But it wasn't shock or dismay. It was something else. *Like wonder. Like gratefulness.*

Mom and Charlotte had vanished.

Trust Charlotte to give me privacy to be an absolute brat.

"Why didn't you tell me?" he had cried. "I tried to find you. You weren't in the phone book. I went to the bars. I hung around the hospital in the city, hoping to catch you. I visited your parents."

Paige had stood there with her hands on her hips, her voice a little loud and challenging. "Why did you want to find me so badly, Reese? Was there something you left behind? A little residual deposit?"

It was so romantic.

"Look," he said, not rising to her bait. "I haven't thought of anyone else since that day in March. I was happy for the first time in years."

"I made you happy?"

"You did. And then you disappeared."

"Like Cinderella?" The thought made Paige smile. "You went around looking for me?"

"Come here, Paige." Reese held out his arms. "If this baby is a girl, I will have to brush up on my fairy tales." His body was tall, and she was short, and yet she fit nicely in his arms. Too nicely. *She didn't deserve this.*

"I wonder what Leslie will have to say." Paige pushed him away.

"Paige," Reese said, reproachfully. "If you'd give me half a chance, you might get a husband out of this."

A husband! "With you and Leslie planning to run off together, Keith and I watching from the sidelines, waiting for the shoe to drop? I think not."

"You have quite the imagination. You obviously don't know me at all. And who is Keith?"

"Don't try to be funny!" She stamped her foot.

There was a long silence before Reese said, "How long will it take for you to cool down? One hour? Two days? Or are you a person who stews and stews?"

Paige heard him get into his vehicle and drive away. She sat on the deck chair and cried. She didn't want to be a person who stewed. She didn't want to be a person who carried a grudge.

Reese had returned an hour later when the cabin deck was full of people. Paige introduced him to Alex, Joshua and Beth, then quickly led him far enough away so he wouldn't hear the excited speculation of her family. She was determined not to be a brat. She was excited and hopeful and joyous. *And truth be told, a little turned on.* She and Reese sat on a park bench by the lake. Their conversation wasn't the "getting to know you" kind of conversation, trivial on substance, heavy on innuendo. No. Right away it was as if they were in tune with each other.

"Your mother told me you lived with Karen Anders but I couldn't find Karen's number," Reese said.

"Her number is unlisted. I never asked why. A lot of things are mysterious about Karen." Paige hesitated. "Did you and Karen ever have a relationship? After Leslie?"

"No. I had nothing to do with anyone or anything connected with Leslie. I was angry for a long, long time. After the night I spent with you, I stopped being angry. It was like the switch turned off. Why did you give up on me so easily?"

"Because I am the kind of girl who cuts off her nose to spite her face. It's a bad quality I have. I may as well put all my bad qualities out in the open."

"When you found you were pregnant you didn't come to find me."

"No." Paige had looked down, ashamed. "You had a right to know."

"What were you planning to do with the baby? Give it up for adoption? Or raise it yourself?"

"I was going to keep it. I don't always think ahead. At least that's what my family tells me."

Spending time with Reese became a daily occurrence. They talked and talked until every taboo topic was exhausted. They both agreed to feel zero remorse about betraying Leslie.

Reese became her best friend. Paige never had one before.

He insisted on accompanying Paige to her ultrasound appointment. The technician took such a long time measuring and writing and rechecking that Paige panicked. *Is there something wrong?* Reese waited with her at the apartment for the call from Paige's obstetrician regarding the results.

No wonder she was so big. Twins. She couldn't tell if Reese was upset at the doubled responsibility, or proud.

"I am gob-smacked with overwhelming joy," he said, when asked. "There is no way you can raise two children on your own. We have to get married."

"If that's your idea of a proposal, it sucks," Paige joked, trying to alleviate the seriousness of the situation. "Why don't you take one and I take the other. Like the Parent Trap." Paige had to explain how thirteen-year-old identical twins plotted, successfully, to get their parents back together.

"Why put off the inevitable?"

Reese was practical. Paige liked that about him. Still, he needed to pass some tests before Paige would make a commitment. The first test had been with Karen. Paige wasn't sure why this encounter was important or what it had been intended to prove, but it needed to happen. Karen was a link to Leslie, a reminder. If any fond memory was to be triggered, best get it out of the way.

Paige had invited Reese to the apartment. She prepared what she remembered was one of his favourite meals. She wore an apron. Her stomach bulged out like a tray and caught splatter when she mashed potatoes with the hand beater.

"Come on up," she called into the intercom when he buzzed his arrival. "It's number 512." Several seconds later she opened the apartment door. "Are you ready to meet with one of your old high school friends? Karen will be home from work shortly. I told her I had a surprise."

"I'm the surprise?"

"Well, the supper too. Usually she cooks."

Karen, dressed in her nurse's colourful and shapeless uniform, arrived ten minutes later. Her hair was pulled back and she wore no makeup. Paige was glad she hadn't warned her roommate ahead of time. Karen, when dressed to the nines, was a knockout.

"Reese Dunn." The tiredness vanished from Karen's face. "You are a sight for sore eyes. Let me get out of these clothes and I can give you a proper welcome." She laughed. "Well, that sounded just dirty."

Before Karen could get the wrong idea — or any idea for that matter — Paige patted her belly. "Reese is the father."

"Well, fancy that," said Karen without missing a beat. "And now he wants all of you, I presume. I was looking forward to having a baby in the apartment. We could have been like two moms. But I see this is better. When will the two of you move in together?" She didn't wait for an answer but headed to her bedroom and closed the door.

"That's a good question," said Reese. "We should live together before the babies are born."

"The problem is — you live in your brother's house. No more basement suites for me."

"I'll start looking for a house. And a better paying job," Reese promised.

The dinner party went off without a hitch. Not once did Reese veer into "the good old days" when he had been with Leslie.

The marriage proposal came later. At the farm, in front of her parents, Reese had gone down on one knee and held out a ring. His face wore an expression of earnestness Paige found unattractive.

"Get up. Not in front of Mom and Dad."

"Rachel Paige Dewhurst," he said. "I don't have a university degree, but I have common sense and a strong back. I'm a hard worker and I have money in the bank. I will provide for you and our children. I believe we could make a happy life together. Will you marry me?"

"What about love? I didn't hear any mention of the word love."

"Love, if nurtured, could bloom and flourish," Mom said.

"These two young ones don't need us here." Dad led Mom away.

Reese had remained on one knee. "I do love you. I believe you will come to love me too."

"What about sex?"

Reese grinned, the look of earnestness gone. He stood. "I don't believe we'll have a problem in that department. But let's do it right and wait until the wedding night."

"You are such a romantic."

"Say yes, Paige."

"Yes Paige."

He removed the ring from the box. It was a solitaire. He attempted unsuccessfully to put the ring on her finger. "We will have to get this sized."

"Wait until after the babies. My fingers are swollen."

When they entered the farmhouse the first question her mother asked was, "So, when's the big day?"

Paige looked at Reese. "Valentine's Day is such a romantic day."

"Valentine's Day it is."

"Valentine's Day, a destination wedding," Paige elaborated. "Like Mexico or Jamaica."

"Destination wedding it is." Reese's smile didn't waver.

"There is no way you can take a newborn to a tropical country," her mother had said.

Pshsh. Typical of my mother to throw cold water on my dreams. "Pioneer women had babies all the time. Took them along on horse-drawn caravans to the west."

"And many of them died," her mother returned pointedly. "And what about the dress you want to wear?"

"Something big and flowing," Paige replied. "I want Aunt Debra to stand up with me. And Reese will ask Dad."

"Are you sure you even want me to come along?"

From the hurt look on Mom's face, Paige knew she had hit a nerve.

As she walked away, she heard Reese say to Mom, "Next summer, we'll have a big party. You can plan it all."

"You have to be nicer to your mother," he said, when he found Paige sulking in another room.

"She's not that nice to me. She's never on my side."

"We have to model for our children."

Paige struck a ridiculous modelling pose and Reese laughed.

Sitting on the bed upstairs, Reese played with her hand, rubbing her fingers, giving her time to think. He never got angry with her. He never told her what to do.

Paige wondered for the hundredth time what she had done to deserve this happiness.

They looked at the Fields' house and discussed its possibilities. They talked about becoming farmers. Two weeks later, they looked closer at the house, yard and land. With the help of the Dewhurst family lawyer, they drew up a bid and submitted it to the Fields' lawyer. They were not to expect the results until December.

Patience had never been Paige's strong suit, but Reese managed to distract her.

On November 28, before the Justice of the Peace in a Prince Albert courthouse, Reese and Paige were married. In attendance were their parents, Dan and Elsie Dewhurst, Ray and Selina Dunn.

Reese had not wanted the babies born out of wedlock.

"Such an old-fashioned word," Paige had laughed. *Out of wedlock.*

On December 12, the twins were born, each weighing over six pounds. Reese was handed the babies, one after the other as they were pulled from Paige's body during a scheduled C-section. A son named Daniel Raymond after the two grandpas and a daughter named Cassandra Elise, the second name a combination of Selina and Elsie.

Tuesday's children. Full of grace.

"Reese," said Paige. "What was I thinking? We can't have a ceremony in the Dominican Republic. We can't take our babies out of the country so soon."

"I'll phone our travel agent first thing tomorrow morning and cancel everything."

"I'm sorry we'll lose the down payment."

"It's a small price to pay."

"Maybe we should tell the rest of the family the truth. That we're already married."

"I have another idea. Let's have a big summer wedding in your family's farmyard. We'll say our vows in front of all the neighbours and friends and family. Your mother would like that."

"But in the meantime, those same family, friends and neighbours will think we're living in sin."

"But we're not. And what an amusing secret for your mother to keep. She'll have the last laugh when she announces later it's all for show."

To everyone's surprise — and not the least Paige's — motherhood came naturally. She was so happy she could weep. And she did, often and uncontrollably, the first week she was home. Despite the exhaustion and emotion, her cup of love overflowed. She was determined to mend all the fences in her life. With Reese by her side, everything appeared do-able.

Except one thing. And it was a doozy.

"Jorden Wilks needs to be charged," Reese said, bringing up the topic once again. "He changed who you were. Teachers are supposed to be professionals. They are not supposed to take advantage of students. How old were you? Sixteen? Do you think you're the first student to ever be in love with a teacher? He stole part of your childhood. He kept you quiet in a little basement apartment, like a sex slave."

"It was hardly that. He said he was in love with me." She turned away so Reese could not see her face. She could not imagine testifying about some of the most intimate moments in her life. She did not want her parents to know how enthusiastically she had participated.

"And are you sure you were the only one?"

No, Paige was not sure.

Other girls had had a crush on Mr. Wilks. Other girls had flirted. Schools were full of silly selfish teenage girls. "You have an obligation to protect future victims. Think of our beautiful little daughter. What if Cassie has a teacher like Jorden Wilks? What would you do?"

Paige remembered being deflowered on the cold classroom floor. The humiliation, the tears, the total lack of romance.

"I'd kill him," she said furiously.

"So we will deal with this together? This needs to be resolved."

"Yes. I promise. Just not now. After the wedding." Paige put her fingers out in a gesture of quotes for "wedding."

She knew Reese was right, but the thought of a confrontation made her blood go cold with fear. Perhaps she could push it off indefinitely.

"Trust me," said Reese. "I'm on your side."

Chapter 39

Wendy

December 1995

"You won't be home for Christmas?"

The disappointment in Mom's voice was evident and Wendy felt her resolve to be assertive waver.

"We're going to Disneyland with friends," Wendy said into the telephone receiver. "Eve and Jeff McDougall and their children. Eve went to school with Alex, and her husband used to play hockey with him. Did I never mention them to you?"

"I don't recall you ever talking about the McDougalls. And haven't you and Alex been to Disneyland?"

"We can go more than once. And the McDougalls moved away from St. Cloud and we lost contact. And then they came back. I bumped into Eve at Molly's dance studio."

Literally bumped into.

She and Eve had stared at each other in delighted recognition and made a date to meet for coffee.

"Without children, so we can catch up," Eve said, and added, "Jeff got the principalship at the St. Cloud Elementary School. We moved home this summer." She paused. "Sorry I didn't let you know. There was a lot going on in our lives."

"My life, too."

They met for coffee and Wendy told Eve about her separation from Alex and their reconciliation. She hadn't minced words.

"That Glennie," Eve had said, when Wendy finished. "She needs to get a life. There's something seriously wrong with her, like she's stuck, or something."

Mom's voice on the phone broke into Wendy's remembrance. "This vacation is rather hasty."

"Yes, it is," Wendy agreed. Hasty decisions alarmed her; she was not unlike her mother that way, but she wasn't going to admit it. "The opportunity for this vacation came up unexpectedly. I was telling Eve about Paige's cancelled destination wedding, and the travel credit. And she said, 'The travel agent is a friend of mine. Her office is half a block down the street. Let's see what's in the offering.' As it turned out, Mom, there was a discounted chartered flight to Los Angeles leaving Saskatoon on December twenty-third and returning on the twenty-ninth. The hotel has a restaurant and a swimming pool with a water slide. It's within walking distance of the Disneyland entrance. How could we possibly turn that down?"

Mom didn't reply. It was a rhetorical question anyway.

"We'll be back in time for New Year's," Wendy said. "We'll come to the farm on the first."

"Are you sure you want to travel in your condition?" Mom threw in a parting shot.

Two months ago, when the family had gathered for Thanksgiving, Mom had caught Wendy discreetly throwing up her dinner in the upstairs bathroom.

"Please don't say anything," Wendy had begged, wiping her mouth with a tissue. "Let Paige have her moment. Alex and I have time enough to tell the family."

Her mother had brought a small glass of ginger ale and a sleeve of saltine crackers. "Here. This helped settle my nausea when I was expecting you."

"You won't say a word? Promise?" Wendy had begged, and her mother hadn't.

Until now.

"I'll be fine, Mom." Wendy's voice was harsher than she intended it to be. Truth was, she wasn't sure she wanted to travel while pregnant, but if she and Alex waited a year, this third baby would be seven months old and more than likely out of sorts with routine thrown to the wind. Joshua would be in a more demanding hockey schedule, one that included practices and games during the Christmas holidays. And, the travel credit would have expired. If they were ever going to get away this was the time.

"Would you like to watch Joshua's hockey game on the

nineteenth?" Wendy asked, to change the subject. "Milford is playing Hatfield. It's our last game before we leave."

"Dad and I would love to come."

Wendy smiled into the receiver. "I'll talk to you soon about the time and the place. I need to get supper started before Alex returns with the kids. Gotta run. Goodbye." Wendy put down the receiver and sat on the couch in the living room. Confrontations made her weary. She closed her eyes.

She hadn't been completely honest with her mother. There were two other reasons, personal reasons, why going away at Christmas was opportune.

The timing of the Disneyland vacation provided a legitimate reason to avoid an unpleasant holiday reunion with the Warrens.

Alex's brother and mother had made harvest extremely difficult. There had been long nights, longer days — and Stuart refused or "forgot" to do some of the more mundane jobs. Wendy kept out of all of it, but it was hard not to be able to protect Alex from his brother's vindictiveness and constant criticism. Now Helen and Murray Warren were trying a different tactic to keep Alex and Wendy in line, a tactic of conviviality, by hosting Christmas dinner and inviting everyone. Alex's sister, who usually avoided the family, was said to be attending. Although it would have been interesting to see what kind of cook her mother-in-law was, Wendy never wanted to be in the same room with Stuart. All the "peace on earth" and "goodwill to all men" was not enough to change her mind. Alex supported her decision.

Wendy had heard Alex say to his mother over the telephone, "We won't be home for Christmas. But thanks for the invitation." He had hung up before falling into the trap of explanations and too much information. Rick, the marriage counsellor, had equipped him with some verbal and emotional tools to help him deal with his difficult family members.

Wendy was proud of Alex. He was learning to stand up to them.

Her second reason for wanting to avoid Christmas with her family was something she would not admit to anyone.

Not in a million years.

She was jealous. And she was embarrassed for being jealous. She had everything she wanted — children, her husband, a beautiful home away from her in-laws.

Paige and Reese with their two beautiful babies would be at the Dewhurst farmhouse for Christmas. They were so happy and optimistic, more so now that their bid on the neighbour's farm had been accepted. They were making plans to renovate their new home. *How perfect the Fields' farm would have been for us.*
But Wendy could never, never admit it to anyone, not even to Alex. The opportunity had presented itself first to Paige, and Wendy would do nothing to undermine her sister's joy.

Disneyland was busy and the lineups were long; California was so different from Saskatchewan, with its sparse population and big empty spaces. It was fun, but Wendy resolved never again to spend Christmas away. Without the church service and religious aspect, the occasion was diminished into just another day. Christmas supper was eaten in the hotel restaurant. No one thought to pray.

Despite this, the family holiday went well. There were no mishaps, not even a scraped knee or a nosebleed. Everyone got along, more or less well. Jeff and Alex — their friendship going back to the days they played hockey on the St. Cloud team — never became juvenile. There was no drinking, no flirtations with waitresses, no need for male posturing. This was a family holiday and Alex treated it as such.

Best of all, Wendy returned home with the flutter of new life safely within her.

At the St. Cloud Town Hall on New Year's Eve, Glennie was grinding her tiny body into every male around, checking to see whether Alex was noticing. It was so obvious and embarrassing and pathetic.

What would happen if I took her aside? Wendy thought. *Talked to her 'man-to-man' as my father used to call it. Would she laugh in my face and say she would forever be a threat? Or would I be ignored, as if I didn't exist?*

Or could a new irony be found — Alex's women becoming friends over their common interest?

Wendy grinned at the absurdity.

"I'd like to talk to you," she said, approaching Glennie when Alex, clueless of her plan, was sitting with some friends.

"Come outside." Glennie did not appear surprised with Wendy's request. "Damn, you can't smoke anywhere inside anymore."

Wendy hesitated. It was cold outside. She grabbed her coat off the rack and followed.

"Have a smoke." Glennie thrust her pack of cigarettes in Wendy's face.

"No, thanks."

Glennie lit a cigarette and inhaled deeply. "So, what did you want to talk to me about?"

"I want you to stay away from my husband."

A slow smile flitted across Glennie's face. "Or — you'll what?"

Wendy realized too late the futility of being forthright. "It's embarrassing to him the way you keep putting yourself in his sight. He shouldn't make avoiding you his top priority." *Or mine.*

"Avoiding me? His top priority?"

Wendy wished she hadn't said that.

"There will always be girls like me. Girls who get their kicks out of taking away another woman's man." Glennie started singing a Dolly Parton song. Her voice rose to a wail in the chorus.

Wendy stared. Other smokers started to snicker.

Suddenly, Alex was outside. Without a word he guided Wendy back into the hall. "Are you okay?" he shouted over the music. "I came to find you before the countdown." He took her to a corner of the hall where it was less loud and held her tightly. "You never, ever have to worry about Glennie. I don't want crazy in my life. I want you. You have to trust me."

Over Alex's shoulder, Wendy could see Glennie had followed them and was watching.

"Ten, nine, eight ...." the crowd shouted. "Five, four, three, two, one! Happy New Year!"

Wendy grabbed Alex and kissed him passionately. No longer was she going to play defence.

"Let's go home," Alex said.

Chapter 40

Elsie

January 1996

Now that she had been given carte blanche to make wedding plans, Elsie — in an act of diplomacy — wanted Selina Dunn to participate in the decision-making. After all, they shared two grandchildren, and accommodating each other's schedules would work better if they were on acceptable terms.

Elsie invited Reese's mother to meet her for lunch. She chose a modest restaurant in downtown Prince Albert, thinking a fancier place might put Selina on the defensive, as Elsie had been the first few times she met Keith's mother. The game of economic one-upmanship with the unpretentious Kim Hamilton had been in her own imagination.

She could see Selina sitting in a booth by a window when Dan dropped her off.

"Thanks for meeting me," Elsie said, sliding into the seat across from her. Selina's greying hair was molded in a tight perm but the style made her pointy face look younger and less angry. Elsie found this encouraging. "I've always wanted to tell you what a fine young man you have raised in Reese."

"He was my easiest to keep out of trouble."

That he was. Easy and good-humoured compared to the oldest boy. And the youngest? Well, best not to talk about him. His death would be an endless ache for his mother.

The waitress approached and handed plastic-covered folders to each of them. "Could I get you something to drink?" she asked.

"Water for me," Elsie said.

"Water for me," Selina echoed and the waitress left.

"Since I invited you, I would like lunch to be my treat." Elsie thought money was likely still tight in the Raymond Dunn household.

"I can afford my meal."

"Well, yes. I'm sorry. I never meant to imply ..." Elsie wished she had asked Dan to stay. He almost always knew how to prevent conversations from stalling.

In silence, the women studied the menus. When the waitress returned with their water, Selina ordered a Reuben sandwich with a side of fries. Elsie ordered the same.

"You are probably wondering why I asked you to meet me," she said to Selina. "It's about the wedding celebration."

"I guessed as much."

"When Leslie got married in Winnipeg, I had no say in any of the details. I want you to feel free to share ideas." Too late Elsie ascertained her mistake in mentioning Leslie's name. Her smile froze on her face.

"How is that oldest girl of yours?" Selina asked. "Still got her nose in the air?"

A mother's natural instinct was to defend her offspring, but Elsie often thought the very same thing. "Yes," she admitted. "She still has her nose in the air."

Selina's face softened. "So, what do you have in mind for this wedding?" she asked.

"We've booked the minister for June 22nd. I'm thinking a wedding in our yard. Peonies in shades of pink will line the lane to the house. The vows will be said in the backyard by the patio, where the irises will be in full bloom. Paige and Reese would like a fiddler to provide the music for the dance later in the evening." Elsie paused, hoping Selina would provide some enlightenment of that particular request.

"I'm not much for ideas. The only thing I can think of is a horse-drawn carriage bringing Paige and her bridesmaids."

It wasn't the suggestion Elsie had envisioned. *A horse-drawn carriage is so cheesy.* "I don't know anyone who has a team of horses and a carriage."

"Lots of people around Hatfield have horses. You just have to know who to ask."

"I'll look into it," Elsie said. Maybe she would have no luck and could report back, regretfully, she had tried but had not succeeded. "Is there anything else you think would be nice?"

"No. Like I said, I'm not much for ideas."

"If there is, we could meet again. And discuss this further."

"We could. Or I could phone and save you a trip."

There was nothing left to say to each other. If it had been Judy sitting across from Elsie, the conversation would have flowed. They would have interrupted each other amid constant laughter, new topics would be jumbled in confusion, all in a rush to get clarified. Their problems would have lessened. Their children's endearing peculiarities would have been enjoyed.

When Judy had heard about the return of Reese Dunn into the Dewhurst lives, she had been sufficiently jubilant. Elsie told her about the City Hall marriage vows. She knew Judy could be trusted not to spill the beans.

Selina's reticence made Elsie uneasy, made her prone to wild imaginings.

How many people has Selina told? Is she happy about the marriage? How does she feel about Paige? Does she even like her a tiny bit?

The waitress brought their order and the women nibbled away at their sandwiches. Every once in a while, Elsie smiled at Selina and encouraged a short exchange of words, but that was where the conversation sputtered and died.

Judy would find the humour in Elsie's situation and find empathy for Selina Dunn at the same time. *Better to have an awkward relationship than no relationship. Better to keep on trying.* That would be Judy's advice. *Keep on trying, for Reese's sake.*

Dan arrived early and Elsie gave a sigh of relief.

"Hello Selina," he said pleasantly. "Did I come at a bad time?" He sat beside Elsie.

"That's nice. To give your wife a lift."

"Well, it would be a long walk if I didn't." Dan laughed. "Can we offer you a ride home?"

"No, thanks. I live only a few blocks from here. I thought it was nice of your wife to choose this place so convenient." She put down the remains of her sandwich, picked up her coat and walked away without saying goodbye. Elsie stared after her, bewildered by the abruptness.

"A difficult meeting?" Dan asked.

"Not the easiest," she admitted, turning to him. "I don't know if she's a little slow or socially awkward. Or maybe she doesn't like me. Or maybe all three." Elsie passed the few fries left on her plate to Dan. "Her only suggestion is for Paige to arrive in a horse-drawn carriage. Dan! How are we possibly going to make that happen?"

"Imagine it," said Dan. "Picture the first carriage, arriving with Wendy, Charlotte and Leslie. The bride arriving with me in a second one."

"In my mind's eye, the horses bolt and everyone tumbles from the carriage. Bones are broken. The wedding is ruined."

Dan laughed. "Imagine the minister in his white robes, inspiring everyone with his words about love and renewal. Imagine the day. A gentle breeze, mid-twenties temperature. The food, hot and delicious, brought into the yard by Lila Gladstone — I've heard her catering business is doing well. We have to hire her, you know."

Elsie chuckled at the last bit. "Oh Dan. About Lila's new business venture. She asked me to be her supplier of dill pickles for next year. I'm now officially employed!"

After a seemingly endless round with lawyers and bankers, the financial and legal papers were signed and witnessed in early March. A house, a yard, four hundred and eighty acres of land, was now owned by Paige and Reese Dunn — and the bank that held the mortgage.

Half a million dollars! Elsie felt faint at the cost. She and Dan had been debt free for several years. She had to remind herself that this was not her problem.

"I was able to make a substantial down payment," Reese said, with a weak grin, after the celebratory dinner Elsie had prepared. "I always believed I needed money available for something important. What could be more important than a home for my family?"

"With lots of room for our children to play outside," Paige said.

"I hope you'll let me help plan your yard," Elsie said. She had never been impressed with Patti's flower beds, "When you live in a zone 2 - 3, like we do, there are limitations what we can grow. Peonies and lilies do especially well."

"No one around here has a yard like this." Paige gestured to the scene outside the window. "I'll gladly accept your advice. Even now, the yard looks attractive with nothing growing."

Elsie glowed with the compliment. A winter garden was a new concept. *In a province that has snow for sometimes six months of the year, why hadn't anyone thought of it before?*

"But first to get the house painted and new carpets installed. Would you mind if we stayed with you while we work on our house? Could we leave the twins for small stretches of time?"

"Of course you can." This new relationship she had with Paige was the answer to Elsie's prayers. "When do you hope to move in?"

"As soon as we can."

It was a wet, cold spring. When the hot weather finally arrived in late May, Dan and Reese worked around the clock to get their fields seeded. Germination was immediate in the moist warm soil and the fields became green overnight, as if to make up for lost time. Elsie prayed Reese's first farming venture would be a success.

She had bad luck with the peonies. They took their sweet time to bud and thwarted Elsie's careful planning of flowers in bloom for the wedding ceremony. She confessed her frustration to a friend, who managed to wangle the loan of unsold pots of flowers and hanging planters from the local nursery.

Further throwing off Elsie's careful planning was her newest grandchild, due in mid-May. He delayed his arrival by two weeks.

"I wanted to give you some help with the newborn," she told Wendy.

"It's my third. I can handle it." Wendy laughed. "Alex said we should name the baby Warren. He thought Warren Warren sounded like a jock's name."

"Thank goodness you settled for Owen Warren." Elsie wasn't fussy about that combination either, but she kept her mouth shut.

On top of the delayed seeding and the lateness of Owen's birth, there were mosquitos. Excess water and hot June weather provided the perfect breeding ground for the insects. Elsie had to douse herself liberally with strong repellent every time she went outside, and shower it all off when she came back in. She wanted Dan to spray the yard before the wedding but was reluctant to nag, seeing as he was trying so hard to finish the farm work.

She feared the ferocity of mosquitos might be the main topic of conversation at the wedding. There would be no one to blame but herself if this venture were a flop.

Chapter 41

Charlotte

June 1996

Charlotte caught the late flight out of Toronto and arrived in Saskatoon before ten. She had made arrangements with an old friend, Carrie McCombs, to be picked up at the airport. The two went to a restaurant and talked well past midnight before driving home through the dark. Charlotte was surprised at how easily their friendship had refreshed after several years of sporadic correspondence.

It was two in the morning when Charlotte quietly let herself into the farmhouse. She had not told her parents of her "earlier than expected" arrival. If the door had been locked, she knew where the spare key was hidden.

Mom was unloading the dishwasher when Charlotte crept downstairs. She straightened in astonishment and, to Charlotte's dismay, began to weep. It wasn't the reaction for which she had been hoping.

"Mom. What's wrong? I came early to help you get things ready."

"I'm so happy. All my girls will be together. I can't remember the last time that happened." Mom wiped her eyes with a tissue. "Leslie and her family will be arriving Wednesday and they are bringing Kim Hamilton. Kim and I have become good friends."

"As good as you and Aunt Judy?" Charlotte teased.

"Ah no. That's special. My friendship with Kim is different."

"I remember a time when you didn't much like her."

"I was intimidated by her. I was wrong to be."

"You admit to being wrong?" Charlotte laughed.

"Oh Charlotte, if you ever knew." Mom blew her nose. "I thought she was a snob. A person with more class than I have. Silly, isn't it? My own personal bias. I now wonder if perhaps I am intimidating to others as well."

"Whom do you think you frighten? I'm curious."

"Selina Dunn. I hope, over time, she finds me to be a pleasant surprise."

Charlotte remembered her mother's boastful "I run a tight ship" routine and how she had especially targeted Selina. *Not the time to bring that up*, Charlotte thought, pouring herself a cup of coffee. She sat at the kitchen island. "There's something about my life I need to tell you."

A frown of concern wrinkled Mom's brow. "You're not pregnant, are you?"

Charlotte smirked. "No. It's about my career. Remember I told you our little radio station was bought out by a larger network?"

"That was months ago. You said it didn't affect your job."

"Bill McKnight, my boss, wasn't able to work under the new owners — for various reasons, one being creative differences — and so he started looking for employment elsewhere. A television station in Liverpool offered him a position as producer of a small half hour show. And he took it."

"Why is your boss's new job of interest to me?" Mom asked. "Unless he asked you to work for him. Oh Charlotte, you're going to move far away, aren't you?"

"Bill is leaving in three weeks and yes, he wants me to go with him. I said yes."

"Liverpool? Oh, Charlotte!" Mom turned toward the sink and scrubbed a pan.

"A plane ride away. Like to Toronto but a tad longer."

"But not in Canada."

"No. But the country is English-speaking and relatively civilized. You could visit and see what the relatives are up to. Both the Dewhurst and Holden ancestors hail from Great Britain. Don't you want to see the old country?"

"Not particularly."

"There's something else," Charlotte said, gently, to Mom's

back. "Bill and I are a couple."

"A couple! That man is too old for you. Isn't he asking a lot?"

"He has a name, Mom. Bill McKnight. And he's in his forties."

"How and where exactly do you and this Bill McKnight plan to live in England?"

"We'll figure that out when we get there." Charlotte was weary now, and impatient. The conversation was rapidly deteriorating. "Now that my sisters are properly tethered to their lives of domesticity, am I to be the main focus of your concern? 'Poor Charlotte, whose life is not complete because she doesn't have a man. A career alone can never satisfy her cold and empty bed?' Well, now I have a man. I thought you might be happy for me."

Mom turned. "You are mocking me. Please, tell me everything, and I promise not to overreact."

"Thank you." Charlotte studied her mother's face. The lines and wrinkles had all been earned, but on the hardship scale her mother had been handed small potatoes. *No point in saying that. It will only make her defensive.* "You remember I came home last year on a break from my job?"

"We knew something was wrong but we didn't want to press. And later there was so much else going on we forgot."

"At the time, I wasn't sure if I had a job to go back to. Those were bleak days for me. I loved my job and it was something I was good at."

Her leave of absence had stretched six weeks, until one morning in late September still at the family farm, Charlotte had answered the telephone and was surprised into speechlessness at the sound of Bill's voice.

"Charlene Faulkner has been fired," he had said, without preliminary salutations. "Please come back. We miss you here at the station."

An unexpected rush of resentment had surged through Charlotte. "No, thank you."

Bill phoned a day later and offered her a raise in pay.

"I'll think about it." Charlotte was still angry enough to cut off her nose to spite her face. *Not unlike Paige in that way*, she reflected, without amusement.

He had phoned a third time — from a hotel room in Saskatoon, wanting instructions how to get to the farm. Charlotte met him in the city.

Paige, had she known, might have said, "It's so romantic," but Charlotte hadn't told anyone, and it hadn't been romantic.

She took her mother's hand in hers. "Bill McKnight is thirteen years older than I and has been married once before. He has two teenage children who live in Liverpool with his ex-wife and her second husband. Bill thinks this opportunity is perfect to be more accessible to them." She paused. "My personal relationship with him is in the courting stages and I have no idea how far it will go. About marriage, I can offer no certainties." Charlotte thought of her conversation the night before with Carrie McCombs who was a single parent. "I am aware my own biological clock is ticking, but whether or not I'll have children is my decision alone."

After a long moment of silence, Mom said, "You are a capable and intelligent young woman."

"Thank you." Charlotte appreciated the effort it took her mother to say those words. "I believe I am. Bill is coming to the wedding, by the way. I want you to meet him."

"I will be cordial and respectful. You can count on that." Mom's tone was serious, but she surprised Charlotte by breaking out into a grin. "If this relationship doesn't work out, you can always return to Hatfield. There's a rumour the town will soon have a radio station and you would be a wise choice in any capacity. You could marry some desperate bachelor farmer if you were worried about spinsterhood."

"Now you're teasing me."

"I am. I'm sorry."

"It's a satisfying way of life, isn't it? Living on a farm. You were born a city girl yet you embraced rural living."

"I developed talents and interests I never knew I had."

"I could live in the country if I had to, but I don't believe I would thrive. I'm a city girl."

"There are plenty of cities closer to your family than Liverpool! So far away!"

The circle of conversation was about to start its second go-round. Charlotte was relieved when her father entered the house.

She would tell him of her plans privately. She could count on him not to overreact.

Chapter 42

Elsie

June 1996

*B*e *careful what you wish for.*
On the day of Paige's celebration, nary a mosquito could be found. A cold wind blew in unexpectedly as the guests arrived, whipping tablecloths into knots and toppling table arrangements. The ceremony was delayed as everyone worked together to move the tables and chairs off the lawn and into the shop, which had been emptied of equipment and tools, and painted.
Just in case.
"Always have a plan B," Elsie had said in the spring to Dan and Reese, when it had been too wet to seed and time had hung heavy on their hands. "The shop could use a fresh coat anyway."
She often had a plan C and D in her back pocket as well, a by-product of her worry. Charlotte told her she was "hyper-vigilant."
Who knows what problems we've avoided because of my imagination?
It was a small wedding. Fifty-two guests. Fifty-two, like a deck of cards, without the troublemakers: the Warrens, and Rod Hamilton, who was separated from Kim. Elsie did not feel any guilt for excluding them.
Reese's number of guests was small: his parents, his brother, sister-in-law and their three children. No friends. A contrast to Elsie's other two sons-in-law who had so many friends. She worried a little, wondering if that deficiency might pose a future problem.
But Paige didn't have a lot of friends either. She invited only one. Karen Anders.

Leslie shrieked when she saw Karen. "How long has it been?" she asked. "Twelve years?"

"The irony," Charlotte said, in an aside to Elsie. "First the former boyfriend and second, the former best friend. Paige has really done a number on Leslie."

"I have never understood irony." Elsie was determined not to worry, at least on this day, about anything that could possibly crop up later, like petty jealousies and competitive flirtations. She plastered a smile on her face and enthusiastically welcomed each guest.

On the Dewhurst side were Paige's sisters and their families, two sets of grandparents, aunts, uncles, cousins, Kim Hamilton and an assortment of the Dewhursts' closest neighbours. Elsie's sister, Debra, brought a date and so did the eldest Rasmussen cousin.

And there was Charlotte's "plus one," Bill McKnight.

Elsie's smile did not waver. Dan extended his hand and Charlotte's "not so young" man grasped it firmly.

Bill McKnight is not unattractive. He did not have the fresh face of Alex, the elegance of Keith, or the handsomeness of Reese, but Elsie liked the way he rolled up his sleeves and helped move the chairs and tables to the shop.

Her smile did not waver fifteen minutes later, when the horse defecated as Dan helped Paige out of the carriage. The steaming mess was cleaned immediately. *But still, what bad timing.* The Rasmussen cousins couldn't stop laughing and even Dan couldn't control his amusement. Elsie had to give him a poke in the ribs when he came to stand beside her.

Paige wore white.

No one here has come to judge. Elsie couldn't help cringing as she wondered what her mother-in-law was thinking.

Paige's dress was unadorned, chaste, and if it weren't for the coy smile that hung on her lips, she looked almost virginal. Around her shoulders was a silk shawl, also white — something borrowed last minute from Lila Gladstone, who had rushed home to retrieve it after noticing the goose bumps on Paige's bare arms.

After the short ceremony, Paige and Reese mingled with their guests. A bar was set up in the shop with Keith and Alex acting as bartenders. At some point in time, Lila and Pete Gladstone left to bring the food from their ovens and coolers. Elsie assured them there was no rush, there was no schedule needing to be followed. She knew from past experience Lila was a perfectionist and everything would be fine.

In the evening after the meal, after the wine and the toasts, after the impromptu speeches with the three babies crying in unison, the fiddler arrived and rosined up his bow.

"Let's par-tay!" Alex shouted, when the music began. He picked Beth off the ground and spun her in a polka. The little girl gave a shriek of delight. On the gravel driveway in front of the shop everyone stopped to watch the laughing child and her fun-loving father.

Elsie shared her look of satisfaction with Judy, the only other person who knew of her intervention to save the Warrens' marriage.

"Elsie, let's dance." Dan grabbed hold. Together they whirled faster and faster until the smiling faces around them blurred.

"I won't let go," Dan promised.

"I won't let you," Elsie replied, breathless and elated.

After that first frenzied dance, they stood together hand in hand and watched the others having fun. The wind had diminished and everyone was warming up with the lively music.

"What a fine life we have built, Elsie. You and I."

"Despite our imperfections."

"We have gathered enough stones for a firm foundation."

"You and your damn stones. To me they represent worries." *There will always be something imagined. Or real.* She shook her head. *But for today, everything is alright.*

She saw her girls. She saw her grandchildren.

She saw Bill McKnight laughing with Troy Rasmussen. Who knew if he might become someone important in her life? Someone she could come to love, as she had come to love Alex.

She saw Judy talking to Reese's parents.

Dan must have followed her gaze. "I'm going to ask Selina Dunn if she'd like to twirl around the dance floor."

"Good idea. And I'll dance with Ray. He looks like he could shake a leg."

About the Author

Roberta Sommerfeld is the pen name for a writer who has lived her entire life on the Canadian prairies. She was born and raised in Saskatoon, but her first teaching job took her to a small town. Roberta married a farmer; together they raised four children.

Roberta has two university degrees from the University of Saskatchewan, as well as a Writers Diploma from St Peter's College. Now retired from teaching, she devotes much of her creative energy into writing.

Roberta lives on the farm with her husband and dog. She keeps busy with her yard and garden, spending time with her family, and travel. She enjoys several hobbies and is almost never bored.

Roberta can be reached at robertasommerfeld.com

Made in the USA
Monee, IL
07 May 2021